STRIKING RANGE

ALSO AVAILABLE BY MARGARET MIZUSHIMA

The Timber Creek K-9 Mysteries

STRIKING RANGE

A Timber Creek K-9 Mystery

Margaret Mizushima

NEW YORK

Published in the United States by Crooked Lane Books, an imprint of The Quick Brown Fox & Company LLC.

Crooked Lane Books and its logo are trademarks of The Quick Brown Fox & Company LLC.

Library of Congress Catalog-in-Publication data available upon request.

ISBN (hardcover): 978-1-64385-746-6
ISBN (ebook): 978-1-64385-747-3

Cover design by Melanie Sun

Printed in the United States.

www.crookedlanebooks.com

Crooked Lane Books
34 West 27th St., 10th Floor
New York, NY 10001

First Edition: September 2021

10 9 8 7 6 5 4 3 2 1

To Terrie Wolf, my agent, my friend,
and a lover of puppies

ONE

Finally . . .

Today Deputy Mattie Cobb could interrogate the man who had once tried to kill her. She parked her K-9 unit outside the prison gates as she scanned cars that had already arrived. She leaned forward, fingers hovering over the key in the ignition, her stomach churning with a mixture of dread, anticipation, and yeah . . . some sort of deep satisfaction that she was about to meet face-to-face with the man who'd once tried to burn her alive.

And he would be left behind bars after her interrogation, while she would be free to walk away.

With hours left to go before regular visitation, there were very few vehicles for her to sort through. She was looking for Jim Hauck, a cold-case detective from San Diego who was investigating the shooting death of Douglas Wray, Mattie's biological father. Her dad had been killed almost thirty years ago, and the case had never been solved. The circumstances around his death were complicated, most of the facts still hidden, and Mattie was determined to uncover the truth.

All the cars were empty. Hauck had said they should enter the prison together, so she assumed she'd arrived before him. She switched off the ignition and settled back in her seat as she glanced into the rearview mirror. Her German shepherd partner, Robo, heaved himself up from his cushion where he'd been sleeping and dropped his shoulders into a long stretch. His pink tongue curled and his sharp teeth glistened as he yawned until his throat squeaked.

"Did you have a good nap?"

He came forward to stand on the other side of the heavy-gauge steel mesh that separated his compartment from the front part of the Ford Explorer that had been converted into their K-9 unit. His tail hung at half-mast, no wag at all to it, and he looked sleepy. It had taken hours to drive to this Colorado state prison from Timber Creek, most of it during the darkness before sunrise.

He plopped his rump down into a sit while she opened the gate at the front of his cage to stroke the soft black fur between his ears. With a predominantly black coat and dark-tan markings, Robo weighed in at around one hundred pounds. This high-energy male shepherd was her constant companion, not only her partner but also her best friend. They'd been paired together over a year now, and they represented the only K-9 unit in Timber Creek County, a large chunk of land in Colorado that boasted a much higher number of mountainous acres than residents.

Talking to Robo always settled her nerves, so she explained to him what was going to happen next. He tilted his head and listened, pinning his ears back when she got to the part about how he was going to wait here. While she talked, she tested to make sure the rear compartment air-conditioning system was operating correctly and set at the right temperature. Even though it was seven o'clock on an October morning, she didn't want to take a chance on heat building up inside the car in case she was delayed inside the building.

She eyed the prison. An eight-foot chain-link fence topped with razor wire surrounded the brick-and-concrete walls that housed about 750 inmates, one of whom was John Cobb, the man who'd tried to end her life several months ago and who'd succeeded in killing her brother.

It was no coincidence that she shared a last name with this criminal. John and his deceased brother, Harold Cobb, had abducted Mattie, her brother, and her mother when Mattie was only two years old. Until recently, she'd thought that Harold Cobb, who'd tormented and abused them, was her father. The best thing that had resulted from the night that his brother,

John, had tried to kill her was that she'd discovered these two scumbags were *not* related to her at all.

Since then, at the insistence of her boyfriend, Cole Walker—Timber Creek's only veterinarian and Robo's doctor—Mattie had reunited with her blood relatives through a DNA database. She'd learned of her real father's death, which had occurred the same night she was kidnapped, and she believed that John and Harold Cobb were responsible—either they'd killed her father themselves or they'd belonged to the gang who had. Today, she and Detective Hauck would be able to confront John with the evidence they had against him, scarce as it was.

Her hope that she could perform well in the interrogation and help Hauck elicit vital information from Cobb had kept her awake last night and set her nerves on edge this morning. Since the authorities, Hauck included, believed her deceased father had been a dirty cop, she feared his case had been placed at lowest priority.

Mattie had information—the source of which she couldn't reveal—that her father had been threatened and coerced into working with Cobb and his gang of gunrunners and drug smugglers. Even if she could get Cobb to confess to only that much, it would change the overall picture of the case and help clear her father's name.

A plain black sedan glided past and parked up front close to the gate in a spot reserved for prison personnel. Mattie spotted the white shock of hair that made Detective Jim Hauck easy to recognize. After the driver's side door of the sedan opened, he unfolded his tall, lean frame and exited the vehicle. He wore a navy suit with a light-blue shirt and tie. His eyes went directly to Mattie's Explorer, telling her he had seen her. He lifted his hand in greeting.

Her heart rate picked up as she returned his wave. Telling Robo, "I'll be back soon," she left her SUV and clicked the key fob to lock it. Robo sat at the window and watched her as she turned to walk away.

She'd been waiting to interview Cobb for months. Detective Hauck had connected with her soon after she'd learned he was working her father's case. But despite promising that he would follow the lead Mattie had given him, he'd become embroiled in another one of his cold cases that had broken wide open and consumed his time until he'd wrapped it up.

Though the fact that Hauck had solved his case spoke well of him, the delay had chafed Mattie. But now the day had arrived when it was a go.

As she strode toward the detective, Mattie felt her features settling into her cop face. But Hauck smiled a greeting when she approached, so she allowed herself a thin smile in return.

She extended her hand, and they exchanged a quick but firm grip that stood for a handshake. "Glad to see you, Detective. Did you have a good flight?"

The crow's-feet around his slate-colored eyes deepened as he smiled. "I did. It was uneventful, which is always good."

Hauck's voice was deep and rich with a quality that Mattie had found soothing when she'd first talked to him on the phone a few months ago. When they met in person soon after, she'd found him to be approachable and interested in her story. He'd been the one to suggest that they interrogate John Cobb together.

Mattie saw no reason to continue the chitchat. "How do you want to work this?"

Hauck's face sobered. "How do you feel this morning? Are you nervous?"

Under the circumstances, it was a legitimate question. Mattie paused, guessing that her response would be important and would figure into how they proceeded. "I'm excited to get a chance to meet with John Cobb face-to-face. Maybe a little nervous, but that will settle as soon as we start."

"I appreciate your candor." Hauck turned toward the sidewalk, and together they began walking to the gate. "I want to start out talking to him alone, and we'll bring you in later. You'll be able to observe behind the mirror."

"All right, but I do want my time with him."

"I understand. When you come into the room, it's important that he sees we're united. That you're a part of this investigation too."

"Sounds good."

"I'll make it clear to him that I'm investigating the shooting death of border guard Douglas Wray out in California, and I'll glean what I can before we introduce you. It should come as a surprise to him that we know Wray was your father."

"Introduce me as Wray," Mattie said, wishing the paperwork she'd initiated to change her name had been finalized. "He knows me as Deputy Cobb."

"All right. What does your ID say?"

"It still says Cobb."

"Okay, we'll reserve the use of Wray for inside the interrogation room to avoid confusion among the prison guards."

"Agreed."

Hauck paused outside the gate and turned to face her. "Does the thought of being in the same room with him frighten you?"

This time Mattie didn't hesitate. "Not at all."

Hauck studied her face. "Good. I don't want him to think he's intimidating to either of us."

"He won't get that from me."

Hauck nodded, turned, and strode up to the guard. "Detective James Hauck and Deputy Mattie Cobb here to see one of the prisoners," he said as he took his badge and identification from the inside pocket of his suit coat.

The guard, a burly guy with a dark beard and a mop of unruly hair, scanned the ID. "Did you bring your service weapon with you, sir?"

"I did."

"You'll have to check that in at the front office."

"No problem."

Mattie could see a slight bulge under Hauck's coat where his weapon remained concealed, while she wore her full khaki uniform and carried her Glock openly on her duty belt. She showed her own ID, nodded when warned she would also need to check her service weapon, and then followed Hauck through the gate.

Hauck waited for her before turning to walk down the sidewalk toward the brick building. "Must think this is our first rodeo in a state penitentiary," he murmured as she fell in beside him.

Mattie nodded, though truthfully, this *was* her first time to visit this prison, not to mention interview a prisoner. Harold Cobb, the man Mattie had once believed to be her father, had died here ages ago, but she'd never been inside the building herself.

When Mattie was six years old, she'd called the police one night when Harold had beaten her mother senseless and threatened to kill her. After being incarcerated in this very prison, Harold had been shanked and killed by another prisoner. Mattie had learned about the incident later but when she was still young enough to feel responsible. Thank goodness those days were past and she no longer felt a need to bear that burden.

Anything bad that happened to the Cobb brothers, they'd brought on themselves.

Hauck held open the door and stood back to allow her to enter first. As she stepped inside the lobby, she scanned the austere room, furnished only with industrial-looking aluminum chairs, their seats covered with plastic upholstery, and stray end tables scattered here and there. A female attendant dressed in uniform sat behind a Plexiglas screen with a metal vent in it for conversation and a cut at the base for exchanging ID. Mattie deferred to Hauck, stepping aside so that he could approach the woman.

A blonde with dark roots, she narrowed eyes heavily outlined in black and raised one darkly penciled eyebrow. "Yes?" she said in a tone that indicated she couldn't be less pleased to have to bother with them.

"Good morning." Hauck remained pleasant and flashed his ID. "Detective Hauck and Deputy Cobb here to interview prisoner John Cobb."

"Just a sec," she said, raising her index finger. She tapped a few keys and searched her computer screen before leaving her chair and disappearing behind a door on the far side of her area.

Hauck looked at Mattie, quirking one brow upward. "Just a sec," he murmured.

Mattie liked his subtle sense of humor. They stood in place and waited until the attendant returned. The woman remained silent as she took her seat, while a door opening farther down the wall drew Mattie's attention.

A woman dressed in a dark-gray pantsuit with a silver blouse leaned through the doorway and beckoned for them to come. Mattie followed Hauck toward her.

"I'm assistant warden," the woman said, offering a handshake. "Shanice Donahue."

Mattie returned the warden's firm grip while studying her. Donahue stood a couple inches taller than Mattie's five foot four. Long-legged and short-waisted, she appeared sturdily built, and her handshake suggested a self-contained strength. Her dark-brown skin was smooth and unwrinkled and her hair jet black, giving her an ageless quality, but the sharpness of her brown eyes indicated she wouldn't miss much that was happening in her environment.

"Come inside and I'll check you in," she said, holding the door open. "We were expecting you."

"Good," Hauck said. "It's nice to meet you, and we appreciate your cooperation."

Mattie crossed the threshold into a space filled with lockers secured with built-in digital locks. A couple benches were anchored to the floor, and an open shower occupied one corner along with a toilet and sink. The room reminded her of a dressing room in a gym, except with less privacy.

"Check your weapons here," Donahue said, giving them each a code to a locker. "Then I'll escort you to the interrogation room and have the guards in John Cobb's pod bring him down."

"What kind of a prisoner is he?" Hauck withdrew a Glock from a shoulder holster beneath his jacket. "Is he any trouble?"

"He's compliant." Donahue kept her gaze unwavering and her expression neutral. Her demeanor spoke of professionalism, through and through. "Sticks with a small group of older men in gen pop, doesn't mix much. Stays out of trouble as much as he can."

"He's in his sixties?" Hauck asked.

"Sixty-two."

"In good health?"

"For the most part. No chronic conditions."

Mattie placed her service weapon and Taser inside the locker and then shut the door and tapped in the code. "Is he involved in drug use or dealing here inside?"

Donahue's gaze shifted to Mattie, and if she was offended by the assumption that there might be drug infiltration inside the prison, she didn't show it—the problem was common enough. "None that we know of."

Donahue handed them both a visitor ID, which they each clipped to their collar in plain sight, then escorted them through another door to exit the room. They entered a hallway that ended in a locked door, where Donahue pressed a button and they all waited for master control to identify them through a camera built into the wall.

With a series of clicks and a hum of machinery, the gate opened by rolling sideways, revealing a narrow space with a second locked door designed to prevent anyone from slipping through either way. The first door clanged shut behind Mattie, and while they waited for the second door to open, she felt a tingle of dread as her ongoing problem with claustrophobia threatened to kick in. She focused on keeping her breath slow and even.

They continued to follow Donahue down another corridor past a series of closed metal doors, stopping at one on the end. She keyed in a code on the outside lock and opened the door, stepping aside so they could enter. The room was even starker than the interrogation rooms at the Timber Creek sheriff's station. A metal table that had a steel ring bolted to the top sat against one wall, anchored to the floor. Chairs were also bolted into position so that the prisoner was seated in full view of the interrogator at all times. Recessed camera lenses were positioned high on the walls, and apparently nothing inside the room could be used as a weapon.

Donahue gestured to a two-way mirror. "There's an observation room with recording equipment behind that wall. The door into it is down the hall. I'll stay in there and handle the equipment for you."

"We appreciate your time," Hauck said. "Deputy Cobb will start out in the observation room with you. I'd also like to observe John Cobb before I enter the room."

Donahue nodded. "Both of you come with me, then, and we'll get set up. The guards should arrive with Cobb any minute."

Mattie and Hauck followed Donahue out into the hallway, waited while she unlocked the neighboring door, and then shuffled inside the small, narrow room. Light filtered into the darkened space through the two-way mirror from the adjoining room, revealing chairs lined up against a shelf under the window and audio and recording equipment near the far wall.

Claustrophobia tightened Mattie's chest. She tried to inhale without calling attention to herself. *Not this. Not now.*

Donahue was showing them how the equipment worked, and Mattie tried to focus on the demonstration instead of the walls that were closing in on her. "Detective, if you want, I can give you an earbud receiver so we can speak to you."

"Sounds like a good idea."

While the two were occupied with rigging him up, Mattie snatched a few moments to use her yoga breathing to center herself in as discreet a way as she could. *Inhale through the nose, slow exhale through the mouth.*

Harsh, repetitive blasts erupted from an alarm in the hallway, and she almost jumped out of her skin.

Donahue's head came up and her eyes narrowed as she listened. Then she darted toward the doorway, brushing past Mattie in the narrow space. "Stay in here," she ordered as she left. She closed the door behind her.

A faint click from the doorknob echoed through the room like a gunshot. Adrenaline made Mattie's heart pound. She tried the knob, but it wouldn't budge. "She locked us in," she said, her voice tight with tension.

"Here, let me see." Hauck pushed past her, nudging her hand aside.

Mattie moved back a step and bumped into the wall. *Trapped.*

"Well, damn," Hauck muttered as he rattled the knob. "The whole prison must be on lockdown."

TWO

Cole Walker snatched toast from the toaster, stacked it on a plate, and hustled it over to the table, where his daughter Sophie was already seated. Getting the kids ready for school each morning before he hurried off to work was like lining up horses at the gate before a race—everyone wanted to run off in a different direction, and sometimes someone balked at going anywhere.

He plopped the plate of toast down on the table and started swiping butter onto each piece—except for Angie's. She would want hers dry. At sixteen, his teen had developed a lot of rules about food. Blond and willowy, Angela looked a lot like her mother, while nine-year-old Sophie, who was built short and solid, seemed to take after him.

Sophie liked her toast the way he did—slathered with golden goodness. He handed her one of the warm slices topped with melting butter. "Thanks," she murmured as she reached for the jelly jar in the center of the table.

Their Bernese mountain dog, Belle, finished eating her kibble and came to the table to lie down beside Sophie where the pickin's were good. Bruno, their Doberman pinscher, had already positioned himself in his spot between Sophie's and Cole's chairs, where he watched Cole's every move, his beautifully sculpted ears pricked.

"What do you have planned at school today?" Cole asked, bumping the jar closer to Sophie.

She tipped her freckled face up to meet his gaze with brown eyes flecked with amber. Her dark curls were tamed somewhat by a recent encounter with her hairbrush, slicked back and still damp with water and tied with a red scarf, her signature color. "We're working on a science experiment. Today we have to weigh and measure all the plants."

As she spread jelly on her toast, she chattered about doling out different measurements of fertilizer, water, and artificial sunlight to an assortment of potted bean plants. Cole knew science was one of her favorite subjects and she was just getting warmed up. Sophie could talk the wire off a fence post if you let her.

Mrs. Gibbs, their resident housekeeper, was at the stove fixing eggs. "We've got fifteen minutes till bus time, young lassies," she called out, her Irish lilt music to Cole's ears.

Angie rushed into the room with their five-month-old Siamese kitten, Hilde, slung over the crook of her arm. Hilde's periwinkle eyes—almost the same color as Angie's—blinked within her dark-brown mask. The kitten appeared completely relaxed and happy being toted around. *Lord knows, she's barely set her paws on the floor since we brought her home.*

The fawn-colored kitten immediately drew Sophie's attention, stopping her monologue midsentence. "Do you want me to get her special morning breakfast?"

"No, I'll do it." Setting the kitten on the floor, Angie bustled over to the refrigerator to retrieve a partial can of soft cat food. Cole allowed Hilde soft food once a day—which the kids called "special morning breakfast"—while a bowlful of crunchy bits sat beside her water dish for her to graze on at all times. Angie spooned a serving of food into a clean bowl and headed toward the utility room with it, the kitten scampering in front of her. To keep the dogs away from Hilde's food, they'd set up a feeding station on the utility room countertop with a step stool positioned beside it for the cat to climb up on. This many pets in the house made things complicated, but Cole loved being surrounded by animals and he appreciated the responsibilities their care taught his kids.

"Don't forget to scoop the litter," he said, catching the grateful smile that Mrs. Gibbs tossed him as she spooned scrambled eggs into a bowl.

"I won't." Angie disappeared inside the adjoining room. When Cole and Angie had brought the kitten home, the typically amenable housekeeper had made it clear that litter box chores did not fall within her purview.

Mrs. Gibbs carried the bowl of eggs to the table, putting a spoonful on Sophie's plate before setting the rest on the table.

His phone jingled in his pocket. Caller ID told him it was a call forwarded from his office, and he answered it as he went to the refrigerator to retrieve the orange juice. "Timber Creek Veterinary Clinic."

"Dr. Walker, this is Ruth Vaughn." The speaker's words were clipped and tense.

Cole didn't need his client to say anything more. "Is it Sassy?"

A hush fell over the room as Mrs. Gibbs and Sophie stopped their chatter to stare at him. Angie, her brow creased with concern, came from the utility room to listen.

Aware that his family was hanging on to his every word, Cole tuned in to what Ruth was saying.

"I'm sorry to call before office hours."

"That's okay, Ruth. Is there a problem?"

"Sassy started labor around midnight, and so far we've had no puppies. She's panting a lot, and well . . . she acts like she's in a great deal of pain."

Alarm nipped at Cole, but he worked at projecting calmness. "The length of labor isn't too unusual for her first litter, but I think I'd better take a look at her."

Ruth released an audible sigh of relief. "I was hoping you would. I'm afraid for Sassy. We love her so much, and we can't afford to lose these puppies."

Cole knew that Ruth depended on the income these pups would bring. A superb example of the German shepherd breed standard, Sassy had achieved an excellent rating for hip soundness from the Orthopedic Foundation for Animals, an organization that provided radiographic examination and counseling for canine hip dysplasia. Her pups would bring top dollar.

More importantly, these puppies had been sired by Robo, who'd also earned an excellent rating, and they were his first litter as well. Some of these pups would probably have bright futures in the working dog industry as well as in the show arena, but they would bring a gift of joy to Cole's family and Mattie as they grew into sturdy little replicas of Sassy and Robo.

"Bring Sassy into the clinic so we can do an ultrasound," Cole said. "Come in now, and I'll meet you there."

"Hannah wants to come. I hope that's all right." Ruth sounded stressed, and he knew she'd had a tough time of it since they'd met last summer. Her teenage daughter, Hannah, had been a staunch source of support for her mother during their transition from living in a strict religious compound to taking up residence in their new home in town. She was also a friend of Angie's.

"Of course she can come. I'll see you soon."

Cole disconnected the call and turned his attention to his family, who were waiting with bated breath, including Mrs. Gibbs. "Sassy's in labor."

Sophie squirmed in her chair, her face lit with excitement. "Can we go to the clinic with you and watch her babies be born?"

Cole shook his head. "You have school, little bit. The bus will be here in five minutes."

"I'll take her to school, Dad." Angie suppressed her excitement more than her little sister did, but Cole could tell it bubbled beneath the surface. "Could we just go to school late this one time?"

"Ple-e-e-ease. Please, Dad. We never get to miss school."

Cole had to admit this was true. Both his daughters held perfect attendance records so far this year, and they were both A students. He decided that delivering puppies would be an experience they couldn't get in the classroom. And besides, this birthing was special. He wished Mattie were in town so that she could watch too.

"Okay," he said.

The word unleashed Sophie from her chair. She sprang up, her dirty dishes in hand, and rushed them over to the sink. "Mrs. Gibbs, do you want to come?" she asked, her dark eyes sparkling.

"No, I think I'll stay home," Mrs. Gibbs said. And then to Cole, she added, "Do you want me to call the schools and let them know the girls will be late?"

"That would be a big help." Cole followed Sophie's lead and cleared his dirty dishes from the table. "Angie, grab a piece of toast or something. You girls, go get your jackets."

Within seconds, they exited through the door into the garage. Cole pressed the button, and the double door to the outside world rolled up with a clatter. A cool, fall breeze swept in, carrying some dried yellow and brown leaves with it. Angie and Sophie ran around to the passenger side and loaded up in front, crowding together in the bucket seat. Since the clinic sat only a couple hundred yards down a private lane, Cole allowed their makeshift seating arrangement, exchanging ultimate safety for time efficiency.

He fired up the engine, backed out, and listened to the ding of the seat belt alarm as he drove to the clinic. Once there, they piled out while he hustled to unlock the front door. He flipped on the lights inside a lobby furnished with chairs for waiting clients and a reception desk, which Angie typically manned after school and on weekends.

"Angie, would you call Tess and see if she can come in a few minutes early? Tell her what's up and that we might need her help." Cole went through into the exam room. "I'll set up the ultrasound machine."

Sophie piped up. "What can I do?"

"You can help me." She followed, skipping close on his heels through the swinging door.

In the back of his mind, Cole continued to be concerned about the situation, although he didn't want to let that show. If Sassy or her pups were in distress, this could mean a C-section delivery, and he would need all hands on deck. Sassy's last ultrasound, just a week ago, had revealed a litter of seven babies, all apparently healthy and thriving. Big pups—and that's what had him worried.

"They're here, Dad," Angie called through the pass-through from the lobby.

"Okay," he called back as sounds from the front door filtered through. He murmured to Sophie, "Let's see what those puppies look like."

She rushed to the swinging door to hold it open. "Hi, Hannah and Mrs. Vaughn. Come in."

When Hannah led Sassy into the room, Cole assessed the dog's level of discomfort with a glance. The beautiful black-and-tan shepherd, a bit smaller than Robo, swept into the room frantically, her tongue extended in a rapid pant, so different from her usual laid-back demeanor.

The fearful expressions on his clients' faces spoke of their concern, and fatigue had left darkened smudges under their blue eyes. Hannah and her mother resembled each other, both sandy-haired blondes. Though they'd once belonged to a religious group and worn old-fashioned dresses and shoes from the past, they now blended more into Timber Creek society; Hannah wore a T-shirt, jeans, and tennis shoes, while Ruth was now clothed in plain leather loafers and a modest denim dress that she'd most likely sewn herself.

Cole projected a practiced air of calm, trying to put them at ease because he knew how much they loved this dog. "Good morning. How long have you two been up?"

"Sassy woke Hannah about midnight," Ruth said, swiping back a strand of hair that had escaped the bun she wore at her nape.

Cole and Sassy were familiar with each other, but she might not be herself under this amount of stress. He approached her quietly, his hand extended low and palm-down for her to sniff. She didn't bother. Instead, she moved restlessly at Hannah's side, another indicator of her level of distress.

Cole reached for a muzzle made from red nylon straps. "Hannah, we need to put this on Sassy. She's in pain and might be more snappish than usual."

Hannah had been in the clinic often enough to know the routine. She helped Cole put on the muzzle and adjust the straps. "Do you want her on the table?"

Cole took his stethoscope out of his pocket. "Let me listen to her heart and lungs first."

The rapid rate of Sassy's heartbeat was another indicator of pain, but the beats were regular and strong and her lungs sounded clear, all a relief to Cole. "Everything sounds good, Hannah. Let's move her to the table now."

Hannah wrapped her arms around the seventy-pound dog's chest and lifted while Cole picked up her hindquarters. Sassy stood quietly on the stainless-steel tabletop until Hannah encouraged her to lie down.

"You and Sassy are a couple of pros," Cole said, as he rolled his ultrasound machine up to the exam table. He snapped on a pair of latex gloves. "She can rest on her side, just like we did last time."

After squirting the ultrasound gel on Sassy's belly, Cole flipped the switch on his machine and nestled the probe between the swollen mammary glands, now filled with milk. Hannah gently lifted Sassy's hind leg to give him better access. "That's great, Hannah. Let's see what we can find."

As he rolled the smooth probe over the dog's skin with one hand, he adjusted the dials on his machine with the other to sharpen the images. Puppies, each in their own amniotic sac, began to take shape on the screen—small forms, their ears flattened against their heads, bodies rounded, little paws tucked up close. The sight never ceased to thrill Cole, especially when he could see the tiny hearts beating.

Sophie sidled closer to the ultrasound machine's screen to get a better look. In the hushed stillness of the room, Cole marveled that the images had been enough to silence even *her* chatter.

He moved the probe against Sassy's belly, repositioning it as he went lower, trying to get an accurate count. "Let's turn her a little more onto her back and hold her there."

Sassy cooperated while Hannah gently rocked her backward, lifting her hind leg higher and making soothing sounds. Sassy seemed to relax a bit as Cole circled her belly with the probe, making him think the massaging action might've made her feel better. Everyone's eyes were glued to the ultrasound screen as Cole counted aloud.

When he neared the dog's pelvis, he saw two pups, heads down, both vying for space in the birth canal. Typically, he could wait and let them sort themselves out, but these were big pups. Cole hesitated, taking a good look at the situation. He held the probe steady and snapped a picture of the image of the two large pups at the base of the uterus.

The puppies had been growing since he'd last viewed them, and if he considered their size along with the level of Sassy's distress, he believed a C-section was the best route to take. He didn't want to risk losing even a single puppy.

He looked at Ruth. "I think she's going to need our help to deliver these puppies. I recommend we do a C-section."

Ruth closed her eyes for a brief moment, her face tight with worry. "Is that dangerous for Sassy?"

He pointed at the still shot he'd taken, which remained on the screen. "At this stage, it's risky to let her go much further on her own. These two pups look like they could get lodged together in the birth canal, and we could lose one or both of them. I hope to avoid that."

Ruth placed her hand on her daughter's shoulder. "Hannah, I think we should let Dr. Walker do the surgery."

Hannah caressed Sassy's fur, hesitating only a moment. "Me too, Mother."

Angie had been standing against the wall behind Hannah, and now she stepped forward to put her arm around her friend's waist. "It'll be all right. We've done this before. We'll take good care of Sassy."

Angie's care for her friend brought a lump to Cole's throat. He was saved from having to respond by Tess coming in through the back door that opened into the kennel room.

"Hi, hi," Tess called out in a singsong as she breezed into the room. Tess always made everything better, her personality as bright as her spiky red hair. "Looks like I almost missed the party. Sorry, but it took me a few minutes to get Tom and the kids organized for the day."

"The party's just getting started," Cole said, glad for his assistant's cheerful presence. "We're going to need to do a C-section on Sassy."

Tess nodded and moved over to the cabinet to start laying out supplies.

"Could Hannah and I stay?" Ruth asked.

There were many reasons why Cole didn't allow clients to participate in surgery. "It looks like you both need some rest, so it's better if you go home. I'll call you as soon as the surgery is over, and you can come back."

Tears brimmed in Hannah's eyes, but she leaned over Sassy to give her a hug and kiss. Ruth did the same and then placed her arm around Hannah's shoulders as they headed toward the door. Angie escorted them, murmuring words of reassurance.

Meanwhile, Tess had been busy setting up, laying out hair clippers, suture, and other paraphernalia on the countertop and placing a sterile surgical pack on a stainless-steel tray that she'd rolled up next to the surgery table. But she turned her attention to Sassy after the Vaughns said their good-byes and enlisted Sophie to help soothe and calm the dog as she lay on the exam table, panting.

Cole drew up a dosage of atropine, which would decrease secretions during surgery, injected it subcutaneously, and then stroked Sassy's head while he waited for the drug to work. The responsibility of delivering these puppies safely and keeping this beloved mama dog alive weighed heavily, and while he smoothed her fur, he rehearsed the upcoming procedure in his mind.

He couldn't let anyone down during the process.

THREE

The alarm's blare filled Mattie's head. A red bulb near the observation room's ceiling began to flash, casting an eerie scarlet strobe inside the dimly lit space. The sensory bombardment created a panicky feeling that threatened to overwhelm her.

Hauck reached inside his suit coat to retrieve his cell phone as the flashing red bulb cast menacing shadows over the hardened planes of his face. After a couple swipes, he put the phone back inside his jacket. "No signal in here. Walls must be too dense. Or maybe they have some type of system to block cell phone signals."

Mattie swallowed hard against the tightening in her throat and tried to project a calmness she didn't feel. Claustrophobia made her want to throw herself against the heavy steel door until she broke it down, but instead she cleared her throat and spoke in a voice that reflected none of her turmoil. "Could you flip the switch on the overhead light? It's there beside you."

Hauck turned to locate the switch.

A bright overhead bulb obliterated the malicious shadows in the corners. Though the alarm kept blasting, at least the light gave Mattie a sense of relief. She turned toward the wall of equipment filled with knobs, video screens, and switches. "Let's see if we can find a way to contact the front office."

Hauck moved up beside her.

"Technology isn't my strong suit," she said as she gave him more room.

"I'm that generation where it's not mine either," Hauck muttered as he scanned the equipment, touching a knob or a button here and there.

Mattie guessed that his age hovered around sixty. "I don't have that excuse. I just wasn't exposed to it until I was an adult. Unless it has something to do with the outdoors, it doesn't interest me."

She'd already told Hauck about her past. He knew that her mother had left Willie and her to be raised in foster care, only for them to be separated and lose touch with each other until shortly before his death. It was one of the great regrets of her life.

"There might be some kind of panic button, but I can't find one." Hauck straightened to scan the room. "We might as well sit down and wait until Donahue comes back. Short lockdowns happen in these prisons, and visitors get locked down right along with everyone else."

Hauck pulled one of the folded metal chairs away from the two-way mirror and sat. "I tell you what," he said with a smile. "If someone besides Donahue or a guard comes through that door, I'll tackle him and you jump on him from behind."

She realized Hauck was joking and that her initial fear was unjustified. Though she had to admit to herself that she'd thought inmates might be taking over the prison, his quiet demeanor made her realize he thought the lockdown a matter of routine. She pulled a chair a few feet toward the back wall and focused on relaxing while she sat. The distraction of their conversation had taken the edge off her claustrophobia.

The alarm still blared in the corridor. Mattie shrugged her shoulders slightly to release their tightness. She tried to keep her movements small and inconspicuous, but when she looked up at Hauck, she realized he was watching her.

He spoke when their eyes met. "Are you okay?"

"Just making sure I stay loose."

Hauck gave her a nod of approval. "If you have to be locked inside a small room, it's best to be with someone who isn't going to panic."

He didn't know how close she'd come, but she was better now. Mattie let the conversation die. It was hard for them to hear each other over the noise in the hallway.

Hauck cleared his throat and projected his voice. "Have you talked to your sister or your grandmother lately?"

"I talk to Julia almost every day." Mattie's sister and grandmother lived together in San Diego, but when they'd all reunited, they'd bonded immediately.

"Has any additional information come up that I should know about?"

"No, we've shared everything we know."

"No information on Ramona's whereabouts, then?" Hauck gave Mattie a penetrating stare that reminded her of the one used by Stella LoSasso, the detective she worked with in the Timber Creek County Sheriff's Department.

"Ramona" was Mattie's mother—Ramona Wray, currently hiding in a small village in Mexico, still terrified of the gang that she'd watched shoot her husband and other innocent bystanders almost thirty years ago. After Mattie had told Hauck what she knew about their abduction, he'd said Ramona was an important witness to the shooting. And Mattie knew for a fact that he was correct.

During the one time she'd met with her mother, Ramona hadn't been able to provide names or useful information about her father's murder, so Mattie honored her mother's request to keep her location a secret. "My sister and grandmother haven't heard a word from her for decades. As far as I know, John Cobb is the only witness that can help us."

Hauck studied her face as he let the moment pass. She wondered if he suspected she knew more than she was saying.

Suddenly the clamor from the alarm ceased, leaving its echo to fade in the resulting silence. They both rose from their seats, and Mattie watched the door, listening while her muscles tensed. A series of clicks shot through the room as someone on the other side of the door tapped in the lock's code.

The door opened to reveal Shanice Donahue, and even though Mattie had expected to see the assistant warden, relief washed through her—perhaps at just having the door opened.

"Sorry for leaving so abruptly, but all visitors must remain in place when the prison goes on lockdown." Donahue's face had hardened into a frown. "We've got some serious shit going on that involves you."

"What happened?" Hauck asked.

"We've had an incident in John Cobb's pod. He's dead."

Hauck cursed under his breath.

Mattie's heart plummeted. Her hopes, goals, and everything she'd planned to accomplish today dissolved into thin air. "What happened to him?"

Donahue looked grim. "When the guards went to get him, he was found dead in his cell."

"Dead how?" Hauck asked. "Shanked?"

"Apparently not. No physical wounds. Manner of death is under investigation. Could be natural causes, might be an overdose on something." Donahue bit off the words, her jaw hardened.

Hauck exhaled in a way that showed his frustration.

Mattie didn't want to give up on learning something—anything—of value today. She stepped forward. "Could we see his body . . . and his cell?"

Donahue's gaze slid away from hers. "I'm not sure I can do that."

Hauck spoke up. "I suspect you have this entire facility under lockdown right now, so we won't encounter any of the prisoners. John Cobb was the only known witness in the case we're investigating. We'd appreciate being able to take a look at him and his cell."

Donahue hesitated, apparently thinking it over. "All right," she said, turning on her heel. "You'll wear caps and booties. I'll be right back."

This time Hauck hurried to the door and caught it before it closed. He stepped out into the hallway, holding the door open for Mattie to follow. They waited in silence until Donahue returned, carrying paper hair coverings that resembled shower caps and booties to cover their shoes.

"Our investigator is already at Cobb's cell, and I've notified him that we're coming." The assistant warden marched swiftly down the corridor, her long strides making Mattie hustle to keep up. Hauck followed. Donahue stopped at the end of the hall, pressed the button for master control, and lifted her face to the camera for identification. The bolt clicked and the door rolled back, opening into another hallway.

They moved past a guard and into a large, rectangular cell block filled with a scattering of metal tables and benches that were anchored to the floor. The room was empty of prisoners. A two-tiered row of cells lined the walls all the way around with metal staircases at the narrow ends of the room leading to the second floor. The walls and doors into the cells were solid instead of bars, and men's faces peered from small, reinforced windows in some of the cells.

"How many men to a cell?" Mattie asked quietly as Donahue began to lead them up one of the stairways.

"In this pod, only one."

"Was Cobb out here mingling with the population before he was found dead?" Hauck asked.

"Inmates eat their meals out here," Donahue said. "Unless an inmate is being disciplined or ill, they eat together. So yes, Cobb ate with the group and then went to his cell. That's where he died."

"Sounds suspicious," Hauck said.

"Yes. Everyone in this pod will remain on lockdown until our investigator can sort things out." Donahue had reached the top of the stairs and threw them a frustrated look over her shoulder before turning down a narrow walkway with a wire mesh railing high enough to restrict inmates from throwing each other over it.

"Was he found in his bunk or on the floor?" Mattie asked.

"On the floor. He's still there." Donahue took another turn and headed along the walkway that stretched down one of the long walls of the rectangle. "His body will be left in place until our coroner can get to him."

Mattie spotted a door that was open midway down the wall. A guard holding a notebook and pen stood outside. When she passed one of the cells, a face leered at her from behind the small window and the man made an obscene gesture. She stared him down as she walked by but averted her eyes from the other occupied cells so she wouldn't provoke another inmate response.

A man dressed in a brown suit and tie stepped out of the cell and waited beside the guard for them to approach. A paper cap covered his hair, but his iron-gray moustache and swarthy, weathered complexion pegged him at about Hauck's age, although he was short and stocky as opposed to Hauck's tall and lean. Donahue introduced him as Detective Russo.

Russo stripped off his latex gloves and offered handshakes. Hauck gave him a business card, and Mattie followed suit.

Russo glanced at her card and then raised a brow. "Cobb?"

"No relation," she said, not wanting to get into the complicated history.

"Thank you for allowing us to take a look," Hauck said. "Did Warden Donahue explain that we believe this man was an important witness to a cold case I'm working?"

"She did. Don't touch anything when you go into the cell, okay?"

"We'll keep our hands to ourselves," Hauck said, glancing at Mattie.

She nodded.

Donahue handed them the protective gear she'd been carrying. Eager to go inside, Mattie slipped on the cap and booties. The guard appeared to be taking notes, and she figured he was in charge of the crime scene record.

She followed Hauck into the room. She peered beyond his tall frame and spotted John Cobb lying on the floor next to a bunk, faceup. Hauck skirted around Cobb's body toward a horizontal steel tabletop and single bench seat, both anchored to the floor. A steel toilet and small sink occupied the other corner of the room.

After Hauck moved deeper into the room, Mattie had a full view of the corpse. Cobb's death hadn't been easy. His mouth gaped open and his features were set in a mask of pain. His face was a ghastly shade of gray, with a bluish tint around his mouth and lips. She felt no sympathy whatsoever for the man. All she felt was a need to determine how he'd died.

Mattie looked at Russo. "Was he in this position when he was found?"

"No, he was facedown and a little closer to his bunk. The guard turned him to determine if he was breathing."

Mattie squatted next to the body to study Cobb's features. Hauck's knees popped as he knelt across from her on the body's other side.

A chill seeped through her as she gazed upon the face of the man who'd once shot an animal tranquilizing dart into her back, abducted her, and tormented her as he tried to elicit information from her that she didn't even know. He'd aged, his hair whiter, his face more lined. He'd changed more than the five months since she'd last seen him warranted, and she hoped prison life had been hard on him.

A pinkish discoloration at the edge of one of Cobb's nostrils caught her eye. She leaned closer for a better look.

"No touching," Russo warned.

"I won't touch him," Mattie murmured as she studied the frothy substance inside both nostrils.

Hauck reached inside his suit coat jacket and withdrew a slim case, from which he extracted a pair of wire-rimmed glasses. He slipped them on and leaned closer to study Cobb's face. "What do you make of that?" he asked Mattie quietly.

"What do you see?" Donahue asked from the hallway outside the cell.

Mattie had seen the foamy substance tinged with pink only in pictures. Many of the K-9 handlers in the state of Colorado met for group training sessions monthly with Sergeant Jim Madsen, the officer who'd originally trained Robo. Madsen had shown photos of individuals who'd died of respiratory failure from opioid overdose, and he'd cautioned them to avoid touching or letting their dogs touch both the substance and the skin of the corpse. Opioids could be absorbed through the skin or inhaled, and such an exposure meant immediate danger of suffering the same fate.

"Foam cone in the nostrils," Mattie said, answering Donahue but making eye contact with Hauck. "Probably from pulmonary edema resulting from respiratory failure."

She stood and turned to the warden. "So you're sure he didn't have any chronic lung conditions? COPD? Congestive heart failure?"

"Nothing like that."

"This could be death by opioid overdose," Mattie said. "No one should handle this body without wearing gloves and protective gear. Make sure the guard who turned him is okay."

"If he followed protocol, he would've worn gloves," Donahue said.

"Unfortunately, not everyone follows protocol. I hope that he did."

"I checked. He did," Russo said, telling Mattie he'd already noticed the presence of the foam cone. He was standing just inside the cell doorway, arms crossed over his barrel chest as he watched. He gave her a nod when their eyes met, as if to confirm her assessment of the death.

Mattie sensed that Cobb had not died of an accidental opioid overdose. She believed someone had killed him. *And there are dozens of inmates and guards who are now suspects that were within striking range*, she thought.

She turned her attention back to Cobb's body: orange jumpsuit with no pockets, white socks, black slip-on canvas shoes with a thin sole. No clothing stains that would indicate vomiting. She examined his outwardly flung arms and his hands, which lay open against the floor. No lacerations or scrapes. No bruising on the surfaces she could see that would indicate defensive wounds or a fight. *Someone close to Cobb must have delivered the drug somehow, possibly in his food or drink.*

Hauck also stood. "Could we get a copy of the ME's report?"

Russo nodded. "That should be possible. Have your department send a formal request."

Mattie scanned the room, noticing books on a small shelf built into the wall over the desk. Curious as to what Cobb had been reading, she moved closer to look at the book titles—one on US history and one on hiking trails in Colorado. The latter caught her attention.

Why had a book about hiking trails in Colorado been of interest to Cobb? She rose on tiptoe to scan the top of the book and could see where the pages had been dog-eared. What trails had Cobb marked?

Mattie looked at Russo. "Could I see inside this book? It looks like Cobb earmarked some of these pages, and I'd like to see which ones."

"Let me handle the book." Pulling on latex gloves, Russo crossed the room and pointed. "This one?"

"Yes." Mattie moved close. "Right there where the first page is dog-eared."

He opened the book and held it up for both Mattie and Hauck to see. The chapter heading appeared in bold letters: **Trails in Timber Creek County**.

Mattie's anxiety started to rise. She reached into her pocket to withdraw her cell phone to take a picture. "Next page."

Russo turned the page carefully. Mattie focused on what she saw rather than the coldness that was starting to gather at her chest. *Redstone Ridge*—the title made her skin crawl.

Redstone Ridge was the beautiful spot high in the wilderness area where John Cobb had killed her brother Willie and then tried to kill her. Cobb had drawn a star at the top of the page and then placed an X at spots on the trail diagram—one near the base, one about midway up where the trail divided, and one at the top near the bottom of the ridge.

And there was another X drawn in a spot on the backside of the ridge, far away from the trail and out in the forest. An eerie feeling crept over Mattie. Though she hadn't returned to this spot since May, just thinking of it drove a cold chill into her solar plexus.

There was a cave there where she'd been held captive, and the surrounding trees would be charred. Cobb had built a fire pit intended for burning her alive, only to have the wind carry sparks away to ignite a forest fire that had provided cover for her escape.

She shut down her mind to turn off the flood of memories, but she had trouble shutting down her body's reaction. She had to suck in a breath to loosen the tightening in her chest.

"What's wrong?" Hauck asked, evidently sensing her distress.

Staring at the page, Mattie shook her head. "I'll tell you later."

Tightening her fingers to keep them from trembling, she reopened her cell phone and positioned it to take a picture.

She planned to hike to the places that John Cobb had marked, including that cave of horror on the backside of the ridge. Why would he mark these spots? What was their significance?

She didn't know the answers yet, but she did know one thing for certain—she was going to find out.

FOUR

Cole scratched Sassy behind the ears while he made sure everything he needed had been set out. The surgical pack with sterilized instruments lay on the tray, waiting to be opened. Clippers, packs of suture, syringes, iodine, scrub brushes, cotton, medication bottles, and everything else he might need had been taken from cupboards and placed on the countertop.

Tess was busy preparing a makeshift incubator to put the pups in once they were safely delivered and breathing on their own. She'd placed a heating pad set on its lowest setting beneath layers of terry cloth towels in the bottom of a box, and she was draping a clean towel over the top to retain the heat.

He addressed his kids. "Okay, troops, let's review."

"I get to wear a mask, right?" Sophie hopped in place.

"Yep, that's right." Cole shared her excitement. In his opinion, delivering puppies was one of the most rewarding experiences of his job. "Now, you guys have done this before, but let's go over the most important parts. Listen up, Sophie. Wait a minute and look at me."

Sophie's attention had drifted as she'd bounced over to the countertop to find the box of surgical masks. She paused midreach, withdrawing her hand and stiffening her shoulders like a soldier as she gave him eye contact.

Cole gave the kids step-by-step instructions, ending with, "Sophie, once I get scrubbed up, I'm clean and you're dirty, right? You can't touch me from that point on. You got that?"

Sophie nodded, her eyes sparkling.

"Good. We've all got to move fast. Since Sassy is getting anesthesia, we won't have time to waste. Any questions?"

"No, sir!" Sophie said.

"Are there seven pups, Dad?" Angie asked.

"That's what it looks like, but we could be surprised. Ultrasound views aren't always clear enough for an accurate count. Okay girls, go ahead and put on your gear."

Tess tied the straps on Sophie's surgical gown while Angie managed her own. Meanwhile, Cole shaved a patch over the vein in Sassy's foreleg for insertion of the IV, and then Tess held the leg to occlude the vein, providing a thick, wormlike target for Cole to tap. After withdrawing the needle and leaving the flexible catheter tubing in place, he fixed the IV line to Sassy's leg with surgical tape.

He glanced at his daughters. "You guys ready?"

"Ready!" Sophie said, while Angie murmured a quiet, "Yes."

"All right, let's get started."

Tess and Cole moved Sassy to the surgical table, and Tess held her in place while stroking her on her side. Sassy appeared as relaxed as she could possibly be under the circumstances.

He drew up a small dosage of propofol, a fast-acting sedative that he used to facilitate intubation. Since the sedation effects of the drug were transient, it shouldn't hurt the puppies, but he would need to act fast to get Sassy onto the anesthesia machine.

He glanced at Tess, and she nodded. Cole injected the drug into the buffalo cap on the IV. Sassy went down within seconds.

The clock started ticking. Cole checked the time—7:20.

He rolled the limp dog onto her chest, and Tess gripped her head on both sides below her ears to straighten her neck. Pulling her tongue forward, he depressed it with the leading end of the endotracheal tube and guided it into her airway. Moving quickly, he inflated the cuff, connected the tube to his anesthesia machine, and started the isoflurane gas and oxygen.

Cole waited a minute while the gas and oxygen mixture did its work. As oxygen saturation occurred, there was always a moment when respirations slowed, usually stopping completely until the machine took over. He observed Sassy until the transition had taken place, then tapped her eyelid to check for a blink reflex. Lack of it told him she was deep enough, so he adjusted the dials on the gas and the oxygen to hold the sedation at that rate.

"Let's move her into position."

Tess and Angie helped him roll Sassy onto her back and fasten the soft restraints that would stabilize her. The clippers whirred while Tess began shaving the dog's belly, being careful not to nick the swollen mammary tissue. When done with that, she would wash Sassy's stomach with a Betadine scrub chased with alcohol.

Isoflurane would pass through the placenta to the puppies, so the race was on. Cole moved to the sink to scrub and put on his sterile gear. Angie closed the ties at his back, and he moved to the surgical tray to open the inside wrap on the sterile pack, first lifting the sterile drape to cover Sassy's belly and then opening the wrap to reveal the gleaming surgical instruments inside.

Tess turned on the overhead lamp and adjusted its beam. Cole selected a scalpel and made the skin incision two inches below Sassy's umbilicus, where he continued to carefully incise to find the fibrous line of the linea alba, a sheath of fascia that joined the muscle layers in the midline of the abdomen. Cutting through this layer resulted in little blood flow and gave him access to the abdominal cavity.

The turgid uterus lay exposed, a strong muscular organ filled with puppies. While keeping the uterine connections intact, Cole lifted the uterus through the skin incision and laid it on the sterile drape. He pulled sterile cotton gauze from one of his packs and tucked it under the organ to absorb its fluid contents when he opened it. If he encountered a dead puppy, this would prevent bacteria from invading Sassy's abdominal cavity.

"Okay, girls," he said. "Get ready to rock and roll."

A muffled "Eep!" came from behind Sophie's mask, while Angie looked on with her steady blue gaze. A little over a year ago, his daughters had never even come to the clinic to watch him work. Now they behaved like seasoned professionals. Well, Angie at least; Sophie needed a few more years to mature.

Cole made the final incision into the uterus near the base of one of the uterine horns, close to a lump that would be a pup. Fluid gushed, and he quickly replaced the gauze beneath the uterus. He worked the puppy through the incision, feeling elated when he delivered the tiny form into the world.

He cradled the pup in the palm of his hand and gently removed the amniotic sac. Each puppy came equipped with one—individual bubbles of protection. Not for the first time, he marveled at Mother Nature's way as he placed the newborn in the warm towel that Tess held open in her palms, ready to receive.

Going for the next puppy, he turned his attention back to Sassy while still keeping an eye and ear on Tess's progress. She used a nasal bulb to suction amniotic fluid from the newborn's mouth and nostrils until it uttered faint sneezes and snuffling sounds. She used the terry cloth towel to stroke and rub the wet puppy, simulating a mama dog's licking and nuzzles that would encourage the baby to breathe on its own.

"It's a boy," Tess announced as she started to hand the pup, towel and all, to Angie.

"Let Sophie take the first one," Angie said, moving over to allow her little sister to get closer to Tess.

Sophie skipped into place, a wondrous expression in her eyes as she took the puppy into her hands. Cole trusted his nine-year-old to handle the puppy the way she'd been taught. Once Sophie had scrubbed the puppy gently to ensure that it was breathing on its own, she placed it in the warm holding box Tess had prepared earlier.

By this time, Cole had found another puppy and worked it toward the incision by massaging the outside of the uterus. He moved it through the opening, removing the amniotic sac before handing it to Tess.

Tess suctioned the baby. "This one's a girl," she said as she passed it on to Angie while Cole found the next pup.

In this relay fashion, they worked together as a team until Cole had delivered seven puppies. The sniffling, squeaking vocalizations that came from beneath the covering on the box made Cole happy. These were big, strong pups, and he had high hopes that they all would survive.

Sophie, Angie, and Tess stood over the box, peeking under the towel, murmuring their delight.

"Four boys and three girls," Tess was saying.

"That big one that's mostly black looks just like Robo," Sophie said, while the others agreed.

As he palpated the uterus to make sure he'd found all the pups, Cole enjoyed watching how thrilled his daughters were with the process. "Are they all black and tan?" he asked.

Angie was bending over the box. "I think so, although some of them have more black than others."

Cole encountered a small lump at the far end of the left uterine horn. As he milked it down the horn toward the incision, he realized it was another puppy.

"We've got another one, kids," he said, making Sophie squeal as she and Angie moved closer to watch.

Cole removed the limp pup—so small compared to the others—and sheltered it in the palm of his hand while he stripped off the amniotic sac. The little form was slick with amniotic fluid, but he could see no signs of decomposition or decay, so he dared hope the baby was still alive and viable.

He handed it to Tess while he turned back to Sassy. It felt like he had all the pups this time, but he found it worrisome that there were still no sounds of life coming from the last newborn.

"Try draining it with gravity," he told Tess when the suction still hadn't brought any results.

She cradled the puppy head down between her hands and swung it gently downward and back up like a pendulum. Then she tried again with the suction.

"Angie, turn the knob on that oxygen canister there in the corner and bring it close so that Tess can place the mask over the pup."

Angie scurried to follow his instructions while Sophie stood by, her face tense. *This is the downside to having the kids help here at the clinic*, Cole thought, fearful that the pup wasn't going to make it.

A delicate sneeze came from the puppy, and Tess moved it under the oxygen mask, tipping its head down while she continued to rub its fur and massage its rib cage with gentle downward strokes, trying to milk fluid from its lungs.

Though he wanted to take over, Cole restrained himself. Sometimes he had to break his sterile field to help with resuscitation, but this wouldn't be one of those times. Sassy's health and her ability to bear future litters were of utmost importance, and he knew that Tess was doing everything possible to save the pup. He needed to let her do her job.

He eyed the pack of absorbable suture that Tess typically opened for him. "Angie," he said, and she turned her attention from the pup to him. "Could you peel open that packet of suture without touching the inside? Peel it back like a banana and then hold it close so I can take it from the packet."

Angie looked stressed as she scanned the boxes on the counter, trying to locate the right one.

"Don't worry, we're not in a big rush now that the pups are out. We can take our time." Cole hoped to reassure her as he told her which box to open. He glanced at the clock. Only twelve minutes had passed, not too long, although the last puppy had probably been affected more by the anesthesia than the others.

Angie peeled open the packet. He selected a needle holder from his pack of sterile instruments and grasped the needle at the top of the packet. As he pulled it free, the prethreaded suture unraveled and came with it.

"Thanks, Angie," Cole murmured. The puppy was making mewling noises that were barely audible. "How's it coming, Tess?"

"We've got breathing established—sort of."

He could tell that she was still not sure the pup would make it. "Keep doing what you can. Angie and I can finish up here with Sassy." His eyes briefly connected with his daughter's above their surgical masks.

Focusing on his work, he closed the uterine incision before repositioning the organ back within Sassy's abdominal cavity. Then he worked quickly and carefully to close each layer, first the linea alba and then a layer of subcutaneous tissue. Even though this was the first time Angie had assisted him in surgery, she followed his instructions perfectly.

"You're doing a great job, kiddo." And then, fearful that being this close to the insides of an animal might make her queasy, he added, "You holding up? If you need to step back, that's okay."

"I'm fine," Angie said.

He could tell by her facial color above her mask that she was being truthful. He'd been on the receiving end of fainting customers enough to know the signs. Once he'd had to revive a six-foot-four cowboy who'd tilted over like a felled tree at the sight of a syringe and needle.

By this time, the sniffling sounds coming from the puppy had increased in volume, and a quick glance told him that Tess had placed it below the oxygen mask while still rubbing it with a warm towel. Though weak, the little one was beginning to squirm. That was a good sign, but Cole knew they weren't home free yet. These smaller pups that some folks called "runts" might not have received enough nourishment in utero, and it could be touch and go to get them to thrive.

Sophie was still standing beside Tess watching, her tension obvious by the way she held her small shoulders.

"Take a breath, Sophie. Looks like that puppy is making progress. You need to relax a little if you can."

"Okay," she said, her voice tight, and Cole saw her shoulders rise as she tried to follow through.

"It's okay, Sophie," Tess murmured. "This one is going to make it."

"I need that last cartridge of suture now," Cole said to Angie, gesturing toward it with his head. Time to close the skin, which he would do with an intradermal suture pattern, burying the absorbable suture beneath the top cutaneous layer so that none of the stitches would be visible. Since the pups would be rooting around Sassy's belly with their sharp baby toenails, this would be the best way to protect against infection as well as prevent rupture of the incision.

Once he'd finished closing the skin, he went ahead and broke his sterile field by grasping the knob on the anesthesia machine and turning off the isoflurane gas. He adjusted the oxygen flow to support Sassy while she came out from under the anesthesia. "Great job, Angel. Thanks for helping."

"I'm glad it worked out okay." She glanced over at the tiny puppy. "Or I hope it did."

While waiting for Sassy to start breathing on her own, Cole injected her with a dose of antibiotic and an analgesic to make her feel better when she awakened. Though dogs were well known for their stoic nature, he wanted Sassy to be able to begin mothering these pups without delay, and he didn't want pain to be a barrier to her nursing the babies.

He went to peer over Tess's shoulder. The tiny puppy, about half the size of the largest pup, lay beneath the makeshift oxygen tent, the mask tilted so that Tess could stroke the baby's fur and massage it with the warm terry cloth towel. The once-limp little body was beginning to gain tone and weak movement.

"Great job, Tess," he murmured as he reached to touch the puppy. Tess moved the towel back so he could see, giving him his first peek at the semidry pup.

He was surprised by what he saw. "Is that one a sable?"

"That's what it looks like." Tess gave him a quick smile before turning back to massage the puppy's fur with the towel.

Sophie tipped her face up to him. "What's a sable?"

"It's a German shepherd color pattern, different from the black and tan that Robo and Sassy have and not as common. It's a mixture of gray and brown or tan throughout the coat with a black tip on the end of each hair. Must be a throwback to an earlier dog in the bloodline."

"Wow," Sophie murmured, apparently still full of wonder from the entire experience. "Is it a boy or a girl?"

"A girl," Tess said. "A little girl."

And let's hope she survives, Cole thought as he tapped Sassy's eyelid, noting that her blink reflex had returned. It wouldn't take long now for her to wake up. "Once Sassy wakes up, we need to make a bed for her in the kennel room. I'm going to keep her here until that last puppy is able to nurse on her own."

Now that everything had calmed down, he thought of Mattie. He loved her, and she would love these pups. He couldn't wait to show them to her, including this little sable fighter that reminded him of Mattie herself—someone who'd overcome the odds and fought to establish a good life.

FIVE

Mattie felt discouraged beyond words as she stood outside the prison gates with Hauck. Except for her mother, Cobb had been the only known witness to her father's death, and now they'd lost everything he knew.

A sharp breeze sliced through her uniform shirt, making her shiver. A glance at her unit told her that Robo had awakened and was watching her from the side window. *No panting; he's fine.*

"Let's sit in the car for a minute and decide where this investigation is going next," Hauck said, turning toward his black sedan as he clicked the key fob.

Mattie had been uncertain how motivated Hauck would be to pursue the case any further, and his willingness to move forward with the investigation reassured her. She followed him to his car, welcoming the break from the wind as she entered the passenger's side.

"Damn." Hauck settled into the driver's seat. "How do you Coloradans stand this cold? You don't even have on a coat."

"I didn't want to deal with it while we were inside, but I think the temperature dropped during the last hour. We have a storm coming in."

Hauck twisted in his seat to face her, his face serious. "Well, that was the shits. I can't believe that happened."

Mattie decided to express the belief that had taken shape in her mind. "The timing was impeccable. It had to be related to our interview today."

Hauck broke eye contact while he considered her words. "Maybe."

"Harold Cobb, John's brother, was killed in this very prison after he was incarcerated here decades ago. There's someone on the outside who's been able to get to them."

Hauck frowned and gazed out the window.

Mattie remembered how her own teammate, Stella LoSasso, always lectured others about jumping to conclusions. She drew a breath and slowed down. "Okay, so I have no proof of that, and it's just a theory. But it's a theory we should consider."

"I'll give you that. Let's talk about what we know for sure."

He turned to look at her, but she waited, wanting to know what *he* was thinking.

"Harold Cobb was killed with a shiv by an inmate who later said he had a beef with him. Staff who investigated that death thought there was more to it, but they never could prove it."

Mattie nodded. The sheriff of Timber Creek County, Abraham McCoy, had shared this information months earlier, and they'd speculated that someone in the Cobb brothers' original smuggling ring had arranged the hit. Until today, that theory hadn't seemed significant—old news. Now, however, Mattie had to wonder if the person or persons who'd arranged Harold's death had also ordered John's.

Hauck paused, but Mattie waited him out, deciding it best to withhold comment until she knew where he was coming from.

"It looks like John Cobb died from some type of opioid, but possibly by a self-inflicted, accidental overdose." Hauck raised his left brow, looking skeptical. "At this point we don't actually know how he died or what killed him, right?"

"That's right. But John Cobb has been imprisoned here for five months, and it seems like a huge coincidence that he would die the morning he was scheduled for an interview with us. I'm not a fan of coincidences. And Donahue said Cobb had no known history of drug use during his stay here, so accidental overdose seems unlikely."

"I hear you. I'll get us the autopsy report as soon as possible. That should tell us something."

It was a relief that Hauck planned to keep her in the loop, but she still intended to ask Sheriff McCoy to request the report as well. "I wish we could have interrogated the men he ate breakfast with and his guards. It would have been easy to slip something into his food or drink."

"I know, but Russo didn't want our help. Not our jurisdiction."

"Do you think he'll share information with you?"

"I think so. I'll follow up tomorrow and see where he's at."

That sounded good. "When do you go back to California?"

"I'm scheduled to fly home this evening." Hauck gave her that speculative look of his. "But I'm thinking of changing my plans."

"Oh?"

"What do you think of that trail map in the book? The one with the markings."

"I think there's something significant about it and it might be a lead."

Hauck frowned. "There was something about that map that upset you. You said you'd tell me later."

By this time, Mattie had recovered from the shock of seeing the mark on the spot where she'd been taken to die. She tried to remain detached while she spoke. "One X was on the place where John Cobb took me when he tried to kill me."

Hauck's eyes narrowed, and he withdrew his cell phone from his inside coat pocket. He swiped and tapped and then held up the screen, showing her the photo he'd taken of the map. "Show me which one."

Mattie pointed to the X on the backside of Redstone Ridge. "Cobb built a fire pit intended for me that night, but sparks from the flames set fire to the forest instead. Investigation of the area afterward didn't reveal anything. But now I wonder if something's there, maybe hidden or buried."

Hauck cursed under his breath as he leaned back in his bucket seat. "How did you get away?"

"I fought him."

"He's about my age, but he appeared to be a pretty strong guy. You must be one hell of a scrapper."

Mattie would've laughed if she hadn't had such a tight feeling in her gut from the memories of it. "I had my share of practice growing up as a kid."

Hauck studied her for a moment, as if taking her measure. "So . . . I'd like to go up to that area to look around."

That surprised her. "The trail's long and it's steep. Are you used to hiking?"

"I stay fit."

"But you're not used to this altitude. It makes a difference."

"I think I can do it."

Mattie wasn't so sure. "We have a sheriff's posse that supplies horses for us when we go on a mission up into the high country," she said, thinking of Cole. "We could arrange for you to go on horseback. Are you okay with that?"

He smiled. "I'm okay around horses. Used to have a couple myself until I moved to San Diego and it was too expensive to keep them."

His enthusiasm to continue to investigate excited her. "Let's go, then. It'll take about four hours to drive to Timber Creek. Do you want to follow me?"

"I'm going to need to buy some hiking boots." He tapped the steering wheel. "I have navigation, so getting there shouldn't be a problem. I'll come after I do some shopping."

"Will you want to stay the night in Timber Creek so we can get started early in the morning?"

"Sure," he said, quirking his eyebrow again. "Is that a problem?"

"There's only one motel. I'll make sure they reserve a room for you."

He released a quiet snort. "Small-town Colorado, huh?"

"You'll see."

"Give me the name of the place, and I'll make my own reservation."

Eager to get on the road, Mattie gave him the information he needed and said good-bye. After getting out of his car, she closed the door, the sound evidently loud enough to alert Robo. He popped back up in the side window, and as she approached, he began his happy dance, a silly grin on his face.

Hauck's plan to come to Timber Creek and her dog's greeting had done much to restore her spirits. She opened the hatch to give Robo a hug and splash fresh water into his bowl from his supply. She petted him while he slurped and exchanged waves with Hauck as he drove past on his way out of the parking lot.

Hauck stared at Robo on his way by. Her dog was an eye-catcher all right. She'd grown used to people being afraid of him, but she knew he was a pussycat at heart—though she would never take his protectiveness for granted. He wouldn't hesitate to put his life on the line to save hers, and she would do the same for him.

She snapped a leash on his collar and invited him out of the vehicle. As he gamboled beside her, she led him to a grassy area, her mind churning with unanswered questions. She was certain that John Cobb had been murdered. Who'd killed him? And why?

"Take a break," she murmured to Robo when they reached some bushes.

She continued to mull things over while Robo took care of his business. What secrets had Cobb known that someone wanted to keep hidden? Were there still active members in the smuggling ring that he'd been a part of decades ago? And if so, what were they into now? Drugs? Guns? What?

Her phone vibrated in her pocket, and she took it out to check. It was a text from Cole: **Puppies delivered by C-Section this morning. 4 males, 4 females. Sassy is fine. Come see them when you can. They'll be here at the clinic until tomorrow.**

Her spirits skyrocketed. "You're a father, Robo!"

Evidently latching on to her mood, her dog responded playfully, rising up on his hind feet to place his paws on her shoulders. She gave him a quick hug before making him get down. "Four boys and four girls, papa."

To help Robo expend some of his energy—and hers—she decided to take a few laps around the parking lot before the long journey home. She told him to heel and jogged off with him at her side, feeling more joyful than she would have believed possible under the circumstances.

But then, what could bring more joy than a litter of puppies?

★ ★ ★

A stiff wind buffeted the side of Mattie's SUV as she reached the top of the last mountain pass that stood between her and Timber Creek. It had been dark when she'd driven through here earlier this morning, but now the view of the forest rolled out before her in a display of gorgeous, Colorado-autumn splendor. Aspen groves stood out amid healthy green pine in pockets of gold, yellow, and orange. Groves of blue spruce complemented and enhanced the fall display—a panorama of shifting colors.

Thirty minutes more to reach home. Even though she'd been born in California to Ramona and Douglas Wray, Mattie considered Timber Creek home, and she was eager to get back. She'd ended up here after the Cobb brothers abducted her, her mother, and her older brother William. She had very few memories of her life with Harold Cobb, because the abuse she'd suffered at his hands had created a mental barrier to that time. Counseling and practice in relaxation and meditation techniques were gradually opening her memories back up to her.

Her long day of driving had given her too much time to think, usually not a good thing. She felt tired and depressed despite the conversation she'd had with Cole earlier about the puppies. She worried about her family's safety. John Cobb had thought her mother had stolen his money, and he'd tortured her brother William to find out where Ramona was hiding. Willie hadn't known where Ramona lived at that time, but now Mattie did. And so did her sister Julia and their grandmother.

If her father's killers were still out there somewhere, actively pursuing illegal business, would someone try to go after Ramona again? And if so, would they also target Julia and their grandmother?

Mattie hoped to get to the bottom of the mystery surrounding her father's murder and uncover any remaining scumbags who might threaten her family. She knew the danger was real, and she couldn't rest until her mother, sister, and grandmother were safe.

She steered around a long downhill curve, loving the sight of the blue-tinted mountain layers in the distance. The sky had darkened, promising a storm. Frothy clouds hung low over snowcapped peaks, and wind blasted her car from the north-west, scattering dried leaves from nearby aspens across the road. She hoped a storm wouldn't interfere with taking Hauck up to Redstone Ridge tomorrow.

Though she was off duty, she felt a need to check in with the office. She activated her Bluetooth system and said, "Call Stella."

The detective answered right away. "Hey, Mattie. Are you on your way home?"

"I'm about twelve miles away."

"How did the interview go?"

"When they went to retrieve John Cobb from his cell, he was in there dead."

The silence on the other end of the line lengthened.

"Stella? Are you there?"

"Damn, Mattie! You've got to be kidding me."

"Nope. I wish I was, although frankly, that's not a subject I'd kid about."

"My gut reaction?" Stella paused for a few seconds. "Who got to him?"

It was gratifying to hear her teammate express the exact same thought that she'd had. "That was my reaction too. There was evidence of opioid exposure, and Detective Hauck mentioned the possibility of accidental overdose. But I think that's unlikely."

"That man was not a drug user. Cartel lieutenant, trafficker, dealer? Yes. End user? No."

"I think we know our guy better than Hauck does."

"What's next?"

Mattie could imagine her friend pushing her reading glasses up to rest in her long auburn hair as she rocked back on the spring pedestal of her office chair and pursed her lips—her thinking mode.

"The prison investigator wouldn't let us interview inmates or guards, but he'll share the autopsy report when it comes in. I'll ask Sheriff McCoy to help expedite getting our hands on it."

"I'll take care of that. I'm sure he'll agree."

"Cobb had a book of Colorado hiking trails in his cell, and he'd dog-eared pages of Timber Creek County. He'd marked places on the Redstone Ridge trail. I need to go up there and check them out."

"Huh . . . I don't like the sound of that. You haven't been up there since, have you?"

Mattie knew Stella meant *since you almost died*. "Right. It's time I take Robo up to investigate that area more thoroughly. He's never done that."

"Yeah, but it's been five months."

"I've still got to search. You know how he's been trained to find things outside of the environmental norm. He might come across something humans have missed."

"Then I'll go up there with you."

Mattie knew that mountain hiking and even horseback riding weren't Stella's thing, making her even more grateful for her friend's offer. "Detective Hauck decided to come out and take a look. He'll go."

"So he wasn't totally convinced that Cobb overdosed, huh?"

"I think it was his way of saying I shouldn't jump to conclusions."

"Got it—we do need to avoid that. But I think it's safe to theorize that someone succeeded at getting a hit on Cobb, and that implies we've got some scary folks still in the game."

"I'd thought of that." Mattie hated the uncertainty of the situation. "And I've got to wonder if Julia and my grandmother are at risk. I guess I need to call Julia and warn her, even though I hate to frighten them."

"I think you should call. Better safe than sorry."

She felt glad to have a chance to confirm her feelings with someone she trusted. "I need to let you go. I'm almost at Cole's, and I think I'll call Julia before I get there. Oh, I almost forgot! Sassy had her puppies this morning. I'm going to stop at Cole's clinic to see them before I come to the station."

"Whoa! That's exciting. How many?"

"Eight. Four boys and four girls."

"Take some pictures of them, okay? Robo becoming a daddy is a first for our department. We need something to celebrate, and a puppy party sounds like just the thing."

"Will do. I'll be in soon."

"But today's your day off. You don't need to come in until tomorrow."

Mattie slowed as she reached the turnoff to Cole's clinic. "Since Hauck is on his way here, I want to talk to the sheriff and plan for tomorrow. I need to ask his permission to use Robo to help search that trail, and he might want me to do that on my own time rather than the department's."

"I think the evidence points to criminal activity within Timber Creek County, though whether it's in the past or present remains unknown. But with John Cobb's death this morning, signs point to the possibility of there being current concerns. Sheriff McCoy will probably agree that this is departmental business."

Mattie pulled over to stop at the top of Cole's lane. "Maybe so. I'll see you soon."

SIX

Cole opened the door between the exam room and the lobby to greet his next client. Despite it being afternoon, Angie sat at the reception desk, and Sophie was in the kennel room with Hannah, Sassy, and the pups. Like Ruth, he'd decided to let his daughters skip the whole day of school, partially because they were so excited about staying with the puppies and partially because he needed their help. Tess had left early to take her sons to a dental appointment.

Friday felt like a great day to play hooky. Maybe there was still a bit of the boy he used to be left in him. He liked to believe he hadn't turned into one of those grim adults who felt life was all work and no play, though he knew his ex-wife and daughters might disagree.

"Dr. Walker, this is Tonya Greenfield and her dog Kip," Angie said, playing her role as receptionist.

Cole smiled at her before turning to his new client, a young girl—looked like she was still a teen—who appeared close to nine months pregnant. The girl was holding an eager-looking border collie who tugged her across the room to deliver a tail-wagging greeting.

"Whoa, Kip! Don't pull your mama down." He blocked Kip's attempt to jump up on him by bending to hold and pet. Kip's color pattern was perfect for the breed standard—black with a white collar around the neck, white strip on the face, white lower legs and paws—and the dog's high-energy personality matched the breed standard as well. "Is Kip male or female?"

"A girl," Tonya said. She seemed skinny for someone with such an advanced pregnancy, all belly above twiggy legs. A riot of red hair curled around her thin, wan face, and dark smudges marred the skin below her blue eyes. He could tell with one glance that her peaked demeanor was no match for the energetic dog.

A woman with sandy hair and a sprinkling of freckles across her cheeks rose from one of the lobby chairs. "I'm Eliza Greenfield, Tonya's aunt," she said, extending a handshake. "We need to get Kip's shots up to date. I'm afraid she didn't have her last puppy shots, so she's way behind."

Angie handed him a booklet from a vet clinic in Nebraska that detailed Kip's vaccinations to date. "I copied this into our records already."

"Thanks, Angie." The birth date told him the dog was over a year old, and there was no record of inoculations after six weeks of age. "No rabies yet?"

Eliza pressed her lips together as she shook her head.

"I couldn't afford to take her in for shots," Tonya said with a little-girl tone. "Aunt Eliza said she'd take care of it for me."

"Here, let me take Kip's leash." Cole gave the booklet back to Tonya. "She's a little excited, and I don't want her to pull you over."

"She's always excited," Eliza muttered, placing a hand against her back as if it pained her.

"Border collies have a lot of energy." Cole stroked Kip's side and tucked her in close to his left heel. He told her to sit, but instead of sitting, she wagged her tail and looked up at him with loving eyes. "Is it okay with you if I give her a treat to make friends?"

"Sure, she loves treats." Tonya's smile lit her pale face.

Cole reached into the pocket of his lab coat, palmed a treat, and repeated the *sit* command while giving Kip a gentle push on her rump. After she sat, he immediately gave her the treat.

When Cole invited her into the exam room by opening the door, Kip surged forward, but he'd already shortened the leash and made her walk beside him while Tonya, Eliza, and then Angie followed. Once he'd moved into the room, he tucked

Kip close to his heel and told her to sit again. The intelligent dog plopped down without needing a touch and stared at his hand as if awaiting her treat.

Which Cole delivered happily. "You've got one smart dog here, Tonya. Border collies are known for their intelligence. I think she's ripe for obedience training."

Tonya looked pleased. "I've been kind of sick with this," she said, rubbing the bulge of her belly. "I haven't been able to give her the attention she needs."

"Maybe Ben could help train her while you're staying with us." Eliza looked at Cole. "Ben's my son, Tonya's cousin."

As Cole glanced up from Kip, he caught the look on Angie's face. Her eyes were downcast and rosy patches had blossomed on her cheeks.

Wait . . . what did Eliza just say? Oh yeah, she mentioned her son. "Does Ben attend high school here in town?"

"Yes, he's a senior. We hated to move him this summer right before his senior year, but he seems to like it okay. Better than I do." Her displeasure with Timber Creek was apparent on her face; in fact, Eliza seemed to wear an irritable frown in general.

Cole glanced at Angie again, who was busying herself by gathering all the supplies he might need and then some. "Have you met Ben yet, Angie?" he asked, trying to sound nonchalant.

She gave him a murderous look before turning away to retrieve bottles of vaccine from the refrigerator. "He's in my history class."

In light of his daughter's flushed cheeks, he'd bet the cool air from the fridge felt good. As far as he knew, this might be Angie's first crush—he'd worried that her parents' divorce might have soured her views on romance, but maybe it had just taken a new kid in town to snag her interest. Cole suppressed a smile and changed the subject to take the pressure off her. "If Ben is willing to help, you might take him up on it. Do you have a way for her to get plenty of exercise?"

Eliza answered for Tonya. "Kip has the run of the backyard. And *run* is the right word. She runs up and down the fence all day, barking and ruining the lawn."

"That's often what you see with these herding dogs. Is there someone in the family that can take her out for a walk or a run?"

Tonya looked at her aunt. "Maybe Ben?"

Eliza's frown deepened. "Maybe, but she's not Ben's dog. She's your responsibility."

Eliza was the one who'd brought up Ben helping to begin with, but he could tell the dog was a bone of contention between aunt and niece. He didn't want to go there with them.

"Well, whatever you work out will be temporary until the baby's born anyway." Cole picked up his stethoscope. "Looks like that might be soon?"

"Next week. I can't wait for it to be over," Tonya said.

Cole felt sympathy for the kid—she did look like she'd been through the wringer. "It'll be worth it. But then the sleepless nights begin."

"Oh, I won't have to deal with that. I'm not keeping the baby. I'm not ready to be a mom."

Cole's heart took a nose dive. He should've realized that might be the case and watched his words more carefully. But Tonya didn't seem to mind, and he covered his own discomfort by putting the stethoscope's earpieces in place and bending over Kip to listen to her heart and lung sounds. He made certain he did a thorough job as he gathered his wits. "Everything sounds good. Let's put her on the exam table."

He bent to lift Kip while Angie hurried to help, though the dog was light enough he didn't need it. Angie stepped in to steady Kip by taking hold of her collar and petting her. He examined Kip's eyes, which were bright and clear, and her ears, which were clean and free of parasites. "She's in good shape, Tonya. You keep her well groomed."

"That's one thing we can still do together. She likes to be brushed."

Cole drew up vaccine in a syringe, took hold of the scruff of Kip's neck, and injected it. Kip looked surprised by the sting but gave him a panting smile as he told her she was a good girl and stroked her firmly on the back. He could tell all was forgiven. She truly was a lovely little dog, and he hoped Tonya could give her a good life.

"So what's next, Tonya? After the baby. Are you going to stay in Timber Creek?" He'd asked purely out of curiosity about Kip's future.

Tonya shook her head. Her face became more animated and her tone lowered slightly, sounding more adult. "I'll move back home with Mom and Dad for a while, but I'm supposed to go to college in Lincoln in January."

"University of Nebraska?"

"Yes." Tonya pumped a small fist. "Go, Huskers."

Cole grinned at her, beginning to like this girl and her openness.

"I had a scholarship to be on the track team, but then I got myself knocked up and couldn't participate. They gave me a pass, and I hope to be ready by spring semester."

Cole immediately thought of Mattie. She'd been a cross-country state champion in high school. Out of the corner of his eye, Cole could see that Eliza looked annoyed, but he directed his conversation at Tonya. "Good for you. What's your specialty?"

"Short distance, mostly—one, two, and four hundred meter. And I also do relay."

"Maybe you can run with Kip when it's time to get back in shape. I have a friend who won the Colorado state championship in cross-country when she was in high school. She still runs all over these hills around town with her dog."

"Oh yeah?" Tonya's brows lifted as if she was impressed.

"She and her dog make up the K-9 unit at the sheriff's office."

Eliza straightened, moving her hand to her back again. "And who is that?"

"Deputy Mattie Cobb." Cole heard the door open and close in the other room. He hadn't realized he had another client scheduled, but he'd better end the chitchat and get ready to move on. As he grasped Kip around her chest to ease her down to the floor, Angie headed toward the doorway to see who had arrived.

After Kip's paws reached solid ground, she began to celebrate, gyrating at the end of the leash in a dance that made Cole
smile and shake his head at the same time. "You've got your
hands full with this one, Tonya. She's a real live wire."

"She's usually more chill than this."

"Let's get you checked out." Cole led Kip toward the lobby.
When he reached the door, he could hear Mattie talking to
Angie on the other side, and his heart lifted. He always felt
lighter when Mattie was around.

He might be wearing his heart on his sleeve, but he could
feel a goofy grin taking over his face as he opened the door.
Seeing Mattie and Angie together, both with smiles on their
faces, did his soul good. Angie had come around to the idea of
him having a relationship with someone new, and she was able
to let her affection for Mattie show. Both his daughters seemed
to care for this woman, a big relief that made his love for her
less complicated. It was tough enough falling in love with a cop
without needing to factor in his daughters' unhappiness.

"Hey, Deputy Cobb," he said, and Mattie turned her beautiful smile his way, giving his heart a tug. "I have someone I'd
like you to meet."

Mattie's eyes had gone to Kip, who apparently had never
met a stranger. Kip wagged her way to the end of the leash to
greet Mattie, who squatted and received the border collie with
open arms.

"Well, you're a friendly one," she said as she gave the dog a
quick hug before rising to stand when Kip turned up the volt-
age on her greeting. Mattie threw a grin Cole's way. "Easily
excited too."

I love this woman, he thought as he turned to introduce his
clients. "You've already met Kip, but here are her people—
Tonya Greenfield and her aunt Eliza. Tonya is going to school
on a track scholarship this spring at the University of Nebraska.
Short-distance specialist."

Mattie's face lit as she shook hands with the two. "Congrat-
ulations, Tonya. That's quite an achievement."

They chatted about running while Angie and Eliza settled
the bill. By this time, Cole was certain that Eliza suffered from

back pain and that he shouldn't turn Kip's leash over to either her or Tonya.

"Wait here a minute," he told Mattie before opening the door to exit. "I'm going to take Kip outside, but I want to go with you to the back."

He hurried to load Kip into the car, waved good-bye to the Greenfields, and went back into the clinic, where he found Mattie and Angie waiting for him.

He wrapped his arms around both of them to give them a tight hug, his way of welcoming Mattie home while including his daughter. "Wait till you see these pups." He guided them toward the exam room door. "They're beauties, aren't they, Angel?"

"Yep. Seven of them are doing real well, but Hannah just texted me that the little one still didn't eat." Even though the girls were inside the same building, they had been in different rooms and texting each other updates all afternoon.

Cole was worried about the wee pup. Any anesthesia exposure should have worn off by now. He feared there might be other problems that were making it so weak.

He held the door open for Mattie and Angie to enter the kennel room, then hurried forward to watch Mattie's face as she approached Sassy and her pups with awe. It thrilled him to share in her sense of wonder.

Sassy lowered her head and gazed at Mattie through upturned eyes, showing she would submit to her presence but wasn't happy about it. Angie stood back a few feet, giving Mattie a chance to move close to see the new puppies. Cole had warned the kids to keep their distance so that Sassy could mother her pups without being stressed, and the girls had placed dog cushions about six feet away where they could lean against the wall. Sassy had taken to motherhood well, licking her puppies to keep them clean and nursing them frequently.

Mattie murmured soothing words to Sassy while stroking her head. Since the two were familiar with each other, Sassy relaxed, heaving a sigh as she stretched out on her side. The pups awakened and began to wriggle blindly toward their mama's food supply—all of them except the smallest.

The expression on Mattie's face turned to concern. "She's really tiny, isn't she?" she murmured.

Cole nodded. "So the little one hasn't nursed yet," he said to Hannah.

The girl looked distressed. "I've been trying to get her to latch on like you showed me, and she opens her mouth, but she gives up after a few sucks. Maybe I'm doing it wrong?"

Cole rubbed the puppy gently to stimulate her to wake up. Sassy raised her head to see what he was doing and then rose into a sternal position to lick and nudge the puppy herself. Once the baby began to move, Cole found a free faucet on Sassy's belly and tried to get her to suckle, but as with Hannah, the pup gave up after only a few tries.

"You're not doing anything wrong, Hannah. I think she's too weak to eat this way." Cole looked at Sophie. "Don't you have a doll bottle at home? I think I remember one with a soft nipple."

Sophie's face lit. "Yeah, Mom gave me that bottle for my sixth birthday."

It amused him that she remembered the exact date. "Do you think you could find it?"

Looking excited, she rose to her feet. "I think so."

"Run to the house and get it. I have some powdered dog milk replacer we can use. This pup needs some nourishment."

Sophie ran through the back door. He could imagine her short legs churning as she sped to the house. She'd been sitting in the kennel room all day, and it was good to send her on an errand that would give her some exercise.

"Do you think she'll take a bottle, Dad?" Angie's concern was as apparent as Hannah's.

"It's either that or tube feed her. But if we can strengthen her suckle, she'll have a better chance of converting to nature's way of eating."

"She has a sable coat," Mattie murmured, her eyes on the pup.

"Dr. Walker said it must be a throwback in the bloodline," Hannah said.

Mattie nodded. "It's said that the German shepherd breed started with a sable-colored dog back in 1899, Hannah. Did you know that?"

She shook her head.

"A man from Germany discovered the type of dog he was looking for among German sheepdogs and registered the first official German shepherd sire. That dog fathered a lot of puppies, so the sable color pattern is in our dogs' DNA. German shepherds are descended from wolves originally, and this mixture of tan, gray, and black-tipped hair comes from them."

"Wow," Hannah said softly. "So she's special."

"Yes, she is." Mattie reached out to give Hannah a quick hug. "But they all are, aren't they?"

Cole loved this exchange. It was apparent how much Mattie loved kids, and she was a natural with them. But he'd known that already—it was part of the reason he'd fallen in love with her.

"Are you going to let Robo meet his pups, Mattie?" Angie asked.

"Eventually. We'll see what your dad thinks about the timing." Mattie glanced up at Cole with a soft smile.

"I don't think Sassy will want Robo around for a while," he said. "She'd probably growl at him."

They chatted about the pups until Sophie returned. She banged her way in through the back door, making Sassy startle.

"Oops, sorry about that." Looking sheepish, Sophie held up the doll bottle to show Cole.

"Great. C'mon, little bit, let's go mix up some dog milk for this tiny girl." As he headed back to the exam room with Sophie, his thoughts went to Tonya, whose petite stature had been accentuated by her pregnancy. A girl of that size seemed at risk for a tough labor and delivery, and he hoped all would go well for her next week.

SEVEN

Mattie spent more time at the clinic than she'd planned to, but she'd stayed to see if the pup would eat. Cole had worked patiently to elicit a few sucks and swallows, and he seemed pleased with his progress. He said he would try again in a half hour.

As she drove to the end of the lane, Mattie told Robo about his new offspring. When he yawned, she smiled at him in the rearview mirror. "You don't care about any of this, do you?"

But at the end of the lane, she stopped and poked her hand through the mesh to pet him, and he *did* seem to care very much about the scents left on her from Sassy and pups. His wet nose tickled her inner arm all the way up to her elbow, and she tousled the fur at his neck.

While she was waiting for a string of oncoming cars to go by before she turned onto the highway, a black SUV from the end of the line swerved into the other lane to pass the slower cars, picking up speed as it went.

She grabbed her radar gun and trained it on the receding vehicle, clocking it at thirty miles above the speed limit. She flipped on her overheads and pulled onto the highway to chase it, while cars in the string moved to the shoulder one by one to let her pass. She caught up to the SUV as it rounded the last curve into Timber Creek and settled in behind it until its driver slowed and stopped.

Leaving on the overheads, Mattie parked her unit so that it would partially protect her from oncoming traffic. While she radioed the department's dispatcher to notify her of her location and activity, the slower cars passed, giving them a wide berth. Traffic had picked up recently because it was the second week of elk season, and hunters were invading the high country around town.

Traffic stops were routine for law enforcement—until they weren't. Approaching a vehicle that had been stopped for speeding could be one of the most dangerous parts of the job. There were many unknowns about what might be waiting inside.

She ran the Nebraska plate on her mobile data terminal, and the results filled the screen—car registered to Cutter Smith, address in Lincoln, a black Lexus SUV with no stolen-vehicle report. A quick peek at the driver's license she pulled up for Smith revealed physical details of black hair, brown eyes, six foot three, two hundred pounds. No arrest warrants.

She powered down the window on the passenger side so that if she needed her partner for backup, she could release him with one touch of the popper button on her utility belt. It would open his cage door, and the open window would give Robo a way to exit.

Frigid wind blasted through the window, making her shrug on her Carhartt jacket with the Timber Creek Sheriff's Department insignia on the sleeve.

Knowing that Robo would be watching, she left her vehicle and approached the driver's side of the car. She noted three people inside, and they'd opened all four windows, an odd thing to do, considering the strong winds.

As she reached the car, she realized why. Her educated nose picked up the skunky odor of burning marijuana. No wonder they were trying to air out their car. The back compartment of the Lexus contained a variety of colored bags filled with what looked like camping gear, and the side window had a rack loaded with canvas-covered long guns, probably hunting rifles.

"Hello, Officer," the driver said, leaning out to greet her. He wore the full beard that many hunters grew to protect their faces from freezing temperatures in the high country, his matching his black hair. "Was I going a little too fast?"

"Yes, sir." Mattie told him his clocked speed as she bent slightly to check the eyes of the driver and then the passengers.

The familiar redness that she was looking for colored the whites around the green irises of the back seat passenger in particular, although any smoking joints had magically disappeared. All the men were bearded, their hair color ranging from ginger on the red-eyed guy in the back to brown on the front seat passenger to the driver's black.

"I'm sorry." The driver gave her a smile meant to be charming. "I must've missed the speed limit sign. I'll slow it down and be more careful."

"I need to see your license and registration, sir."

"Sure thing."

Mattie watched his hands as she rested her right one lightly on her service weapon. But he fished out only his wallet from his back pocket, worked for a few seconds to coax the card out of its plastic sleeve, and handed it to her. He also handed her a paper registration from inside his console. One glance told her it was indeed Cutter Smith driving his own vehicle, although the photo on the driver's license showed him minus the beard. But the dark-brown eyes and smile in the photo obviously matched the driver's—he was a good-looking guy.

"I need for you to step out of your vehicle, Mr. Smith."

His brows knit. "Is there something wrong, Deputy Cobb?" He'd evidently read her name tag.

"The strong odor of marijuana in your vehicle suggests that you could be driving impaired." Mattie moved away from the door so that he could open it. "Step out of your vehicle, please."

"But I haven't been smoking," he said as the click from the door handle told her that he intended to comply. The door opened and he heaved himself out of the SUV. He was big, standing almost a foot taller than Mattie's five foot four.

She stepped back to maintain a safe distance between them. "The smoke inside the vehicle could have affected you, sir. I need to make sure you're safe to drive. Do you have any weapons concealed on you?"

"Absolutely not." His original joviality was beginning to fade, typical of this type of traffic stop. Folks were always friendly in the beginning, but they turned surly as soon as they realized that law enforcement was onto whatever they were doing wrong. Dressed in camo and fleece, he stood with his hands shoved into his pockets, bracing against the wind, his shoulders scrunched up.

"Please move to the rear of the vehicle." Mattie watched him walk steadily toward the back of his Lexus, stopping him when he reached a spot between their two cars. "Turn away from me and place your hands on your head. I'm going to do a quick pat-down."

Smith scoffed, shaking his head in disgust, as he complied. The pat-down revealed nothing, and she began directing him through a roadside sobriety test: heel-to-toe walking and fingertip-to-nose touching while she observed his muscle coordination.

"I made Reagan keep his window rolled down so I wouldn't be affected," Smith muttered as he completed the test with no apparent problems.

"That was smart of you." It would've been even smarter if he'd maintained the speed limit—then she would've never known—but she wasn't going to tell him that. "I appreciate your cooperation, sir, and you can return to your vehicle."

Once he was inside, Mattie spoke through his window to the passengers. "I need to see everyone's identification, please." Though Smith's license had indicated he was thirty-three years old, she needed to make sure the passengers were of legal age to smoke weed. A quick glance through their driver's licenses told her that all were within legal limits, including the red beard named Reagan Dawson. They were all from Nebraska.

"All right," she said to Cutter Smith. "I'm going to write you a warning and let you be on your way. I hope you'll keep your promise to slow down and observe the speed limit signs more carefully."

He looked relieved and nodded, some of his friendliness restored.

"Where are you headed?" Mattie asked him.

"Somewhere west," he said, lifting his hand to indicate that direction. "We're here to hunt elk."

She bent lower to speak to everyone in the car. "I know you're from out of state, but you all need to know it's illegal to open marijuana packaging and use the contents inside a moving vehicle. I'm going to cite Mr. Dawson for that."

A chorus of groans arose.

"You should know Colorado state law if you're going to buy weed and use it here. No transporting of marijuana is allowed across state lines, no smoking in public places including outdoor parks, and no smoking on federal lands including national forests and campgrounds."

"Shit," Dawson muttered from the back seat.

"Just giving you fair warning." Mattie gave him her cop face as well. "Your best bet is to find a motel that allows smoking. The one in Timber Creek does not, so you might as well keep driving." She straightened. "I'll return in a few minutes."

The smooth whirr from the power windows told her they were raising them as she walked back to her Explorer, their driver's licenses in hand. Robo greeted her with a few bouncing steps as she approached the car, followed by sniffing at her through the mesh when she stepped up into the driver's seat.

"You smell what's going on, don't you?" Robo had been trained to detect narcotics and gunpowder, which was why she didn't need to use him to sweep this particular vehicle. She already knew he would hit on both. The illegal use of marijuana gave her probable cause to search inside the vehicle for other drugs if she wanted to, but she believed these guys weren't drug runners and had honestly come into the area to hunt. They had all the gear for it, including the beards.

She ran a quick check to make sure the two passengers had no arrest warrants, wrote out the citations including the speed warning, and returned to the Lexus to deliver them. Smith rolled down the window and tried to stare her down as she handed him the citations, but she didn't let him.

She bent forward to address them all. "Drive safely and slow it down. Be careful to observe state laws for marijuana use, and you should have no more trouble. Good luck with your hunting."

She really didn't care whether they bagged an elk or not, but she said it as a gesture of goodwill. Out-of-state hunters and tourists could sometimes be a nuisance in Timber

Creek County, depending on their behavior. They brought much-appreciated income to the town's merchants, but some of them also brought trash, alcohol, and mischief. These were the types that gave the respectful outsiders a bad name, and Mattie had to wonder about these guys, since they'd already broken the law.

Smith gave her a sardonic smile. "Thank you, Deputy Fife . . . oh sorry, I mean Deputy Cobb." His passengers snickered at his joke.

Clever, never heard that one before, Mattie thought, but she kept the retort to herself. "Be safe out there, Mr. Smith."

She turned on her heel and walked away before he could take another shot at her. Providing law enforcement in a small town had its share of challenges, this type of ribbing being only one. It was offensive, but Sheriff McCoy held his officers to a high standard of professionalism, and he wouldn't accept excuses for public displays of temper.

"Smartass," she muttered as she climbed back into her SUV, and that would be the only reaction she allowed herself. She checked back in with dispatch to radio an all clear while she waited for the Lexus to drive away.

Smith used proper signals before pulling into the lane. She followed several car lengths behind as he made a point of creeping the last quarter mile into town. When he turned onto the highway to Hightower, she stayed with him until she reached the last street in Timber Creek, where she turned and drove around the block to set a course toward the station.

County cruisers and the sheriff's Jeep filled the parking lot, telling her it was shift change and time for afternoon report. She unloaded Robo, and he trotted ahead to the door, his tail waving. He paused to let her enter first, which she rewarded by saying, "That's right," before telling him it was okay to follow her inside.

It was a small thing but one that he'd tested her on in the past, often crowding her at the door. With Robo, she had to stay on top of him to remind him who was boss. With these high-drive male dogs, you didn't dare let discipline slip or it could take weeks of retraining to regain their respect.

Once inside, her dog knew he had the run of the place, and he beat it over to the dispatcher's desk, where Mattie's friend Rainbow sat with her headset on. She stripped it from her head so she could lean over Robo to give him a hug and a kiss and coo sweet nothings in his ear, her long blond side braid swinging forward. The two had a special relationship, and Mattie had given up on keeping them apart during their first greeting of the day. As long as her dog didn't allow his rambunctious behavior to spill over to others, she let him enjoy the love.

"Hey, Mattie." Rainbow glanced up, laughter lines crinkled at the edge of her blue eyes. "You're not supposed to be here today, much less making traffic stops."

"I know, but the guy was busting thirty over the limit outside of town, and I couldn't let that go." Mattie watched while her dog nuzzled Rainbow's arm, asking for more petting, which the dispatcher seemed happy to provide. "You spoil him."

"We're buds, aren't we?" Rainbow giggled while Robo stole a kiss, swiping his tongue against her cheek.

"That's enough." Mattie intervened, telling Robo to settle down before he tried to climb into her friend's lap. "Anything happening around here that I should know about?"

"Nope, just the routine. Brody's doing report. Stella said to look her up when you stopped by. She's in the sheriff's office."

"All right." Just routine meant no known trouble brewing, which might lead to Sheriff McCoy's allowing her to investigate the Redstone Ridge trail tomorrow with Hauck. "Robo, you have to come with me, even if you don't want to."

Rainbow gave him one more kiss on top of his head. "Do you want to come out to my place for dinner this weekend? You guys haven't been out forever."

Her friend lived just outside the city limits west of town in a small cabin built beside the actual stream called Timber Creek from which the town derived its name. "I'd love to, but a detective from California is coming here, and if the sheriff approves, we'll probably be spending this weekend up in the high country."

"Detective Hauck?"

"Yeah."

"He just left. Stopped by to talk to Sheriff McCoy and Stella and then said he was going to go check into the motel." Rainbow grinned. "The Silver Fox."

Mattie nodded. With Hauck's white hair and movie-star looks, she thought it an appropriate nickname. "The name fits."

"Friendly guy. He even stopped on his way out to visit with me."

Mattie agreed that visiting with a dispatcher wasn't typical detective behavior, but she thought something besides friendliness might have come into play. Rainbow didn't realize it, but she was very pretty.

"What did Detective Hauck want to talk about?" Mattie asked, thinking he might have been flirting.

"You."

That was a surprise. Mattie frowned. "What did he want to know about me?"

"Well, he wanted to know about you and Robo, I guess. He said he didn't know you were a K-9 handler until this morning. So he mostly wanted to know about Robo and what he does for the department." Rainbow gave her a fake frown. "Don't look so concerned, Mattie. I just told him general stuff that he could learn from anyone. I didn't reveal any of your deep, dark secrets."

Mattie knew she was being teased, but truthfully, Rainbow didn't even know her deep, dark secrets. Stella did, and because of past circumstances, the sheriff and Brody did too, but Mattie had never shared everything with Rainbow. She kept her past history private whenever possible. She responded by teasing back. "That's good. I trust you'll keep my secrets safe in the future. So he wasn't flirting with you?"

Rainbow scoffed. "Are you kidding? He's older than my father. He just seems like a nice guy."

Mattie agreed. "I'd better go join Stella and the sheriff. Robo, come with me." Robo fell in beside Mattie as she crossed the lobby to the door of McCoy's private office. With a hand gesture, she signaled for him to sit at heel before she tapped on the door.

"Come in." The sheriff's voice, rich and deep in timbre, came from inside. When she opened the door, he greeted her with one of his smiles that made her feel warm and accepted. Abraham McCoy's age was beginning to show, with a sprinkle of gray at the temples of his closely buzzed black hair, but aside from the crow's-feet at the corners of his brown eyes, the dark skin of his face remained smooth and his jawline taut. The man exuded a trustworthiness that voters evidently recognized, which kept him in office. "Have a seat, Deputy. We were just talking about how we could support you with Detective Hauck's investigation."

As she settled onto one of the chairs in front of McCoy's desk, Mattie exchanged glances with Stella. Robo sat beside her, ears pricked, as he appeared to scope out the sheriff's office. It was unusual for him to be invited into this inner sanctum. "I heard that Detective Hauck stopped by."

"Right." McCoy leaned forward, forearms on his desk. "Since John Cobb was killed outside our jurisdiction, he seemed to want to make sure I would allow you to help investigate. I told him that wouldn't be a problem. We're the ones who arrested Cobb in the first place, and those markings on the map you found bring the investigation right back to Timber Creek County. We need to go see if we can find anything."

"I'm glad you feel that way. Cole said he would arrange horses and a posse member to take Hauck up into the high country. How many of us do you plan to send?"

"Just you, Robo, and Hauck. We'll make further adjustments if you turn up something."

"Hauck seems motivated to see if he can tie John Cobb to your father's death, Mattie," Stella said. "Maybe he'll be able to make some headway where others couldn't."

"I hope you're right." Mattie thought her father's case had been allowed to sit on the shelf for years. "I wonder why John Cobb marked that trail in the places he did."

"Hauck shared the photo of the page with us," Stella said as she and McCoy both picked up their cell phones and swiped their screens. "I'll enlarge and print it."

"Thanks." Mattie pulled her cell phone from her pocket to open the same photo while Robo settled down beside her, resting his head on his front paws. They were all familiar with this trail, having excavated Willie's grave site near the base of the ridge a few months ago. "Do you associate anything with these markings?"

"The obvious, I guess," Stella said. "Something buried? The Cobb brothers' history might suggest firearms, money, or even bodies."

McCoy looked grim. "We investigated that area beneath the ridge with Robo when William's grave was discovered, so I'm not sure we'd find anything new there. But the X on the backside of the ridge corresponds to the area where Cobb took you, and it bears further investigation. Even though we searched there after Cobb was arrested, we didn't use Robo at the time. Cobb must've hidden something up there before we arrested him. Maybe you can get a sense of how we should proceed after you explore tomorrow."

Mattie thought about the wilderness involved. Miles of forest surrounded Redstone Ridge in the high country west of town. Secrets lay buried up there for decades—perhaps forever. Unless she and Robo could bring them to light.

EIGHT

Saturday morning

On the back of Cole's red roan named Mountaineer, Mattie followed Garrett Hartman as he led their small party toward the north side of Redstone Ridge. Named for a shade of rose quartz that ran through the striated rock on the cliffside, this ridge was arguably one of the most beautiful spots in the state of Colorado, despite the forest surrounding it being marred by fire. But for Mattie, its beauty had been destroyed by her brother's death.

She settled deeper into her well-insulated coat, a wind- and rain-resistant brown winter jacket supplied by the department. The frigid air pinched her cheeks, and she pulled its faux fur collar up to shield them. Mountaineer needed little to no guidance as he followed the lead horse, so she was able to relax in the saddle, leaning forward and shifting her weight to maintain her balance as they moved upward on the steep trail.

The cold front brought in by yesterday's wind had lowered the temperature at least thirty degrees. Clouds hung low around peaks cloaked by snow, and frost flocked the needles of spruce and pine, but snowfall had yet to accumulate at this elevation. Their journey had been unimpeded and they'd made good time this morning, riding in tandem through the trees' shadows—first Garrett, followed by Mattie and then Jim Hauck.

Robo ranged from front to back, sometimes blazing the trail and oftentimes exploring the outskirts deeper in the forest but always coming back to trot beside Mountaineer for a while. At this rate, he would cover two miles to their one.

Cole had wanted to come, but puppy care prevented it; and Mattie understood, especially since his kids were involved.

When they'd checked in with each other this morning, he'd told her he loved her before saying good-bye, and despite earlier struggles with saying the words, she now found them easy to repeat, a simple thing that lifted her mood when she faced a tough day like today.

They were entering the area destroyed by fire. Garrett Hartman—a tall, lanky cattleman who served on the sheriff's posse—turned in his saddle, his gray-blue eyes showing his concern. He'd been part of the group who'd helped find her the night this area burned. "How are you holding up?" he asked, his voice laden with care.

"I'm good. Don't worry." Mattie felt almost as close to this man as she did to Cole, although in a completely different way. She'd met Garrett a little over a year ago when investigating the death of his teenage daughter. He'd developed a fondness for both Robo and her, treating Mattie like he was a protective older brother—a trait that she found endearing, which surprised her. She wasn't used to accepting protection, a duty she considered an important part of her own job description.

Garrett turned to face forward again as his gelding humped up another steep incline, stones rolling under the horse's churning hooves. The pack behind Garrett's saddle contained supplies they would need for the day, a foldable camp shovel tied on top.

Mountaineer followed at a safe distance, and Mattie grasped the saddle horn as she leaned forward. Blackened tree trunks, stripped of their branches, spiked the landscape. At first they were scattered among healthy trees that had evaded the fire, but as they rode deeper into the burnt area, she could see where the devastation took over and filled the mountainside with very little but the charred debris of dead trees.

The odor of charcoal still tainted the air as they left behind the clean scent of the living forest. Robo came back and stayed close beside her as lowering clouds weakened the sunlight. Mist wrapped around the crags, readily apparent in the distance now that the forest no longer blocked the view.

Mattie knew what lay at the base of those crags—a cave where she'd fought off her captor and escaped. A chill breeze quickened, and without the shelter of the evergreen forest, it hit her square in the chest. She shivered, not only from the harsh wind but also from the memories of that cruel night.

How the wind had howled! She'd stumbled from that cave, still partially under the influence of a disabling drug, and disappeared into the trees. Equipped with night-vision goggles, John Cobb probably would have been able to find her if it hadn't been for the forest catching on fire. A blessing in disguise for her; utter destruction for the backside of Redstone Ridge.

The clang from the horses' shod feet rang out as the trail transitioned from forest floor to patches of granite slab. She remembered being transported up here the last time, slung over a saddle, moving in and out of consciousness, her senses reeling from the tranquilizer that John Cobb had delivered by shooting a large animal dart into her back.

Garrett turned to check on her again, and she pasted on her cop face as she met his gaze. She sensed that he knew how she felt, and he sent her an empathetic look before turning away. She didn't want him to worry about her, and she vowed she'd keep her emotions under control.

"This is godforsaken land." Hauck, breaking a silence he had maintained most of the way up, projected his voice from behind. "When did this fire happen again?"

Garrett turned in his seat to answer. "Last May. Not enough time to recover much."

"There's a little bit of green coming back," Mattie said, pointing out the places where grasses and brush had taken hold during the past summer.

Robo trotted ahead as they covered the last bit of rocky ground that led to the area where John Cobb had set up camp. As Mattie approached, she could tell that the pit he'd intended for her was still apparent. Steely anger at the man's brash stupidity—building a huge fire during a windstorm—filled her with strength.

"This is where the fire originated," Garrett told Hauck as he rode past the pit a short distance and then reined to a stop. "When we could get back in here after the fire, the cave was searched thoroughly. But not with Robo."

Evidently hearing his name, Robo trotted up to join their little group, wagging his tail as Mattie dismounted and then pressing his body against her legs. She patted his side, making a thin cloud of black dust fly from his fur as the odor of scorched wood filled her mind with a flashback from when Cobb had tried to brand her with an ember on the end of a smoking stick.

Though sorry she'd missed her chance to interrogate him, she was glad he was dead and he'd never be able to torture or kill again.

"Were you part of the party that searched here, Garrett?" Hauck asked as he dismounted.

"I was. I was up here the night of the fire and a couple days after."

"So was the search primarily visual?"

"That's right."

"What did you find?"

Garrett looked at Mattie, obviously passing the question to her.

Mattie kept her words even and free from emotion. "They found and took into evidence the rope John Cobb used to bind me and the bola I made with it to protect myself after working my hands free. A charred stick that he intended to burn me with. And they took samples of vomit I left behind when the tranquilizer he used on me made me sick."

"Good lord," Hauck muttered as he searched Mattie's face.

She turned away to untie her pack from behind her saddle before he could find any cracks in the mask she'd put up to hide her turmoil. "I'll take Robo inside the cave and see if he can turn up anything." She glanced back at Hauck. "He's trained to search for narcotics, gunpowder, and anything outside of the environmental norm. The cave is the best place to start."

"It makes sense that if Cobb buried weapons or drugs up here, he might do it inside a cave," Hauck said. "You know, to protect it."

Mattie placed her pack on a boulder that wasn't sullied with ash. She found Robo's collapsible bowl and filled it with water from her supply. He slurped noisily. She replaced his everyday leather collar with one made of blue nylon that he wore for evidence detection.

As soon as she buckled it on, he gazed up at her with his intelligent eyes, awaiting her direction. She could tell he already knew his mission. It was tied to the equipment: collar meant find an object, harness meant search for a person. Although she'd been his partner now for over a year, his cleverness still amazed her.

She told him to heel and led him toward the mouth of the cave, hearing the men's footsteps crunch the gravel on the rocky path behind her—sounds identical to the ones John Cobb had made as he came into the cave that night with the intent to torture her.

The noise raised an alarm within her solar plexus that was purely driven from cell memory, a phenomenon she'd discussed with her trauma counselor. Triggers from past trauma could activate the flight-or-fight response in survivors at the most unexpected times.

Well . . . today she'd expected to be triggered, but that didn't help her control the surge of adrenaline that hit her system right now. Robo brushed against her leg, prancing on his front feet as he gazed up into her eyes, probably trying to figure out her problem. Her emotions always traveled down the leash to him. She stopped before entering the cave and bent to stroke the velvety black fur between his ears, taking a moment to center herself.

That night, she'd lain on the floor of the cave, listening for Cobb's footsteps, her bola tucked beneath her, the rope wrapped over her hands as if they were still tied. The cave spun in cogwheel-like freeze frames, and she had feared that vertigo would overcome her and she wouldn't be able to fight. But the alternative had been certain death. The adrenaline that hit her system that night gave her the ability to fight off her captor and escape; today she needed to disperse the energy another way. Deep, steadying breaths.

Stroking Robo's ears settled her somewhat, and she led him the rest of the way into the cave, an alcove shallow enough for natural light to reveal the interior. She did a visual sweep of the rocky walls and the floor, which was littered with shale and stones. The dank odor of animal scat and decayed remains wafted from its forty-foot depth, creating another feeling of déjà vu from that night.

Her experience as a law enforcement officer and K-9 handler drove back her fears. She told herself this was just a cave—a rock room twenty feet wide, forty feet deep, and ten feet high. Nothing more.

She eyed the cave's floor and decided it made sense to do a grid search. She clipped a short leash to Robo's collar and leaned over him to thump his sides and deliver the chatter he loved so well, the words that raised his prey drive and turned him into a sniffing machine. When he began to dance with anticipation, she straightened and spoke the command they used for an evidence search: "Seek!"

She used her free hand to point to the cave's floor, and Robo lowered his nose to the ground, his delicate lips fluttering as he vacuumed up scent. Mattie had already created a grid in her mind, and now she applied it, walking Robo to the end of the cave. He sniffed a three-foot swath, his head moving side to side as he quartered the area before moving back to the cave's opening. Back and forth, left to right, they covered the floor without any indication from Robo that he'd found something outside the environmental norm.

Until they reached the right wall. There, about halfway down, Robo pawed the stones, whiffed the depression he'd made as if double-checking his work, and then he sat, staring hard at the place he'd sniffed—his signal of a hit.

A healthy surge of adrenaline punched her already activated system. Since she trusted Robo's sense of smell completely, she tousled her dog's ruff and told him, "Good boy," as she moved him back a few steps. Even if all he'd found was some buried trash, he'd still done his job. She glanced at Hauck, who'd waited at the mouth of the cave with Garrett. "He's got a hit, but I don't see anything."

Hauck came into the cave to stand beside her, his eyes fixed on the depression that Robo had made within the stones. "Should we dig here?"

Of course they should. His question showed his lack of experience with her dog. Deputy Ken Brody, who usually backed her, would already be down on his knees snapping photos.

Mattie used hand signals to tell Robo to sit and stay. "First we take pictures, and then we'll dig."

"I'll get the shovel in case we need it," Garrett said, leaving the mouth of the cave to head for the horses.

Eager to uncover whatever was hidden, Mattie took out her cell phone and began taking shots of the cave's interior and close-ups of Robo's mark.

Hauck soon joined her, taking pictures with his own phone. "What do you think he found?"

"Weapons, ammo, or drugs would be my guess."

"Not money?"

Mattie shrugged. "I doubt it. If bills or coins are just below the surface, Robo might hit on them, but I think that's unlikely. Then again, you never know with this dog. Sometimes he surprises me."

"How about explosives?"

"That's not Robo's training. Like I said, just gunpowder." Mattie considered the possibility of a trap of some kind. Was it possible some type of explosive had been planted? Should she wait and ask for a bomb team to excavate the stash? "I suppose we should be concerned about explosives. But what would be the point? I mean, why set a bomb here in the back of a cave?"

Hauck nodded, taking one more picture before he lowered his phone. "I agree. I think it's most likely that he hid something and planned to come back to get it. I guess we'll see. Why don't you let me do the digging and you stand back a ways?"

"No, I'll do it." Mattie withdrew a pair of gloves from a pocket in her coveralls and put them on. "I'll push back some of the shale and soil and see what's beneath. My guess is that whatever Robo hit on isn't very deep."

She knelt, feeling the sharp edges of shale bite her knees. She gently scooped back the loose stones to clear a space about two feet square in size. The soil beneath the shale brushed away easily, as if something had been buried there recently. She dug only a couple inches deeper and stopped when she felt the slick surface of plastic beneath her fingertips.

"I've got something right here," she told Hauck. "Would you take photos while I dig it out? I don't think we'll need a shovel."

"Sure." Hauck moved closer, holding his phone ready.

Mattie scraped back the soil, careful not to damage anything beneath. Wiping away dirt and pea-size gravel, she cleared the top of a package the size of a gallon bag made of dark, heavy-duty plastic.

"Let's get a shot of this." She leaned back so that Hauck could take the photo, and then she continued to unearth the bag. After a few quick swipes, she was able to lift it. She felt its contents shift beneath her fingers like fine sand, or in this case, most likely powder.

"My bet is narcotics," she said to Hauck. "Feels like powder, so maybe cocaine. Could be a variety of things."

"That's a big bag." Speculation crossed Hauck's face. "Worth a lot on the street."

"I'd say so."

"Shall we open it to see what it is?"

Mattie remembered the foamy substance in John Cobb's nostrils—residue from pulmonary edema secondary to respiratory distress. "I think we should have the lab open it in a controlled environment. This could even be what Cobb was exposed to yesterday, and I only have two doses of Narcan in my pocket."

Narcan reversed the effects of opiates such as fentanyl, one of the street drugs most dangerous to narcotics detection dogs. It saved the lives of dogs, their handlers, and even addicts after accidental exposure or overdose. Nowadays K-9 officers carried two doses, one for their dog and one for themselves. If they were exposed to fentanyl inside this cave, she would treat Robo first. She would always treat Robo first.

Mattie scooped away some more dirt but didn't find anything else. Garrett returned to the cave, carrying the bag that held the sat phone as well as the shovel.

"I heard the satellite phone ring before I got to the horses to answer it, so I brought it for you," he said.

"Thank you." With a sense of alarm, Mattie rose from her knees to take the phone outside where she would get a better signal.

NINE

With renewed hope, Cole watched the puppy suck and swallow from the doll bottle. After spending the night in the clinic with the kids, trying to feed the wee pup every two hours, he felt like a horse that had been "rode hard and turned out wet," an old cowboy expression. It had been a long morning after a hard night, but it looked like their efforts were beginning to pay off.

"I think she's got the hang of it, Hannah," he said.

Dark circles colored the fragile skin beneath Hannah's blue eyes, but her smile lit her face. "Do you think she'll live now?"

"I can't guarantee it, but her chances are much better now than they appeared to be last night."

"Should I see if she'll latch on to Sassy?"

"Let's let her drink her fill from the bottle. The more nourishment she gets, the better. Maybe by this afternoon we can transfer her to Sassy."

"I'll call my mom when she's finished." Hannah continued to cradle the small pup while she fed her.

Ruth had remained home with her other children, but Hannah had updated her frequently.

"She'll be glad to get the good news," Cole said.

Sophie stood up from her cushion, the only one in the crew who'd slept through most of the feedings. She looked full of energy while Angie and Hannah gazed wearily from bleary eyes. Cole felt certain his stinging eyes looked just as tired as theirs.

"Should I go home and get us some lunch?" Sophie asked. "I'm starving."

Cole had returned home to shower and get ready for the day before he began his office hours in his clinic. He'd brought breakfast and snacks for the kids, but apparently all that food had been eaten. "You know what, little bit? I think it's safe for all of us to take a break. Let's go home for lunch, and maybe you girls could lie down for a couple hours between feedings."

"I'm not a bit tired," Sophie said, and indeed, with the exception of her tousled curls, she looked ready to take on the world.

"That's good to hear." Cole wrapped an arm around her to give her a quick hug. "The rest of us didn't fit on our cushions as well, so we're beat. After you have lunch, you can read a book or watch some TV, whatever you want. Why don't you run up to the house now and warn Mrs. Gibbs that we'll be there soon. See if she needs your help. Tell her Hannah is coming too."

Sophie left just as the pup began to sputter, clamp her jaw, and try to get away from the nipple.

"She's done, Hannah," Cole said, holding out his hand. "Let's see how much she ate."

A good half of the bottle was empty. "That's a fair amount for a puppy this small. Let's put her back down so Sassy can clean her up."

"She's not as wet this time," Hannah said with a tired smile. "Sassy might not be as happy to have her back."

It had been their nighttime joke, watching Sassy eagerly receive the pup to lick the milk replacer from her fur. But yet again, as Hannah gently put the puppy back down beside Sassy, the mama dog greeted her with her warm tongue. Cole felt certain that Sassy's unwillingness to give up on this baby was part of the reason it still lived.

And now maybe he could relax some of his parental instincts with his kids, including Hannah. He'd stayed with them the last twenty-four hours out of concern that the puppy might die, and he hadn't wanted them to be alone if that happened. It would have been hard enough on them without their having to bear the burden of ultimate responsibility. He'd needed to be present and in charge.

So he'd stayed with the kids instead of going up to Redstone Ridge with Mattie, even though he knew how hard the trip would be for her. Returning to the place where you had faced death would be hard on anyone.

As they headed outside, Cole put his arm around Angie's shoulders. "Hey, Angel. What's going on between you and this guy Ben Greenfield?"

"Da-ad!" Angie threw him a scowl.

But Hannah gave him a knowing smile, and he squeezed Angie's shoulders. "I only have one thing to say, girls. When you have a boyfriend, make sure he treats you with respect. Don't ever accept anything less."

"Geez," Angie muttered, although she let him keep his arm around her shoulders as they walked out to the truck. But Hannah gave him eye contact and nodded—maybe that was the only agreement he was going to get.

"And if either of you ever need me to come help you with any situation, just call, anytime, day or night." This time they both nodded, and he decided to be satisfied with that.

★ ★ ★

Mattie reached Sheriff McCoy on her first try.

"Mattie, I want to update you on some changes we've had in the plan. But first tell me where you're at and what's going on up there."

McCoy typically referred to his deputies formally, calling her Deputy Cobb. But recently he'd begun calling her Mattie, and she didn't mind at all. It was as if he realized the name Cobb no longer fit. Even Brody, someone she considered less sensitive than the sheriff, called her Mattie nowadays. And she felt herself moving away from the name Cobb as well, detaching from all the pain the name had caused her.

She was glad she had good news to share. "We've hit the jackpot in the cave. A bag filled with a powdery substance, buried just under the surface. My bet is it's some type of narcotics."

"That's great news. And I think you'll like what I have to tell you."

"What's that?"

"Sergeant Madsen has several dogs in training that he wants to bring to help us."

"Wow." The news pleased her indeed. Madsen had been Robo's trainer, and he was someone she admired tremendously. "When can we expect him?"

"He's rounding up handlers, but he thinks he can arrive by evening. He's got a variety of specialties in the works, including a couple cadaver dogs and one trained on explosives. He said he's got a dog trained on narcotics that he'll bring to back up Robo, so we have the whole spectrum covered."

There couldn't have been better news. Although Robo had been able to find corpses in the past, it wasn't his specialty. Sergeant Madsen had told her that Robo had been exposed to cadaver training briefly before they focused on narcotics detection, and her dog was smart enough to remember everything he'd ever been taught.

"I was worried that we might miss buried human remains," Mattie said. "And with John Cobb, that scenario could be possible."

"Agreed. Finish up what you can today. Snow is forecasted for above eight thousand feet this evening, so I want you all down from there before it hits. I wanted you to know you had the cavalry coming in to help tomorrow with the lower elevations, in case you run out of time today."

"Couldn't be better, sir. Thanks for letting me know." As she signed off, Mattie reached out to stroke Robo's fur. She buried her cold fingers in his ruff. "We're getting some help, buddy. How about that?"

Robo bumped his nose on her belt pocket that held his tennis ball.

"All right." She replaced the sat phone in the bag. "Playtime now, and then we'll check on the others."

She climbed uphill beyond the cave to find a spot that had been spared from fire. A cold front had blown in from the northwest the night of the fire, driving sparks and the blaze in a southeasterly direction. The fire had spread downhill from where it first ignited, but the forest uphill and to the north remained relatively untouched.

Robo gamboled at her side as they climbed the steep slope. She removed the tennis ball from its pocket and threw it. Robo scrambled after it, tucked into the challenging footing of the slope. The ball landed in some bushes and lodged there while Robo homed in on it, thrusting his nose into the golden brush. The ball glowed neon yellow against his black lips as he carried it jauntily back to her.

Though Robo could play like this forever, she limited him to five minutes before going back to the cave. Dark heavy clouds had filled the sky in layers, and the wind showed no sign of letting up.

Garrett waited outside in the shelter of the leeward side of a boulder, and she downed Robo beside him. Once inside, she saw that Hauck was using the shovel to excavate the remainder of the right wall and the entire back edge of the cave's floor.

She paused at the mouth of the cave. "Have you found anything else?"

Hauck quit digging and stepped back from the end of the cave so he could straighten and stretch his back. "Nothing. I think we can safely say we've found everything buried here."

Mattie went farther inside to examine the tightly wrapped bag lying on the cave floor. "This looks like about a kilo. Depending on what we have here, it represents a lot of dirty cash. Our lab can have an answer for us by tomorrow." She went on to tell him about Sergeant Madsen and his dogs.

Hauck frowned. "Now . . . who is this guy?"

Mattie explained the sergeant's role as a K-9 trainer.

"I don't want this turning into a circus with a bunch of dogs running around," Hauck said.

"It won't." Mattie let her abrupt reply show what she thought of his concern. She turned to Garrett. "Sheriff McCoy says this front is bringing in snow at eight thousand feet. We need to finish up and get down lower before it hits."

Garrett nodded. The light inside the cave had grown dimmer and dimmer.

"I'm going to send Robo out to search this area around the cave."

"I'll follow up with a visual search," Garrett said.

Mattie nodded. "Thanks."

Hauck turned to the back of the cave to pick up the bag they'd found. "I'll put this in my saddlebag."

"The chain of custody starts and stays with me," Mattie said. "We'll pack it out in my saddlebag."

Hauck's brow lifted. "All right, Deputy. I guess it *was* your dog's find."

Mattie signaled Robo to come with her as Hauck carried the bag to the horses. She packed it into the saddlebag that had been lashed behind the cantle of her saddle, enjoying a few moments of respite from the harsh wind behind Mountaineer's warm body.

Although Mattie figured that after five months there would be nothing in the area with human scent on it, she banked on the hope that Robo might still be able to find something outside the environmental norm. She freshened his sniffing equipment by offering him more water, and after a few laps he looked at her as if he knew he had more work to do. One thing about Robo—he was always ready to go.

He watched her face as she chattered to him about finding something. When she felt he was set, she paused, raised her arm, and lowered it in a sweeping gesture to encompass the entire landscape. "Seek!" she told him, and sent him on his way.

She jogged after him as he began to cover the burnt forest, fanning out toward the right to search and then moving left. She suspected that if John Cobb had hidden anything else up here, it would be underground, limiting the possibility that Robo would find it. If snow didn't bury this country tonight, she would try to bring Sergeant Madsen and his dogs back up here tomorrow.

Together Robo and Mattie searched the area. Blackened dust infiltrated her boots and darkened the ends of her pant legs. Gray puffs rose like ghosts from beneath Robo's paws as he traversed the dead forest.

He went back to one spot by some boulders near John Cobb's old campsite and sniffed it thoroughly twice, giving it enough attention for Mattie to take note. Though he didn't alert on it, she marked it with a short piece of orange flagging tape attached to a small spike that she set into the ground. The tape shuddered in the wind, blowing sideways like a flag at a ninety-degree angle.

Mattie followed her dog as they crisscrossed the mountainside, first with the wind at their backs and then with it blasting into their faces. Her body warmed while her cheeks and nose suffered. She wished she'd brought a ski mask to cover them. After covering a radius of approximately one hundred yards from the cave, she decided to call a halt. Her intuition told her that they'd already found the reason for John Cobb's mark in the cave—the drugs—with the possibility of something else having been buried at the spot she'd marked.

Snowflakes pelted her face, alerting her that the predicted snowfall had arrived early. She feared blizzard conditions would set in fast. She called Robo, ending his search with praise and hugs instead of playing with the ball. Snow had already begun to coat the windward side of grassy tufts and rocks, and they didn't have time to waste.

"Come with me," she told Robo as she jogged back toward the cave where the others were taking shelter.

Mattie spoke to Garrett. "Do you think it's safe to take a few minutes to dig in one spot?"

His face showed his concern. "I don't know, Mattie. This is a full-on blizzard. We need to get down to a lower elevation before we're forced to hunker down in this cave for shelter."

They hadn't brought camping gear, and that was the last thing she wanted. "Ten minutes, no more. I just want to see if there's anything close to the surface. We can come back after the storm if it warrants further investigation."

Garrett hurried to get the shovel. After Mattie led the way to the spot, he bent his back into the work and within no time had dug a hole about two feet square and a foot deep.

Mattie noticed a certain amount of looseness in the soil. "Does it feel like there's been recent digging?"

"I think so." Garrett dug down another six inches. "How deep do you want me to go?"

"That's deep enough." She pulled her orange stocking cap down over her ears as snowflakes spattered her face. "We need to move out."

"But something could be buried here," Hauck said, evidently not wanting to quit.

"I don't know. Robo didn't actually hit on it—he just seemed interested. We'll come back after the storm passes when we have reinforcements. It's not worth taking a risk by staying here longer."

Hauck frowned. "Won't this area get buried in snow?"

"Can't really say. This is the first snowfall of the season, and the forecast is for sunshine by tomorrow." Mattie looked at Garrett. "Thanks for digging."

"No problem."

The horses were eager to head downhill. Wind blasted the snowfall in sideways, so thick it reduced their field of vision to mere feet. The trail disappeared rapidly under a blanket of white, but Mattie knew from experience that Mountaineer would stick to the trail no matter what the conditions.

"Do you want Mountaineer to take the lead?" she shouted forward to Garrett, the wind carrying her voice.

He turned in his saddle to shout back at her. "We'll be all right."

She shivered and hunched deeper into her coat. When they reached the living forest, it was like escaping the fury of hell. Pine and spruce grew thick enough to break the cruel wind and catch some of the snow. The trail wound downward through boulders that also provided brief respite from the storm as their short string of riders plodded past. Mattie kept her eyes on Garrett's back, hoping the lower altitude would give them a break.

But even when they reached the midway point where the trail divided, snow continued to fall. Garrett turned to her again. "I know you wanted to stop here to search, but I think we'd better keep moving."

"Agreed. Let's go down and search the area by the trailhead." Mattie turned to Hauck. "You doing okay back there?"

He replied by waving her forward with a gloved hand, although she didn't miss the way he'd set his jaw, as if preventing his teeth from chattering. A crust of ice clung to his eyebrows. She needed to bear in mind that the older man was used to a much warmer climate and might actually be done for the day, ready for a warm heater in the car and his motel room where a hot shower awaited.

Another half hour in the saddle and the snowfall finally lightened; fifteen minutes later and the wind drove merely a smattering of flakes at their backs. The trail was wet but clear of accumulated snow. Mattie breathed easier, stealing another glance at Hauck as Mountaineer navigated a switchback in the trail. The detective looked better, not quite so grim. "We're almost down," she said to him, and he nodded.

As they reached the lower altitude, they rode through groves of aspens, their golden leaves dancing in the wind, and then cottonwoods and willows, whose fallen leaves scattered across the trail. "Hold up a minute, Garrett," Mattie called out. And when he stopped, "This is the area where the X is on the map, isn't it?"

"Maybe the top boundary," Garrett said. "I'd say that X covered from about here on down."

Mattie dismounted and bent to pet Robo. "I'm going the rest of the way on foot so Robo can search."

Garrett turned his mount to use the slope to his advantage, stepping down from the saddle on the uphill side. He took Mountaineer's reins so Mattie could get Robo's equipment from her pack. Hauck dismounted as well, subtly stretching his legs.

Stiff from the unfamiliar horseback riding, Mattie knew exactly how he felt. "Are you game for more searching, or do you want to ride on down and warm up in the Explorer?"

Hauck stamped his feet. His boots looked warm and rugged, but his feet and legs were evidently as chilled as hers. "I'm game. Just need to move around a little."

Though the detective was out of his element, Mattie admired his ability to hang tough. She nodded before turning away.

"We'll stick to the trail but try to keep you in sight," Garrett said.

"I'll search the hillside the best I can on the right side. There'll be some places too rugged for me to follow Robo into, but we'll keep coming back to the trail." She unzipped the top part of her coat and pulled out her cell phone. "Let's see if we have a cell phone signal here."

Garrett checked his phone. "I do."

"Me too. If I don't see you when I come back to the trail, I'll call." She thought of something else. "Would you call the station and let dispatch know we're safely out of the high country? Tell Rainbow we'll search the base of the trail before we come back to the station."

"Will do."

After taking time to give Robo his water, she slipped on his evidence detection collar, patted him down, and chatted him up. When he was ready to go, she cast him out into the forest. It felt good to be back on the ground and moving again.

Watching for loose stones, bushes, and roots, she ran behind Robo, keeping one eye on his body language. Though wet snowflakes continued to spatter her face, melting as soon as they hit, the rugged terrain had her heart pumping within minutes and her body warmed. Robo disappeared into ravines, behind huge boulders, and down into dry creek beds too filled with brush for Mattie to enter, but he always popped back into sight and kept moving. If he found something, he would sit and wait for her, so she let him search on his own.

With Robo out in front, she followed him down a path obviously made by humans, which led to an empty campsite by a small stream. Robo took a moment to explore the stone fire ring filled with cold ash, passed it by, and trotted on down toward the water before disappearing within the tall grasses. When he didn't come back, Mattie hurried to find him.

He was sitting beside a bag of trash. *For Pete's sake, whatever happened to pack out what you bring in?* But when she drew near, she could smell the stench of rotting meat. Or was it flesh?

After replacing her gloves with a pair made of latex, she opened the bag cautiously, peering into it. As the odor intensified, she discovered a partial chicken carcass amid other discarded food and paper trash. Relieved, she closed the bag and placed it out on the trail, rewarded Robo with praise and a hug, and sent him on his way. She called Garrett to tell him where she'd left the bag and asked if he would ride by and pick it up for them to take down to the dumpster. She continued to search as the snowflakes thickened.

She was jogging back toward the trail behind Robo when her cell phone jingled. She paused, fishing it out of her pocket as she called Robo back. It was Sheriff McCoy.

"Got your message that you're at a lower altitude," McCoy said, an edge to his voice. "Where are you now?"

"Almost down to the trailhead. So far we've found nothing but trash down here."

"I need you to head to the campground between the Redstone and Balderhouse trailheads. How long would it take for you to get there?" McCoy definitely sounded grim.

"I can get there within fifteen minutes."

"Good. Detective LoSasso and Deputy Brody are already on their way. Some hunters there have found a body."

TEN

No matter how many times Mattie had been called with news of a dead body this past year, the words still opened a pit in her stomach. Garrett and Hauck were equally alarmed, and Garrett led them down the hill in record time.

Trotting her horse, Mattie followed Garrett toward his truck and trailer, where she could dismount. "Could you take Detective Hauck back to the station so he can get his car?" she asked.

"Sure. But will you need me to bring the horses to the campground?"

"I don't think so, but check in with Sheriff McCoy."

Hauck reined up and dismounted. "Why don't I go with you? Maybe I can help."

Mattie didn't think that was a good idea. This was Stella's crime scene, and she didn't want to step on her toes by bringing another detective uninvited. "I'll mention your offer to Detective LoSasso and let her make the call."

Hauck gave her that squinting stare of his that made her feel he was taking her measure. "All right."

Mattie realized she was now in the same position as that of Shanice Donahue and Detective Russo. She turned away and plucked at the knots in the leather ties that held her saddlebag and pack in place. She would secure Robo's find inside her unit under double locks and either take it to the station herself later or send it with another officer.

She shrugged on her pack and lifted off the saddlebag. "Go to your motel to warm up. If Detective LoSasso wants to bring you on board, she'll call and you can drive to the campground. It's just off the highway, so you won't need four-wheel drive."

"Okay. In the meantime, I'll check in with Russo and see what he'll tell me about Cobb's autopsy." Hauck moved toward the back of the trailer to load his horse.

"Sounds good," she said as he walked away.

Robo trotted over to the Explorer and stood at the rear hatch. Looked like he was ready to go home—little did he know that more work awaited. She thanked Garrett for his help and carried the saddlebag to her unit, where she stored it in her evidence locker. Robo hopped up into his compartment and checked his empty water bowl, which she promptly filled for him.

She fired up the engine and turned toward the highway. It would take only five minutes to reach the campground, not even long enough to warm up the car for Robo. But he had a thick coat and was already digging at a spot to lie down in on his cushion in the back. He would probably nap while she assessed the situation.

As she drove, the windshield wipers swiped away snow-flakes that had turned to sleet, their rhythmic thump mesmerizing. She hardened herself against the images she knew she was about to face. Though she knew nothing specific about this scene, death investigations were tough, no matter the circumstances.

By dusk, the temperature would plummet and ice and snow would coat the asphalt. They needed to figure out what they could about this death and send the corpse to the medical examiner as quickly as possible.

Up ahead, two sets of flashing lights marked the parking lot that was her destination. As she approached, she could tell the lights came from Brody's and Johnson's cruisers, Johnson being the other deputy on duty today.

She tapped the brake before turning into the paved lot, and her unit's heavy-duty tires responded with good traction. Beyond the flashing lights, she spotted Johnson, tall and lean with his orange stocking cap visible above the crowd. He was inside a covered picnic shelter surrounded by about twenty campers who'd evidently come out of their tents and RVs to watch the show.

"Good grief," she muttered under her breath. "At least Johnson's here to deal with that."

Robo popped up in her rearview mirror as soon as she parked her vehicle.

"You're going to stay here," she told him, to which he responded by yawning and plopping down to sit. She climbed out of her unit, locking the doors as she turned to leave.

She left her vehicle and climbed the short rise toward Johnson and his crowd. The Redstone-Balderhouse Campground was one of the official camping areas near Timber Creek, maintained by Colorado Parks and Wildlife. Each campsite had a picnic table, a metal ring and grill for fires, and a spot for pitching a tent or pulling in a camper. The grounds stayed full during the summer but emptied out around Labor Day, only to fill up again during fall hunting season.

As Mattie approached Johnson, she scanned the faces in the crowd. At first she didn't recognize anyone, but then her eyes were drawn to someone familiar—Ginger Beard Man from the car she'd stopped on the highway yesterday for speeding. He appeared to recognize her as well, his expression turning bitter as she quickly found his two companions.

She gave no indication of recognizing the threesome and let her eyes drift through the crowd and then back to Johnson. He moved several yards away from the onlookers to meet her.

Turning his back on the group, he spoke in a low voice. "Stella and Brody are just beyond this rise. Take the first fork to the left. Yellow tape is up. You can't miss it."

"You need help keeping these campers away, Johnson?"

"Nah, they're staying where they're supposed to. Stella said to send you over when you got here."

"Any family members here to identify the body?"

He shook his head. "Negative. Still unknown unless Stella found ID."

"Is the person who found the body still here?"

"Yeah, he's in the crowd. Stella told me to keep these guys here so she can interview them later if she needs to. Not everyone came out of their campsites. Garcia will be here soon to help us canvass the entire campground."

A huge task in itself, and it was getting dark. Garcia was the night deputy and a seasoned member of the force. Mattie still thought of Johnson as the rookie, since he'd been added to their department last summer straight out of the academy, though he'd seen his share of action this past year and was becoming a fine officer. "Okay, I'll leave you to it."

She hurried up the wide gravel road that led over the rise. The roads and pathways were well tended, at first wide and lined with stones and then narrowing and unlined as they branched off to the various campsites. Mattie took the left fork as the slope leveled off and wound downhill past a vault toilet. Its stench stung her nostrils as she hurried around it, spotting in the distance the glow of the yellow tape.

A faint two-track road wound through the trees to an isolated area used for tent camping. This part of the grounds appeared relatively empty compared to the RV and camper sites at the front. As she drew near, she realized that the pine and spruce thickened to shelter the area beyond the yellow tape, blocking view of it from the road.

The dim light of dusk had ebbed, and the temperature had dipped along with the setting sun. Her breath hung in a fog in front of her face before fading into the frigid air. She narrowed her eyes against sleet that pelted her cheeks and tugged her own orange stocking cap low on her forehead and down below her ears. This would be a miserable night to process the scene of a dead body.

The only two people at the scene were Stella and Brody, both dressed in heavy coats, light from their flashlights trained on the corpse. Stella glanced at Mattie as she ducked under the tape. "You got here fast."

"We were near the base of the trail when the sheriff called." Mattie went to stand beside Stella so she could see the body. Brody, shining his light on the dead girl's face, lowered his large frame to squat on the other side, his bare head damp from snowflakes that melted into his dark buzz cut.

The body lay faceup, eyes closed. Young—perhaps no more than a teen. Long, red curls surrounding the girl's face grabbed Mattie's attention. Snowflakes and sleet had begun to gather within her tresses and were catching on her closed eyelashes and cheeks.

Recognition slammed a sucker punch to Mattie's midsection. She'd met the girl before—at Cole's clinic yesterday.

She needed a second to catch her breath. "I think I know who she is," she murmured, squatting down to get a closer look, wanting to make sure.

"Be careful. Notice the pink residue at her mouth and nostrils," Brody said, training his flashlight's beam on the girl's pale face. "If you do know her, that would give us a huge start."

She'd already noticed the pinkish discoloration smeared beneath the girl's mouth and nostrils by the wet conditions, and she wouldn't touch this body without gloves. The pink streaks reminded her of the foam cone she'd seen inside the nostrils of John Cobb.

What was the likelihood of seeing this symptom on two unrelated bodies two days in a row? First at the Colorado state prison and now at a Colorado state campground, miles away from each other. Opioid deaths were climbing in the state, but still . . . this seemed like too much of a coincidence.

The girl looked so cold, dressed only in jeans and a long-sleeved tee that was pulled low to cover her hips, a coat wadded up under her head like a pillow. Mattie wanted to cover her to protect her from the elements, though she knew she couldn't. Pale and stiff, the young woman lay in repose with her lips parted—an ice maiden. Mattie scanned the rest of her body, and an incongruity struck her. This girl wasn't pregnant like the one she'd met yesterday. Perhaps she didn't know this ice maiden after all.

"So, don't keep us in suspense," Stella muttered as she hunkered down beside Mattie. "Who is she?"

"Now I'm not sure. I met a girl with hair just like this yesterday at Cole's clinic. Tonya Greenfield. But Tonya was about nine months pregnant, and this girl obviously isn't."

Already wearing latex gloves, Stella reached to gently push the bottom of the girl's tee upward, revealing a soft spandex maternity panel at the top of the jeans and thin legs below, a bulge left where a pregnant belly might have once been. "Maybe it *is* the girl you met," she murmured.

Mattie felt sick to her stomach. Tonya, the girl who wanted to give her baby a better life through adoption, who planned to start fresh this spring with her track scholarship. Someone so vital and full of life . . . and full of love for her dog. Kip, wasn't it? Where was Kip now? And more importantly, where was the baby? And why was Tonya lying here dead in this campground?

"Theories?" Stella said. "What are we looking at?"

"The obvious is opioid overdose," Brody said, "but I'm not saying that's what it is."

"And if overdose is what we're looking at, was it accidental or a suicide?" Stella looked at Mattie as if she might have the answer.

"I can't say, but I don't think suicide. The girl I met appeared to have a plan for her future." Mattie scanned the area. "No car?"

"Not that we've found here close by," Stella said. "Let's treat this like a homicide and a body dump. I don't want us to miss something."

Mattie shared what she knew about Tonya, including the information about the baby's adoption and the scholarship. "I would have never thought depression or even drug use, for that matter. That girl seemed focused."

"Okay," Stella said. "So where's the baby?"

"Right." Brody raised his gaze to make eye contact with Mattie. "Could Robo find a baby out here?"

"I think so." Mattie's pulse quickened with hopefulness, but the temperature was below freezing and no telling how long ago the baby might have been born.

Brody nodded. "Finding this baby, whether it's alive or dead, is top priority."

"Agreed," Stella said. "While you and Robo do your work, we'll process this scene so we can move this girl's body as soon as Dr. McGinnis is done with her."

McGinnis was the county coroner, charged with verifying death and estimating time of death at the scene. Since their rural county didn't have a medical examiner, bodies found inside its boundaries were transported to a neighboring county for autopsy.

"I'll contact Sheriff McCoy," Brody said. "He'll try to find this Tonya Greenfield and see if she's missing."

"Have him call Cole," Mattie said. "He'll know how to reach her."

Mattie rose and jogged down the rise, passing Johnson as she headed to her unit in the parking lot. A white Chevy Tahoe was turning off the highway and rolled forward to park next to her unit. The beam from its headlights swept her car, highlighting Robo's silhouette as he stood to stare at the newcomer from the back window.

Mattie recognized the mop of gray hair atop the man's head before he tugged on his cap and lowered the earflaps. That thick mane cut in Beatles style from the sixties belonged to Dr. McGinnis. He waved at Mattie as he exited his Tahoe and then opened the back door to retrieve his bag from the back seat.

As she approached, he turned to face her. His horn-rimmed glasses fogged in the frigid air, and he took them off, giving her a view of the concern in his dark eyes. "Do we have an ID yet?"

"Maybe." She felt certain of the girl's identity but still didn't want to believe it. "We're going on the assumption that this is a girl I met yesterday at Dr. Walker's clinic, Tonya Greenfield. But if so, that girl was pregnant, and this one isn't. She's wearing maternity clothes, though, so . . ."

"Is the baby with her?"

"No. I'm going to see if Robo can find it."

The doctor took a sharp intake of breath. "For heaven's sake."

"Brody's having Sheriff McCoy check to see if Tonya's missing. Brody and Stella are up there at the scene. You can drive a little closer if you want to."

"No, I'll walk. I don't want to disturb anything in case we have another homicide on our hands."

She gave the doctor directions, and he left to head up the rise, his shoulders bent as if beneath a heavy burden. Robo greeted her with his happy dance, evidently reenergized after his short rest. She opened the back hatch, and he pressed against her for a hug.

"Are you ready to work?" She ruffled his fur and patted his sides in solid thumps. He swiped her cheek with his tongue, and she gently pushed his nose away.

Her heart grew heavy as she considered how to prepare him for the job that lay ahead. In the end, she decided they would be searching for a human infant, either alive or dead, so she would dress Robo in the tracking harness he associated with searching for humans.

But at the last moment, she decided to add his Kevlar vest. Neither of them had worn body protection today, but there was something about this scene that felt off—and they were surrounded by hunters with rifles. Brody would be busy processing the scene with Stella, so no one would be at her back. She shed her coat and slipped on her own Kevlar vest before zipping her coat back on. The added warmth felt good after the brief exposure to the cold air.

She gave Robo his water and invited him to jump down from the unit. He circled her ankles and gave her the eye contact that meant he was ready to work. After clipping on a short leash, she told her dog to heel and turned to jog back uphill with him. They would begin the search near the girl's body.

As she passed the first picnic shelter, some of the folks in the crowd were stomping their feet against the cold and looking restless. Though she wondered how long Johnson was going to have to manage crowd control, she couldn't help but think the wait outside in the elements might be a legitimate price to pay for their initial curiosity. She wished they could use the bystanders to help search for the baby, but without knowing for certain that no one in the crowd was a killer, she felt it best to search on her own.

Dr. McGinnis had donned gloves and a protective respirator mask to examine the girl's body, and with his glasses back in place, he looked like an alien from another world bending over her lifeless form.

"Air temperature has been falling rapidly all afternoon," he was saying, his voice muffled by the mask. "I'll do my best to measure body temperature and current ambient air temperature for the medical examiner to decide. Rigor's set. I'm guessing this girl's been dead at least three hours, maybe four. The cold temperature might have slowed down the onset of rigor."

That seemed counterintuitive to Mattie—wouldn't the cold stiffen a corpse?—but she knew that the rigidity of rigor was part of the decomposition process, sped up by heat and slowed down by cold.

"We have access to temperature recordings for the day," Stella said to McGinnis. "Once we know when this girl was last seen alive, the ME can track it."

"I suppose so."

Brody and Stella were both standing back but lighting the body for McGinnis. "See here," the doctor said as he raised the girl's shirt. "There's a pattern of lividity here that doesn't match up with her lying on her back. It looks like she might have been moved after her death. Let's get some photos of this if we can."

Lividity referred to a discoloration of the skin associated with blood settling in the lowest parts, making it useful to determine body position shortly after death. This incongruence supported homicide. Though it wasn't a surprise, Mattie shivered from a chill unrelated to air temperature.

She squatted beside Robo, wrapping her arm around his neck and hugging him close. She decided to keep him on his leash so she could be near enough to protect him if necessary.

"We need to find someone," she told him as she stood to thump his sides. Then she gave him the command used to find a person: "Search!"

He looked up at her as if expecting a scent article. When she didn't offer one, he put his nose to the ground, sniffing the area near their feet and a few paces beyond. He seemed to quickly pick up a scent and began trotting up the path, back toward the parking lot. Mattie jogged behind him, trying to keep slack in the leash so she wouldn't slow him down.

Robo appeared confident, driving forward, giving the ground an intermittent sniff. The minutes were ticking by, and Mattie hoped they would find a living baby at the end of this track.

ELEVEN

Cole was alone in his clinic, finishing up some computer work before closing for the day. He yawned, rubbing his gritty eyes. The past twenty-four hours had been long but, by the end, very rewarding.

He tilted back on the spring of the desk chair he was sitting in, rocking and thinking about the kids. Hannah had worked diligently getting that weak puppy to eat, and Sophie and Angie had supported her efforts, mixing the milk replacer and cheering her on all day. He was proud of them all.

By midafternoon, the puppy had finally latched on when Hannah transferred her from the doll bottle to Sassy. Though Cole had to stifle Sophie's initial boisterous celebration, more restrained high fives had followed all the way around. An hour later, the puppy had nursed again, and Cole had high hopes that she wouldn't backslide. He felt like they'd turned a corner.

When he'd discharged Sassy to return home, he'd given Hannah and Ruth instructions to make sure the little one latched on early during feeding time so she wouldn't get aced out by the stronger pups, and he felt like she was in good hands.

As he was pushing himself up from the chair, his cell phone rang. He picked it up from the desktop and saw it was Sheriff McCoy calling. "Hello, Abraham."

"Cole." McCoy cleared his throat. "I'm not calling with good news."

Cole's heart leapt to his throat. "Is Mattie okay?"

McCoy spoke in a rush to reassure him that Mattie was fine. Cole's relief made him miss the next few words, but the sheriff had snagged his attention again by the time he finished his sentence: ". . . found a body."

"Hold on a second." Cole opened his eyes wide in an attempt to clear the cobwebs from his tired brain. "You said *who* found a body?"

"Some hunters up at the Redstone-Balderhouse Campground. I'm sorry to say that Mattie thinks the deceased might be one of your clients. I'm calling to get contact information."

Cole reached behind him to stabilize the rolling chair so that he could sit again, bracing himself for the next part of the conversation. "Who does Mattie think it is?"

"A girl named Tonya Greenfield."

Shock took the wind from his sails, and he ended up speechless. *My God*, he thought, *it can't be*. But Mattie had met the girl just yesterday, and she probably wouldn't mistake the identity of a young woman with a headful of curly, red hair and almost nine months pregnant.

"The deceased isn't pregnant, though there's some evidence that she might have been," the sheriff was saying. "I need to call her or her family to see if she's missing."

Cole didn't hesitate. "Let me give you the phone number I have." He opened his client tracking system, tapped a few keys, and brought up Tonya's record. "Here, I have Tonya's mobile number and a home phone that belongs to her aunt and uncle. She's staying with them until after the baby's born."

"Thanks, Cole. I appreciate it. And her aunt and uncle's names?"

"The aunt is Eliza Greenfield. I don't have the uncle's name." Cole paused for a moment. "Sheriff, call me back and let me know what you find out, all right? I won't be able to sleep tonight unless I know that girl's okay."

After disconnecting the call, Cole stared at the record he'd pulled up on his computer screen. Tonya and her dog Kip . . . the record displayed spare details about this duo, but his memory held so much more. The friendly dog, a young woman on the brink of starting a new life, an aunt who seemed willing to help her wayward niece up to a point but didn't seem too happy about it. He prayed Tonya wasn't the girl in the campground.

Cole stood, placed his cell phone in his pocket, and shrugged into his coat before going outside to take care of evening chores. He flipped on the yard light and headed for Mountaineer's corral, ducking his head against the mixture of sleet and snowflakes that spattered his face. Garrett hadn't returned the horse yet, but Cole tossed hay into the gelding's feed bunk and checked to ensure there was plenty of water in the heated stock tank.

He noted that the chickens had water and feed, indicating that Sophie had already cared for her pets, though the hens had taken shelter now inside the coop. She'd been good about handling their care.

His phone rang, and he snatched it from his pocket. Abraham again. Cole connected the call. "What did you find out?"

"Eliza Greenfield says Tonya left this morning to go to her routine midwife's appointment in Hightower. She had not started labor before she left. Even though Mrs. Greenfield hasn't heard from Tonya all day, she said she hadn't been worried because the baby's father showed up yesterday and she believed Tonya was with him. So Tonya is unaccounted for, and she's not answering her cell phone."

"Oh no." Cole's hopes sank like an anvil dropped into a lake. "Now what?"

"Dr. McGinnis is at the scene, and an ambulance is five minutes away. There's evidence that we're dealing with a homicide. We're going to transport the body to the ME in Byers County as soon as possible to get cause of death. I'll have the Greenfields go over and confirm identification." McCoy paused to draw a breath. "I've already activated the search-and-rescue volunteers to look for the baby. We need to search that entire campground, including inside RVs and campers, to make sure the little one isn't out there somewhere."

It seemed like an astronomical job. "I'll go help. Do you need the riders in the posse?"

"No, the canvass would best be done on foot. There are buildings to search through as well."

Cole envisioned the vault toilets, toolsheds, and picnic shelters. "I'll gather up all the flashlights I have and head out there right away."

"Deputy Garcia radioed in that black ice is beginning to form on the highway. Be careful."

"Will do." His fatigued brain awhirl, Cole disconnected the call and headed back to the clinic to lock up. Poor Tonya. He hated to believe that the girl was dead but trusted Mattie's ability to identify her. He thought of his own kids—they were safe and sound, tucked into their warm home with Mrs. Gibbs.

But this comforting thought dissolved as parental concern kicked in. How would this impact Angie when she learned that her new friend's cousin had been killed? He knew very little about this family who'd moved into town recently, and he wondered what they were really like. Eliza Greenfield had seemed unhappy and in pain. Was something wrong within the family? Was this kid, Ben, safe for Angie to be around?

Suddenly his daughter's first crush didn't seem so cute and innocent after all.

★ ★ ★

Robo didn't pause. He led Mattie up the path toward the shelter where Johnson waited with the hunters. Even as she reached the midway point, she knew she'd made a mistake. She hadn't communicated their mission clearly enough to her dog, and he'd picked up the freshest scent at the scene. She knew where he was headed, but she needed to let the track play its course. She didn't want to stop or correct him, because this was what he'd been trained to do. He knew his business, and she didn't want to mess that up and confuse him for the future.

Johnson looked surprised as she and Robo drew near. Robo breezed past him, out in front with Mattie trailing behind at the end of his leash. He went directly through the crowd toward Reagan Dawson, the man with the red beard. As Robo came at him, Dawson looked frightened. He threw out his hands as if for protection and stood up from where he'd been sitting at a picnic bench.

Robo stared at Dawson and sat near his feet, while everyone else in the shelter stared at Mattie. She called Robo back, telling him what a good boy he was as she rubbed his fur and hugged him close to her leg.

She spoke to Dawson. "Yours was the freshest scent near the body, and my dog picked up on it."

Dawson had lowered his hands, and he stammered a few times before his friend with the brown beard spoke up. Mattie remembered him as Wyatt Turner.

"Reagan found the girl," Turner said. "He was right there about an hour ago."

She'd suspected as much. "Who else was there?"

Cutter Smith, the guy who'd been the driver, stood. "I was close, though I didn't go as near as Reagan did."

Mattie knew it was best not to engage right now; she needed to move on. "All right. Detective LoSasso will need to speak with you, and we appreciate you waiting here."

"Okay," Dawson said. Relief had replaced his fearful expression. "Your dog singled me out because I found the body?"

"He did." There were a few murmurs of admiration for her dog from others in the crowd, who seemed impressed.

Mattie scanned the group. "Thank you all for your cooperation. We'll be searching this area, and we'll need for you to return to your campsites after Detective LoSasso and Deputy Brody are finished talking to you."

She didn't tell them they would be searching their trailers, campers, and RVs. No need to give them warning so they could hide anything.

"How did the girl die?" one of the campers asked, his deep voice resonating from the far side of the shelter.

"We don't know at this point," Mattie said, searching him out.

He was a large man with a dark, heavy beard and dressed in camo, and he persisted in trying to get information. "Did someone kill her?"

Mattie stared at him for a few beats. "And your name, sir?"

"Dusty Spencer," the guy said, clasping his hands at the front of his big belly. "From Nebraska."

The three guys she'd stopped yesterday were from there as well, and for that matter, so was Tonya. Another coincidence? She swept her hand in a gesture that encompassed the three-some but spoke to Spencer. "Do you four know each other?"

Spencer shook his head, as did Cutter Smith. "No, ma'am," Spencer said.

"I have no information that I can share with you right now, Mr. Spencer. You'll have a chance to talk with Detective LoSasso soon." Mattie turned away to leave the shelter with Robo. As she passed Johnson, she spoke to him in a low voice. "Be sure Stella talks to Mr. Spencer as well as the other three who found the body."

Johnson dipped his head in a nod.

The wind was coming from the northwest, and for Robo's sake, she wanted to start downwind with the scent coming toward their faces. As she jogged off toward the southeast, red-and-blue strobe lights flashed from the highway. Headlights pierced the snowflakes as an ambulance turned into the parking lot.

Mattie felt relief that the young woman would be secured inside the ambulance soon, out of the elements. It seemed like a small thing, but somehow thinking about it gave her comfort. She hoped the baby was alive and sheltered from the elements too, away from this cold campground, safe and sound in a warm place where they would eventually find it.

A Timber Creek County cruiser that Mattie knew would be driven by Garcia followed behind the ambulance, turning in right behind it. Reinforcements were starting to arrive. She radioed Brody as she continued down the path, and his voice crackled to life from the transmitter at her shoulder.

Mattie spoke into the mic. "Garcia has arrived."

"He'll help you search."

"I'll get him started."

"Volunteers are on their way," Brody said before they signed off.

At that bit of news, her relief factor ramped up quite a bit. She hurried toward Garcia, who met her halfway up the path. Built like a fireplug, Garcia had quite a few years on him, but no one on the force could fault his endurance. He might be slower than some, but he could hike a trail to its end.

"Good to see you." Mattie held her flashlight beam low, away from his eyes.

"We think there might be a baby out here, Mattie?" His voice carried his concern.

"It's possible. It's up to us to make sure there's not." She faced the campground, pointing toward the southeast side. "I'll start on that edge so Robo can face the wind. I'll sweep the grounds and the buildings that I come to. You start on the opposite side. Knock on doors and question the campers."

"Do I tell them we're looking for a baby?"

Mattie considered it for only a moment. "Yes. Ask if they've heard a baby cry or any sounds of struggle or cries for help from the woman who was found dead. Make note of anyone who seems to act evasive or suspicious, and Stella will follow up."

"So this is a homicide investigation?"

"Looks like it, and we're treating it like one."

"Okay, then. Radio if you need me."

"Same." They parted ways, and Garcia hurried up the path toward the northwest side.

After jogging fifty yards to her edge of the campground, Mattie patted Robo's fur, chatted him up, and prepared him for another go. "Let's find someone," she said, sweeping her arm out to encompass the area. "Search!"

Robo trotted out, sniffing the wind this time, reassuring Mattie that he would be looking for someone besides Dawson. Some dogs trailed people by scenting the air, while others tracked with their noses to the ground—and some dogs were able to do both. Robo fit into the latter group. It made him all the more valuable when searching for humans, whether a missing person or a fugitive.

Most patrol dogs were trained in tracking and apprehension, and Robo was no exception. At one hundred pounds, he turned into a battering ram when he hit a bad guy at full speed. But tracking was tracking, no matter what the need, and sometimes Robo served double duty in search and rescue. Mattie rarely worried that he would get confused and try to bite a missing person at the end of his search, since Robo's apprehension command was "Take 'em" and that's what turned him into a shark, homing in on a fugitive to bite and hold. Besides, he'd also been trained to call off from a bite before it happened.

But tonight, with him dressed in Kevlar, she knew she was giving him mixed messages, so she thought keeping him on a leash was important, even though it slowed their search. She jogged behind him, guiding him through trees and picnic shelters, stopping to use her flashlight to search trash cans and dumpsters when they came to them. With dread building in her chest, she tore at the dark trash bags to open them inside the receptacles. Wearing leather gloves for warmth covered by a pair of latex gloves for cleanliness, she rifled carefully through wrappers and discarded paper products stained with food, hoping to avoid discarded needles. She found nothing but trash.

At the first vault toilet they came to, she opened the door and let Robo inside, following him in as she diminished her breath to mere pants to try to cut the smell. But Robo didn't seem to mind, and he swept the empty area around the covered toilet. Years ago, a kidnapped toddler had been found alive and abandoned down in the vault below a toilet like this in a Colorado campground, and Mattie knew that a copycat was always a possibility.

She opened the toilet lid and shined her light down into the vault, illuminating excrement and paper enough to see that the chamber was halfway full but no infant had been placed on top. She tried not to gag at the thought of what that image might look like as she lowered the lid and moved Robo outside to resume their search.

At this rate, it might take all night to search this entire campground, but she wouldn't give up until she assured herself that the baby was nowhere on these premises. She owed that to the young woman she'd met . . . could that have been only yesterday? What had happened to Tonya since then?

Her cell phone signaled an incoming text, and she paused to strip off her glove to check it. It was from Detective Hauck, and it consisted of one word: **Fentanyl.**

Mattie knew it meant fentanyl was the drug that had killed John Cobb.

She stuffed her phone back in her pocket and resumed her search. Cobb's death had taken a back burner to Tonya's. Finding the baby was top priority now.

TWELVE

Cole arrived at the campground as the ambulance was heading into the campsites, the high-profile vehicle swaying on the gravel road. He parked his truck beside Mattie's SUV and followed the red taillights on foot as the ambulance drove up the incline. A skiff of snow now covered a layer of ice, and he slipped on the treacherous footing, forcing him to slow his pace.

Deputy Johnson gave him a salute of recognition as he passed the first picnic shelter, and Cole waved back. The deputies in the county seemed aware that he was part of the sheriff's posse and therefore allowed to proceed into areas not open to the public. Cole guessed he'd paid his dues, considering the many times he'd helped with body retrieval during this past year.

He squinted against the snowfall, scanning the area to look for Mattie but not finding her. The ambulance lumbered through trees into the far reaches of the campground, sound from its engine muffled by the accumulating snow. Cole felt the isolation of this spot, and it made him flinch, wondering if it had been used as a body dump. Was it even possible that Tonya Greenfield had been murdered? If so, who would do such a thing to a vibrant young woman and her unborn child?

Flashlights up ahead filtered through the pine boughs, meeting the headlights of the ambulance to illuminate the scene. People clustered around a yellow tarp, which had apparently been used to cover the body. Mattie wasn't among them.

Stella looked up to greet him as he approached. "Cole, thanks for coming out in such terrible weather to help."

Ken Brody acknowledged him as well. "Doc," he said, as he extended a handshake.

"Sheriff McCoy said he needed volunteers to search the campground. Do you know where you want me to start?"

"Deputy Garcia has started canvassing the area," Stella said. "Could you take charge of assigning volunteers to work various quadrants of the campground as they get here? Mattie and Robo are already out there searching the bushes. We need people to search buildings and talk to the campers. Ask if they've heard or seen anything, that sort of thing."

"All right," Cole said, his eyes drawn to the lump covered by the tarp. "I'll go back down to the parking lot and catch folks as they arrive."

"Before you go, are you up to taking a look to see if you can identify the deceased?" Stella asked.

He'd suspected they would ask that of him, and he approached the task with both dread and the desire to make sure the young woman was indeed Tonya. "I am."

EMTs dressed in protective gear had unloaded a wheeled stretcher and were carrying it around the ambulance. Brody squatted beside the tarp and uncovered the girl's upper body while Cole moved closer. Curly red hair matted and wet from exposure, pale skin that looked frozen and hard as alabaster. He knew from experience that this image would haunt him for months, one of the downsides of working with the sheriff's department.

"It's Tonya Greenfield," Cole said, lifting his eyes to meet Brody's. "Or her identical twin."

Brody nodded and covered the girl's face again. They both stepped back to let the EMTs place her in a body bag and transfer her to the stretcher. Cole turned away, saying to Stella, "I'll go down to meet the volunteers as they arrive."

"The first wave should be here any minute," Brody said.

Feeling sad and unsettled, Cole trod back downhill to the parking lot, carefully making his way through the ice and snow. *Where is Tonya's baby?*

And despite desperately wanting to know the answer to that question, he hoped the infant wouldn't be found out here in this campground. No newborn could survive these conditions.

★ ★ ★

Several hours after beginning her search, Mattie trudged through about four inches of snow toward her unit with Robo and Cole at her side. The cold front had blown through and the storm had passed. The air was still, and stars popped in the sky as the clouds cleared—but the temperature had fallen to well below freezing for the first time in the season, and their breath hung in the air.

Though the accumulation of snow wasn't deep, the layer of ice that lay beneath it made for treacherous conditions on the highway, and Deputies Garcia and Johnson had left earlier to respond to pleas for help from stranded motorists. Campers had returned to their shelters, and after Tonya's body was loaded for transport, Stella and Brody had begun their rounds to question them, which they'd not yet completed.

Once again, the Timber Creek volunteer search-and-rescue squad had proven itself invaluable. Despite the cold, wet weather, ten people had shown up, Garrett Hartman included, and they'd scoured the campground in teams of two. Mattie and Robo had also combed through the entire area, and Mattie could now end their search knowing that there was no baby out here to be found.

That knowledge didn't answer the question uppermost in everyone's mind, and she voiced it now to Cole. "Where is that baby?"

"I wish I knew. I'm afraid it might have died." Cole sounded tired and discouraged. "But I think we can rest easy that we're not leaving a live infant out here to suffer."

"Me too."

Cole took hold of her elbow as they crossed a particularly slick patch of ice where the sleet had formed a thicker layer near the edge of the parking lot. Unimpaired by the hazardous footing, Robo trotted toward the back of the unit, looking eager to load up.

"He's probably covered twenty miles today," Mattie said. "I fed him earlier, but I bet he's hungry again. I'll give him more food, and he can eat while I wait for Stella and Brody to finish up."

With his gloved hand, Cole brushed snow off her SUV to reveal a layer of ice covering the car's surface, windshield, and windows. "It'll take some work to get this off. Let me have your scraper, and I'll get started."

His truck was also coated. "I'll be here longer than you will, so I'll start my vehicle and turn on the defroster," she said. "Let's clear your truck first."

"Good idea. I'll start my truck too and then sit with you inside your car so we can warm up while we talk."

Mattie opened the rear hatch, and Robo hopped inside. She unbuckled and removed his search harness and Kevlar vest, finding the fur beneath smashed flat but dry. She ruffled it up for him, giving him a good scratch and massage as he stretched. His sides looked sucked in around his belly, the look of a working dog when he'd been at it all day. She always kept food and fresh water for him in her unit, because she never knew when they would have to work late.

The engine in Cole's truck fired and revved as she scooped a large amount of kibble into Robo's bowl. He chowed down, crunching the nuggets. She removed the skim of ice from the water he'd left earlier and was happy to see that the supply in his jug still poured freely.

Cole left his truck running and joined her at the back of her unit. Smacking his lips and chewing, Robo looked up at Cole, warming Mattie from the inside as she recognized the trust reflected in her dog's eyes.

Cole must have appreciated it too; he stroked Robo's ears and along his back while he murmured praise for Robo's good work. "He really is one of a kind, isn't he?" Cole said quietly to Mattie.

She nodded agreement as tears stung her eyes. It had been a long, hard day without much to show for it. She gave Robo's ears one last stroke and stepped back to lower the hatch. "Let's start warming up my car."

After climbing inside the Explorer, Mattie started her engine, flipped on the back window defroster and the seat warmers, and turned off the heater fan until the engine had a chance to warm. Her thoughts jumped to a different compartment in her life. "How did it turn out with Sassy's pup?"

"The kids are calling her Velvet. And after a lot of work, she finally started nursing. Things are looking good."

"Great news. And I love that name, though it doesn't sound very ferocious, does it?"

"What? Are you thinking she'll follow in her father's pawsteps and grow up to be a police dog?" Cole pulled off his glove and reached for her hand.

Mattie stripped off her gloves, tucked her left hand inside her coat pocket, and slipped her right inside Cole's warm palm. It was the first skin-to-skin contact they'd had all day, and it felt good.

She leaned back in the warmth of her seat and sighed. "I don't know if she'll be police dog material, but she has the bloodline for it. Maybe she'll go into narcotics or explosives detection without being trained for patrol."

"Or maybe she'll grow up and be another pet for Hannah or one of the kids. Too early to tell."

Mattie turned to face him as their eyes met and they shared a smile and a quiet moment. Cole raised his hand to touch her cheek and then settled back in his seat, chafing her hand between both of his to warm it.

"Why don't your hands get as cold as mine?" she mused.

"Cold hands, warm heart."

"Does that also mean warm hands, cold heart?" she asked with a smile.

He shook his head and held her eyes, giving her that special look that spoke of the love he felt. "Nuh-uh. No, ma'am. Nothing like that."

Not wanting to remove her hand from his, Mattie leaned forward so she could turn up the heat and defrost to full blast with her left.

"What happened up at Redstone Ridge today?" Cole asked. "Was that hard to go back?"

They sat holding hands while Mattie summed up her day. It surprised her that she could tell him exactly how tough it had been to return to the cave. In the past, wild horses couldn't have dragged that type of confession from her, but with Cole, the words flowed easily.

"I should've gone with you," he murmured.

"No, you were exactly where you needed to be. You and the kids probably saved our little Velvet."

A semicircle of bare glass had appeared at the bottom of the windshield, opening their snug cocoon to the world. Mattie leaned forward to peer through it. A dark shape materialized against the white snow on the road coming down from the campsites.

"Someone's coming," she said as she removed her hand from Cole's and flipped on the headlights to light their way. The extra illumination showed the newcomer to be Stella, and within seconds, the detective slipped, her arms waving outward for ballast before she tipped backward.

"Oh no." Mattie opened her door and hopped out. "She fell."

She heard Cole's door open as she crossed the icy patch near the asphalt to gain the more secure footing of the gravel road. With Cole following, she sprinted uphill. "Stella, are you okay?" she called as she drew near.

The detective struggled to sit, swearing under her breath as Mattie knelt beside her.

"Yes, yes, I'm okay." Stella sounded more mad than hurt. "Damn ice. It's slicker than snot out here."

Mattie hovered, wanting to pick up her friend but knowing she should give her a minute.

Cole squatted beside them. "That was a nasty spill. Are you sure you didn't break anything?"

"I don't think so." Stella raised her hand to rub the back of her skull.

"Did you hit your head?" Mattie asked.

"Shit, yeah."

"Are you nauseous?" Cole asked. "Dizzy?"

"No, just shaken up." Stella reached a hand out to Mattie. "My butt's cold. Would you help me stand?"

Both Cole and Mattie lifted Stella to her feet. She swayed slightly before she appeared to gain her bearings. "Damn boots," she muttered. "I need to get me a pair like yours."

Mattie looked down at Stella's feet, lit by the headlights from her car. Her friend's boots were more stylish than hers, but they lacked the heavy tread. "We'll make sure you get some," she said quietly, still supporting Stella's arm. "Can you walk?"

With Cole and Mattie on each of Stella's arms, the detective hobbled down the incline toward the parking lot, her head lowered to watch each step. When they reached Mattie's unit, Cole opened the door on the passenger's side, and warm air washed over them.

He helped Stella into the seat and leaned close to look at her. Mattie worried about the bump on Stella's head, and apparently Cole did too.

"How are you feeling now, Stella?" he asked. "Take a minute to look around. Are you dizzy, seeing double, nauseous?"

Garrett Hartman had taken months to recover from a blow to his head that had caused serious visual problems at first. Mattie knew that was what concerned Cole. A concussion could be serious—not to mention bleeding inside the brain.

"No, Cole." Stella trembled, and her face took on a determined look, as if she was trying to suppress her shivers. "I'm going to be fine, okay? I'm just cold and worn out."

"I'll be back." Cole left to go to the mobile vet unit on the back of his truck.

Mattie took his place beside Stella and knelt so they could be eye to eye. "You wouldn't lie about how you feel, would you?"

Stella gave her a thin smile before closing her eyes and leaning back in her seat. She tipped her head back against the headrest and sighed. "This warm seat is heaven. My head's sore, okay . . . but I'm fine. Not dizzy, not sick, no double vision. I just need to sit a few minutes and rest. Don't make a big fuss and embarrass me more than I already am."

"No need to be embarrassed, Stella. A fall like that could happen to anyone."

Cole returned, and Mattie moved out of his way. Stella opened her eyes and looked at him as he knelt beside her. He showed her a penlight that he held in his palm. "Look straight at me for a few seconds. I want to look at your pupils."

"Oh, for the love of God," Stella muttered, but she did as she was told.

Cole splayed the light across Stella's face, moving it back and forth from each eye. "Even size and responsiveness. Did you lose consciousness?"

"No, Cole, I didn't!" There was a warning in Stella's voice. "Now quit fussing over me before I have to get out of this warm seat and whip your ass."

Cole burst into laughter and looked at Mattie. "Are all you cops this stubborn about your injuries?"

She knew he was referring to the many times he'd been concerned about her scrapes, bruises, and burns while she'd insisted she was perfectly fine. "It comes with the badge," she replied, giving him a half smile.

"All right," he said to Stella. "If you have a headache, take Tylenol, not aspirin, and don't fall asleep for a couple hours."

"I know all that," Stella grumbled. "And I'll be lucky if I get any sleep tonight."

"Okay, let's close this door, so you can warm up." Cole stood and stepped back, but paused when Stella reached to take his hand.

"Thanks, Cole," she said, looking up at him. "You're a good man, and I shouldn't take my frustration out on you. Thanks for helping us tonight. Now get out of here and go home."

"Yes, ma'am."

Mattie caught the twinkle in Cole's eyes before he closed the door on the SUV and the interior light went off. "We all appreciate your help, Cole," she said. "You're beat. I'll keep an eye on Stella while we wait for Brody. You should head home."

"At the risk of getting my ass whupped, I'll check Stella again before I leave. After I scrape the windows."

"Do you need help with that?"

"No, go ahead and sit inside."

Mattie rounded her vehicle while Cole opened the door to his truck to grab an ice scraper. She slipped inside, relaxing into the warmth as she closed the door on the harsh scraping sound Cole made as he went to work.

Stella turned against the headrest to make eye contact. "Sorry I'm so cantankerous."

"I'm used to it." Mattie smiled to soften the words. "Don't worry about it, but you *are* going to have to let Cole check your pupils one more time before he leaves. Hey, it's more convenient than me running you in to see Dr. McGinnis."

Stella sighed and closed her eyes. "I suppose so."

Mattie looked through the widening gap of clear windshield as the defroster continued to do its job. She would have to scrape only the side windows, since the rear window heat tape had already cleared the back. She sat with Stella in silence, watching for Brody to come down the hill and realizing that Cole had moved on to clear the ice off Brody's cruiser.

After a few minutes of silence, Stella roused and opened her eyes, though she continued to let the headrest support her. "I didn't get a chance to tell you, Mattie, but the EMTs and Dr. McGinnis found fentanyl patches on Tonya's inner arms."

"Patches?"

"Yeah, Dr. McGinnis said it looked like four times the normal dose for pain."

Fentanyl, the same drug that killed John Cobb. Different method of delivery, though. She'd suspected Tonya's death might be opioid related, but still . . . Her chest felt heavy with sorrow and anger. "John Cobb died from fentanyl overdose too. Speculation on how the patches were put on Tonya?"

"Self-dosed or someone dosed her? Accidental overdose or on purpose? Those are the questions." Stella closed her eyes again. "I'll get started tonight by going to interview her aunt and uncle."

"It's after midnight. You're still going?"

"Yeah. The sheriff notified them that two people who knew Tonya had identified her body. They'll go over to Byers County morgue in the morning to make identification official, but I want to get some details tonight and get started."

"I'll go with you."

Stella smiled as she looked at her. "Sheriff McCoy is still on duty, and he could do it, but I appreciate it when *we* work together. And no telling what tomorrow morning will bring. I hear that Madsen and his cadre of dogs and their handlers have arrived, and they're bunking at the Big Sky."

The mention of the local motel made Mattie think of Detective Hauck. "I forgot to tell you earlier that Jim Hauck wanted to come with me to this scene. I told him to wait until I got clearance from you, but then I forgot."

Stella pursed her lips as she turned to stare at the wind-shield. "That was for the best. But I wonder . . ."

Loud scrapes at the side window made Mattie jump. She'd been concentrating so deeply on her conversation with Stella that she'd lost track of Cole, and now he'd moved over behind her to finish clearing her car.

"That man's an ice-scraping machine," Stella murmured.

Mattie turned to retrieve her own scraper, but she paused to share her thoughts before leaving to help Cole. "Two deaths by fentanyl in two days? I have to wonder if there's a connection between Tonya and John Cobb."

"Yeah. We'll talk to Hauck about it, but with what little we know at the moment, the chance that these cases are linked appears to be slim to none."

THIRTEEN

Early Sunday morning, after midnight

Cole yawned as he pulled out of the parking lot onto the high-way. His truck fishtailed as it hit the black ice, and he turned into the skid to correct it. Creeping along, he lowered the heat and cracked a window so he wouldn't fall asleep on the drive home. On second thought, noise from the radio might also be in order.

He tuned in to his favorite country music station just in time to listen to the weather report. ". . . ice is a real problem, so stay off the highways tonight. Take shelter wherever you are and drive home in the morning, because we've got a big change in store for the rest of the week. If you don't like the weather in Colorado, folks, don't worry, things will be entirely different within twenty-four hours. This storm has blown through, and tomorrow will be sunny and clear with a high of sixty degrees. That's right, thirty degrees warmer than our measured high for today."

When the windshield fogged, Cole turned up the defroster and continued to drive with caution as he listened to a classic by Garth Brooks—"I'm Much Too Young to Feel This Damn Old."

How appropriate! His feet and back ached, and at this speed, it would take him at least a half hour to get home. He settled in for the drive, fiddling with the controls to keep the cab warm enough to defrost the windows but not so warm that he'd fall asleep.

A few miles outside Timber Creek, the red-and-blue strobe of an emergency vehicle flashed ahead, and he hoped it was the county road maintenance crew out sanding the road. That would be a tremendous help. But as he drew near, he realized the vehicle was parked on the shoulder, and he slowed even more. His headlights lit the rear of the vehicle—it was a cruiser from the Timber Creek County Sheriff's Department.

Cole pulled to a stop behind the cruiser. His tired brain was picking up on the fact that something wasn't right here. Light spilled from the partially open driver's side door, making a glare on the icy highway. There was no one in sight. The cruiser's headlights pierced the darkness, and its engine was still running, a fine mist of exhaust hanging at its tailpipe.

He set his emergency brake and exited his truck, stepping down carefully onto the ice. With one hand on his truck for stability, he moved with caution toward the cruiser, searching the area around it. *Maybe Garcia or Johnson, whoever belongs to this cruiser, stopped for a bathroom break.* But Cole dismissed the thought as soon as it surfaced, because it didn't make sense. If that had been the case, the officer wouldn't have turned on his overheads.

Cole flat-footed his way across the slick area between the two vehicles and then ran his hand along the cruiser's edge for mooring until he reached the open door. He peered inside but saw nothing out of the ordinary. He dodged around the door to go to the front of the car, and that's when he spotted something that sent his heart into overdrive.

About thirty feet in the distance and lit by the cruiser's headlights, a Timber Creek County deputy lay in the barrow ditch, his legs twisted at an impossible angle, crumpled in a heap. Cole slid on the ice and snow into the ditch and ran as fast as he could manage. Careful not to collide with the officer, he went down to his knees and scrambled to the man's side. He still couldn't tell who it was, because the deputy wore a cap with earflaps, his face turned and partially buried in the snow. But the stillness of this man's body and the horrible condition of his legs spoke volumes. With his heart in his throat, Cole considered what he should do.

He knew he shouldn't move him. He stripped off his glove and carefully worked his fingers to the carotid area of the deputy's neck. Cole's hopes skyrocketed when he felt a thready pulse. He moved his fingers to the man's nose and felt warmth, indicating that he was still breathing. Cole reached for his cell phone but found the penlight he'd used with Stella instead. He must have left his cell phone in his truck.

He pressed the button to turn on the light and leaned forward to shine it on the officer's face. Though the man was unconscious, Cole recognized the youthful features of Deputy Ed Johnson. Leaving Johnson in place, Cole rose and ran toward his truck as fast as he could, slipping and sliding through the snow in the ditch.

He fell hard on his knee as he floundered up the side of the ditch, but picked himself up and lurched to the passenger's side door. He jerked it open, found his cell phone in its holder, and tapped in *9-1-1*. He listened to the ring on the other end while he flipped the front seat forward and fumbled through the items in the back, looking for anything warm that he could use to cover the injured deputy.

A female voice answered the call. "Nine-one-one, what's your emergency?"

"Rainbow, is that you?"

"Yes."

"Cole Walker here. I'm out on Highway Twelve about three miles from town. Deputy Ed Johnson is injured, unconscious, on the side of the road. It looks like he might have been struck by a vehicle. His legs appear to be broken. He might have other injuries. I'm afraid to move him." Even as he spoke, Cole snatched up a pair of insulated coveralls, a coat, and two hoodies from a plastic storage tub on the back seat.

Although Rainbow had always struck Cole as a free spirit, he'd seen her in action during emergencies before. Though she must be reeling from the impact as much as he was, she appeared to take the news in stride. "I'll send an ambulance right away, Cole. Sheriff McCoy is here at the station. I'll notify him. We'll get help to you as soon as possible. Do you need instructions for CPR?" Ticks from a keyboard sounded in the background.

"He's breathing; his pulse is rapid and weak. No CPR needed now, but I know how to do it." He closed the door to the truck, slid down into the ditch, and headed toward Johnson. "I'll try to keep him warm."

"I've got the sheriff here, Cole. He wants to talk to you. One second while I patch him through. Hang in there."

A click and then McCoy's deep voice filled the receiver. "Cole, I'm heading there now. Is there anyone else with you?"

"No, I left the others at the campground. Mattie, Stella, and Ken." His breath formed a cloud of mist as he ran toward Johnson.

"All right. We'll notify them as well." The sound of the sheriff firing his engine came over the phone.

"I'm closer to town than I am to the campground. Tell that ambulance to be careful. Conditions are horrible."

"They chained up to get back from Byers County, so they'll be okay."

Cole reached Johnson and sank down on his knees in the wet snow beside him. "I need both hands now to cover Ed. I'll try to keep him as warm as I can."

"I'll be there soon." The sheriff disconnected the call.

Cole shoved his phone into his pocket. He shook out the insulated coveralls first and placed them over Ed's torso, tucking the edges into the snow gently. The kid was lying on snow and ice, but Cole didn't dare move him. Spinal cord injury seemed likely with his body twisted this way. He opened the coat and laid it across Ed's hips and thighs, not daring to tuck it around the mangled limbs. He spread the hoodies on Ed's legs.

He leaned forward to assess Ed's breath and pulse, praying that the young man would hold on. If CPR became necessary, there would be no way he could protect the positioning of Ed's spine and legs. The warm breath and rapid heartbeat against Cole's chilled fingertips gave him some small measure of relief.

He rocked back on his heels to wait, knowing that the three miles from town would take an eternity for the ambulance to navigate under these conditions. He had no idea if Ed had suffered a brain injury in addition to broken bones, but he supposed his decreased level of consciousness was a blessing in disguise. Because when he woke up, this poor kid was going to be in a world of pain.

★ ★ ★

When Brody came down from the campground, Mattie had transferred chain of custody for the package that Robo had found in the cave to him, so he could take it to the station while she went with Stella to talk to the Greenfields.

Now she was following the two red dots of his taillights as they drove slowly toward town on the slick road. Warmed by the heater and tired from the long day of physical exercise out in the cold, she fought being hypnotized by the glare of lights on the ice. She couldn't let her guard down, because one second of inattention could result in a slide into a ditch.

They were still about seven miles from town when the announcement came over the radio: "Code 10-33. Location, three miles west of Timber Creek on Highway Twelve. Ambulance en route. All units, report your location."

She glanced at Stella and their eyes met, the detective's brow lowered with concern. Code 10-33 meant officer in trouble—emergency. Mattie keyed on the transponder to report their location at the same moment that Stella's cell phone rang. She missed the beginning of Stella's conversation as she responded to the radio communication but tuned in as soon as she ended her own transmission.

"We're still a ways out," Stella was saying.

"About seven miles," Mattie murmured, aware that she knew this area better than the detective, who'd moved to town within the past year.

"Seven miles," Stella repeated into the phone before pausing to listen. "All right. Brody's just ahead of us. It's slow going, traveling about thirty miles per hour."

Mattie glanced at Stella's face, which had been taken over by a grimace.

Stella was still talking to her caller. "The ambulance has arrived. Okay, Sheriff, we'll get there as soon as we can." Another pause as she listened. "All right."

Stella disconnected the call. "Cole found Johnson injured by the side of the highway three miles from town. Not sure about the extent of his injuries. Both legs look broken. He's unconscious."

The description made Mattie wince.

"The sheriff said to not take any chances trying to rush there," Stella said. "The ambulance has arrived and Sheriff McCoy too, so Cole has help. We're to take a look at the scene and see if we can find clues as to what happened."

Brody's taillights were pulling farther ahead, so Mattie assumed he'd also been given the bad news. She focused on the road instead of the ache in her stomach. The thought of Johnson lying at the side of the road, his body broken, sickened her. "And no cars in sight when Cole arrived?"

"Right." Stella leaned forward in her seat, one hand on the dashboard as if that would speed up their arrival. "This has to be a hit-and-run."

"How so? What did the sheriff say?"

Stella told her how Cole had found Johnson with his cruiser running and his overheads flashing.

Sounds like a traffic stop to me, Mattie thought. "Johnson didn't check in with dispatch before making a stop?"

"Evidently not. He'd been out on patrol since he left the campground."

No longer sleepy, Mattie turned on her overheads and focused on keeping her vehicle on the road as she picked up speed. They drove in silence until she spotted flashing lights on the horizon.

"There," Stella said as she zipped up her coat.

Despite their hurry, or maybe because of it, it seemed like it took hours to reach the scene. Mattie pulled up behind Brody's cruiser, checking on Robo in the rearview out of habit. He didn't even rise from his cushion, apparently still asleep from the exhaustion of his long day.

She stopped and set the parking brake, bailing out of her unit a split second behind Stella. Worried about the ice rink beneath their feet, she couldn't help telling Stella, "Be careful on this ice."

"Tell that to my boots." Stella moved forward, keeping one hand on Brody's vehicle while they approached Cole's truck.

The ambulance had already left, taking Johnson with it. Sheriff McCoy and Cole stood beside Cole's truck, their grim faces lit by Brody's headlights. Brody was already at Johnson's cruiser, searching the road around it with a flashlight. Mattie turned back to retrieve hers from her unit, and Robo stood and yawned when she opened the door and the interior lights came back on.

"It's okay, buddy. You can lie down."

He stood and watched as she found the flashlight in the console.

"You're going to stay here."

Robo yawned again and sat, telling her he knew he was off duty. He would rest while he could. She shut the door, leaving him in the warm car while she made her way carefully back toward the others.

McCoy and Stella were talking to Cole, and she searched his face as she approached. She'd never seen him look so ashen and stressed. Waiting for help with someone injured as badly as Johnson must have taken its toll. Their eyes met, and she reached out a hand to squeeze his. Her colleagues knew how she and Cole felt about each other, and there was no need to hide it. "How are you doing?"

Cole returned the hand squeeze before letting go. "Relieved that Ed was still alive when the ambulance got here."

"Did he say anything?"

"No, he roused, but he seemed confused. He was in a lot of pain."

"And did you notice anything that might help us determine what happened?"

He gestured toward Brody, who was still searching the road in front of Johnson's cruiser. "Some tire marks in the snow on the shoulder and possible skid marks on the ice that Ken's looking at. There's damage to the front of Johnson's cruiser."

Mattie turned to McCoy. "I can work with Brody, unless there's something else I should do."

"We need all eyes on the scene before any evidence melts and disappears. And we'll need to look at it again in daylight. Cole has volunteered to stand guard, but he's done enough for one day."

Their small department was already stretched to the max. With Johnson out of the picture, they needed more help. The sheriff's posse provided a pool of trained citizens, and maybe the sheriff would call on one of them to fill in.

McCoy spoke to Cole. "Go ahead and go home. We'll cover this."

Cole glanced at Mattie.

"Go home," she said. "Your day started a long time ago."

He nodded as he extended a handshake to McCoy. "I'll leave you to it, then."

"Thanks, Cole," McCoy said as the two shook hands. "Deputy Johnson couldn't have been in better hands."

"I don't know about that, but I hope it was enough." Cole reached for Mattie's hand to keep her from following McCoy as he turned away. "Call me when you're done?"

"We have a full night's work ahead of us. Go to bed and get some sleep. Call me in the morning when you wake up."

Cole nodded, squeezing her hand again before they parted. She wished they'd had time to let him debrief after his terrible experiences tonight. He looked like he could use it. More often than not, their relationship took a back seat to their jobs.

She set her thoughts aside as she approached her teammates. Stella and Brody had knelt to photograph tire prints in the snow, so she joined up with the sheriff.

McCoy pointed to skid marks and scratches in the ice. "See right here. It looks like someone reversed and then sped up."

She trained her flashlight on the area and could see how he'd arrived at that conclusion.

"They must have rammed into Johnson's cruiser, possibly trapping him there," McCoy said.

His comment made her gut tighten.

Lighting up the road, its shoulder, and the ditch, Mattie and the sheriff searched for signs and prints left in the ice and snow, though any footprints leading from the icy skid marks into the ditch had been obliterated by the ambulance and EMTs. They found slide marks where people had gone down into the ditch from the road, a couple of them near the place where Cole had parked his truck. She imagined him floundering down to the ground where he could gain better traction while trying to help Johnson, and an ache of sympathy formed in her chest.

"Let's photograph the skid marks, but I doubt we can capture an image very well under these conditions," McCoy said.

"I'll get my pad and make a sketch of them." Watching her footing, she trudged back to her unit while she pondered the marks left on the ice. It was always possible that a car could strike an officer out on the highway during a traffic stop—that was why parking a few feet to the left so the cruiser could act as a shield was so important. But the skid marks looked like someone had reversed and then taken off again.

The tracks indicated someone had hit Johnson on purpose. Did they actually reverse to run over him? She hadn't eaten since noon, but her empty stomach rolled.

Why would someone try to kill a patrol officer that way? And could it be related to Tonya Greenfield's death and her missing infant?

FOURTEEN

Eventually Mattie had asked Robo to work again, thinking he might turn up something in an evidence search by using his sharp sense of smell in the snow. But she'd been disappointed— if someone had exited the hit-and-run vehicle to check on Johnson, there was no trace of it.

She led Robo back toward her Explorer, leaving Stella to creep along on the ice behind them until she reached the passenger side. Mattie loaded up her dog, removed his gear, and offered him a treat, which he swallowed after a few quick chomps. Her partner had not voiced a single complaint about having to work overtime in the ice and snow.

After climbing back into her seat, she glanced at Stella to see how she was holding up.

Stella's head was tipped back and her eyes closed, but she heaved a sigh and turned her head toward Mattie, moving slowly as if the small movement required great effort. "This night is never going to end."

"How are you doing?"

"Other than having a splitting headache, things are peachy."

Mattie didn't reply, figuring her friend deserved some prickly behavior. She rummaged through her console until she found a bottle of Tylenol, which she handed to Stella along with a bottle of water.

"Thanks," Stella murmured, as Mattie turned on the engine and adjusted the heater.

She plugged the Greenfields' address into her navigation while Stella shook tablets from the container and swallowed them with the water. She emitted a breathy "Ahh . . ." after chugging at least half the bottle.

"Four ought to do it." Stella placed the pill bottle back inside the console. "I'll call the Greenfields to let them know we're on the way."

"Do you want me to call them?"

"I'll do it, so you can focus on your driving."

Mattie pulled onto the asphalt, steering around McCoy's and Brody's vehicles. Deputy Garcia and Frank Sullivan, the posse member who'd responded to their call for help, had parked on the opposite side of the road and were being briefed before the others left. A local rancher like Garrett, Frank responded to calls more often than not and was someone the sheriff could count on.

After Stella made her phone call, she leaned her head back again and appeared to be dozing, so Mattie concentrated on her driving in silence, her thoughts pinging from Johnson to Tonya to John Cobb and back, making no firm connections. She also thought of the traffic stop she'd made yesterday, wondering if the hunters from Nebraska were involved with Johnson or Tonya in any way.

Stella roused when they reached the Timber Creek streetlights, and Mattie was glad to see her alert so easily. She felt confident that even if Stella's bump on the head had given her a concussion, it would be mild and she wouldn't need to see a doctor. Stella would have to be hog-tied to get her to Dr. McGinnis anyway, so Mattie felt relieved that she could strike that job off her to-do list.

Mattie followed her navigation system's directions to the development outside of town where the Greenfields lived. The road took them up a forested hillside where new homes had been built on five- to ten-acre lots. Timber Creek had taken a turn toward population growth during the past year, bringing with it new families and new faces, and the Greenfields were among the many she'd not met.

Stella took the band from her ponytail and shook out her hair, which tumbled down to a few inches below her shoulders. Mattie glanced at her to see her wince as she rubbed the back of her scalp.

"How's the headache?"

"Better." Stella massaged her temples before scraping her hair back to recapture her ponytail at her nape. "Sorry if I was a bitch."

Mattie snorted. "Quite all right. I didn't take it personally."

"You shouldn't." Stella leaned back in her seat as a pleasant voice from the Explorer's speakers told them to make a right turn in one hundred feet.

Since navigation had led Mattie the wrong way more times than not out in these new developments, she hoped they'd arrived at the right place. But porch and yard lights filtering through the trees guided her up the long driveway to a house where most of the lights were still lit. At two in the morning, this had to be the Greenfield place. She pulled her unit into the driveway and ratcheted on the parking brake.

Built of log and stone, the sprawling home blended into the surrounding forest, and the huge windows that graced its front would afford a gorgeous view during daylight. *This house cost a pretty penny.*

A tall, lean man opened the door and stepped out into the spotlight on the front steps. Salt had been thrown onto the icy concrete of the driveway and sidewalk, and it felt good to have traction under her feet as she and Stella made their way to where the man waited.

"I'm Corey Greenfield," he said, offering a handshake. His face was haggard and drawn, reflecting not only a lack of sleep but also sorrow. "Thanks for coming."

Stella shook his hand. "I'm sorry for the delay, but it couldn't be helped. Thank you for waiting. This is Deputy Cobb."

Mattie gripped his hand in a firm shake, and their eyes met. His were red rimmed, and the light cast shadows on the planes of his face, the lower half covered with stubble from a long day's growth. He wore his blond hair short, and he was dressed in sweats.

A woman that Mattie recognized as Eliza came up behind him and opened the door wide. "Come in, come in. Get out of the cold."

As Stella and Mattie stepped into a slate tile entryway, warm air enveloped them. Faux logs flamed with gas fuel in an open hearth set in the middle of a great room with a vaulted wooden ceiling. Comfortable-looking sofas and chairs were arranged on one side, and it looked like the space beyond the fireplace served as both kitchen and dining area.

Eliza's eyes looked tired and her lids sagged at half-mast, but they didn't appear swollen or reddened from shedding tears. Mattie made no judgment about that; it was just an observation. This family had received notice of Tonya's death hours ago, and though Corey looked like he'd been weeping recently, tears might come and go during the hours after losing a loved one.

"I'm Eliza," the woman said, offering a handshake, which was brief and soft. She did a double take when she looked at Mattie. "We met yesterday at the vet clinic, didn't we?"

As Mattie confirmed that they had, the border collie Kip scampered into the room from a hallway off to the right, followed by a teenage boy. The kid resembled his father, except he wore his hair in a buzz cut. He appeared to have the broad build of a football player or wrestler, making Mattie think he might be into weight lifting, common enough among both male and female students involved in the local high school athletic program.

Kip greeted Mattie with a great deal of tail wagging and smiling, and Mattie was relieved to see the dog safe and sound here where she would be taken care of until Tonya's parents could take her home. The thought of it made her heart ache for them. Though she hoped the girl's parents loved the dog as much as Tonya had, Kip would be no replacement for their daughter.

Corey introduced the boy. "This is our son, Ben."

Ben came forward to shake hands, and Mattie noticed that he looked like he might have been crying recently as well.

Eliza led the way toward the cluster of seats, her steps slow and careful, her posture bent, same as Mattie had noticed yesterday at Cole's clinic. Stella sat on one end of a plush sofa, looking tired and drawn as she sank into the cushions, while Mattie took a seat at the other. As Ben sat in a chair beyond a glass coffee table, Kip zeroed in on Mattie, coming to sniff her pants thoroughly.

"You smell Robo, don't you?" Mattie leaned forward to scratch Kip behind the ears until Ben called her over to him and told her to sit at his feet. The border collie did as she was told, and Mattie murmured, "Good dog," before settling back on the sofa.

Corey remained standing with one shoulder against the stonework of the fireplace, his arms crossed. "What can you tell us?"

Stella answered. "I think Sheriff McCoy has already told you that we couldn't find any sign of an infant at the campground. I wish I had better news to report."

Mattie watched Eliza settle onto the edge of a straight-backed chair. Her eyes held a dreamy look as she eased into her seat as if trying to get comfortable. *She's on something for pain*, Mattie thought, wondering how or if that related to Tonya.

Stella continued, "We hope you can provide us with some thoughts on this situation, Mr. Greenfield. What was going on in Tonya's life? Who are the people she might have interacted with today? That kind of thing."

"It's Corey—no need for formality here. As I told the sheriff, Tonya has only been with us for a few weeks. She's my brother's child, and they live in Nebraska. They're devastated, but as soon as this weather clears, they'll drive here. Hopefully, they can make it tomorrow."

"The forecast calls for a warm-up. The roads will probably be clear by midmorning." Mattie tried to project her sympathy as she removed a notepad and pen from her shirt pocket. "We've been told that Tonya had a midwife appointment this morning. Could you tell us more about that?"

"Tonya left home about seven fifteen to make an eight o'clock appointment in Hightower." Corey looked at his wife as if for confirmation, and she nodded vaguely. "I gave that name and phone number to the sheriff earlier."

He paused for a moment before going on. "She connected with this midwife even before she moved here and has been seeing her once a week. Tonya wanted a nonhospital delivery, which this midwife offers in a birthing center that she built as an extension to her home. The adoptive parents live in Willow

Springs, so Tonya thought it would be more convenient for them to come get the baby if she delivered here instead of Nebraska. She said she didn't want the little one to have a long ride home after coming into the world."

That bit of information made Mattie's chest ache.

Sorrow was evident on Stella's face, something the detective rarely allowed herself to show. "We need the names and contact information for the adoptive parents."

"Eliza, do you have a phone number for the Thompsons?" Corey asked.

"I'll get it." Eliza stood and straightened carefully, placing her hand on her lower back.

Ben spoke for the first time, his voice deep but tight with tension. "Tell them about Skylar, Dad."

Mattie studied Ben for a few beats. He'd leaned forward to brace his elbows against his knees, and he looked taut as a cat ready to pounce.

Corey glanced at his son. "I was going to mention him next. Skylar Kincaid is the baby's father. He arrived in town last night."

Their stress set off Mattie's alarm system. "Was Tonya expecting him?"

"Not at all. In fact, she was upset that he was here," Corey said.

Ben gripped his knees with both hands, his knuckles white. "She was pissed. She didn't want anything more to do with him."

Stella straightened, looking much more like herself. "Tell us who Skylar is and where he's from."

Corey answered, although Ben looked like he had something to say too. "Skylar is a student at the University of Nebraska, where Tonya planned to go in January. They knew each other from high school, although he's a year older than she is." His shoulders slumped. "Uh . . . was."

Mattie wanted to hear more from the son; she would bet the two teens had bonded while Tonya lived here in this house. "Ben, what did Tonya say about Skylar?"

Ben appeared eager to talk, and the words spilled out of him. "When she first found out she was pregnant with his kid, he wanted her to get rid of it. Told her he'd pay. It pissed him off when she decided on adoption. He told her he didn't want someone else raising his kid. When he showed up last night, Tonya was upset. She didn't know what he wanted from her. They were supposed to meet and talk after her midwife appointment."

"Trouble comes from bad choices," Eliza murmured to her son as she came back into the room. She handed a slip of paper with the Thompsons' phone number on it to Stella.

Though the mother might have wanted to take advantage of a teachable moment, Mattie thought it inappropriate under the circumstances. And clearly Corey as Tonya's uncle and Ben as her cousin had felt more connected to the girl. *What are Eliza's feelings toward her niece?*

"Geez, Mom, would you give it a break?"

Ben's response partially answered Mattie's question. It looked like Eliza hadn't been completely on board with sheltering the pregnant girl here at her home, and Mattie couldn't help but wonder how her attitude had affected Tonya. But this Skylar kid seemed like a solid lead, and they needed to find him ASAP. "Where did Skylar stay last night?"

"I don't know," Corey said.

"He was going to sleep in his car." Ben narrowed his eyes as if thinking. "I think he planned to stay in the park next to the gas station."

The cold front had moved in during the day, so car camping seemed possible last night. Typically, Garcia moved squatters out of the park, but if the kid had moved his car around, he might have gone unnoticed. Mattie wrote a note to herself to see if Garcia had encountered Skylar or had recorded a license plate number for someone who'd appeared to be loitering during the night.

"Do you have a phone number for Skylar?" Stella asked.

"No, but Tonya had his number in her phone." Ben's eyebrows rose in a hopeful expression.

Stella shook her head. "We didn't find a cell phone at the scene. We have a bulletin out in the region to be on the lookout for her car, but so far no one's seen it. Did she have a locator on her phone?"

"I can ask my brother. Maybe he'll know. He wanted me to call him after I talked to you, so he'll be waiting." Corey drew his own cell phone from his sweatpants pocket. "I've got Tonya's number right here, though."

He read it aloud while Mattie recorded it. They could try pinging the phone if there was no locator on it.

Corey looked at Stella. "I can call my brother now. He might know how to contact Skylar. Do you want to talk to him?"

"I do, but let's finish up with you first, and then I'll call him as we drive back to the station. What's his number?" Stella and Mattie both jotted it down before Stella went on. "Is there anyone else we should know about who could have played a role in Tonya's death?"

Corey frowned. "None that I know of. Another question for my brother."

Ben leaned forward to pet Kip. "There's an old lady Tonya met at the midwife's who acted all judgy about private adoption. She really hurt Tonya's feelings."

"It's good to think about this from all angles, Ben," Stella said. "Was this woman one of the patients?"

"No, she works there. Tonya said she told her to think about using an adoption agency instead of selling her baby. But it was nothing like that. Tonya found someone who would help with her medical expenses, but she wasn't getting money for the baby. I told Tonya to tell the midwife—she needs to know what her people say to her patients."

Mattie wondered if this could lead to something. "And did Tonya complain to the midwife?"

Ben shook his head. "I don't know. If she did, it would've been this morning at her appointment."

Retaliation such as murder for a patient complaint would have been a huge overreaction. But still . . . it felt like something they should follow up, and now Mattie believed a trip to Hightower would be in order. "You've been a big help to us, Ben. Is there anything else you can think of?"

He shook his head, his expression sad. "I can't believe someone would hurt Tonya. Everyone liked her, and she always wanted to have fun."

"Maybe too much fun," Eliza murmured.

"How can you say that, Mom? What's wrong with wanting to have some fun?"

"Ben! That's enough."

The sharp words from Corey made Ben glance his father's way before bending to pet Kip. Mattie wondered how the family dynamics had affected Tonya. Had the girl been uncomfortable living here? And were Tonya's parents as disapproving as Eliza appeared to be? Did any of this figure into the girl's death? It felt like information to tuck away.

Stella stood, reaching into her pocket for a business card, which she gave to Corey. While she told him to call if he thought of anything else that might help their investigation, Mattie gave one of her own cards to Ben. He seemed to know Tonya best, and he also seemed to care about her the most. Perhaps he would eventually recall something that would help solve this case.

Kip rose and Mattie leaned down to pet her, murmuring a question to Ben. "What will happen with Kip?"

"Uncle Gibb might take her home. I wish I could keep her, but Mom won't let me."

Mattie nodded, hoping Tonya's parents would provide a good home. Border collies like Kip needed a lot of attention to thrive, and this little dog would make a delightful pet for someone, especially someone who had lots of room for her to run.

"Could we see Tonya's room before we leave?" Stella asked.

Eliza's lips puckered with distaste. "It's a mess."

"That doesn't matter. We need to see if we can find anything that might give us access to her friends or anything that might point to an enemy."

Eliza led them into the hallway that Ben had come down earlier. Kip dogged Mattie's heels until Eliza paused at a closed door, and then she ran forward, tail wagging. The dog's eagerness to enter the bedroom she probably shared with Tonya almost broke Mattie's heart.

The bedroom *did* look like a whirlwind had come through: clothing scattered around and in piles on the floor, the bed covers rumpled and drooping off the double bed, a variety of cosmetics strewn across the dresser top. Kip jumped onto the bed and scraped the rumpled sheets with her paw to make a nest until Eliza shooed her off. Mattie wanted to intervene, but she knew it wasn't her place and kept silent.

Kip retreated to a dog cushion on the far side of the bed while Stella and Mattie quickly searched the room, finding nothing that would provide information for the case. No purse, no diary, no address book or calendar. But Mattie felt she'd gained a sense of the stark life Tonya had led in this house with only her clothes and some toiletries to call her own.

Mattie decided to take advantage of being with Eliza. "I couldn't help but notice that you might be having some back pain, Mrs. Greenfield. Is it severe?"

Eliza looked at her, her eyes half closed. "It's been bad. I think I'll have to have surgery."

Mattie was thinking of the fentanyl patches. "Are you able to take something for the pain?"

"I hate to, but I have a prescription for OxyContin. Not what I want to take, but nothing else seems to touch the pain."

Another high-powered opioid, commonly abused. "Have you ever used fentanyl patches?"

Eliza squinted at her, shaking her head slowly. "I don't know what that is. I take pills."

Mattie nodded and closed the subject as she and Stella ended their search and walked toward the door. Eliza called Kip from the room, and the border collie trotted back to Ben, making Mattie glad that the dog still had a friend in the house.

They said their good-byes, and as they reentered the Explorer, Stella leaned back in her seat with an audible sigh.

Mattie knew she was risking life and limb, but she couldn't help but ask, "How's your headache?"

"I'm okay, Mattie. I really am, so quit worrying. It's just this case that's getting to me." Stella pulled out her cell phone and opened her notebook, evidently getting ready to make the call to Tonya's parents. But she hesitated, turning to face Mattie. "Have you ever been pregnant?"

The question surprised her; Stella wasn't one for digging into someone's private life. The thought of pregnancy gave

Mattie a mild chill, and she wondered why Stella had asked about it. She tried to treat the question lightly as she backed out of the driveway. "No, that's one thing I've never had to deal with."

"I was once."

Though it was the last thing Mattie had thought she might hear, she tried not to react, pausing to shift her car into drive while her gaze connected with Stella's. She didn't know what to say. When Stella turned away to look out the windshield, Mattie decided to begin the drive downhill.

Stella spoke in a voice that was flat and void of emotion. "Right after I decided to divorce my husband, I discovered I was pregnant. I never told him, but it complicated my own decisions tremendously. At first I was horrified and mad that I would be linked to this man forever by a child."

In the midst of everything going on, it seemed weird to be having such a private conversation. Mattie remained silent during a long pause, expecting that her friend would next tell her about a decision to have an abortion.

"But then I kind of got used to the idea of being a mom," Stella continued, sounding more like herself. "I thought I could just tell the creep that the baby belonged to someone else. It would tick him off to think I cheated, which was exactly what he was doing, but hey—I couldn't have cared less about that at the time."

Stella paused, which prompted Mattie to ask, "What happened?"

Stella shrugged. "One day at work, I started to cramp. By that evening, I lost the baby. There was no reason for the miscarriage—it was just one of those things. I hadn't started to show yet, so no one even knew. It was probably one of the saddest days of my life."

"I'm sorry it went that way for you," Mattie murmured, feeling an ache deep in her chest for her friend. "You would make a great mom."

"You think so?" Stella sounded surprised as she turned to study Mattie. "I ended up thinking it was all for the best, because I would have sucked at being a parent."

Despite her sadness, Mattie tried to smile. "You might be Momzilla, but you would raise great kids. Maybe you will someday."

Stella scoffed as she raised her phone and swiped it on. "No, that ship has passed. No more tripping down memory lane—time to call Tonya's father."

FIFTEEN

At the station Mattie parked between the sheriff's Jeep and Brody's cruiser, their vehicles splattered with grime from the highway. She unloaded Robo, and she and Stella trudged along the salted pathway that led to the door while her dog trotted briskly ahead. He waited under the spotlight at the door, alternating between staring up at it as if willing it to open and watching them approach.

"Open sesame," Stella murmured with a quiet chuckle.

Mattie was always grateful when Robo lightened the mood. This had been a long day, starting with the hard trip to the backside of Redstone Ridge and ending with the unresolved tragedies of Tonya's death and Johnson's attack. A lot of moving parts had come into play today, perhaps none of them connected.

But the possibility of connections swirled in her mind, dangling as if on strings that were waiting to be tied together. She needed time to think and to discuss these possibilities with her teammates.

They entered the brightly lit lobby, and Mattie spotted Rainbow sitting at the dispatcher's desk across the room. Robo hurried over to greet her while Mattie and Stella followed at a slower pace.

Mattie noticed that her friend still had on the same clothes she'd been wearing . . . could it have been yesterday afternoon? She watched her dog fawn against Rainbow's legs while she patted him. "Why are you still here?"

Rainbow glanced up, the pale skin beneath her eyes marred by ashen half-moons. "Pulling a double shift. Sam is sick."

Sam Corns, the night dispatcher. "Oh no, what are you going to do? You can't work all weekend."

"I have someone lined up to take a shift in a few hours. I'll go home, then, unless the sheriff needs me to stay."

Stella turned away to go toward the staff office. "Can I get you some coffee, Rainbow?"

"No thanks, but I made a fresh pot," Rainbow called to the detective's retreating backside.

Stella spoke over her shoulder. "You're a lifesaver."

Rainbow flashed a pleased smile as she looked up at Mattie, but then she sobered and spoke quietly. "I feel terrible about Ed getting hurt. I was swamped with calls from stranded motorists, and I lost track of him."

The dispatchers usually checked in with their officers if they hadn't heard from them in a while. "Has it been crazy here?"

"I've been trying to find places for people to stay."

"Sometimes you can't keep up with it all."

Rainbow shook her head and sighed. "The ambulance is back, but we haven't heard anything about Ed since he made it to the hospital. Garcia is coming back to the station. Everyone finally seems to be off the roads. The Big Sky Motel is full, and so are the bed-and-breakfasts."

"It's been a tough night. You haven't heard from a young man named Skylar Kincaid, have you?"

Rainbow frowned in thought as she referred to a list she'd made on a stenographer's notepad. She scrolled her finger down the names before shaking her head. "No, although I did talk to several people before I thought I should start making a list. I'm sorry, Mattie; it's been such a busy night, and I don't have complete records. My fault—I should've done a better job."

"Hey, we're shorthanded and you can't cover everything. It's not a big deal, and I doubt if he would call in for help anyway."

Rainbow was scanning her computer screen. "I do have all the calls from stranded motorists logged in here, and he's not among them."

"Thanks for checking. So the sheriff and Brody are here?"

"Yeah, the sheriff wants to meet as soon as you can. I'll let him know you're here."

"Right. I'll grab some coffee and get Robo settled. Would you ask Garcia to come to the briefing room when he arrives?"

"Sure will." Rainbow lifted her phone receiver and punched the intercom button for the sheriff while Mattie turned away to head for the staff office with her dog following behind. She met Stella in the hallway, carrying her coffee mug decorated with a caricature of Sherlock Holmes, one eye huge as he peered through a magnifying glass.

"The sheriff wants a meet soon," Mattie warned her as they passed each other.

"Sounds good."

Robo trotted into the room ahead of Mattie and pounced on the red cushion beside her desk. She gave him a treat with the intent of getting him settled for bed, but with his pricked ears and wide-open eyes, it looked like he was ready to go again. His nap in their unit must have been all he needed. She fixed coffee for herself, lacing it with almond-flavored creamer, snatched up some notepaper, and headed for the briefing room, saying, "Come with me, Robo."

Stella was already there with her laptop open, tapping keys and scrolling through screens. Brody, carrying his laptop with him, came in right behind Mattie, and McCoy followed soon after. Mattie rolled the whiteboard over to a spot near Stella before taking her seat and settling Robo on the floor beside her. It was time to summarize Tonya's case.

But McCoy started elsewhere. "Just got an update from the hospital. Johnson's injuries are mostly orthopedic. He was able to tell the ER doctor his name and where he worked, so that's an excellent sign. He didn't seem to know what happened to him, but maybe that will come back to him—then again, maybe not. He's in a lot of pain, so they have him heavily medicated."

Stella looked solemn. "What are the orthopedic injuries?"

"Both legs broken in several places, a fractured pelvis, and a few fractured ribs. Bruising across his torso but no ruptured spleen or internal bleeding. Small miracle there. The doctor thinks someone hit him and then ran over him."

Stella released an audible breath.

"That's the story at the scene too," Brody said, his voice a growl. "He's lucky to be alive."

McCoy rubbed his temple. "It's possible he dragged himself off the shoulder and rolled into the ditch. He might have saved himself."

"The EMTs tromped down the edge of the ditch above him, so I couldn't tell if he did that or not," Brody said, "but it seems possible."

"I'll release a media bulletin asking for citizens to come forward if they have any information about a hit-and-run involving one of our deputies." McCoy opened the notebook he'd placed on the table in front of him. "I'm also offering a reward for information leading to an arrest, including the report of bumper or fender damage as well as any suspicious behavior or verbal confessions related to the incident."

Mattie thought that was a good move, though McCoy looked as discouraged as she felt. Most hit-and-run accidents went unsolved, much less hit-and-runs that had been done with malicious intent.

The sheriff passed his hand over his face, rubbing the dark stubble on his chin, where Mattie noticed that patches of gray stood out in contrast against his dark skin. The sheriff had always been a mentor to her and perhaps even a father figure; it bothered her that he was beginning to show his age and that it might lead to his retirement before she was ready.

"Okay, let's discuss Tonya Greenfield," McCoy said. "What do we know, and what are our leads?"

Stella rose from her chair, opening her notebook before rolling the whiteboard closer. She picked up a red marker and wrote *Persons of Interest* on the upper right side of the board. "First of all, we need to find a young man named Skylar Kincaid. He's the baby's father."

Brody leaned forward, narrowing his eyes as he watched Stella write the name on the board. "Did he agree with the adoption?"

Mattie thought that an astute question—Brody was apparently of the same mind-set as she and Stella.

"Evidently not." Stella went on to summarize the information they'd learned about Skylar's surprise appearance in Timber Creek. "According to the Greenfields, Tonya planned to meet with Skylar after her midwife appointment. We need to track this guy down as soon as possible. Unfortunately, Tonya's father didn't know how to reach him. Her father doesn't think her phone has a tracer on it either. We've got the number, though, so I'll see if we can ping it, and I'll get her records from her provider."

"If we can't locate Kincaid some other way, we can put a BOLO out on him in the region, including Nebraska. It's possible he's already headed home." McCoy made a note in his spiral book before looking at Brody. "Could you see if you can track down a vehicle registered to that name?"

Brody nodded, already typing on his keyboard.

Stella tapped the marker against the table. "Tonya's father gave me the name and phone number of her best friend. I've left a message for her to call me, and I'm hoping she can give me information about how to contact Skylar. Or anyone else we need to talk to."

"All right," McCoy said. "Keep me posted."

Mattie spoke up. "I asked Rainbow to have Garcia check in with us when he gets here. Ben Greenfield thought Skylar was planning to sleep in his car in the park Friday night, and I thought Garcia might have spotted him either there or somewhere else here in town."

McCoy acknowledged her words with a nod.

Brody turned his laptop so they could see the screen. "No car registration under that name, but there's a driver's license. Here's his picture."

His face stony, Skylar's most outstanding feature was his hair—long and bleached on top with dark, buzzed sides. He also had a scruffy dark beard and hazel eyes. Using his birth date, Mattie calculated his age at twenty years and some odd months, and she jotted down his address, which was in Omaha.

Stella was writing *Employee at Midwife's* on the whiteboard. "I don't have a name for this woman yet—she's a lead we got from Ben Greenfield. Apparently she didn't approve of Tonya's adoption plan and said so. This might be nothing, but we need to talk to the midwife anyway, and we might as well interview this woman at the same time."

McCoy referred to his notepad. "The midwife is Carla Holt, and here's her number." He rattled off the digits.

Mattie made a note of the name and number in her pocket notebook. This would be a good place to start come sunrise.

And then Stella wrote *Reagan Dawson* on the board, the name of the ginger-bearded man who'd found Tonya's body. She added his cronies Cutter Smith and Wyatt Turner to the list below his name.

They keep turning up, and evidently Stella didn't clear them after their interview. "What do you think of those guys?" Mattie asked her.

"They seemed to check in with each other a lot, lots of shifting eye contact. They hadn't been out hunting yet and they didn't have a campsite. Dawson said he was walking through the far ranges of the campground looking for a place to car camp when he found the girl. They were also in a hurry to leave. They said they didn't have camping gear that would hold up to the elements, so they'd called to make a reservation at the Big Sky. I made an appointment for them to come in and talk to me some more here at the station at ten this morning."

"They agreed to that?"

"They did. I figured if they didn't show up, that would tell us something."

"Did you find any other persons of interest there?" McCoy asked.

"I have a list of everyone who is camping there and their contact information. It's a tough situation. No one seemed to notice a vehicle drive into the area and go back to that site. Most of the campers said they were away for the afternoon, hunting up in the foothills."

Brody cleared his throat. "Stella and I both talked to Dusty Spencer, the guy you were concerned about, Mattie. Then I followed him back to his RV to take a look inside. He was at the campground all day and didn't go up to hunt with his buddies. Said he was in charge of cooking dinner, but there didn't seem to be any evidence of cooking. He had his own vehicle there, so he could have left the campground without taking the RV . . . that made me wonder if he could've left, brought the girl back, and dumped her. Long shot, I know, but still."

Stella wrote *Dusty Spencer* on the whiteboard. "Let's leave him on the list for follow-up. It's hard to think someone would dump a body in their own backyard, but it happens. Especially when folks are unfamiliar with the area."

A tap came at the door, and Garcia poked his head in. "You wanted to talk to me?"

"Come in, Deputy," McCoy said.

Garcia entered, his strides quick and assertive as he approached the table. Mattie had seen Garcia in action when they once broke up a bar fight together, and she knew that although the heavily muscled man might be short in stature, he was mighty. He drew himself up to his full height as he stood beside the table.

His posture triggered the same response in Mattie, and she straightened too. "We're looking for a guy from Nebraska who might have tried to sleep in his car in the park Friday night. I wondered if you noticed someone on your rounds," she said.

Garcia's eyes narrowed and he reached for his pocket, drawing out a spiral notebook similar to Mattie's. He flipped open the pad and read from a page. "Eleven PM, Community Building parking lot, black Jeep Grand Cherokee, Nebraska plates."

Mattie recorded the plate number he gave them in her own notebook. "Did you talk to the driver?"

"No, the car pulled out almost as soon as I drove into the park. Nothing wrong with the vehicle and no reason to stop him. I recorded the plate in case I saw the same car loitering in town later."

"Which you didn't." Mattie guessed there had been no such luck, or Garcia would've filed a report.

"That's right. Looked like there were no passengers, so I guessed it was someone driving through town that thought he might catch a few *z*'s before moving on. Or he'd already had a nap before I moved in on him. I followed him to the highway, and he turned toward Hightower. Didn't see him again."

"Thank you, Deputy," McCoy said. "Do you have any other information about that particular vehicle?"

"No, and that was the only car with Nebraska plates that I noticed that night."

Brody cleared his throat, his eyes on his screen. "Here it is. That vehicle is registered to Roger Kincaid of Omaha, Nebraska. Here's an address and phone number."

"I'll call it," Stella said, pulling her cell phone from her pocket. They waited in silence while she dialed and listened. Mattie felt disappointed when the detective ended up leaving a message saying they were looking for Skylar Kincaid and for someone to call her back.

"Is that all you need from me?" Garcia asked. "I hear a cup of coffee calling me."

"After you get your coffee," McCoy said, "go out to relieve Frank Sullivan at Deputy Johnson's crime scene. I'll take call on patrol for the rest of the night. That's all, Deputy."

Garcia gave a casual salute as he turned and left the room.

Stella eyed the whiteboard. "That's all we have on the list so far. Tonya's father didn't know of anyone who might have caused Tonya harm."

Mattie recalled Eliza's disapproving words, which seemed inappropriate under the circumstances, and thought she needed to say something. "I don't think the aunt, Eliza Greenfield, would have necessarily harmed Tonya, but she evidently disapproved of her, and she seemed unhappy about Tonya and her dog staying at her house."

"I noticed that too." Stella raised her arm to write on the board but then lowered it. "I don't think it warrants adding her as a person of interest. Let's just keep her in mind as we go. I'll add her later if it looks like we should."

Stella wrote *COD* for cause of death on the whiteboard, followed by the words *Fentanyl Overdose* and a question mark. "Dr. McGinnis found four fentanyl patches on Tonya, which supports the conclusion that overdose is what caused her death, but as you know, it hasn't been confirmed yet by autopsy. Manner of death? Could be accidental overdose—she might have been in pain after giving birth and self-medicated. It's a prescription med, though usually given to cancer patients or people with intractable pain."

I wonder if that's what Johnson is on right now, Mattie thought.

Stella continued, "We need to find out if and where she might have obtained the patches. Her father said he had no idea where they might have come from and to his knowledge, Tonya had never used the medication before."

Three of the strings that Mattie wanted to tie together dangled in her mind. "I know the John Cobb homicide probably has nothing to do with Tonya, but Hauck notified me that Cobb's death was caused by fentanyl, and we know Tonya's death was also caused by fentanyl. We don't know yet, but I suspect it was fentanyl that we found buried in the cave at the backside of Redstone Ridge."

"Oh," Brody interjected. "I ran a presumptive field test on the contents of that bag before I sent it to the lab for confirmation. It was positive for fentanyl."

"Good to know," Mattie said.

"We've had an increase in deaths by fentanyl across the state during the past year, though none in Timber Creek," Brody muttered. "Tonya's would be a first. And then to find a stash of the damn drug that we assume John Cobb hid outside of town—doesn't seem so far a stretch to make you wonder if they're connected."

As they talked, Stella had continued writing. Under the heading *Manner of Death*, she'd written *Accident*, *Suicide*, and *Homicide*, all followed by question marks. "Let's strike off suicide," she said as she drew a line through the word, "but we have to wait for official word from the ME regarding the other two. Mattie, we need to see if the midwife prescribed fentanyl patches for Tonya, although I can't imagine that she would."

Mattie couldn't imagine it either, not for a pregnant woman. "Can a midwife even prescribe that type of opioid? You know what I mean—is it within her scope of practice if she's not a licensed physician?"

"Good point." Stella squinted at her as she rubbed the back of her head.

Mattie could tell Stella felt off her game. It was late, and even a mild concussion could slow her thinking. "And another thought I had about Johnson. It seems odd that he would be attacked on that stretch of road between the campground and Timber Creek on the night a body was found. I can't help but wonder if Johnson's case is related to Tonya in some way."

Stella nodded. "As in, did he pull over to help a motorist who actually had something to do with Tonya's death?"

"Exactly."

"We have a lot of questions tonight that I hope will come clear soon," McCoy said. "And Mattie, one more thing about the John Cobb investigation. Sergeant Madsen arrived with three other dog handlers this evening, and they're all staying at the Big Sky. They can go out with Detective Hauck tomorrow to continue the search. He was able to bring dogs with the specialties that he wanted."

Mattie was relieved at the news, because she already knew her assignment would be to work Tonya's case. She wished she could join up with the dog teams, but she trusted Jim Madsen to do a thorough job. "They'll have it all covered."

"And Cole and Garrett plan to go with them. I hear you have an area up high that still needs some excavation. If they start low and work their way up, they should be able to reach the high country by midafternoon. Or at least I hope so. There's no way of knowing how much snow Redstone Ridge got this evening."

"We didn't have time to search the middle area where the trail forks, so they'll have plenty to do in the morning."

McCoy addressed the group. "I think you all need to go home and grab some sleep. Be back here by seven in the morning. By then, we should be able to reach some people and get some answers."

McCoy and Brody left the room, and Mattie gathered her things while watching Stella write notes in her spiral pad. At one point, she frowned as she stared at the page for several seconds, apparently searching for what she wanted to remember before jotting it down. Not at all Stella's typical brisk demeanor, and her face appeared drawn and haggard.

Mattie waited until Stella looked up at her. "You're coming to my house to sleep. You can have my bed, and I'll take the couch."

Robo stood and ambled toward the door, where he stopped, staring at Mattie as if willing her to come.

"Oh no." Stella winced as she shook her head. "That's not going to happen. We only have a couple hours, and we'll sleep better in our own beds."

"Okay . . . Robo and I will stop off at our house, grab a few things, and I'll be over to sleep on your couch." Mattie turned to leave.

"Why? It's not necessary."

"I need to keep an eye on you. I'm not going to let you slip into a coma tonight from a brain bleed."

Stella scoffed. "I'm not going to have a brain bleed. You're overreacting."

Mattie opened the door to leave the room. "I'll see you at your house."

Stella released an exaggerated sigh. "I'll come stay with you. It's easier for me to make a change than for you and Robo. But I will take you up on your offer to sleep in your bed. I've been on the couch before, and it kind of sucks. Are you sure you want to do this?"

"Absolutely."

Mattie heard Stella mutter, "Stubborn cop," as she left the room, and it made her smile. *It takes one to know one*, she thought as she followed Robo back to the staff office to get her coat.

SIXTEEN

Mattie awakened Stella at six, the prearranged time for them to rise in time to get ready to be at the station by seven. The detective roused easily and color had returned to her face, which relieved Mattie's concern. Maybe she'd worried unnecessarily, but she wouldn't have done anything differently. Sleeping on the couch was an easy sacrifice for peace of mind.

Stella left to drive to her own home, but not before giving Mattie a hug and a thank-you. Mattie showered and dressed in record time, still giving her a half hour to share her routine Sunday morning breakfast with Mama T, the foster mother who'd raised her during her teen years and whom she'd grown to love as if she were her own mother.

As usual, Robo was waiting at the front door by the time she'd retrieved her service weapon from its safe in her bedroom closet and gathered her things. He waved his tail, his eyes eager as she opened the door for him to go outside.

"Okay, buddy. Let's load up." He beat it over to the back of the Explorer while she used a slower pace to navigate the icy stone pathway that led from the porch of her small stucco-covered adobe home. Paved roads and curbs did not exist on this side of town, and her parking spot was a pull-in at the side of the gravel road. She loaded Robo and started her engine before grabbing the ice scraper from its pocket on the back of her seat.

The sun was just beginning to brighten the horizon, and Mattie's breath turned to vapor as she scraped a light layer of frost from her windshield. Stars still shone in the cloudless sky.

It took only a minute to drive the few blocks to Mama T's home, the tires rattling over pebbles, which gave her some traction. She hoped the sun would come out bright and warm as predicted today so that everyone could get on the road early. There was a lot of work to be done, but with the addition of those who'd arrived with Sergeant Madsen, there were enough capable officers to accomplish it.

She parked in front of Mama T's house and made her way past the ice-enshrouded pansies in the flower bed, their last splash of autumn splendor ended by the storm. The ceramic chipmunks and squirrels that her mama was so fond of scampered in frozen poses in the yard.

Mattie slipped down the side wall of the house to the kitchen door, tapped twice, and then stepped into the warm embrace of a room laden with the wonderful aromas of her teen years: spicy green chili, scrambled eggs, and homemade tortillas. Mama T had made huevos rancheros, her specialty that she prepared each Sunday. Their time together was one of the treasures of Mattie's life.

Teresa Lovato, a small plump Latina, her black hair shot with silver and scraped back and twisted into a bun at her nape, looked the same as always, wearing a blue calf-length housedress faded from many launderings. She turned away from the stove to greet Mattie with a hug and a smile. "Good morning, *mijita*. How do you like the beautiful ice storm we had last night?"

Though it always warmed Mattie's spirit to be called *my little daughter*, she knew her foster mom had no idea what havoc the ice storm had wrought. As she fixed her plate at the old wood-burning stove that Mama T chose to keep despite Mattie's offers to buy her a modern one, she summed up some of the things that had happened the night before when others were sleeping, though she spared her mama the gruesome details.

The two settled at the table with plates of huevos rancheros and hot coffee in thick white pottery mugs. Mama T stared at Mattie, her brown eyes wide. "A dead girl, a missing baby, and an injured patrolman. What a terrible night you had, *mijita*."

"And you know Stella. She fell on the ice and hit her head. I made her stay at my house to sleep last night in case she had problems."

"A bang on the head can be serious. How is she?"

"I think she'll be okay. She looked much better this morning."

They savored a few bites in silence, sipping their coffee, and Mattie felt the tension ease in her shoulders. Being with her mama reminded her of the good in the world.

"Yolanda called," Mama T said, her brow lowered. "She and Julia are frightened for you with this John Cobb thing."

Apparently Yolanda, Mattie's grandmother, had already shared the news about Cobb with her mama. The two had become fast friends since they'd met last summer, and they spoke on the phone often. "I'll be okay, Mama. I'm surrounded by police officers all day, and my home is well fortified. I still think there's an active gang working out of California, so I'm more worried about Julia, her family, and Abuela—you know, since they live there."

"Julia moved them all to a condo a friend loaned them near the beach. It's close enough that her husband can still go to his work and the boys can go to school."

"I'm relieved. I don't know how long they can keep that up, but maybe the detective who's working the Cobb case can give us some answers soon." As long as her father's killers were free, Mattie worried that neither she nor any of her loved ones were entirely safe.

Mama T clucked her tongue and wagged her head in dismay. "This is a terrible thing."

"I know, Mama. I hope Detective Hauck is the one who will finally catch the people involved in my father's murder. Then we could relax and live our lives in peace." She didn't add that maybe her mother could come out of hiding, because she didn't want Mama T in on the secret. The less her loved ones knew, the better, and she would never want to put her mama in harm's way.

They chatted about the kids who were currently fostering with Mama T—still asleep upstairs—and about Riley Flynn,

whom Mattie had hired as her foster mom's helper, a relationship that appeared to be working well for both of them. The
half hour sped by, and when Mattie glanced at the clock, she
realized she had only five minutes to get to work on time.

"I have to go, Mama." Mattie stood and began clearing the
dishes.

Mama T made a shooing gesture with her hands. "You go.
I can get this."

Mattie placed her dishes on the counter near the sink, gave
her mama a hug, and hurried to her vehicle, where Robo was
waiting, his eyes locked on the house. He wagged his tail as she
climbed inside, and she gave him a pat through the mesh at the
front of his cage. As she pulled onto the street, she realized she
didn't have time to call Cole and touch base with him as she'd
planned.

Remembering how upset he'd looked last night, she hated
to miss talking to him. She dialed the sheriff.

"Good morning, Mattie." His deep voice resonated through
the Bluetooth connection.

"I'm on my way to the station but thought I'd check in
and see if I have time to stop by the motel to brief Sergeant
Madsen."

"That would be fine. Detective LoSasso is trying to contact Carla Holt to see if she can make an appointment. I think
you can spare about twenty minutes before you need to be
here."

"Sounds good. I'll be in soon."

She dictated a text to Cole as she drove: *Are you awake?* Her
phone rang in her hand with a call back from him.

When she connected the call, he greeted her with, "Did
you get any sleep last night?"

Even hearing his voice lifted her spirits. "A couple hours,
but I slept hard. How about you?"

"Like a log until about five this morning. Couldn't go back
to sleep after that. I'm glad you called."

"I wish I could've talked to you last night. That was a hard
thing, taking care of Johnson while you waited for an ambulance. It must've been awful."

"Well . . ." His breath released with a sigh. "The whole evening was awful, but not as hard on me as it must've been on you."

"It was probably a draw. But how are you this morning?" She wished she could *see* him to tell how he was really doing.

"I'm holding up. And you?"

"I'd be better if we could get some answers about Tonya and her baby. Did you get the latest update on Johnson?"

"I called Abraham this morning. I guess Ed is stable but heavily medicated for pain. He doesn't remember being struck."

"So the same as last night. I hear you're going up Redstone trail with the dogs today."

"Yeah. Is there anything in particular you want us to look for?"

"There's a spot up by the cave that needs to be excavated. If you can make it up there in the snow, Garrett and Hauck know where it is."

"Mattie, there's something I need to ask you," Cole said, sounding serious.

She was approaching the motel and could see the officers exercising their dogs in an open lot next door. She needed to end the call but couldn't after what he'd just said. "Sure, what is it?"

"I think Angie has a crush on Ben Greenfield. You know, Tonya's cousin. I guess I need to tell her about Tonya's death before I leave today."

She hadn't known about Angie and Ben—no wonder Cole sounded disturbed. "It's best she hears it from you."

"But . . . I'm also worried about Angie's safety." Cole went on in a rush. "Here's a kid I don't know anything about, and his cousin turns up dead in a campground. I don't know anything about his family either, except Eliza seemed to dislike her own niece, a kid I thought was trying to make the best out of a tough situation. Do I need to tell Angie to stay away from him and his family?"

Mattie tapped into her gut reaction about the Greenfields. "I met Ben last night. He looked like he'd been crying before we got there, and he seemed eager to share information that might help us. But Eliza I'm not so sure about."

"I need to talk to Angie."

"I agree. It's okay to tell her you're worried. Tell her to take it slow with Ben, and we'll keep her in the loop as much as we can."

Cole released an audible breath. "Thanks, Mattie. I guess it's always best to just talk things over."

"It is, and Angie seems mature enough for you to be honest. I hadn't noticed that she and Ben have made a connection when I've been at school." She visited the high school regularly for her Just Say No program.

"I don't even know if they have yet, but I think she's interested. The girls plan to go to Hannah's today for puppy watch, so she'll be occupied."

"Sounds good." Mattie had passed the dogs and pulled into the U-shaped courtyard at the motel. It was full of cars, so she reversed and drove onto the highway's shoulder to park. "Cole, I hate to end our call, but I'm going to have to."

"No problem. I'll talk to you this evening."

As they said their good-byes, Mattie thought about the text grapevine between teens. If Angie and Ben were a couple already, they would be in contact with each other, no matter what Cole told her.

By now the sun was an orange glow on top of the horizon, shedding enough dim light to reveal four dogs running around their handlers in the snow. Mattie picked out the large form of Sergeant Madsen, who was waving at her. As she left her unit, Robo bounced around in back, evidently excited to see the other dogs. In his experience, this meant a group training session, which he loved.

Madsen separated from the group, leading an eye-catching bloodhound as he came forward to meet her. The dog's black muzzle stood out against his coppery coat and wrinkled face, and Mattie thought she recognized him.

"Is this Banjo?" she asked as she and the sergeant greeted each other with a firm handclasp.

A tall, burly man with a shaved head and a police badge tattoo above his right ear, Madsen spoke with a southern drawl. "Nope, one of Banjo's pups. This is Fritz, and he's training to be a cadaver dog."

Mattie wanted to pet the bloodhound as he sat calmly at his handler's heel, but she refrained from taking such a liberty. Handlers didn't appreciate others reaching out toward their dogs unless invited or given permission.

She went on to tell him about the drug she and Robo had turned up the day before. "Field test says it's fentanyl, and we should get confirmation today. So be careful."

Madsen nodded as he pointed at a beautiful dog that had the solid build of a shepherd and a tawny coat with a black facial marking that covered his muzzle and spread up toward his eyes like a mask. "That Belgian Malinois is cross-trained for patrol and narcotics detection." He went on to point out the other two. "The black Lab over there has explosives training, and the yellow Lab is experienced in cadaver work. We can handle it all."

"You sure can."

"It's a great training opportunity, not knowing what or even if something's buried up there." Madsen waved the others over to introduce them to Mattie, and they talked about the day's plan. The sergeant told her that he'd met Detective Hauck already and that they were all leaving as soon as the ice had melted enough on the road.

The dawn light promised that the sun would warm the highway, and the temperature had already started to rise. After Mattie filled them in regarding the terrain they should expect to cover, it was time for her to exchange handshakes all around and go to the station.

She would have loved nothing more than to take her dog up into the high country with the team, and she knew Robo would feel the same way. Sharing a mutual mission and camaraderie with fellow dog handlers cemented a special bond among K-9 officers. But the need to investigate Tonya's death overruled any personal desire to work on her father's cold case.

Her cell phone rang in her pocket. It was Stella. "Skylar Kincaid called me back. He's come in, so we can talk to him before we go to Hightower."

Mattie's hopes lifted at the good news. This guy seemed like one of their most important leads. "I'll be right there. I'm just a couple minutes away."

"I'll go ahead and get started."

SEVENTEEN

A black Jeep Grand Cherokee covered with road sludge and bearing dirty Nebraska plates was parked at the station beside Stella's Honda. Clearly, this vehicle had been on the road during the storm yesterday, and Mattie wondered what story Skylar Kincaid would have to tell about it.

Robo was bouncing around from one window to the other, apparently still worked up about seeing the other dogs, so she decided to leave him in his compartment while she spent the next half hour in the interrogation room. He was more likely to keep out of trouble here in their unit than if she tried to make him stay alone in the staff office. Telling him she'd be back, she made sure his climate control was set for automatic, though she doubted the temperature would rise enough to turn on the air conditioning.

She found Stella inside an interview room with its door ajar, where she tapped before entering. Skylar stood and offered a handshake, apparently a nod to social etiquette, as Stella introduced them.

"Go ahead and leave the door open, Deputy Cobb," Stella said. "I've explained to Mr. Kincaid that we're just needing some information and he's free to go at any time."

Mattie left the door the way she'd found it, and after she and Skylar took their seats, Stella got down to business. "Mr. Kincaid stayed in Hightower last night at the Sleepy Owl Motel," she said.

"Call me Skylar, please," he said. "Otherwise, I'll think you're talking to my dad."

"You're here in Timber Creek early," Mattie said.

"My dad woke me up, said the police were looking for me. He suggested I check in with you."

Skylar looked older than the twenty years stated on his driver's license. He wore clothing suitable for the outdoors: jeans, a flannel shirt covered by a down vest, and heavy hiking boots. He was of average height but muscular and compact.

"I appreciate you coming in to talk to us," Stella said. "You must be wondering why I called."

"Absolutely. What's going on?"

So Stella hasn't informed him of Tonya's death yet, Mattie thought, watching Skylar carefully.

Stella placed her hand on the case file in front of her. "We want to talk to you about Tonya Greenfield."

He narrowed his eyes. "All right. What do the police have to do with Tonya?"

Stella ignored the question. "Did you see Tonya yesterday?"

"I did. We met yesterday morning in Hightower right after her doctor's appointment."

"Where did you meet, and what time?"

"We met in the parking lot by that little discount store— Double Dollar or something like that—at about ten o'clock." An impatient look crossed his face. "I'm sorry, but I don't know what this has to do with you."

Stella tapped the file lightly with one finger. "Tonya was found dead just outside of town yesterday evening."

Mattie observed him closely as he collapsed back in his chair and his eyes widened in astonishment. He opened and closed his mouth before speaking. "Are you sure?"

"Yes, completely sure." Stella leaned back in her chair as if to match his posture. She remained silent, and Mattie waited with her for Skylar to speak.

He shoved back his chair. "What about the baby?"

"Tonya was no longer pregnant," Stella said. "We don't know where the baby is."

Skylar leaned forward, bracing his elbows on his knees. "This is unbelievable."

They waited as he seemed to turn things over in his mind.

Stella broke the silence. "Where did you and Tonya go after leaving the parking lot?"

His face shut down as if to hide his emotions. "We didn't go anywhere together, if that's what you mean. We sat and talked in her car for about a half hour, I guess."

Mattie decided it was time for her to throw questions at him too, to establish a rhythm that sometimes seemed to force people into saying more than they wanted to. "What did you talk about?"

"I told her I wanted the baby. I have rights as the baby's father."

Which was absolutely true for adoptions in Colorado, but it was strange that this conversation had occurred so late in the game. "You want to raise the baby?"

"My sister does. I told Tonya we would exert our rights to get the baby." His face had flushed with what appeared to be anger. Though he was still trying to hide his emotion, a clenched muscle at his jaw gave him away.

"Why talk about this so late in the pregnancy?" Mattie asked.

This time he scowled openly. "I tried to talk to her a month ago, but she reacted by leaving town. It took me this long to find out where she was."

Stella jumped back in. "And what was the result of yesterday's conversation?"

"Tonya told me to get out of her car." He bit off the words. "I called my sister, and she said she would consult an attorney first thing tomorrow morning to see what we can do to stop the adoption."

Interesting—so they planned to intervene legally. "Did you tell Tonya that's what you were planning to do?" Mattie asked.

"I sure did."

"What happened then?"

"She got mad. Screamed at me to get out of the car."

Looks like he's still mad about it today, Mattie thought as he continued to scowl. *Mad enough to kill?* "What did you decide to do then?"

"I'd slept in my car the night before, so I was beat. I got a room in Hightower to wait. I figured that's where Tonya planned to deliver the baby anyway. I spent some time figuring out which doctor she might be seeing and which hospital she might go to. I zeroed in on that birthing center by the discount store, because that's the direction she came from when we met."

"Did some detecting, hmm?" Stella said.

"Damn right." The muscle at his jaw bulged again. "Now what's happened? Why is Tonya dead and the baby gone?"

"Those are questions we have as well." Stella tapped her finger again on the case file. "What do you think might have happened?"

He threw up his hands and shouted. "How the hell am I supposed to know? I'm just the baby's father."

"From what I've been told, you didn't want the baby to be born," Stella said, her voice especially quiet in the wake of his.

He clenched his fists on his knees. "Shit! Who told you that? Tonya? That's old news. What . . . a woman can change her mind, but a guy can't?"

He was getting worked up, and there was something in Mattie that wanted to needle him more, but she decided it best to let Stella carry on, since the detective seemed to be trying to deescalate.

"Look," Skylar said, still angry, though he'd toned it down a notch. "I didn't want the baby to be born in the beginning, but Tonya didn't want to have an abortion, so . . . By the time I told my parents, well, they were shocked, but they didn't want someone else to raise my kid. My sister's a lot older than me. She has two kids already, but she decided she wanted the baby. You know, to keep it in the family."

Sounded like passing on a family heirloom rather than wanting to nurture a child. Though Mattie had an appreciation for the concept, the way this kid expressed it left a sour taste in her mouth. "When did your family come to this conclusion?"

Skylar gave her a scornful look. "I told you, about a month ago."

Mattie nodded. "You said that's when you talked to Tonya."

"And so . . ." His words dripped with sarcasm as he slowed his words way down. "That's when we decided—that's when I told Tonya. Does that make sense?"

"Oh, it makes sense." Mattie could feel her irritation starting to build; this kid's air of entitlement didn't sit well with her. "I'm just curious about the decision being made so late in the pregnancy. After Tonya had already made plans."

His eyes darted off to the side. "It took a while to figure things out."

"Or maybe it took a while to tell your family about it?" She knew it was a dig as soon as she said it, implying that it had taken time for him to work up the courage. Maybe it was because she was tired, but she couldn't help herself.

"I can understand that," Stella said. Mattie leaned back in her chair to let Stella take over. "So your family's on board, and you tracked down Tonya here in Timber Creek. Was it your intention to wait in Hightower until Tonya delivered the baby? Did you plan to intervene?"

"Damn right. I planned to find out who she was giving the baby to so I could stop it. You can't just give a baby to someone else if the father wants it."

"So you got a room at the Sleepy Owl. What did you do the rest of the day?"

"I slept and I figured out where Tonya was going to deliver the baby. I had dinner and turned in early. When I woke up this morning, my dad had left me a message that you'd called. And I came to *you*, Detective. You didn't have to track *me* down."

He sent Stella a scorching look that Mattie thought made him look comical. She decided to dig a little deeper into how Skylar had spent last evening. "Is that your Jeep parked in the lot?"

He narrowed his eyes at her. "It is."

"It looks like it was on the road during that storm that moved in yesterday afternoon." In an effort to keep her statement neutral, she didn't add, *instead of being parked outside a motel room.*

It still seemed to prod a nerve—that muscle in his jaw bulged again. "It was messy on the road this morning."

"The sludge was pretty heavy. Did you drive anywhere on the highway yesterday afternoon or evening?"

His eyes slid sideways before coming back to meet hers. "I got dinner out, and I drove around town to find the birthing center and the hospital. Otherwise, I was in my motel room."

Mattie had a niggling feeling that he was lying. If he'd stayed in his motel room most of the day, why had he been so tired that he'd had to turn in early? "Are you sure you didn't come back to Timber Creek?"

"I didn't." He looked at her for a few beats before turning back to Stella. "Am I under arrest, Detective?"

Stella gave him a look of feigned surprise, not one of her finest moments of acting. "Why, no. Should you be?"

"I know my rights. I don't have to stay here if I'm not under arrest." Skylar stood, his face dark with anger. This man seemed filled with rage, and Mattie believed he could be Tonya's killer.

Stella remained seated and spoke quietly. "No, you don't have to stay, but we'd appreciate your cooperation. We plan to find out what happened to Tonya and her baby."

"I hope you do. But I've already told you everything I know about what happened yesterday."

"Do you know anyone in Tonya's life who might mean her harm?"

"I barely know Tonya anymore. We hadn't seen each other for at least six months. I don't even know who's in her life right now."

Though he remained standing, he seemed willing to linger. Mattie wondered if his outburst had been related to her catching him in a lie about where he'd been yesterday afternoon and evening.

"When you and Tonya were together, did she ever use drugs of any kind? Even prescription painkillers?" Stella asked.

"Are you kidding me? You must not know her."

His sneer held derision, as if Stella should have known better, something Mattie thought ridiculous under the circumstances, but it seemed to project that part of his personality that had irritated her earlier—a superior attitude that he just couldn't hide.

Stella remained cool and merely nodded. "I've never met Tonya. I'm investigating her death."

That response seemed to cool him down. "Tonya had no interest in drugs of any kind. When I knew her, she was in training, trying to get a track scholarship. She wouldn't even drink a beer."

And she got that scholarship too. Mattie felt a twinge of pain as she thought of Tonya's lost hopes and dreams.

Stella kept on. "Do you have any idea where the baby might be?"

Skylar looked at the door. "I have no idea what happened to Tonya, and I don't know where the baby is. You need to talk to someone who does."

He was looking antsy, and Mattie could tell they were about to lose him.

Stella began wrapping up. "We need to be able to reach you in case we have information about the infant. Could I have your cell phone number?"

He gave Stella his number, and she jotted it down. "Where will you be today? Are you planning to go back home?"

"I'll be here until tomorrow. My sister's coming from Nebraska, and I'll wait for her."

"Do you think she'll still come . . . considering?"

He shook his head. "I don't know, but she'll want to know where the baby is."

"We need to talk to her after she gets here." After giving him her business card, Stella showed him the way out to the lobby, while Mattie drifted along behind. When the front door closed behind him, Stella turned, one eyebrow raised. "He got pretty short-tempered when you pinned him down about where he was yesterday."

"Look at his Jeep. That vehicle was on the road during the storm yesterday. I think he was lying."

"I think so too." Stella looked out the glass door. "Interesting that he plans to stay around. I wonder why."

"Do you think he knows something about the baby?"

Stella sighed. "Your guess is as good as mine. He's got a lot of anger against Tonya—maybe because she dared to prevent him from getting his way. He struck me as someone who was used to that. And his innocent act wasn't very convincing."

"I can see him wanting to make sure that no one else got that baby, but his sister seems more motivated to give it a home than he does. If they were willing to take legal action, they would have probably prevailed over the adoptive couple. So why kill Tonya? Unless it was an act of rage."

"And maybe the baby is in someone's hands getting medical attention? But . . . that seems unlikely."

Mattie watched Skylar as he walked to his Jeep and got in. She noticed that Robo stood inside the back of their unit watching Skylar too, even as he drove away. She wondered what her dog thought of the young man. No telling what type of intuition Robo had about people.

EIGHTEEN

Since the highway was still icy in spots, Mattie drove carefully toward Hightower for their appointment with Carla Holt at her birthing center. Stella rode shotgun, and Robo was catching his first nap of the day in back.

Stella had already talked to Carla about her employee's criticism of Tonya's adoption plan. Tonya had made it to her appointment yesterday morning, and she'd registered her complaint, so the midwife had been aware of the incident and had already reprimanded the woman involved, Deidra Latimer. Carla had also agreed to ask Deidra to come in to her office to be interviewed.

Stella was writing in her notebook. "Since Tonya's due date was next week, the baby would have been fully developed and able to survive."

"Dr. McGinnis thought Tonya had been moved after death, so it's possible she delivered in a clean, warm environment."

Stella cocked one eyebrow. "Like a birthing center?"

"Yeah, something like that . . . or a motel room. What if Tonya went into labor while she was meeting with Skylar? Could he have assisted in the birth, medicated Tonya heavily enough to cause the overdose, and dumped her body?"

"In that case, where's the baby today?"

"With his sister," Mattie said, thinking it wasn't too big of a stretch for the sister to have driven with Skylar from Nebraska to make sure she could get the baby.

"A homicide planned by brother and sister? I'm not so sure about that."

Mattie had imagined all sorts of reasons a baby might be stolen from its mother, none of them good. "Could we talk about motive for killing Tonya?"

Stella shrugged. "Sure. Sometimes exploring theoretical motives for a case is useful."

"It's just that I've got several thoughts in my head, and it would help me to get them out in the open and see what you think."

"Go right ahead."

"Getting Tonya out of the way gives Skylar and his family rights for custody. No legal battle needed."

"You're right, but motive to get rid of the mother might apply to others, such as the adoptive parents . . ." Stella consulted her notes. "The Thompsons, although the motive could apply to anyone who knew Tonya and wanted that baby. An orphan is easier to take than an infant with a parent who's motivated to claim it."

"True, but Tonya already had an adoption agreement with the Thompsons."

"Yes, but it's not unusual for a birth mother to change her mind during the last days of pregnancy or after the birth. If that happened, the Thompsons wouldn't have any right at all to the baby. So . . . it opens up the Thompsons as persons of interest."

Mattie nodded, thinking that Tonya had not indicated a change of mind when she'd met her. In fact, she'd seemed determined to go ahead with the adoption. "What if Tonya went into labor, delivered at the birthing center, and something went wrong? Maybe Carla Holt lost both Tonya and her baby, and then she tried to cover it up."

Stella pursed her lips and nodded. "That's possible. Let's watch both of them carefully when we mention Tonya's death. See what kind of reaction we get."

Mattie drove in silence for a bit before giving Stella a sidelong glance. "I've thought of another motive that could be related to the midwife and her assistant, or someone else that's not even on our radar. What if someone wanted the baby to sell? You know, infant and child trafficking."

Stella emitted a prolonged, sibilant breath. "Thought of that one too, though the idea of it curdles my breakfast. I need to research any related cases, both solved and unsolved, in the region—a pregnant woman killed at the end of her term with a missing infant. I'll do that later this morning."

"And we need to look at the schedules these two women had yesterday. See what they were doing in the afternoon."

Stella nodded. "I hope the ME can give us an estimated time of death after the autopsy today. That would help us pin down the time frame."

It *would* help, but with the body exposed to the weather like it had been, Mattie doubted he could provide anything more specific than a time window. "One more thought related to the men at the campground yesterday. Tonya might have been killed during some type of sexually motivated assault and losing the baby was collateral damage. In that case, the infant might also be deceased."

"Regarding assault, that's another question the ME might weigh in on. And yes, it's a possibility."

Mattie glanced at Stella, who was staring out the passenger side window. "Any other motives I haven't mentioned?"

Stella answered in a low voice. "I have this wild idea."

"Go ahead . . . tell me."

Stella sighed. "What if this all became too much for Tonya? What if she decided a late-term abortion was the way to go, and the whole thing got botched? That might explain the dosing with pain meds."

"But why dump her body in a campground?"

"Because she had a friend or acquaintance out there willing to help."

Mattie thought about it and couldn't imagine the Tonya she'd met seeking that option. But then, she'd been surprised by human behavior before, and talking to the girl one time wasn't the same as knowing her well enough to predict her actions. "That's part of why you're interested in the Nebraska contingent of hunters at the campground."

"Right."

"And Robo did lead me straight to Reagan Dawson when he picked up his scent by Tonya's body. But of course, I think that's because he's the one who found her."

"Finding the deceased to throw off suspicion and muddy the water isn't a new concept for a killer."

Mattie agreed. "When you talked to Tonya's best friend, did she say something to make you think this could be a possibility?"

Stella turned toward her. "Not in specific words, but she did say that Tonya wavered between abortion and adoption in the beginning. She also said that Tonya had quit calling her back this past week, which made her wonder if she was dealing with something she didn't want to share."

"Hmm . . ." Mattie pondered this bit of information for a brief moment. "But then, there could be all kinds of reasons for the lack of contact. Maybe Tonya was dealing with her home environment, or she didn't feel like sharing her feelings as she moved closer to the adoption. What did her friend say about Tonya's relationship with Skylar?"

"That in her opinion, Tonya had ended it because of his insistence that she get an abortion. She said Tonya wanted to make up her own mind, and once she decided on adoption, she didn't want to hear anything more from Skylar."

Mattie thought things might have changed since early in Tonya's pregnancy—young love could be volatile, especially under such strained circumstances. "Since Tonya agreed to meet with him yesterday, I wonder if she still had feelings for him. Of course, according to Ben, she was upset that Skylar showed up, but still . . . I wonder if she was conflicted in some way and it caused her extra distress."

They passed into the Hightower city limits, and Mattie slowed as her navigation system offered directions for the next turn. She steered into a well-kept neighborhood of newer homes and pulled over to the curb in front of the first one, which had been built adjacent to the back parking lot of the local discount store. A solid wooden fence separated the store from the residential neighborhood, and Mattie wondered if its proximity explained why Carla Holt had been granted approval to run a business from her home. In small towns like Hightower and Timber Creek, the lines between commercial and residential real estate often became blurred.

The house looked like a rambling ranch from the outside, its red brick not an exact match to the rust-colored siding on the new addition, which ran parallel with the street. A metallic-blue Ford Fusion sedan, dulled by road grime, sat parked in the driveway in front of the garage.

Robo woke up as she shut down her engine. She told him he was going to stay before she and Stella exited the vehicle. He yawned and sat to watch them go.

They headed down the sidewalk to an outside entry on the addition, marked with a sign that read **MOUNTAIN VIEW BIRTHING CENTER** in large letters while Carla Holt's name and her credentials were recorded in smaller script at the bottom. A smattering of rock salt was evident on the sidewalk, but the sun had risen well above the horizon, and its warmth, combined with the salt, had melted any residual ice from last night's storm.

Mattie followed Stella up the steps to the doorway, which was also wheelchair accessible via a concrete ramp that ran to the right of the entryway and then doubled back on itself. The entire setup appeared professional and inviting.

The door opened into a lobby appointed with homey furnishings and a counter that separated customers from the receptionist's area. A woman, who appeared to be forty-something and had short, raven-colored hair set off by bleached highlights, sat behind the counter inspecting a computer screen.

The woman rose from her seat and extended a handshake across the countertop. "I'm Carla Holt. Thank you for driving here to talk to me. The roads were such a mess last night, I hated to go back out there this morning."

Stella shook hands first. "So were you out on the road last night?"

As Mattie shook hands, she wondered why Carla would bring up driving during the storm first thing.

"I needed supplies and groceries from Willow Springs, so I got caught out during the storm and didn't make it home until late." Carla smiled as she walked out from behind the counter.

"What time did you leave for Willow Springs, and when did you get back?" Stella evidently decided to go for alibi right off the bat.

Carla looked surprised but replied to the question. "I left home about three and didn't get back until around seven. I often stop at a coffee shop for some down time and to read when I go to Willow Springs, and I got caught off guard. It took me two hours to get home on a drive that usually takes forty minutes."

Mattie knew the road well, and it involved crossing a pass through the mountains. The ice storm would have made the extra drive time quite possible.

Carla waved a hand toward the seating area. "Let's sit. Deidra won't be in for another half hour. I thought that would give us some time to talk privately before she arrives."

"Thank you." Stella glanced at Mattie as they all took seats in the lobby. "You must be wondering why we're here to talk with you."

"Well, when you said police business, I decided it must be important. But I have everything I need in place to run my center—licenses, registrations, and such. I'm not too worried." The lines on Carla's brow belied her words. "But I assume this has something to do with Tonya Greenfield, since she's the patient you were asking about."

Stella nodded. "I'm sorry to bring you bad news, but Tonya was found deceased yesterday near Timber Creek."

Carla couldn't have looked more startled; she slumped back in her chair and raised her hands as if to ward off the statement. But was her reaction genuine or was she acting? Mattie wasn't certain.

"Are . . . are you sure?" Carla stared at Stella. "That doesn't seem possible. She was the picture of health when I saw her yesterday morning. Did she . . . did she go into labor by herself? What happened?"

"That's what we're trying to determine. We hope the medical examiner can give us some answers."

Carla's face showed her distress. "I suppose the baby is also gone?"

Is she using the word gone *as a euphemism for dead, or is she asking if the baby's missing?*

Stella evidently wanted clarification too. "When you say *gone*, what do you mean?"

Carla lowered her eyes to her lap, where her hands were clenched. "Is the baby dead too?"

"We don't know," Stella said.

Carla's eyes darted upward to meet Stella's. "So . . . why don't you know if the baby's dead or not?"

"Tonya was no longer pregnant when she was found, but we don't know where the baby is. I understand that Tonya's due date was next week."

"Yes, everything appeared on schedule, but . . ." Carla paused as if thinking. "I suppose I can share some details with you, since my patient is deceased. It would be better if you had a warrant for the information."

Stella unzipped her leather notebook to remove the warrant she'd obtained before leaving Timber Creek, and she extended it toward Carla.

The midwife took it, scanned it, and then nodded as if it satisfied her needs. She drew a breath. "When I examined Tonya yesterday morning, her cervix had begun effacement and dilation. I told Tonya that I thought her labor could begin within the next twenty-four to forty-eight hours."

"How did Tonya respond to that?" Mattie asked.

"She seemed excited . . . scared. I mean nervous . . . you know. She expressed some of the normal fears about a first-time delivery."

Mattie needed to dig more into that fear. "Was Tonya particularly nervous about pain?"

Carla nodded. "I would say so, although no more than some of my young mothers. We do labor and delivery training here, but Tonya had yet to finish all of the classes, since she'd moved here so late in her term."

"Do you use pain medication for labor and delivery?"

"Not unless we have to for extended labor or complications. I have a local family physician on call for my patients. He can step in and prescribe pain meds if necessary."

Mattie glanced at Stella, wondering if it was all right to bring up the fentanyl patches.

Stella took over. "Who is your physician consultant?"

"Nash Rodman. We don't have any obstetricians in Hightower, so when Dr. Rodman joined the local family practice about a year ago, I asked him to consult with some of our mothers. It's been nice to have a young doctor with modern ideas to collaborate with."

Mattie recorded the doctor's name in her notebook.

"Do you or Dr. Rodman perform abortions?" Stella asked.

"I don't, and I doubt if he does, since he's in family practice, not obstetrics. I send my clients who're interested in exploring abortion to an obstetrical clinic in Willow Springs. You'd have to ask Dr. Rodman himself about his policy."

"Did Tonya ask you about exploring abortion as an option?"

"No. Tonya knew what she wanted before coming to our center, and she had her adoption plan in place."

Stella finally turned to the subject that Mattie wanted her to address. "Do you or your physician consultant ever use fentanyl patches as a form of pain control?"

"Not at all. Like I said, we avoid using drugs if possible."

"Do you have samples on hand?"

"Absolutely not. There would be no reason for it."

Mattie wondered if Carla was protesting too much.

Stella changed the subject. "Please give me a rundown on your schedule yesterday, including the time you finished with Tonya and saw her leave."

"You mean my whole day? Why?"

"You and Ms. Latimer were among the last to see Tonya alive. I need to create a timeline for Tonya's day yesterday, and it's routine to establish a timeline for those who had contact with the deceased."

"Wait a minute—are you saying that Tonya was *killed*? She didn't die during childbirth?" Carla's hands were gripped tightly together in her lap.

Stella remained expressionless. "Again, we don't know. I would appreciate everything you can tell me to help us put the pieces together."

Carla looked nervous. "Tonya was our only patient yesterday, and I scheduled her on a Saturday morning so I could teach her the breathing techniques she needed to know before her labor. She arrived at eight and left about ten o'clock."

She paused to swallow, the audible sound revealing tightness in her throat. "I spoke to Deidra about Tonya's complaint, and then she left shortly after. I worked here in the office until about noon."

"Was anyone else here at the time?" Stella asked.

Carla bit her lip as she shook her head. "I closed the center and went into my home for lunch. Like I said earlier, I left for Willow Springs about three and returned home around eight last night."

She said seven earlier, Mattie thought. "Are you sure it was eight?"

Carla waved dismissively. "Seven or eight, sometime around then."

"And did you eat lunch with someone here at your home or have contact with someone before you left for Willow Springs?" Stella asked.

Worry lines appeared between Carla's brows. "I live alone, so no."

Stella nodded, her face serene. "Please give us details as to your stops in Willow Springs and whether or not you have receipts."

Carla mentioned stops at a grocery store, a gas station, and a coffee shop, ending with a drawn-out explanation of why she never got printed receipts, keeping only digital records.

"While I talk with Ms. Latimer, perhaps you can pull up those records to show me."

"I'm not sure the charges I made will be posted on my account yet. I don't think I can show you a record of it today."

Stella pursued the point. "Didn't you mention that you needed medical supplies? What store did you go to for that?"

Carla flushed. "The medical supply store closes at two on Saturdays. I'd forgotten that, or I wouldn't have made the drive yesterday at all. And I paid cash at the coffee shop."

Stella nodded, her eyes slightly narrowed. "Then please send me a record of your purchases at the grocery store and gas station as soon as you can."

The midwife nodded, and a muscle at her jaw bulged as she lowered her eyes. "I feel like I'm a suspect," she murmured.

"You're in the position of being close to the deceased, and as I mentioned before, we don't know yet what caused Tonya's death." Stella kept her tone neutral. "I'm gathering all the information I can so I don't have to backtrack later. And I appreciate your help and cooperation."

The outside door opened, and Mattie glanced over to see a woman enter. Apparently, Deidra Latimer had arrived. She scanned the room and gave them a quick smile before bending to unzip and take off her boots. Her platinum-blond hair draped over her face, but not before giving Mattie a glimpse of one of the most strikingly beautiful women she'd ever met.

"I hope I'm not interrupting," Deidra said.

"No, you're right on time," Carla responded quickly.

Mattie thought the midwife looked relieved to have someone arrive who would take the focus off her.

NINETEEN

Cole sat astride Mountaineer on a rise just above the Redstone Ridge trailhead and watched the team of four dogs and their handlers begin to comb the area. Sergeant Jim Madsen had divided the landscape into quadrants and assigned each quarter to one dog team. Then he planned to rotate through so that each team could use their special talents to search for what they'd been trained to find—narcotics, explosives, or dead people.

Cole had met Madsen last spring when Sophie went missing and the sergeant brought his bloodhound Banjo down from Denver to help search for her. It had been good to reconnect with the intimidating man who had a soft heart. They'd embraced like brothers when Cole arrived at the motel earlier to lead the way to the Redstone trail parking lot.

They'd encountered no problems driving on the highway. The road had been sanded, and the truck and trailer were heavy enough to provide stability. The bright Colorado sunshine was beginning to warm the countryside, eating away the snow that had fallen last evening so that brown patches of dirt and autumn foliage had begun to show.

He turned to look at Garrett, who sat beside him astride his bay gelding. It was great to see his friend back in the saddle after being absent for a couple months. Garrett looked healthy and fit, and Cole couldn't have been more pleased to be working beside him again.

Detective Hauck was riding one of Garrett's horses, and he sat watching the dogs as well, his wrists crossed on his saddle horn. "It's fascinating to see this group of dogs work," he said.

"It *is* that." Garrett turned toward Cole. "But that mean-looking shepherd that looks for drugs might as well take a break. Mattie and Robo covered that area yesterday, and if they didn't find anything, it ain't out there."

Cole smiled. It was well known how much his friend admired Mattie. "That's a Belgian Malinois, Garrett, one of the best breeds in the business for police work. Be careful what you say around him, or he might eat your lunch."

Garrett chuckled. "I'm just saying Mattie and her dog are at the top of this game. And I'll take a friendly German shepherd like Robo any day."

Hauck leaned forward in his saddle to look at Cole. "Those two do make an impressive team. Deputy Cobb covered miles on foot yesterday. I was amazed at her stamina."

"She trains hard for this," Cole said. "And I have to work hard to be able to keep up with her."

Hauck raised one eyebrow. "So you work with Mattie often?"

"When the sheriff's department needs me." Cole decided that was all he wanted to share. He liked Hauck, but it was too soon to tell him his personal business.

Hauck studied him briefly before turning back to watch the dogs.

"We might as well get down and stretch our legs," Cole said as he dismounted. "This might take a while."

The teams were quartering back and forth, covering their assigned areas, often disappearing into the timber. Thinking along the same lines as Garrett, Cole kept his eye on the two Labs and the bloodhound. If explosives or a corpse lay buried, these would be the dogs that would alert.

After about an hour, a commotion arose from within a grove of ponderosa pine. "Over here," one of the handlers shouted.

Cole turned to step back up into the saddle. "Let's ride down to see what he found."

He led the way at a sedate pace, not wanting to ride up suddenly on the dog team. He spotted Madsen and Fritz hurrying through the trees on a course that would take them to the same pine grove where Cole and his party were headed. He slowed so Madsen would arrive first, figuring the sergeant would let them know if he wanted their help.

When he saw the team who'd signaled the alert—a muscular guy who was built like a wrestler, sported a brunet crew cut, and was paired with the yellow Lab—Cole's heart sank. "It's the cadaver dog, Garrett," he said as his friend's horse quickened its stride to move up beside him.

"Yup." The grim lines set on Garrett's face spoke volumes about what he was feeling. His daughter, Grace, had been found in a shallow grave in the mountains a little over a year ago.

"Do you want to stay back?"

"I brought a pry bar and a shovel." Garrett showed no sign of stopping. "They might want to use it."

Cole nodded, riding close enough to hear Madsen talk to the Lab's handler.

"What did she do, Dirk?" Madsen asked.

Dirk squatted beside his dog, one arm around her in a hug as he stroked and patted her side. "She gave me a hit, Sarge. Came here, did a double take over the ground, and then she lay down right on that spot," he said, pointing to an open area inside the grove.

"Good job. Now let's get a second opinion." After Dirk led his dog away about twenty feet, Madsen waved his hand toward the ground. "Let's go, Fritz. Find it for me."

Fritz moved forward, nose to the ground, and within seconds he lay down on the same spot and stared up at Madsen.

"Good lord," Madsen said, looking over toward Hauck. "I think we've got a body."

★   ★   ★

After lining up her boots on a mat beside the door, Deidra straightened and slipped off her coat, leaving her russet knit scarf draped around her neck. The tall blonde glided across the room on socked feet, wearing black leggings and a multicolored tunic, her stride as lithe as a dancer's. Crow's-feet around her green eyes spoke of years that weren't readily apparent in her smooth, flawless complexion. Her makeup seemed artfully applied in a less-is-more strategy. All in all, she projected the appearance of a woman in her fifties who had maintained her youthful looks. She reminded Mattie of Rainbow, making her think *yoga and vegan.*

Carla introduced Stella and Mattie before saying, "This is my assistant, Deidra Latimer."

Almost six feet tall, Deidra displayed perfect posture and a slender yet athletic-looking build. She made complete eye contact, looking self-assured as she exchanged handshakes.

"We appreciate you coming in to talk to us on your day off," Stella said when she shook Deidra's hand.

"No problem. In this business, we're always on call." Deidra smiled softly as she adjusted her muffler. "It comes with the territory, and I love my job."

Carla interjected, her expression sad but determined, "I'm afraid these officers brought bad news about one of our patients."

Deidra sobered and stood still, one hand on her scarf. "Oh?"

"It's Tonya Greenfield." Carla paused before blurting out the rest. "She's been found dead."

Deidra looked stunned as she sank into a chair. "How? What went wrong?"

Apparently having felt the need to deliver the bad news to her employee herself, Carla now relinquished the floor. She set her mouth in a grim line and directed her gaze toward Stella. Though Mattie made note of the dynamic, she categorized it as within the norm for employers who worked closely with their personnel, sort of a protective response.

And Deidra's question made Mattie think that the assistant believed Tonya's death was associated with her pregnancy.

Stella took over. "We're not sure what happened to Tonya, though we plan to find out. We'd appreciate your help."

"Of course. I'll help however I can."

Stella turned to Carla. "Is there a private space we could use to interview Ms. Latimer?"

"Call me Deidra, please," she murmured, looking down at her hands folded in her lap.

"My private office is inside my home, but you're welcome to use it." Carla paused for a moment before standing. "Wait, I do have work I need to get done. Why don't I go to my office, and you can stay here in the lobby where it's comfortable. Deidra, the detective brought a warrant for us to share medical information, so you can talk freely about what you know with them. When you're finished, please knock on the door."

Carla left, and Mattie waited for Stella to get the ball rolling.

"Deidra, when Tonya was found, she was already deceased but no longer pregnant."

Deidra's brows knit. "So she died in childbirth?"

"We don't know."

"When she left our office yesterday, I thought we would see her back here very soon. Her exam showed that her body was getting ready to deliver." Deidra paused. "Have you talked to the people who were going to adopt the baby yet?"

"I've made an appointment to meet with them."

Deidra lowered her gaze to study the floor. "Carla might have told you that I spoke out of turn about Tonya's adoption plan. I regret that. But . . ."

There's always a but *when a person thinks they're in the right,* Mattie thought.

"But I feel passionately about going through formal channels for adoption, and that includes using an adoption agency."

Stella nodded as if in sympathy and leaned forward with an open posture, her body language inviting Deidra to keep talking.

"I'm sorry if I caused Tonya distress. I should've kept my mouth shut." Deidra's mouth set in a line that implied that this was exactly what she intended to do now.

Though Stella waited, Deidra didn't say anything more, making the detective break the silence. "Did you get a chance to talk to Tonya about it?"

Deidra shook her head, looking sad. "I planned to apologize to her the next time I saw her."

Stella changed the subject. "What is your medical specialty, Deidra? Are you licensed as a nurse?"

"Oh, no. I'm a certified medical assistant. My on-the-job experience and training are what give me the obstetrical specialty."

"How long have you worked here?"

"About a year, but I worked for another midwife years ago before I moved to Colorado."

Mattie decided to jump into the conversation. "And where was that?"

"In California, but that clinic closed, and I worked for an orthopedic surgeon for a while before moving here. I'm lucky to have this job, because I'd much rather work with expectant moms and experience their joy when they have babies."

Mattie hoped to nudge her back to the situation with Tonya. "Though not all births are joyful, I suspect."

"True, although there's nothing better than helping a new life come into the world." The smile Deidra offered seemed genuine.

Mattie realized that the information she'd received about Tonya's encounter with this woman had come secondhand from Ben and might have been colored by teenage drama. Though both Deidra and her boss seemed to agree that criticizing Tonya's adoption plan had been inappropriate, Mattie could also see that under the circumstances, it might have touched a raw nerve on Tonya's part. "Did Tonya express any ambivalence about going through with her pregnancy?"

Deidra raised a finely sculpted eyebrow. "No, not at all. She came to us after she'd reached the cutoff for legal abortion and seemed determined to follow through with her plan."

"Do you ever provide pain medication for the patients you follow here?" Mattie asked.

"Oh no, that would be way outside my scope of care. I follow through with whatever Carla suggests for each patient, providing education or facilitating referrals, that kind of thing."

And though they'd already asked Carla about fentanyl, Mattie wanted confirmation from a second source. "And does Carla provide or recommend pain medications?"

Deidra shook her head. "We emphasize pain management techniques that don't include the use of drugs."

"Have you ever worked with a midwife or physician who used fentanyl as a method for pain control?"

Deidra looked surprised. "Not for labor and delivery, although the doctors at the orthopedic clinic I worked at sometimes prescribed it."

Mattie thought again of Johnson and the pain he must be in. "Was that common?"

Deidra frowned as if conjuring up that time. "I'm not sure. It was never my role to discuss or administer medications. I worked primarily as an assistant for exams, you know, setting up and cleaning up, that type of thing. If a patient said they were having uncontrolled pain, I reported it to the nurse or the MD, and they handled it."

Deidra seemed to be providing the right answers, and Mattie felt they'd covered the misunderstanding she'd had with Tonya adequately. She settled back in her chair and allowed Stella to take over.

And Stella seemed ready to move in a new direction. "Tonya's appointment here was one of the last places she went before her death. Did she happen to say where she was headed next?"

Again, that expression of discomfort crossed Deidra's face. "No, but . . . I spoke to her only briefly while I took her vitals . . . before she met with Carla. Uh . . . Tonya seemed reserved, and when I tried to visit with her, she wouldn't engage like she used to. I'm embarrassed to say I know now that she was mad at me."

Indeed, Deidra looked regretful and ashamed as she sat with her eyes downcast, a rosiness moving into her cheeks.

"So you didn't see her again before she left?" Stella asked.

"Only to say good-bye as she walked out the door."

"And what time was that?"

"About ten. Carla had been with her for about an hour and a half, teaching those pain management techniques we talked about. I worked in here loading charges into the computer for insurance billing."

"So what time did *you* leave here?" Stella asked, getting into Deidra's alibi.

Deidra released an audible sigh. "Carla talked to me about Tonya's complaint, so I left here around eleven. I keep a time card, and I could give you the exact time if you want it."

"About eleven will do." Stella leaned back as if lounging in her chair, though Mattie knew she was anything but relaxed. "Could you give us a general outline of what you did for the rest of the day?"

"I was upset that I'd created a problem for one of our patients." The memory of it creased Deidra's brow. "I went to the store to pick up some cleaning supplies and then went home. I was too upset to eat lunch, so I scoured my entire house top to bottom, including the cabinets and the refrigerator."

Mattie could relate to working off emotions with activity. That's why she and Robo ran the foothills around Timber Creek.

"Then I did some yoga practice to try to calm my mind, cooked a nice meal, since I was starving by then, and went to bed early. That was my day, and I have to say, I felt bad about Tonya through most of it." She was shaking her head. "I ended up lying awake, so I watched Netflix before I finally crashed."

"And were you with anyone else yesterday?" Stella asked.

"I live alone. Maybe if I'd called a friend, I could have let go of some of those bad feelings I was having, but I didn't. I don't like to be a burden to my friends."

The strain on Deidra's face as she'd described her day looked genuine to Mattie. She couldn't think of anything else to ask and thought maybe they should wrap things up and move on; perhaps they could interview this Dr. Rodman before having to leave Hightower to make it to their appointment back in Timber Creek.

Evidently, Stella felt the same way, and she ended the interview by asking Deidra to invite Carla back into the lobby. She gave her business cards to the two women and asked them to contact her if they thought of anything else that might be useful.

The sun had risen further in the sky, and drips off icicles that hung from the eaves plopped onto the ground beneath. Mattie paused at Deidra's car and took note of the car's make, model, and license plate on her pad, a habit she'd developed early in her tenure in law enforcement. It was a maroon Mazda CX-5 SUV, and it looked clean enough to indicate that it had been parked somewhere during the storm last night instead of being out on the road.

Robo greeted them exuberantly as they climbed back into the car, and Mattie gave him a thorough petting as she asked Stella if she wanted to try to track down the doctor before leaving town.

"We have time, don't we?" Stella swiped open her cell phone and asked Google to find his number. Within seconds she had his answering service on the phone.

Mattie listened to Stella's one-sided conversation, gleaning enough to know that Dr. Rodman was out of town for the weekend.

Stella disconnected the call. "Well, the doctor might be able to confirm what we've learned about pain management at this clinic, but he doesn't appear to be a lead related to Tonya's death. He's in Denver for a conference, and I'll be able to confirm his presence there easily, since he was scheduled as one of yesterday evening's speakers. He's supposed to be back in the office tomorrow, probably home later today, and I left a message for him to call me back."

"All right." Mattie gave Robo one last pat and started the engine. "That's the Double Dollar next door, the discount store where Tonya and Skylar supposedly met. Let's go see if they have video cameras that might have recorded Skylar and Tonya's meeting."

"Sounds good." Stella began writing in her notebook.

Mattie drove around the block and turned into the lot behind the building, which was almost empty on this Sunday morning. Out of habit, she scanned the few cars that were there, and a grimy, silver Honda Civic with a dented rear bumper caught her eye. Her heartbeat quickened as she read the license plate.

"There's Tonya's car right there," she said, turning in beside it.

"Well, I'll be damned." Stella reached for her cell phone before Mattie could bring her vehicle to a full stop.

TWENTY

Cole didn't have much of a stomach for digging up graves, but he couldn't stand by and let Garrett do it. He dismounted from his horse and rushed over to untie the tools from behind his friend's saddle. "Stay put, Garrett. I'll take these over to Sergeant Madsen."

"All right." Garrett hitched up one hip and turned in the saddle to watch Cole. "I brought that pry bar in case they want to probe the ground below the surface with it."

"Good idea."

Cole carried the tools to where Madsen and Hauck stood talking. Hauck looked excited as he gestured toward the spot that Fritz had just indicated, while Madsen looked grim.

Hauck was saying, "What's the likelihood of anything being buried here? I assume this area was searched months ago after John Cobb was arrested. Why wasn't anything found here then?"

Madsen flung out his arm, gesturing wide to encompass the forest. "Look at this terrain. Without the marks on that map, discovering something buried out here would probably be impossible, even with dogs. And as far as I know, this is the first time this area has been searched by dogs."

Though Cole agreed with Madsen's response, he held back until he made eye contact with the sergeant, then lifted the pry bar. "If you want to probe the ground, Garrett brought this."

Madsen nodded and reached for the bar. It was about four feet long, pointed at one end and bent in a ninety-degree angle with a flattened edge at the other. "We might as well try it."

Hauck stood back while Madsen tamped the bar into the ground. At first it looked like the bar met resistance from hard soil. Madsen tried another spot about six inches from the first and seemed to get the same effect, but this time he leaned into it. The bar sank slowly at first, then shot downward almost its full length into the ground. Madsen released the tool as if it burned his hands. He straightened and looked at Cole. "Feels like open space a couple feet down."

Cole knew what that meant—a grave site with decomposing remains. And he would bet that Garrett recognized it too. He turned to check on his friend in time to see him give a short salute before turning to ride away. Cole felt relieved that Garrett had decided to remove himself from the scene.

"What are the odds of an animal being buried here?" Hauck asked.

"Slim to none." Madsen walked over toward Cole and reached for the shovel. "These dogs are trained to detect human decomp, and that's what they do."

This was police business, and Cole was happy to stand back and let Madsen take over. Madsen went back to the pry bar, bent forward, and tugged it from the ground. It came up easily, bringing soil with it.

A man of substantial size, Madsen bent to the task of digging up shovelfuls of dirt that looked relatively loose compared to the tightly packed, stony soil typical of the Rockies. The odor of decayed flesh began to infiltrate the air.

Madsen stopped digging and looked at Hauck. "We have clothing. We're going to need a forensic team to excavate this grave site."

Hauck nodded as he withdrew his phone from his pocket and began dialing. He stepped away while speaking into the phone. "Sheriff McCoy, we've got a body here, and we're going to need a forensic team to recover it. We're about a half mile up the Redstone Ridge trail."

Hauck's voice faded as he continued to walk away and make plans with McCoy. Cole began to wonder where this would lead. This must be another one of John Cobb's victims. But what did they have going on here? Two bodies within close proximity in two days—were the two deaths connected somehow?

The other handlers had continued searching, rotating through the quadrants as originally planned. A shout came from outside another grove of trees not too far away. "Sarge! Over here! We've got a hit!"

Heart in his throat, Cole whirled and hurried through the forest, searching for the handler who'd called out. He spotted him about fifty yards away near the base of a tall pine. It was the guy with the black Lab, the dog trained to detect explosives.

His handler had him by the collar and was speed-walking away from the spot the dog had indicated, as if afraid it might blow at any minute.

★　★　★

Stella disconnected her call and pocketed her cell phone. "Sheriff McCoy will get a warrant and will arrange covered transport for the car to our lab. I need to go inside and see if we have CCTV out here. Will you stay and guard it?"

"Will do." Mattie peered inside the Honda's windows, taking note of the mess within. Food wrappers, soda cans, and items of clothing littered the back seat and floor, and black and white dog hairs coated the front passenger seat. It would be a challenge for the crime scene techs to sort through all of it for trace evidence. Perhaps they would have some luck at finding fingerprints.

She wanted to sweep the car's exterior for drugs. She didn't anticipate finding anything, but under the circumstances, she thought it prudent to look. If there were fentanyl patches in the car, Robo would probably detect them.

As Stella hurried toward the store entrance, Mattie went back to Robo's compartment. He danced in place as she splashed some water in his bowl and took out the blue nylon collar he used for narcotics detection. Even as she removed his leather collar and buckled on the blue one, he settled into work mode, his eyes pinned on hers. When she clipped on his leash and asked him to unload, he circled her legs and sat at her left heel without needing direction. He stared up at her.

Mattie began the chatter used to rev up his prey drive, thumping his sides as she pulled him close to her leg. It didn't take much to get Robo excited, and soon he looked ready to begin. "Wanta find some dope? Let's find some dope."

Robo's training involved a passive method of indicating, so she knew he wouldn't touch the surface of a vehicle unless she told him to. There would be no paw or scratch marks left on the exterior.

The car looked like it could have been out on the road during the storm last night. She led Robo to the rear bumper first and did a visual inspection of the dents there, both on the bumper and on the upper trunk. They weren't deep or crumpled like those left from metal against metal. Instead, they were shallow and rounded, as if the car had come into contact with something soft.

Like a person. Rear bumper damage would be consistent with the signs they'd read on the ice and snow at Johnson's crime scene last night.

She used one hand to direct Robo's nose toward the underside of the bumper while holding his leash in the other. Her dog, his ears pinned alongside his head, sniffed where she pointed. Then Mattie moved around the car, asking him to sniff the cracks at the trunk, doorways, and hood, paying special attention to the wheel wells.

No hits. If there had been drugs in this car, even if they were sealed, she would bet her next paycheck that Robo would have smelled them. His lack of response supported her theory that Tonya wasn't a drug user, and the girl probably wasn't the type to self-medicate either.

After all, if Tonya had wanted to use pain meds during her labor and delivery, why would she have sought a midwife's services to begin with? She would have gone the more common route of traditional medicine and found a doctor who shared that philosophy.

Hurried and purposeful footsteps sounded behind her, and she turned to find Stella coming back from the store with a steely glint in her eyes.

"They have a surveillance system inside but no cameras out here. They gave me access to yesterday's recordings, though, and I downloaded them on my thumb drive. Maybe we can still pick up something important." Stella paused before adding, "I got a call from Sheriff McCoy."

Mattie could tell that the sheriff had called with some important news.

Stella continued, "The dog team found a shallow grave near the Redstone Ridge trailhead. McCoy has called in the CBI to excavate the grave and an agent to help with that investigation."

Calling in the Colorado Bureau of Investigation was a big step. "John Cobb marked that part of the trail on the map. I think it's safe to assume that sometime before we arrested him, he either killed this person or had a part in disposing of the body," Mattie said.

"That's a fair assumption. Now, if they can only find some proof. There's more—the explosives dog hit on something that they haven't dug into yet. They're waiting for a CBI explosives team to make sure they're not sitting on a booby trap."

"Good grief." Mattie couldn't believe how the Cobb investigation had taken off. "Drugs, explosives, and a body. What next?"

"Who knows? But for now, the sheriff wants us to stay in our lane with Tonya's case. Transport should arrive any minute. We need to follow it back to Timber Creek to make sure the car stays within our custody."

Mattie felt pulled in two directions more than ever. Dog handling and working with the K-9 teams was in her blood, but loyalty compelled her to find justice for Tonya.

"Look at the condition of this car." Mattie pointed to the road grime and dented rear end. "This car was on the road last night, and the dents look consistent with hitting something softer than another car."

"I noticed that too." Stella frowned. "This might be the vehicle that hit Johnson last night. If there's any DNA on the exterior of this car, we need someone to find it."

Mattie studied the upper part of the trunk, imagining the loss of body fluid from the nose or mouth of any victim who had been struck. She hoped that was the case and that the fluid had been preserved and could be swabbed as evidence.

A truck and covered trailer turned into the parking lot and headed their way. Mattie waved the driver over, and she and Stella observed as he used a winch to load the car. Within minutes, they were on the road, following the transport vehicle toward Timber Creek.

Stella's phone rang, and she spoke with a person who Mattie soon realized must be the medical examiner. Stella flipped open her notebook and began taking notes. After ending the call, she turned to Mattie.

"The ME just completed Tonya's autopsy. He's listing her cause of death as cardiac arrest secondary to respiratory arrest and the manner of death as homicide. He found subtle bruising on her forearms and above her ankles as well as a sticky residue that suggests binding with something wide, like duct tape." Stella's distress was evident in her tight voice and the look on her face. "He confirmed a vaginal birth, and there was enough trauma from that to make it hard to tell if there was a sexual assault. Since there was no semen present anywhere, he thinks it unlikely."

"So maybe our hunters aren't implicated after all."

Stella shrugged. "Condoms take care of the lack of semen."

"You're right."

"The ME says four fentanyl patches could cause respiratory failure. He'll let me know when the toxicology results come back with the blood levels. She had edema and congestion in her lungs and airways, enough to inhibit her oxygen intake and stop her heart. He estimates time of death between two and five o'clock PM."

"That means the baby was born between ten o'clock in the morning, when Tonya left the midwife's office, and the time-of-death window. Pretty fast labor for a first-time birth."

"The ME ordered a test for Pitocin," Stella said, referring to the drug used to stimulate labor.

Mattie glanced at Stella. Her friend's face had paled, and she sat hunched with her arms wrapped across her stomach. Though the ME report had been disturbing, Stella's reaction seemed atypical of her usual stoic self. "Are you okay?"

Stella looked out the passenger side window and shook her head. "I'm feeling a little queasy, and my head aches again."

"Do you want some more Tylenol?"

"I brought my own," she said, reaching for her bag. "Probably should take some."

"There's a bottle of water in the console."

Stella lifted her travel mug. "I've got some coffee left over."

"Water's better if you're queasy."

Stella shot her an impatient look but opened the console for the water. "All right, Mom."

Mattie shook her head. "That's hard news from the ME. Want to talk about it?"

"I guess so." The pill bottle rattled as Stella shook out tablets and popped them into her mouth, chasing them with a swig from the water bottle. "Bruising indicates Tonya was restrained before death, possibly during her labor and delivery. Posing her body the way it was indicates she was dumped by someone who knew her, maybe someone who cared about her."

Mattie nodded. "I'm liking Skylar Kincaid more and more for this."

"Right. But one more thing—the ME found a short red hair on Tonya's sweater. He doesn't think it's one of hers, because it's wiry, similar to a beard hair."

"Reagan Dawson." Mattie glanced at Stella, whose nod told her she'd thought of the same person. The man who'd found Tonya's body—and they had an appointment to interview him and his buddies back at the station within the hour. "Well, we'll soon be able to question him about how close he got."

They rode in silence for a few miles, Mattie checking on Stella with sidelong glances. The color in her face returned gradually.

After a bit, Stella spoke. "I can't imagine the pain and terror Tonya felt when she delivered her baby. Restraining her like that must have been pure torture. This is a hell of a case."

A glance told Mattie that her friend felt anguished by the mere thought. "That's a painful thought."

"Even a miscarriage is painful. I can't imagine what it would be like to deliver a full-term infant under those conditions."

Mattie could tell that Stella's torment had something to do with her own loss as well as the case. She raised her hand with the intention of touching her friend's shoulder but lowered it back to the wheel. She wasn't sure what to say that would provide comfort.

After a few minutes, she decided to address it head on. Knowing Stella, if she didn't want to talk about it, she would say so. "Going through a miscarriage is a terrible thing to have to do on your own. Did you have anyone to support you during that time?"

Stella shook her head as she looked out the passenger window. "Not really. I didn't want the jerk to know about it, and we worked out of the same department. You know how cops are—we're at work all the time, so our only friends are the people we work with. I had yet to meet someone like you, someone I could trust to keep my problems confidential."

This time Mattie did touch her on the shoulder. "I'm sorry you had to go through that alone. I know a good counselor I could recommend if you need someone to talk to."

Stella glanced at her, and Mattie gave her a soft smile. They both knew she was referring to the counselor Mattie worked with, the therapist who specialized in trauma counseling that Stella had recommended several months ago.

Stella returned the smile before sobering. "I'm all right. It's just this case that's getting to me, and I can't seem to shake this headache. I'm just not up to par."

Which was all the more reason that Mattie needed to stick to this case and work with Stella. She wanted to assist her in any way she could. "You know what? Tonya delivered that baby before she was overdosed enough to cause her death, so I think it's alive and someone has it."

"That makes sense, and it poses the question: where is that baby now?"

"If we can find it, we'll find our killer."

Stella nodded but didn't comment as she settled back in her seat to gaze out the window and brood. This behavior seemed more typical, and Mattie retreated into her own thoughts.

She realized that tracking down the baby was more easily said than done. She would have to see if the sheriff would put out a press release calling for tips regarding an infant showing up unexpectedly in a family or a community. It wouldn't hurt, and it might actually give them information that would help solve Tonya's case, now labeled for certain as a homicide.

TWENTY-ONE

Cole lingered nearby to see what would be done next. A hit from an explosives detection dog added another level of caution to the equation.

"Are we sure this is a bomb?" Hauck asked.

Rob, the black Lab's handler, spoke up. "Thunder also detects gunpowder. It could be something as harmless as ammo buried here, or it could be a more dangerous type of explosive."

"Okay . . . how deep?"

"Hard to say, but I'd guess anywhere from one to twelve inches, depending on the type and amount of what's there."

"And how often is your dog wrong?"

This question made Rob frown. "He's still in training, but he's been accurate so far."

Madsen stepped in. "These dogs are taken through a protocol that goes from easy to difficult. Thunder has passed every training item with flying colors and is doing field work now to finish up. We should take this alert seriously."

There was a moment of silence before Madsen spoke again. "What's John Cobb's MO? Are bombs his thing?"

The words came out of Cole's mouth automatically. "Guns, drugs, and fire."

Hauck nodded his agreement. "Decades ago, this guy smuggled guns and drugs out of Mexico. In recent years, I'd guess, he was still into drug running. But bombs . . . that's not been a part of his game that I know of."

Madsen looked as though he was turning the information over in his mind. "We still can't take a chance on digging this up ourselves. We have to wait for a bomb squad to recover whatever's down there."

Hauck rubbed the back of his neck. "Are you sure it's not narcotics?"

"Completely." Madsen straightened, staring at Hauck. "Thunder hasn't been trained to hit on narcotics, and he wouldn't. Protecting human life in a case like this is top priority. We'll wait for the CBI team to get here."

Cole wondered how long that would take. If they had to wait until the CBI arrived to take over, the rest of the day might be wasted.

"McCoy is sending Deputy Brody to take over this site so we can move on up the trail." Madsen turned to the dog handlers. "You guys finish up the search while I mark off these sites."

Cole helped Madsen string flagging tape near each site. Within an hour, both Brody and McCoy arrived, Brody on foot and McCoy on the back of one of Frank Sullivan's horses.

McCoy nodded at Cole before speaking to Madsen. "Deputy Brody will take over here. We expect the CBI forensic team and an explosives team to arrive soon. I'll ride up the trail with you to the next spot on the map."

Madsen and his dog handlers led the way to set the pace while Garrett, Hauck, and Cole followed on horseback. Sheriff McCoy brought up the rear. As they wound their way upward, Cole noticed that Garrett was quieter than usual.

Cole's thoughts lingered on Garrett and Leslie's daughter, Grace, and how he and his kids still missed her. That led to thinking about Tonya and how her bright light had been snuffed from this world. Two unrelated and senseless deaths.

Hauck interrupted his thoughts when he turned in his saddle. "So I heard that both you and Garrett were here the night John Cobb abducted Mattie and took her up to the cave at the top of the trail."

"We were. We rode together in a search party and found her sometime after Cobb set the forest on fire." Memories of the roaring blaze that had threatened to overtake them flamed briefly in his mind. Nightmares still haunted him about that towering fire.

"So how did you find her in this huge forest?" Hauck asked.

"Her dog Robo found her. We followed him."

A speculative look crossed Hauck's face as if he were imagining it. "That's pretty amazing," he said, before turning forward in his saddle.

They climbed higher into the mountains. The sun was a brilliant white ball making its way up in the sky, and its heat warmed their backs and began melting the snow. It was turning out to be one of those gorgeous fall days that often followed a Colorado snowstorm.

Cole soon recognized a massive boulder beside the trail and knew they weren't far from the trail's fork halfway up. Within minutes, the K-9 crew had reached the stream at the fork and Madsen was handing out instructions even as Cole and the others approached.

"We might as well stay close to the trail, because this terrain is too rugged to go too far beyond. Dirk, since you've already found one corpse today, you take this section off to the north side that corresponds directly to the X on the map. The rest of us will take sections above and below, with one team covering a narrow strip to the south. We'll rotate through just like we did before."

While the handlers led their dogs off to search the area, Cole thought that although Detective Hauck might not have developed an appreciation for K-9 teams before, he'd be completely schooled in their value by the end of the day. How else could you search for drugs, explosives, and bodies in a rugged, mountainous area like this?

After about an hour of searching, the explosives team had another hit. Madsen left the rotation to collaborate with Hauck and McCoy. He squinted against the sun as he shared his thoughts about what to do next. "We should finish our work here and move on to the site up above. We need to get back to Denver tonight, so we better keep moving."

"I have to go back to Denver tonight too," Hauck said.

"We'll mark the site of the hit and assign someone to stand guard until we can excavate it," McCoy said, glancing at Garrett and Cole.

Cole knew he should volunteer. "I'll stay. Garrett knows the exact spot to show you up above."

But Garrett gave Cole a look that held an appeal. "I'll stay here, Cole. Just get them to the cave, and Detective Hauck can direct you to the spot Robo was interested in."

He must think we'll find another grave, Cole thought as he agreed. He returned to his horse, preparing to lead the others to a place he'd avoided since the night Mattie was taken. A place he'd once thought lovely that now represented nothing but bitterness.

★　★　★

When Mattie and Stella entered the station lobby, Robo trotted toward the dispatcher's desk, obviously expecting his friend to be waiting for him, but he stopped in his tracks when he spotted a stranger sitting there instead. He tucked in by Mattie's left heel and kept up with her as she approached the desk.

Apparently Rainbow had arranged for one of the local EMTs, Nadine Cooper, to cover for her. Nadine, a woman with short graying hair and kind brown eyes, removed her headset and smiled as Mattie greeted her. She'd served on the county ambulance team for years and occasionally subbed in as dispatcher when necessary.

"Hey, Mattie," she said, before nodding at Stella and then speaking to her. "Detective, I heard from the hospital just a minute ago. Ed Johnson's awake, and he wants you to call him as soon as you can. He asked for Sheriff McCoy, but he's up on Redstone Ridge trail and I couldn't reach him by cell. I offered to call him on the satellite phone, but Ed asked for you to call him instead."

"Sounds good," Stella said, and hurried toward her office.

Mattie felt relieved that Johnson was awake, and maybe he'd even remembered something. "How did he sound, Nadine?"

"Weak but alert." Concern creased the EMT's brow. "Compared to last night, I'll take that any day."

This comment surprised her. "Were you on the call last night?"

"I was. It's a relief to know he's awake and making sense."

"It sure is." Mattie paused before changing the subject. "What's going on up at Redstone trail?"

"Deputy Brody is in charge of the lower site. The forensic team and bomb squad have arrived, and the dog teams have gone on up the trail. Oh . . . and CBI Special Agent Rick Lawson should arrive sometime this afternoon."

Mattie knew Lawson; they'd worked together before, and she considered him a decent guy. She glanced at the clock—ten minutes before ten. "And the three hunters we expect from the campground? Are they here yet?"

Nadine shook her head. "No one has come in. Garcia is working a double shift. He's been in and out."

"Okay, I'll be back in the staff office." She turned away as Robo trotted ahead. Mattie thought his response at finding a stranger at Rainbow's desk had been cute. But then, she often thought that of her dog.

As if to fortify his cuteness, Robo pounced on his red cushion and went into play pose, his routine for asking for a treat. As usual, she made him work for it, directing him to the middle of the room for a series of doggy push-ups—commands for "down" and "stand" in rapid repetition.

She'd once watched a video of a group of officers doing push-ups alongside their K-9, all of them in sync. She hoped to duplicate that video with members from the department as soon as Robo could perform his doggy push-ups flawlessly. He was doing great, alternating his downs and ups without hesitation, but now the recording would have to wait until Johnson healed. Her video wouldn't be complete without the rookie.

Stella entered the office, empty coffee mug and notebook in hand, and went directly to the coffeemaker. After filling her cup, she laid down her notebook and leaned back against the counter to blow on her drink, sending up hot steam that carried the coffee's aroma. "Our three hunters just arrived. I put Reagan Dawson in one room and Cutter Smith in the other, and I left Wyatt Turner out in the lobby for now. I want to make them wait a few minutes."

"Okay." Mattie gave Robo his treats and directed him to his cushion, where he lay down. "Did you reach Johnson?"

"I did." Stella looked perkier than she had all day. Talking to Johnson must have lifted her spirits. "He said he spotted the car, saw Tonya's license plates, and thought the car was empty. The next thing he knew, it was backing toward him and pinned him against his own vehicle. He can't remember the rest clearly, but he thinks he slipped on the ice, fell forward, and was dragged a ways. He remembers the pressure of being run over, and then he blacked out. He doesn't recall moving into the ditch, but I think that's probably what saved him."

"Did he say why he didn't call in his location to dispatch before leaving his vehicle?"

Stella shook her head, lowering her gaze for a second. "I couldn't ask him about that. I'll leave that one to Sheriff McCoy to deal with."

"A rookie mistake. Once the kid's back, we'll all give him hell for not following procedure."

"That should do it." Stella and Mattie smiled at each other.

Mattie sobered. "How did he sound?"

"Not too bad, considering. He's in a shitload of pain, but they've got him on a lot of different things to help with that. Right at the end of our conversation, a nurse came in to give him a dose of Dilaudid through his IV, so I'd guess he's in la-la land right about now."

"Geez, I hope he heals okay."

"He told me the doc said nothing was broken that he couldn't fix, so Johnson felt pretty hopeful."

Mattie let out a breath. "Thank goodness for that."

"And now we have a positive ID on the car that hit him. We just need to find out who was driving it."

Another thought had occurred to Mattie. "I wonder if this might not have been done by two people. The car was driven from Johnson's location to Hightower and left behind the discount store. Where did the driver go from there? Was he on foot in the ice storm? Or did someone in another vehicle pick him up? And if someone picked him up, did he call someone already in Hightower for help, or did his friend follow him there to help him ditch the car?"

Lost in thought, Stella took a sip of her coffee. "I like the theory of two people, especially when you think of ditching the car. It also makes sense that the car was used to dump Tonya's body. But there was a long length of time between the body dump and Johnson's hit-and-run—maybe around six hours. Where was Tonya's car during that time?"

"Right. And how does this affect our persons of interest from the campground?" Mattie already had an idea of who could be eliminated as a suspect.

"It eliminates Dusty Spencer. Brody was with him for a long time, and he didn't leave the campsite. But the other three are still on the list. I guess we should get started with their interviews." Stella straightened and picked up her notebook. "They declined drinks. Do you want coffee?"

"No, I've had enough."

Stella lifted her mug. "This is medicinal."

Mattie smiled. "I suppose so."

As she rose from her chair to leave, Robo jumped up from his cushion to go with her. His ears fell when she told him to lie down and stay. She'd skipped his run this morning, so this would be a test of his staying power, but he couldn't join her in the interview room. If Dawson did confess to something, a defense attorney would have a heyday claiming intimidation.

Mattie followed Stella into the hallway.

"This is Reagan Dawson," Stella murmured, stopping at the first door.

The redheaded Dawson glanced up from the table to stare at them as they entered the room.

"Thank you for coming in, Mr. Dawson. This is Deputy Cobb, our K-9 officer."

"We've met." Dawson's lips thinned in a downward arch. "The deputy already took one shot at my wallet."

Mattie gave him an unapologetic nod of acknowledgment.

Stella dismissed his complaint by moving on. "We just want to talk with you this morning to get information about when you found the girl's body last night. What led you to that part of the campground?"

"I told you last night—I was looking for a place to set up camp."

"And where were your friends at the time?"

"We'd parked and all split up to look for a good site. I don't know for sure where they were at the time. You'd have to ask them."

"Okay. And up to the point when you parked, had you all been together in the same vehicle?"

"Yes, we only have the one car. We spent Friday night in that town called Hightower." He gave Mattie a hard look. "At Officer Cobb's suggestion, we found a motel where we could use our weed without breaking any laws."

Mattie smiled at him this time, especially since he'd just admitted they'd been in Hightower. "Well done, Mr. Dawson. What time did you leave Hightower to drive back to Timber Creek?"

"We got a late checkout and came back here in time to eat an early dinner at the pizza place. Then we went out to the campground. You know the rest."

Mattie continued with the questioning. "Had you ever seen or met the deceased woman before you found her?"

"Never."

"And did you approach her or touch her after you found her?"

He shook his head. "I got close enough to tell she was dead. I think I leaned over her to look at her real good, but I didn't touch her."

A stray hair could've landed on Tonya's sweater if he'd leaned close enough. Mattie wondered if he'd known he shouldn't touch her skin since she was loaded with fentanyl. Most people would have probably at least checked her pulse. "Why didn't you touch her?"

He looked astonished. "Why would I touch a dead person? I figured I'd stumbled into a crime scene."

"What gave you that impression?"

He gave Mattie a piercing look. "Didn't you have the same impression? She was lying there like she'd been posed for someone to find."

That was an interesting observation on Dawson's part. "How did you arrive at the conclusion that she'd been posed?"

He shrugged. "You see it on TV all the time—all those mystery shows."

The influence of television. Mattie decided to turn the questioning a different way. "So you're from Omaha. What do you do there?"

"That's where I grew up and where my parents live, so that's what's on my driver's license. But I'm a student at the University of Nebraska, and most of the time I live in Lincoln." He tapped a finger on the table repetitively as if using it as an outlet for his nerves. "It's my senior year."

The same school that Tonya planned to attend and, more importantly, the one in which the baby's father was already enrolled. "Do you know a student named Skylar Kincaid?"

Dawson frowned. "Skylar is one of my fraternity brothers."

Mattie couldn't help herself—her surprise made her glance at Stella, but the detective's face remained as placid as a lazy summer day.

"Have you seen Mr. Kincaid since you arrived here?" Stella asked.

"No, but he's supposed to be down here somewhere this weekend. I guess he's got a meeting with his ex-girlfriend or something."

"Have the two of you spoken on the phone lately?"

"Not at all." He gave Stella a suspicious look. "Is Skylar in some kind of trouble?"

"No trouble, Mr. Dawson." Stella waited.

"Okay . . . if you say so." Evidently Dawson suspected there was more behind this line of questioning than Stella was willing to share—which there was. If these two men were friends, they might have acted together to ditch Tonya's car.

Stella continued along the same line. "So . . . have you ever met Mr. Kincaid's ex-girlfriend?"

He smirked. "Nope. But he's her baby daddy, so I guess he knows her pretty well."

Mattie liked that Dawson seemed willing to talk. "When did you speak with him last?"

He tipped his head back to look at the ceiling for a few seconds as if thinking. "I think we talked about a week ago. We're in the same fraternity, but we don't really hang out. He's a couple years behind me."

She wondered if he'd used the delay to make up his answer. She changed the topic. "What do you study, Mr. Dawson?"

His eyes shifted between Stella and Mattie. "I'm getting a degree in civil engineering and will graduate after the spring semester."

"And Mr. Kincaid?" Mattie decided to test the friend factor. "What's he studying?"

"I have no idea. Skylar hasn't actually moved into the frat house, because it's full of upperclassmen. He'll be able to move in next year."

"Are Cutter Smith and Wyatt Turner students?" Stella asked.

"No, they both graduated years ago. I just met Wyatt this weekend. He's Cutter's friend, and I met Cutter through an internship I did last summer."

Stella leaned forward, giving him her penetrating stare. "So after spending the night in Hightower Friday, what time did you leave there yesterday?"

Stella's intensity appeared to make Dawson squirm. "I don't know."

"Think . . . when did you leave the motel?"

"Well, we made a few stops after we left the motel, so I don't know exactly when we left Hightower. We got a late checkout, so I guess we left around one."

"Did you go anywhere before you checked out?"

He ran his hand through his red beard. "I went to that store next to the motel to get some snacks."

"Which store?" Stella asked.

"Uh . . . I think it was called the Double Dollar?"

The store where Tonya's car was found. "What time?" Mattie asked.

He shrugged. "Must have been around eleven."

Mattie made a mental note to check for him on the CCTV film. It would be easy enough to see if he was telling the truth.

Stella jumped in again. "Where else did you go?"

"That was it—to the Double Dollar and back. Why all these questions about my schedule yesterday? Am I a suspect or something?" His face flushed.

Stella didn't let up. "You left the motel about one. What stops did you make?"

"We got gas."

"Where?" Mattie interjected.

He blinked a couple times before answering. "That gas station right next to the store. I don't know the name of it."

"And you were all together in the same car?"

"Of course. I told you we only have one car."

Mattie didn't like that these guys and Tonya had been in such close proximity before she was murdered, but even though they bombarded Dawson with repetitive questions for another ten minutes, and even though his nervousness seemed to escalate, he didn't change his story and he said nothing to incriminate himself.

And then Stella asked if she could take a DNA sample.

His eyes opened wide in surprise. "Why do you want that?"

"At this stage of the investigation, we need DNA from anyone who came close to our victim's body. Even if it's only to eliminate people."

They were under no obligation to provide their reason, but Stella's answer had been, in part, true. Though Stella didn't mention it, they needed to find out if Dawson had left the beard hair.

"If I refuse, you'll think I did it." Dawson hesitated but then agreed to give a sample.

Stella whisked a DNA kit from her jacket pocket and swabbed his cheek. As she sealed up the kit, she confirmed that she had his contact information and then asked what his plans were for the rest of the day.

"We're going to the campground to set up camp. I don't want to, but the other guys are set on it."

Stella evidently wanted clarification. "You don't want to because . . ."

"Shit, dude. If you found a dead person somewhere, would you want to go back? I just want to forget what I saw."

We go back all the time, Mattie thought. *We don't have the luxury of being able to forget.* As Stella wrapped up the interview, giving Dawson her card, Mattie remembered their victim, a lively girl who seemed to love her dog. She would never forget Tonya.

TWENTY-TWO

Cutter Smith looked as sure of himself as he'd been when Mattie stopped him on the highway. When she and Stella entered the room, he was leaning back in his chair, arms crossed over his chest, legs stretched out in front—a picture of relaxation, except that his narrowed eyes and scowl gave him away.

"I've been waiting a long time," he said.

Stella looked unconcerned. "Sorry about the wait, but we needed to visit with Mr. Dawson first."

"We came down here to hunt, and we're wasting another day."

And it's really not our fault that you spent the entire morning smoking pot in your motel room yesterday, Mattie thought.

"I appreciate you coming in this morning, and we won't keep you much longer," Stella said. "As with everyone else at the campground, I need to verify your schedule yesterday. Let's start with where you stayed the night and go from there."

Smith frowned but didn't hesitate. "We stayed at a cheap motel called the Overnight Inn."

"One room?"

"Yeah, three of us in one room. We left there about one, stopped to get gas, and then drove here to Timber Creek. We got pizza and then went to the campground."

"Were you all three together all morning?"

Smith raised a brow. "Yep."

"No one left the room?"

He shook his head, looked down at the table, and then looked back at Stella. "Well, Reagan made a run to the store for snacks sometime before we checked out. Otherwise, we were all there. We watched a game on television."

Mattie interjected, asking for details. Turned out it was a college game between two rivals, University of Colorado and Colorado State. She already knew about it, and the time frame matched up. "How long was Mr. Dawson gone when he went to the store?"

"About fifteen or twenty minutes. Our motel was right next door." He gave Mattie a sour look. "He walked there, if that's what you're worried about."

Driving while under the influence hadn't been her immediate concern, but hearing the length of time Dawson had been away from the others made her think that either this group of men had nothing to do with Tonya or they all did. "Do you know Skylar Kincaid?"

He met her gaze. "I don't know anyone by that name."

"He's a fraternity brother of Mr. Dawson's."

Smith shook his head. "I've only known Reagan since he interned at my company earlier in the semester. We had talked about him joining me and Wyatt for this hunting trip, but I don't know any of his buddies, if that's what you're asking about."

Mattie nodded, waiting to see if he'd say more.

He leaned on the table with his elbows, his posture open. "Look, I know you're concerned that Reagan found that girl yesterday, and I don't blame you. We know you need to find out what happened to her. But Reagan didn't have anything to do with her death. None of us did. We've been together all the time since we left Lincoln Friday morning, and I'm beginning to regret coming here. We have to go back on Tuesday, and we haven't even set up camp."

Mattie didn't feel sorry for him, but she hadn't observed any deceptive behavior yet either. "And how do you know Wyatt Turner?" she asked.

"We went to school together. He started a construction company in Lincoln, and I'm a civil engineer. We work on some of the same projects. I can give you character references if you want them . . . I'm just hoping to get out of here in time to set up camp and do some scouting before dusk."

"Character references would be good, Mr. Smith," Stella said. "Just another question or two. Do you know a young woman by the name of Tonya Greenfield?"

He shook his head. "Never heard that name before."

"She's the deceased. She's from Omaha and planning to move to Lincoln soon."

He looked puzzled. "I told you I didn't recognize the dead girl last night. I've never heard her name either."

Smith made a more convincing witness than Dawson; he seemed less nervous and more confident, perhaps because of his extra years. Whatever the reason, Mattie believed him and felt they should move on. She was beginning to think these guys were innocent.

Stella wrapped up the interview, gave Smith her card, and told him they would be able to leave soon. Wyatt Turner was now waiting in the same room where Dawson had been interviewed, and it took only about ten minutes to determine that his story matched that of the others and they could send them on their way.

"Well, that seemed like a waste of time, but at least we can check them off our list," Mattie said as Stella followed her into the staff office. Robo leapt to his feet, doing a happy dance on his cushion. Mattie released his stay, patting and praising him for waiting so long.

Stella went to refill her mug. "I don't think I'll cross them off yet."

"I meant cross them off our interview list."

"Oh, right." Stella rubbed her neck. "I don't like the fact that Dawson and Kincaid are fraternity brothers. And I still don't like that there was a red beard hair on her sweater. What's the likelihood of that happening unless he brushed against her while carrying her?"

"It could happen. Stray hair falls all the time. But I agree that it's odd that Kincaid and Dawson know each other. When we look at their stories, though, they were together except for a fifteen-minute window. If they're our guys, I think it has to be all of them or none of them, and it just doesn't make sense that the two older men were involved. What would be their motive to kill this girl?"

"I know. I don't have the answer to that yet." Stella glanced at her notes. "I'll follow up on Smith, make sure he's the businessman he says he is, and I still need to research similar cases. And of course, we've got the CCTV tapes to look at."

"I can help with those." Mattie had noticed that Robo had begun to pace back and forth between her and the door. "Robo really needs a run. It won't take long."

As soon as she said the word *run*, Robo bounded toward the door, whirled, and went shoulders down in a play pose. Mattie knew she could put him off no longer.

Stella smiled as she headed for the doorway. "I can see he's excited about that. Take your time. I'll get everything set up."

Robo trotted behind Stella while Mattie grabbed her jacket. Once outside, she went to the picnic table at the side of the building to do a quick stretch, and Robo capered in the grass, now wet from the melting snow. She told him to heel and headed down the sidewalk toward Main Street. He fell in beside her, a happy grin on his face as she picked up the pace to a fast jog.

Main Street was quiet, with several cars parked at the diner, probably folks out for Sunday brunch. She passed Main and continued her quick pace toward the highway, running through the park on a gravel road littered with fallen leaves, and then took the sidewalk again toward Clucken House, where a group of local men often met for coffee each morning.

When she entered the parking lot, intending to jog through and exit on the adjacent street, she spotted the two SUVs from Nebraska parked side by side—Skylar's Jeep and Smith's Lexus. The sight stopped her in her tracks. Robo halted and came back to stand by her side, looking up as if to see what she wanted him to do. She scanned the log building but didn't see the men through any of the windows on this side.

What the hell? Both Skylar and Dawson had stated that they didn't plan to get together here this weekend. Was this a chance meeting? It could be, but she needed to check into it.

"We have to go inside here, Robo. I think we need some doughnuts."

He was panting happily, she assumed more from exertion than heat, though the day had warmed up nicely, and he stayed beside her as she walked toward the front entrance. Since she knew the owner allowed Robo inside, she let herself in with her dog latched on to her left heel.

She immediately spotted the foursome sitting together at a center table. Skylar was eating a plateful of scrambled eggs, and the other three were drinking coffee.

Dawson glanced up, and his face fell when he spotted her. He murmured something to the rest of the crew before pushing back his chair and heading her way. They all turned to watch. Mattie waited just inside the door for him.

"We decided to stop for breakfast, and Skylar was already here. I swear it." Worry lined his face. "When I told you we weren't planning to meet up with him this weekend, that was the truth."

Cutter Smith joined them, wearing his usual air of confidence. "We needed breakfast, Deputy, and Skylar happened to be here. This is the first time Wyatt and I ever met him."

Now they know the relationship between the dead girl and Skylar, and they want to distance themselves from him. She gave them a noncommittal answer. "I see."

"Did you follow us here?" Dawson asked.

Mattie raised one brow. "Just a chance encounter."

Dawson continued to prod. "Why didn't you tell us the dead girl was Skylar's girlfriend?"

Smith touched his elbow. "Reagan, let's go back to the table. Our food's there now."

Mattie decided to make a point before they could walk away. She kept her voice low but made sure to maintain eye contact with Dawson and enunciate clearly. "If you learn anything about Tonya Greenfield's death and you *don't* report it to law enforcement, you can be charged as an accessory to murder."

"If you think any of us had anything to do with this girl's death, you're wrong." Dawson looked grim as he turned to follow Smith back to their table.

Skylar kept his head down while Mattie purchased a dozen doughnuts to take to the station, and she watched the group openly as she waited for the server to bag her pastries. All four men focused on their plates, those facing her giving her a glance or two, but the conversation at their table had ceased. She paid for the doughnuts and let herself out the door.

She thought the encounter very interesting and was eager to tell Stella. The detective had been right about not marking the threesome from Lincoln off their list too soon. Evidently they didn't know how hard it was to maintain privacy in a small town—lucky for her, not so much for them.

A few steps into the parking lot, she stopped with Robo at her heel to let an incoming car pass by. Recognizing Angie's silver Corolla, she raised her hand in greeting and drifted out to meet her.

Ben Greenfield exited the passenger's side as Angie left the driver's seat and came around the front of the car with a sheepish look on her face, making Mattie think that Cole had spoken to his daughter this morning as planned and delivered his warning to take things slowly with Ben. Right now, though, she believed the men inside the diner were more dangerous than this teenage boy.

A bit breathless, Angie hurried to greet her. "We've been at Hannah's today and came to get some doughnuts."

With four murder suspects gathered at a table in the restaurant, Mattie didn't want the kids going in there. She handed her bag to Angie. "Here, take these. I bought them as an excuse to talk to someone inside, and I don't really want them."

Angie frowned. "Are you sure?"

"Positive." She sidled over to Angie's car, trying to herd the kids along with her. "How are you today, Ben?"

Angie's cheeks flushed. "You guys know each other?"

"We met last night," Ben said, and then to Mattie, "I'm doing all right. It helps to get away from the house for a while and spend time with those puppies."

"I bet." She turned toward Angie, whose face was now rosy. "How are the pups doing?"

A smile eased some of the tension in the girl's face. "They're good. Even little Velvet is eating today, and Sassy is a great mom."

Mattie smiled at both kids. Ben seemed less mournful than he'd been last night. "That's a great name for the little one."

"Hannah named her," Angie said.

Ben leaned against the front fender of Angie's car, and a shadow crossed his face. "Have you found out what happened to Tonya yet?"

What Mattie could share with the kids was limited. "We're making progress, Ben, and we'll talk with your folks later. But right now, we've got several lines of inquiry going and several leads to track down that seem promising."

Ben glanced at the restaurant. Skylar Kincaid came around the front of the building and hurried toward his car. Mattie felt herself stiffen as her protective response kicked in.

When Skylar looked her way, he almost stopped, but then he put his head down and kept moving toward his car. Mattie tucked her thumbs at the top of her utility belt and openly watched him get inside his car and then drive away.

"That car's from Nebraska," Ben said. "Was that Skylar?"

The kid was observant. "It's best not to get involved with the investigation, Ben. We've got it under control."

"Did he kill Tonya?"

"All the elements in Tonya's case haven't come clear yet, but we've had a chance to talk to him. And we know how to contact him if we need to. We'll be able to brief your family again soon."

Angie seemed to be studying her and moved toward her car door. "C'mon, Ben. We need to get back. I promised Sophie we wouldn't be gone long."

Angie was a sharp kid, and she evidently realized that Mattie could only say so much. Mattie and Robo followed the girl to her car door, and at the last second before getting inside, Angie turned to give her a hug.

"Thanks," she murmured close to Angie's ear before backing up out of the way. Robo edged forward to nudge the girl, and she bent to give him his farewell pats as she sank down into the driver's seat.

Mattie hesitated to speak but then decided to say what she was thinking. She leaned inside the car to address both kids. "Would you two do me a favor and stay close to Hannah and Sophie for the rest of today? Until we know more about what happened to Tonya, it would give me peace of mind to know you were all together and safe."

"Okay, Mattie." Angie lifted the bag of doughnuts. "Thanks again for these."

The kids waved as they drove away, and Mattie raised her hand as she watched them go. She tried to suppress her concern over the fact that one of her suspects had seen her with the kids. Even though Skylar might have had motive to kill Tonya, that didn't mean he was a homicidal maniac. And there would be no reason for Tonya's killer to go after her loved ones.

But still, Mattie felt a ripple of apprehension as she jogged through the parking lot to the next street and set a quick pace back to the station with Robo at her side.

TWENTY-THREE

The guys that worked K-9 were all in good shape, and despite a few inches of snow on the trail, they made it to the cave in record time. It made Cole grateful that he'd been on horseback, because he might not have been able to keep up.

He stood at the mouth of the cave, feeling a chill unrelated to the wind as he studied its interior. He didn't want to even imagine what Mattie had gone through here, and he turned his back on it to trail after Hauck and the other officers. They had all stopped near an outcropping of boulders about a hundred yards from the cave.

Dirk and the yellow Lab were standing off to the side while Madsen was leading Fritz over to sniff near the hole that had been dug yesterday.

"The cadaver dog got a hit," Hauck murmured as Cole came up beside him. "Madsen's getting his second opinion."

It didn't take long for Fritz to lie down beside the hole.

Madsen praised his dog and then looked at Cole.

"Do you want me to go get the shovel and pry bar?" Cole asked him. He'd left Mountaineer tied up by the cave.

"John Cobb liked to burn bodies up in this high country, right?" Madsen asked.

"Near the base of the ridge on the other side." He gestured toward the pit the man had dug for Mattie. "And that was his plan up there."

Madsen shook his head, his disgust evident. "We'll have to go slow. If we hit charred wood, we'll back out and wait for the forensic team to excavate it."

"I'll go get the tools." Cole turned away and hurried toward his horse.

★ ★ ★

Back at the station, Mattie took Robo to her office to offer him his bowl of water while she refilled her coffee mug. She regretted not having a bag of doughnuts in hand as she made her way to the briefing room to find Stella. It had been a short night, and a little sugar would have provided some extra energy.

Stella looked up from her computer screen as Mattie and Robo entered the room. "Wait till I tell you what I've found."

Mattie had information to share too, but she let Stella go first. "What?"

"I've been researching similar cases. There's a missing single mother from Denver who disappeared three weeks after delivering a baby boy, and another teenage mom from Colorado Springs who disappeared within a week of giving birth. In both cases, the babies are also missing." Excitement bubbled from Stella as she went on. "I talked to the detective from Denver, and guess what. Carla Holt delivered their missing mom's baby."

Mattie's heart tripped. "You're kidding! Why was this girl living in Hightower?"

"She was staying with her grandmother until after she delivered. Evidently the family didn't want her around their other children while she was pregnant." Stella made a face, shaking her head as if she disagreed with that stance. "This young mom went missing about six months ago, in April."

Mattie pulled out her notepad. "And her name?"

"Rose Marie Harlan, and here's her picture." Stella handed her a black-and-white head shot. "Age nineteen, brunette, brown eyes, five feet four, one hundred sixty pounds at the time of her delivery though typically one twenty. Her baby boy is named Sam."

Mattie looked into the dark eyes of the girl in the photo and thought she recognized a hint of sadness there.

Stella went on. "The detective I talked to said that since Rose had been a patient of Carla's, he interviewed her at the time, and Carla said she knew nothing about the girl's disappearance. Rose was scheduled for a six-week checkup, which would have taken place three weeks after she went missing, but since she'd had no problems during or after delivery, she hadn't been seen at the clinic since the day after she gave birth."

Finding this connection to Carla Holt was huge. "So did he suspect Carla might have been involved in Rose's disappearance?"

"No, not at all. He spoke with her to see if she might have any idea about the girl's whereabouts, which Carla denied. She was never a suspect, because they still aren't even sure a crime has been committed. He said Rose was from a dysfunctional family and under a lot of stress, so he thinks maybe the girl just decided to take off with her baby to get out of her home situation."

"What did her family think?"

"They think she wouldn't have left home without telling someone. And they said she didn't have money or a way of supporting herself if she did. Her baby was only three weeks old."

Mattie was thinking of the dead body west of Timber Creek that was awaiting excavation—the one buried in a spot that John Cobb had marked on a map. If this body turned out to be the missing girl from Denver, it would implicate Cobb in her death or at least in the disposal of her body. "And now . . . what do you think?"

"I told the detective about our DB. He said to keep in touch. If it's female, he can retrieve his missing girl's dental records. I told him to go ahead and get started. I have a terrible feeling about this."

Mattie did too. "What about the case in Colorado Springs?"

Stella handed her a second photo, a candid shot of a young pregnant girl who looked happy. "Kaylee Cunningham, blonde, green eyes, five feet two, one hundred five pounds before pregnancy. Her baby is a girl, named Joyelle."

"And she was also Carla's patient?"

Stella shook her head. "That one isn't tied to our midwife. I've already spoken to the detective that handled her case, and according to him, Kaylee was living with her boyfriend after giving birth, and their baby was two weeks old. She disappeared in March. The boyfriend was at work, which the detective verified, and when he got home, both Kaylee and baby were gone. They traced her movements. Her mother said Kaylee had called to tell her she was going crazy staying at home and had decided to walk to a nearby store to pick up diapers.

"Kaylee was last seen on the store's CCTV checking out at the self-serve cash register. She had the baby in a front pack and was carrying a grocery bag as she walked out of the store. Outside view from CCTV at the next store captured her walking down the sidewalk and turning into the residential neighborhood where she lived, apparently heading home. That was the last camera that spotted her."

"Oh no."

"According to the boyfriend, the grocery bag and diapers were *not* found at their home. Doors were locked, and there was no sign of forced entry or a scuffle. Boyfriend's statement that he was at work all day was confirmed, and his distress over her disappearance seemed genuine. All family members said that Kaylee was happy about having a baby, and they swore she had no plans to leave her boyfriend. Neighbors didn't observe anything that looked like an abduction, but no one noticed her out walking that morning either. This case is classified as a missing person and infant."

"Does the detective think she could have been abducted before she made it home?"

"He thinks it's a possibility, though he doesn't have evidence of it. She might have gotten into someone's car willingly and is happily living somewhere else."

Though Mattie had nothing to base her assumption on, she didn't think that was what had happened. She had a bad feeling that something more sinister was afoot. "What's your take on it, Stella?"

Stella rocked back in her chair and stared forward for a brief moment before looking at Mattie. "I think we have to listen to the families of these girls and give their concerns credibility. Both believe their daughters wouldn't run away and leave their homes willingly. We have to take these reports seriously."

"Agreed, but why do you think these girls and their babies might have been abducted?" Mattie had her own thoughts on the subject, but she wanted to hear Stella's.

Stella's eyes glinted with anger. "What we talked about before . . . infant trafficking. When we include Tonya, we've got three missing babies from different parts of the state. Is it likely the cases are connected? No. But is it possible? Absolutely. You know as well as I do that we have two of the major highways for human trafficking running right through our state."

She was referring to Interstate 70 running east and west and Interstate 25 going north and south, intersecting in the city of Denver, where other major highways branched to create a hub for trafficking of all types, including human. Timber Creek felt secluded within its sheltering mountains, but despite its small size, the town had already suffered the impact of drug running and animal trafficking. Infant trafficking was not out of the question.

The thought caused a shiver to run down Mattie's spine. "Is it time to confront Carla Holt?"

"Not yet." Stella paused, obviously thinking. "I want to see if I can turn up a connection between that Colorado Springs case and Carla's clinic. I have contact information for the girl's mother and her boyfriend, and I need to talk to both of them before we talk to Carla again."

"Sounds good."

"Oh, and one more thing. The lab report came in on the powder you found at the cave. It was definitely fentanyl."

It was good to have the type of drug confirmed, although there were still unanswered questions. When had John Cobb hidden drugs up at the cave, and why? It had to have been before his arrest in May, which was probably what had prevented him from going back to retrieve it. She regretted that she hadn't taken Robo up to search the cave sooner.

"Let me tell you who I ran into at Clucken House." Mattie summarized the apparent meet-up of the Nebraska crew and her subsequent conversation with Reagan Dawson.

Stella was frowning as she listened. "Do you believe their meeting at the restaurant was by chance?"

"It could have been. Skylar was already eating, and the three hunters hadn't yet received their food. But I felt like their reactions were sneaky and covert."

"Could be guilt or feeling guilty about being caught together."

"Right." In light of the information Stella had turned up, Mattie was eager to have that body near the Redstone Ridge trailhead excavated and identified. If it turned out to be the remains of Rose Marie Harlan, then Carla Holt would be associated with two young mothers who were now dead with missing infants. "When will the forensic team from CBI have information for us?"

"Brody called in and said they were getting started. I asked him to call us as soon as the team discovered details from the site." Stella glanced down at her notes. "I need to follow up on that Colorado Springs case. Would you take a look at the CCTV film from the Double Dollar to see what we've got on it?"

It was the last thing Mattie wanted to do; working outside with Robo was her thing, not this office work and tedious fact-finding. But it was important that someone go through the tape. "Sure."

"I've got it set up on the desktop in my office."

Robo dogged Mattie's footsteps as she hurried to Stella's office, and he settled on the floor behind her when she sat in the chair. She rocked the computer mouse to activate the screen, which displayed a still shot of a row of three cash registers, only one of them manned, on the paused footage. The quality of the picture was pretty good compared to some CCTV film she'd seen before.

She noticed a clean pad of notebook paper that Stella must have left in front of the screen and selected a pen from those in the holder. It took a moment to figure out how to run the tape forward and back so she could begin the review process.

The time stamp on the tape said Saturday at 0800 hours, which she recorded on her notepad. She believed the players in question would appear after ten o'clock, but in the interest of being methodical and thorough, she began watching the film from the start.

At first there were no customers present, and the one cashier on duty drifted in and out of the picture, apparently whiling away the time on an early Saturday morning. Whenever a customer approached, she would pop back into place to ring up their purchase. Mattie grew impatient with the lack of action and began to fast-forward until a person entered the frame. Then she would slow the speed and even stop it to see if she recognized anyone.

Around nine o'clock, business picked up and there were more faces to scan, but still none that were familiar. She continued to view the tape in a series of fast-forwards, slows, and stops until shortly before eleven o'clock on the time stamp when Tonya approached the checkout counter. Her sudden appearance on the film snatched Mattie's breath away.

Though the film was black-and-white, she could imagine the fiery tangle of long, red hair that spilled out beneath the girl's stocking cap.

Tonya's face appeared wan and pinched with stress when she first appeared in the frame, but as soon as she engaged with the cashier, the lively expression that Mattie was familiar with returned, transforming her into the beautiful girl she'd met at Cole's clinic. Though there was no sound, the two chatted as Tonya set her items on the counter: a box of disposable diapers, a baby's one-piece sleeper, and what appeared to be a cozy baby blanket.

Tears prickled Mattie's eyes as she froze the frame and recorded the details along with the time stamp. *Mi cielo*, she thought, borrowing an exclamation of dismay she'd learned from Mama T. *My heaven, she's buying things for her baby before she goes into labor. She knows the baby's birth is imminent and she wants to prepare.*

Had Tonya changed her mind? Did she want to keep her baby? Or were these merely farewell gifts as she said good-bye and sent her baby off to its new home?

Mattie's attention was now fully focused on reviewing the film. She switched to another camera and pulled up footage from within the clothing aisles. After fast-forwarding to ten thirty on the time stamp, she slowed the footage, scanning for Tonya's familiar silhouette, a pregnant girl with long hair beneath a stocking cap. There were still only a few customers in the store, and it didn't take long for Mattie to find the person she was looking for.

Tonya strolled the aisle, her gait somewhat heavy with her feet placed wide and one hand low on her belly. She paused at a rack, holding up baby sleepers and putting them back until she made her choice. After placing it in a basket that dangled from one of her arms, she trudged to a shelf, where she selected the blanket and then the package of diapers. With her odd gait, she tottered out of the frame, so Mattie paused the film to make note of the time. She advanced the tape slowly, scanning for any other customers who might have been predators, but no one appeared to follow the girl.

The time had matched up within a minute to the shot at the cash register, so Mattie believed Tonya had left the baby department and gone directly to check out. She went back to the cash register film where she'd left off and watched Tonya continue a conversation with the cashier—*did the girl always engage with strangers, or had she been lonely?*—until Tonya waved her hand, lifted her two bags, and shuffled toward the exit.

"Damn," Mattie muttered, wishing like crazy that the store utilized outdoor CCTV. Who had been waiting there outside? Was it Skylar? Carla Holt? An unknown predator?

When will we get Tonya's cell phone records? Her frustration high, Mattie uttered a few curses, because today was Sunday and the records probably wouldn't come in until tomorrow. Had Tonya phoned someone? Did she start to drive home to Timber Creek but turn back because she'd gone into labor? Did she call Carla Holt's clinic? Where the hell had she gone next?

Mattie continued to advance the cash register film, looking for anyone else who was familiar. Within five minutes of Tonya's departure, Skylar Kincaid appeared in the frame at the cash register. Mattie hit pause so she could record the time, and she captured a shot of Skylar's expression frozen on the screen. The young man scowled at the cashier, his demeanor positively dark.

She advanced the tape slowly, searching for a good picture of the items Skylar was purchasing. What she saw made her gasp. They were almost identical to Tonya's: baby clothes, blanket, and diapers. But there were two additional items on the counter—baby formula and a set of baby bottles.

"Good grief." She drew in a breath and released it slowly to ease the tightening in her chest as she clicked on the forward arrow. Robo stood and came over to nudge her arm with his nose, and she absently stroked the soft fur on his head while she focused on the screen.

Skylar had said that he and Tonya had talked outside in this store's parking lot, but he'd failed to mention that he'd gone *inside* to shop. Had he known that Tonya had gone in there too? Mattie would bet her next paycheck that he had.

He'd obviously planned to take the newborn. Had he followed through with his plan? If so, where had the baby been while he was at the station this morning and then while he sat inside Clucken House to have breakfast? Had his sister already arrived in town to take care of the baby, and had he lied about waiting for her? If so, why was he still hanging around? Why hadn't they both gone home?

Unanswered questions scuttled through her mind like rats as she continued to advance the film. Soon after Skylar left, she found Reagan Dawson, paying for bags of chips and candy. His demeanor seemed calm and composed, nothing remarkable of note, and there was no one with him.

Mattie was thinking she'd probably seen all she was going to when she was surprised to spot Deidra at the register. The pretty woman smiled at the cashier and chatted while she placed her items on the counter. Mattie froze the tape and focused on the objects: a large bottle of cleaning liquid, a package of something that looked like sponges, and rubber gloves. This seemed to corroborate Deidra's statement that she'd stopped to buy cleaning supplies on her way home from the birthing center, and it only made sense that she would stop at the store next door.

Stella appeared in the doorway, a Cheshire cat grin on her face. "Wait till I tell you what I just found out."

"And I've got a bunch of stuff I've discovered here."

"Great. You go first."

Stella frowned with concentration as Mattie summarized what she'd found on the footage so far, and she lifted the notepad she was carrying to begin to take notes.

Mattie picked up her own pad to show Stella what she'd recorded. "I have details and times right here."

"Perfect." Stella reached for the pad and studied it. "So even after Skylar talked to Tonya, he planned to get his hands on that baby."

"That's what it looks like."

"Reagan Dawson's appearance seems to match what he said."

"That's right."

"And Deidra Latimer picked up cleaning supplies."

"Yes," Mattie said. "What did you find out?"

"It's about the Colorado Springs case. Kaylee Cunningham's mother just told me that Kaylee went to Carla Holt's clinic early in her pregnancy. At that time, she was living in Hightower with a friend and working at a shoe store."

"You *did* find a connection. So this shifts us back to Carla and Deidra."

Stella nodded. "Mom says Kaylee's boyfriend is her high school sweetheart and a great guy. She doesn't suspect him of any wrongdoing. After Kaylee told him she was pregnant, he convinced her to come back to Colorado Springs and move in with him. Evidently the two didn't marry right away so they could keep Kaylee on her parents' insurance. But once things settled down and Kaylee was released from postnatal care, the two of them did plan to marry."

"What does the mom think happened? What's her take on Kaylee and the baby's disappearance?"

"Kidnapping. But she has no idea why and she has no idea who would do such a thing. The family has never been contacted for a ransom. She's afraid it was random and fears the worst."

Mattie nodded as she turned over the whole picture. "Kidnapping, yes . . . but maybe not so random. How would Carla or Deidra know the baby had been born?"

"Could've been a birth announcement, either in the news or Kaylee kept in touch." Stella tapped her chin with her pen and looked thoughtful. "I've got to do some tracing out in California, contact the clinic Deidra worked at before. Run some background checks on both Carla and Deidra. And the Thompsons will be here soon for their interview."

Mattie knew she couldn't blame Robo this time. *She* was the one who needed to be on the move. "Can you conduct the Thompson interview by yourself?"

"Sure."

"I want to go find out if Skylar checked into the Big Sky and try to determine if his sister is here in town or not. I want to know if they have Tonya's baby."

"Okay. We'll touch base when you get back."

As Mattie left the station with Robo, she hoped her inquiry would lead her to the baby. Finding the little one would be the best thing she could do for Tonya right now, and she was still convinced that when she found the newborn, she would also find Tonya's killer.

TWENTY-FOUR

Mattie parked about a block away from the Big Sky Motel, opened the front door of Robo's cage, and let him bail out behind her as she exited her vehicle. She told him to heel and strode quickly toward the motel, approaching from a direction where the office would block her from view from the courtyard or rooms.

The owner of the Big Sky, Dale Gray, happened to be one of Robo's biggest fans, so she let her dog follow along as she entered. A bell above the door tinkled, announcing her presence. She scanned the lobby, where a short, plastic-covered sofa and a few matching chairs surrounded a coffee table cluttered with magazines, but fortunately there were no people.

Voices from a television murmured from a room just past the check-in counter. Dale's head, thinly covered with wispy white hair, appeared first as he peeked around the open doorway, his face breaking into a grin when he spotted her. It felt good to be greeted with such enthusiasm, and Mattie automatically matched his grin as she raised her hand in greeting.

"Hey, Mattie." With a slight hitch in his step, Dale walked around the counter. "And there's our boy Robo!"

Robo greeted Dale with a wagging tail and lifted his face to be petted. Mattie enjoyed the results of Robo's community prestige as she watched the two of them. She and Robo had responded several times to Dale's calls for help this past year when he'd had customers who created disturbances that he couldn't settle himself.

A tall, thin man in his seventies, Dale spent much of his day in the room behind the counter watching TV while also keeping a steady eye on his property through a window that looked out into the courtyard. During one of Mattie's visits, he'd shown her how he kept his draperies adjusted a certain way so he could watch unobserved for pranksters and rowdies, a system he'd created since he had yet to invest in CCTV.

She hoped to capitalize on his surveillance today. "How are you doing, Dale?"

"Couldn't be better." Always a sporty dresser, he straightened his bow tie, which was lime green with yellow polka dots, a cheerful addition that conflicted with the lines of fatigue on his face. Last night, he'd probably stayed up late taking care of stranded customers. "What a gorgeous day it's turned out to be, after the worst ice storm we've had in years."

"I heard business was brisk for you here last night."

He smiled. "At least that was one good thing about the storm."

Mattie looked out the office window into the courtyard and spotted Skylar's black SUV parked there pretty as you please, though still covered with highway grime. Several doors down at the bottom of the U, she could see Detective Hauck's dark sedan, also dirty and spattered. Although Hauck had told her he planned to drive back to Denver later this afternoon, he'd evidently left his car parked here for the day.

She gestured toward Skylar's car with a tilt of her head. "I'm interested in the owner of that black Jeep."

Dale's unruly white brows shot upward. "Oh? What do you need to know?"

This was her payoff for having a good relationship with the town's merchants—apparently Dale had no reservations about sharing information with her. "Is he here by himself, or does he have someone with him?"

"He checked in by himself, but he told me he expects his sister to arrive sometime today. Said they'd share the room." He shook his head and quirked one corner of his mouth, looking skeptical. "I don't know if he said that to cover up a rendezvous with his girlfriend, but it makes no nevermind to me. I couldn't care less about my customers' business as long as they pay their bills, obey the rules, and don't trash the place."

Dale bent over Robo, petting him again as he cooed. "And if they don't behave themselves, I have you to help me, don't I?"

"Well, for what it's worth, I think it *is* his sister he's expecting." Mattie stared at the room beyond the Jeep, wishing she had X-ray vision. "He didn't have a baby with him, did he?"

Dale straightened to look out the window, leaving Robo to gaze up at him, his tail waving gently as though inviting Dale to continue his petting. "Not that I know of. He didn't mention one, and I didn't see him carry a child or any of the paraphernalia involved with a baby into his room."

"We're looking for a missing infant," Mattie told him.

"Huh . . . I'm sure it's not the one you're looking for, but there's a woman with a baby in that detective fella's room right now."

Mattie stared at him for a few beats, not sure she'd understood right. "Are you talking about Detective Hauck?"

"Yup."

She hadn't known Hauck knew anyone in Timber Creek. Could someone have come from out of town to visit him here? "Did Detective Hauck register with two people?"

"Nope, just himself."

"I thought he was leaving today."

Dale shook his head. "I don't know what he's doing. He paid for an extra day but said he's leaving sometime this evening. I offered him a late checkout on the house, but he said his department would spring for it. Seems like a nice fella."

Hauck did have a certain charm about him. But before she could construct her next question, Dale continued.

"He seems to be friends with this gal. I think it was her that came last night, driving a silver Honda Civic that had some back bumper damage. Here, I've got her license plate number right in the next room. Thought she was going to squat and share a room with him, but then they both left."

Oh my God, he just described Tonya's car, Mattie thought as she watched Dale limp toward his inner office. Though her heart rate kicked up a notch, she had regained a semblance of composure by the time Dale called out the license plate number from the other room.

It *was* Tonya's car. She struggled to take this in and make sense of everything. "So Detective Hauck and this woman left together last night? In one car, or did they take two?"

Dale came back into the room, stopping behind the counter. "Oh, they took both cars. Like I said, I thought she was gonna stay, so I kinda kept an eye out for them to return. The detective came back by himself in his own car around two in the morning."

Mattie was still suffering shock waves. "You say this woman is in his room now? Where's her car?"

"That's part of why I noticed her." He pointed to an opening between the buildings at the end of the courtyard. "She came in right through there. She must've parked her car in the back." He shrugged one shoulder. "We've had a lot of congestion in the lot here today. It just cleared out about an hour ago."

"What does she look like?"

"Blond hair, tall, real pretty."

Deidra Latimer? With Detective Hauck? "Are you certain she has a baby with her?"

"Absolutely. Carried it wrapped up in a fuzzy yellow blanket. Had one of them diaper bag thingies over her shoulder and a handbag over the other. Had to juggle everything while she let herself into the room. I guess the detective gave her a key to his room last night."

Her mind reeling, Mattie held up a finger as she pulled her cell phone out of her pocket. "Stand by a minute, Dale. I'm going to need your help."

She dialed Stella.

★　★　★

While they waited for Stella, Mattie explained to Dale that she suspected this woman might have the missing baby, though she had no explanation for why the two were now in Detective

Hauck's room. She had her own theory, but it wasn't anything she could share with the motel owner.

With Robo at heel, she skirted around the backside of the motel to do some surveillance, noticing the windows at the end of each unit. Dale had told her to expect a small frosted one placed high on the wall, indicating a bathroom, and a much larger one placed lower that corresponded to a second bedroom at the end of a short hallway. A gravel road ran along the back of the courtyard, where she found a maroon Mazda CX-5 parked on the shoulder. Deidra's car.

Since it was past checkout time, most of the rooms were empty, and when she returned to the lobby, she felt certain she hadn't been spotted. The rooms on each side of Hauck's were unoccupied, but Mattie was concerned that Skylar might be here on the property. Had he come to take possession of the baby?

Keeping an eye on the courtyard, Mattie stood behind the curtain in the lobby window. Soon Skylar exited his room, without luggage, and drove away. Mattie watched him go with mixed feelings. At least he was now out of the way. But would he return and try to intervene when they made their move?

Stella arrived, her movements quick and her attention focused as she joined Mattie at the window. Mattie pointed out the room behind Hauck's sedan. Dale watched them from behind the counter, not even trying to hide his excitement. "Let me know how I can help," he said.

Mattie nodded at him. "You've already helped tremendously."

Her voice quiet yet intense, Stella updated Mattie on what she'd accomplished before leaving the station. She'd reached McCoy to inform him about their situation and Hauck's potential involvement. She'd discovered then that even though the K-9 teams had finished their work and left to return to Denver, Hauck and Cole were still up at the cave.

The news flooded Mattie's system with fear. She tried not to let it consume her thinking processes, because she needed to keep her wits about her if they were to recover Tonya's baby unharmed. She had to leave Cole's safety in the hands of Brody and the sheriff.

As she spoke, Stella seemed to be watching Mattie for her reaction. She must have been satisfied, because she pressed on. "And Judge Taylor gave me a verbal warrant to search that room. Let's figure out the best way to execute it."

★　★　★

With Robo on a leash at Mattie's side, she led Stella around the motel toward the back of the property, where they could remain hidden from view from the front side. Dale had given them two key cards, one that released the doorknob and a master key that released the security dead bolt. Mattie pinned all her hope on Deidra's desire to keep this baby alive, no matter what her motive.

When they reached the corner of the building, Stella spoke softly. "There's a possibility she's armed."

"We should plan on that."

Mattie's amped-up emotional state had traveled right down the leash to Robo, and he danced in place at her side. She drew a steady breath and placed her hand on his head. "Easy," she murmured.

They stole down the sidewalk between the two buildings at the end of the courtyard toward a housekeeping cart that Dale had trundled over and left for them. Mattie kept Robo hidden behind it, and she and Stella ducked their heads, turning their faces away from the window, as they rolled the cart up to the door of the room. The draperies were closed and looked heavy enough to have blocked them from view.

Mattie parked the cart in front of the door, leaving enough room for them to squeeze through. Stella took one side of the door while Mattie took the other, staying out of view from the window. She fished the clearly marked key cards from her pocket while Stella drew her service weapon.

Using a hand signal, Mattie told Robo to stay behind the cart. He pricked his ears and watched her, panting with excitement.

Mattie tapped on the door. "Housekeeping," she said, disguising her voice and hoping that Deidra wouldn't recognize it.

No answer. They needed to announce themselves as police before they entered the room, but if they heard one cry from the baby, it would give them exigent circumstances to move ahead. They'd hoped that Deidra would give herself away as they fiddled with the door.

Adrenaline had already saturated her system, making her heart rate climb. She glanced at Stella, who nodded. Mattie used the key card to swipe at the doorknob. It clicked open, but the security bolt was in place.

"Just a minute," came a female voice from inside.

"Housekeeping," she repeated as she traded out one key for the other. When she swiped the dead bolt, it didn't release.

"I said wait a minute, goddammit." Loud and angry, the color of this voice was nothing like the dulcet tones Deidra had used during her interview.

Inside the room, a baby began to cry—the high-pitched wail of a newborn that pressed at Mattie's heart.

"Sheriff's department!" Stella shouted. "Do you have a baby inside?"

"No," Deidra responded, although the baby continued to cry.

"It's a go," Stella murmured, before shouting at the closed door. "Sheriff's department! Open up!"

Mattie swiped the card again, and this time the door opened. She pushed it back against the wall.

Stella stepped inside. "Hands up where I can see them!"

Mattie entered behind Stella in time to see Deidra raise her hands for a split second and then dive for the bed. She snatched the baby, still wrapped in a yellow blanket, and cradled it against her chest. She whirled and ran down the hallway, disappearing into the back bedroom. The door slammed behind her, and the turn of the lock resounded in the room.

"The window!" Stella shouted.

"Cover this exit!" Mattie darted around the housekeeping cart. "Robo, heel!"

She sprinted down the sidewalk between the two buildings with Robo at her side. When she rounded the corner of the building, she spotted Deidra running full tilt toward her car with the baby clutched to her chest. She heard a crash from the other side of the window, and she figured Stella had just breached the locked door.

"Halt! Deidra, halt, or I'll send the dog!" Though she would never release Robo and endanger the baby, Mattie issued the threat anyway. Mattie ran toward Deidra while Robo ranged out in front, a missile wanting release. She could tell he craved a takedown and was just waiting for his command.

Deidra glanced at Robo and stopped, the baby wailing in her arms. Stella climbed through the window, landing on her feet. She assumed a shooter's stance, her weapon trained on Deidra.

It seemed to be a stalemate, and Mattie feared for the baby's safety. "Robo! Guard!"

Robo crouched about thirty feet from Deidra, his hackles raised and his teeth bared.

The baby's cry swelled as Deidra clutched it against her.

Mattie slowly advanced, holding out her arms. "Give the baby to me, Deidra," she said quietly.

"Get back!" Deidra took a step backward.

"Don't move or my dog will attack," Mattie said in the same soft voice, knowing full well that he wouldn't unless she told him to. "He won't go for the baby. He knows where the threat is. He'll go for you."

Deidra stood frozen in place. "He'll hurt the baby."

"No, he won't." Mattie took a few steps closer. "He'll go for your legs. He'll bite."

Robo was trained to go for the arm when threatened by a fugitive, but Deidra wouldn't know that.

Mattie edged closer while Deidra eyed Robo. The baby's cries echoed against the back of the building, filling the air. It was nerve-racking. Out of the corner of her eye, she noticed Stella inching toward them off to the side.

Robo slunk forward, and Mattie feared she might lose control of him. He really wanted that bite, and the baby's cries were agitating him too. She reinforced him with another command. "Guard!"

She exerted effort to remain calm as she sidled closer. Hoping to fill the woman's mind with doubts, she kept up a quiet chatter. "Deidra, you need to do the right thing and give me the baby. It's over. You're not leaving here. You don't have your purse with you. Do you even have your keys? The baby carrier is still in the room. How are you going to drive and keep the baby safe? If you cooperate, things will go better for you. They always do. I've seen it time and time again."

Hauck had been with Mattie when Tonya died, so she knew he hadn't killed her. Which meant this woman had. Things would not go easy for her.

"Stay back!" Deidra's eyes had grown wild with indecision. They shifted between Mattie and Robo.

It's time to turn up the heat. "Look at his jaws, Deidra. They're powerful. He'll bite you. If you give me the baby, I won't let him."

Mattie glanced at Robo in time to see saliva drip from his mouth. His teeth gleamed, but he was holding steady. *How much longer can this standoff last?* She inched forward, now a mere six feet away.

Deidra was staring at Robo when Mattie decided to take action. She moved near, hovering a couple feet away. Her arms remained outstretched and her hands itched to snatch the crying infant, but she feared her touch would scare the woman and make her flee.

Though Mattie was probably a good six inches shorter than Deidra, she straightened to her full height. "Let me take this burden from you, Deidra. This is an impossible situation. Let me help."

She was near enough to feel the woman's fight-or-flight instinct dissipate.

Deidra's eyes glazed as she stared past Mattie into the distance. "Jim's going to kill me," she whispered.

"We'll protect you," Mattie murmured, though she didn't feel that someone who would kill a young mother to take her baby deserved protection.

"He can reach anyone. Who do you think set up the hit on that man who killed your brother?" Deidra closed her eyes for a beat before looking down at the baby in her arms. "This is all his idea, his doing. I got caught up in it and feared for my life. There was no way I could get out of it."

"That will be taken into consideration. Did you plan to give this baby to its father?"

"What? What are you talking about? Jim plans for us to take her to California. He has parents out there waiting for her . . . a nice, wealthy couple. They'll give this little girl a better home than the Thompsons ever could."

And pay for her too. "Deidra, it's time to do the right thing and let me have her." Making sure she touched only the blanket and not the woman herself, Mattie slowly grasped the warm bundle, supporting the baby with one hand above and the other beneath. She waited, moving slowly, until she felt Deidra release her grasp. She swiftly tucked the infant against her chest as she stepped backward toward Robo.

Stella hustled forward to take charge, telling Deidra to put her hands behind her back and then cuffing her.

"Robo, out!"

Still obviously worked up from the stressful situation, Robo panted and saliva dripped from his black lips. But when Mattie told him to heel, he released his guard and came to her. Not skilled in handling a baby, she held the newborn close with both arms, afraid she might drop her. She told Robo he was a good boy, giving him eye contact, hoping she could pass her love and praise for him through her gaze.

She felt almost faint with relief as she cuddled the child against her, trying to soothe her. The baby girl felt lightweight but solid in her arms, and Mattie thought for a brief moment she would cry along with her.

The baby quieted slowly, her cry fading into hiccups and sobs. The memory of Tonya's sweet face and smile flashed into Mattie's mind, making her heart ache. She wondered if the girl had been able to see her baby daughter before she died.

She peered into the infant's tiny flushed face, damp with tears, and stroked her cheek gently with her fingertip. "You're okay now, sweet one. We've got you," she whispered, bending to press her lips to the moist tuft of red hair plastered with sweat against the small head.

TWENTY-FIVE

Though Hauck and the K-9 teams had left an hour ago, Cole remained stationed at the suspected grave site. Madsen had taken a long time to dig down several more feet, carefully sifting through the dirt. When he'd finally turned up black, charred wood in his last shovelful, the sergeant had stopped, shaking his head.

Cole volunteered to guard the site until the sheriff could send someone to help. Without cell phone service from this spot, he depended on Hauck and Madsen to deliver the news to McCoy, and he didn't have any idea how long it would take for someone to relieve him of his duty.

The sun had reached its zenith and begun its downward arc in the sky. Wind from the northwest lowered the temperature and turned the warm autumn day into a memory. Clouds filled with wind gathered around the peaks and blew ice crystals off the snowfields. Cole scrunched lower in his well-insulated coat, bringing his collar up toward his ears. He decided it would be safe to go to the cave for shelter and to build a fire.

He untied his horse and swung into the saddle. As he approached the cave, Mountaineer raised his head, whinnied, and quickened his pace, his ears pricked forward.

Recognizing Mountaineer's greeting for another horse, Cole first thought someone had already arrived to take over. But then he realized such a quick turnaround would be impossible.

He drew near the cave but couldn't see a horse anywhere. After tying Mountaineer, he walked up the short incline and entered the cave opening. He startled when a shadowy figure at the back of the cave rose to its feet. It was Jim Hauck.

"Detective, I didn't see you arrive. What brings you back here?"

Hauck didn't answer as Cole scanned the rear of the cave where the detective had been kneeling. Several bundles lay at his feet, though the light was too dim for him to tell what they were. But when he raised his gaze again, he could clearly see the gun in Hauck's hand—and it was trained right at him.

"Too bad you had to come snooping back in here, Dr. Walker." Hauck's eyes had narrowed, and he quickly covered the ground between them, stopping six feet away. "Raise your hands or you're a dead man."

★ ★ ★

Virginia Garcia, Deputy Garcia's wife and head of county child protection services, had come to the station to take custody of Tonya's baby girl. It was such a relief to know the child would be sheltered and cared for in the experienced woman's home until her future placement could be determined.

Stella had told Mattie that on the way to the station, Deidra had confessed to accidentally overdosing Tonya after the baby's birth—she said she'd planned only to sedate her—and she denied any knowledge of Skylar. If further investigation proved Skylar innocent of involvement, a paternity test would be ordered, and if that verified him as the baby's father, his sister would most likely end up raising the little girl. Although Mattie had yet to meet the Thompsons, her sympathies went out to them—she figured they would be heartbroken.

But she had no time to dwell on the sorrowful situation or even to sit in on Stella's interrogation of Deidra. Instead, she and Robo were driving west, the lowering sun in her eyes, as she headed toward the Redstone Ridge trailhead to meet with Sheriff McCoy.

Cole, Garrett, and Hauck were still up in the forest. Garrett had been stationed at the trail's midpoint to guard a potential bomb site, and Cole had been left at the cave to guard a possible grave. Though Hauck had originally left with Madsen and his crew, Madsen had reported that he'd turned back, saying he'd decided to stay another day and might as well wait with Cole. And then Madsen and his dog teams had left to drive back to Denver.

So now Cole was up in the wilderness alone with a devious killer. The thought terrified her.

According to Deidra, Hauck was the mastermind behind it all—infant trafficking, John Cobb's death, and helping her ditch Tonya's car. The woman had seemed willing to talk, and Mattie hoped Stella would pry even more details from her.

How long had Hauck been involved with criminal activity? Could he have been part of the smuggling ring that was responsible for her father's murder? If so, could this be why her father's case had never been solved?

Though these questions plagued her, she set them aside as she turned into the parking lot at the trailhead. She parked next to McCoy's Jeep, ratcheted on the emergency brake, and scanned the other vehicles. There were no people present; she figured everyone would be working at the lower site. As incident commander, the sheriff would be there too, coordinating with CBI and calling in further reinforcements as needed. He'd already sent Brody up to check on Garrett and Cole.

She focused on the supplies she would need, making sure she had everything with her before leaving her unit.

Robo danced on his front feet as she opened the hatch. Wanting to harness that energy for a run up the mountain, she spoke to him in a calm tone as she invited him to unload. She emptied a small amount of leftover water from his collapsible bowl and stuffed it inside her backpack, which already contained a bladder filled with fresh water, energy bars, Robo's treats, and some of his food.

And one more item—an unwashed tee of Cole's she'd retrieved from a hook in her closet, a shirt left there after an overnight stay. One of those rare nights when the kids were staying with friends and she and Cole could be together. But now, even a glimpse of the shirt that she'd bagged carefully to maintain Cole's scent made her chest tighten.

Without wasting time, she checked to make certain all was secure on her duty belt. Though she knew her service weapon was locked and loaded, she inspected it quickly before securing it in its holster.

She shrugged on her pack and sprinted toward the trail with Robo at her side. The trail angled upward at a gentle incline into the forest. Her boots slipped on muddy stones, wet from melted ice and snow, making her watch her footing.

She pushed on as the trail grew steeper, her breath coming in puffs of vapor as the sunshine faded and the temperature dipped. Robo scrambled ahead.

They maintained a fast pace until they reached the scene, easy to identify since it was nothing like its natural state. Trees were now marked with crime scene tape, and the area was dotted with people.

As she topped the rise, McCoy strode forward to meet her. "Brody has already started up the trail," he said, his words clipped. "I was able to reach Garrett. He's headed up the trail to the backside of the ridge. I told him to stay put for his own safety, but he refused. Said he couldn't wait around with Cole in danger. He's armed and he thinks Cole is too, for whatever that's worth."

Cole often carried a .38 Smith & Wesson revolver when he rode into the high country. But Mattie could read the alarm on McCoy's face, and they both knew that firearms might not be useful if you were faced with a trained cop who'd turned rogue. Especially one in disguise.

"Is Brody on foot?"

"He's on the horse I rode earlier."

"I'll try to catch up with him."

"He has the sat phone and a radio. He'll check in when he reaches the cave or when he finds the others. Cole and Garrett only have cell phones."

"I've got my radio and my cell. I'll be off, then."

"Be careful," McCoy said, extending a handshake.

"Always." They exchanged a tight grip before she turned to leave.

She picked up her pace to a jog, and Robo trotted ahead. Though she yearned to reach the others at top speed, she knew she had to pace herself. It normally took at least two hours of climbing to reach the cave, though she hoped she could shave off at least a half hour.

The bottom half of the journey was less steep than the top, so now would be when she could make up some time. The trail wound through ponderosa pines with their sweeping, long-needled boughs. Groves of blue spruce, which bore shorter needles, gleamed brilliant blue in the slanting rays of the setting sun.

Alternating a fast walk up the steep slope with a sprint on the more level stretches, Mattie grew warm and her breath came in even cycles. This was what she'd trained for in high school, and this was what she excelled at—the cross-country race, one of the most grueling challenges in track. And her dog could run like this all day; she made sure he stayed fit and lean for this type of challenge.

The words of her high school coach echoed in her mind. "Don't get in your head. Don't get distracted. Watch your footing at all times. Push yourself up that hill; your reward is the downhill on the other side."

She made it to the midpoint within forty minutes. The flagging tape that marked one of the trees caught her eye as she jogged past. She gave Robo water from her supply and then unhooked the water tube from the strap of her backpack, pressing the bite valve between her teeth as she sucked the welcome fluid from the bladder.

She keyed on her radio to check in with the sheriff. "Sheriff McCoy. This is Mattie. Over."

Immediately her receiver crackled. "Copy. Where's your location?"

She pressed her mic. "I'm at the midpoint. No one's here."

"Brody hasn't checked in. He must be between you and the cave."

Mattie assumed Brody hadn't met up with Garrett or Cole, or he would have notified the sheriff. Worry about the two men made her throat tighten, but she knew she couldn't lose focus. She needed to stay alert and pay attention. "Tell Brody I'm not far behind him."

"Copy that."

They both signed off, and Mattie and Robo headed up the trail that led to the cave. The sun had set behind the mountains, though there was still plenty of ambient light. She estimated another hour before twilight and hoped to reach the cave before then.

The temperature felt like it had dropped at least twenty degrees, and a cold breeze nipped her cheeks as she navigated the rocky uphill path. The higher she went, the colder it would be as she made her way toward the snowy peaks. The terrain became more challenging. The ponderosa gave way to towering lodgepole and groves of aspens, their golden and orange leaves shivering in the waning light as they danced in the icy breeze.

Mattie's breath became vaporous clouds, and she pulled her runner's gloves from her jacket pocket and tugged them on. She kept up the fast pace she'd set for herself on the lower part of the trail, though now there weren't many spots where the trail leveled off. It led ever upward, but when she reached a switchback, she did something she hated to do—she left the trail to climb directly to the upper level, a practice she would typically avoid to prevent damage to the forest habitat. But she had no time to spare.

She was sprinting through the last stretch of the living forest toward the burn area when her breath began to hitch. She'd been pushing too hard. Robo was about fifteen feet ahead of her as she faltered. As if he sensed that the distance had grown between them, he stopped, turned to look back, and waited for her to catch up.

"You're so good," she murmured, stroking his head between his ears before shrugging off her backpack. "Let's get you some water."

She partially filled his collapsible bowl, and he lapped the contents greedily. She rehydrated too, and within minutes she felt she'd recovered her breath enough to go on. After repacking his bowl, she slipped on her backpack and took to the trail, this time keeping a moderate pace on the steep parts.

With Robo in front, they passed into the burn area. A patchwork of snow, dirt, and charred debris covered the terrain.

Though the air grew more frigid, its bite stinging her face, she gained more light after leaving the forest. It was a trade-off she welcomed, since she feared she and Robo would be tracking after dark, and she wanted to save the batteries on her head lamp.

When she reached the granite shelf that led to the cave, she scanned the area for Brody, feeling relief when she spotted a horse tied to a tree. He'd waited for her.

As she and Robo breached the last uphill stretch, Brody stepped out of the cave. He raised his hand in greeting, and she did the same.

He came toward her, frowning and carrying a scrap of paper that fluttered in the breeze. "You made good time. I've been here less than ten minutes. Garrett left us a note."

She bent forward, bracing herself against her thighs as she heaved to catch her breath. "What does it say?"

"Says he picked up tracks of two horses headed north toward the Balderhouse trail. He's following them." Brody pointed. "They're pretty easy to see against the snow."

Mattie scanned where he pointed and could make out the tracks leading away from the cave. "Let's go."

"Have you caught your breath? You can take the horse."

"No, I'm ready. I'm better on the ground with Robo."

"Garrett can't be too far ahead." Brody strode off to untie his horse.

Garrett was a born woodsman in search of a friend he believed to be in danger. He would travel as fast as he could . . . but Mattie intended to catch up with him.

TWENTY-SIX

The son of a bitch had taken his gun and his cell phone. Cole's bare hands were bound in front with a zip tie that cut off his circulation. His hands numb, he rode through the trees ahead of Hauck, setting a course for the Balderhouse trail.

Hauck had demanded that Cole lead him to a trail he could take downhill that would bypass the others and end up in a less public place. Cole had convinced him this was the way to go, but secretly he hoped that someone would become suspicious when he went missing from his post at the cave and when Hauck didn't return from the high country.

McCoy, Brody, Garrett, or any one of his buddies on the posse would know his strategy would be to head for the Balderhouse. It was the same trail they'd come down when they'd avoided the fire and found Mattie. And Cole made sure he left tracks in the snow as he rode away from the cave.

Though he'd reined Mountaineer into every patch of snow he could to leave a trail, drifts were getting harder to find as they angled downhill toward the Balderhouse. He welcomed the waning light, because when it grew dark, he planned to make a move. Hauck had held a gun on him the entire way, so it would be dangerous, but if he didn't escape soon, he had no hope of getting out of this alive. Hauck couldn't afford to let him go.

Cole suspected the bundles Hauck had retrieved from the cave held drugs, cash, or both. He must have found them yesterday and had somehow hidden them from Mattie. Cole didn't know how that could've happened, but the snake had disguised himself well enough to gain everyone's trust. She might have left him alone while she and Robo searched outside.

A break in the trees revealed the bare trail, which Cole could hardly see in the poor light.

"Is this it?" Hauck said from behind.

Cole turned to answer so he could see if the gun was still at his back. It was.

"We're almost there." They'd reached the Balderhouse trail, but he lied, hoping to buy just a little bit more time—darkness was his friend. "This will take us to the trail, but the connection is tricky, especially at night."

Hauck waved the gun at him. "Keep going."

Cole scanned what he could still see of the terrain, looking for a spot that would offer cover and a place to hide. He hoped to use the scumbag's unfamiliarity with these surroundings against him. After they went about fifty yards down the trail, Hauck told him to stop.

This is it. Cole tried to breathe through the fear that tightened his gut, expecting a bullet to pierce his back at any second.

But Hauck dismounted and started fiddling with the ties on his saddlebag. He tugged on a pair of white gloves that shone in the dim light and took out a bag of something. "This will fix that dog if he follows us," he muttered, bending to shake out a white line of powder on the trail behind Mountaineer.

This is my chance. Cole fumbled at the saddle horn with his numb hands, unable to grasp it. Changing strategy, he straightened, swung his right leg over Mountaineer's neck, slid off the saddle, and hit the ground running. If he could make it beyond the range of a bullet, he could disappear into the darkness.

Hauck uttered curses while Cole sprinted away toward the left side of the trail. A gunshot rang out and a bullet pinged near Cole's right side, forcing him to dodge left. Dark shadows loomed ahead. Trees, boulders? He couldn't tell, but he kept his legs churning as Hauck fired another shot.

Cole tripped on the stony ground, almost losing his balance. Running as fast as he could, he dodged behind a boulder, hoping to use it for shelter. But then the ground tilted suddenly downward and he fell face first, striking his cheek against a rock.

Stunned, he pushed himself up, bending forward to run, stumbling as he went. Unable to see clearly, he hit an icy patch, slid on some shale, and lost his balance again, gathering momentum as he rolled down a steep incline, rocks striking his face and body.

He threw up his numb hands, trying as best he could to shelter his head as he fell.

★　★　★

Mattie could barely make out anything as they tried to follow the track. Snowy patches where they'd been able to see hoofprints grew smaller and fewer. The quickening wind blew at their backs. It was time to pull out their ace in the hole—Robo's nose.

Brody was in the lead, and Mattie called to him. "Wait up a minute, Brody."

He reined to a stop and turned back.

"It's time for me to put Robo on Cole's scent. I have a scent article."

"That's a relief. We're just about finished with daylight."

She felt pressed for time, but it would take only a few added seconds to do things right. She removed Robo's tracking harness from her utility belt and changed out his equipment before giving him some water to moisten his mucous membranes.

After he'd quenched his thirst, she patted his sides, thumping a rhythm on his rib cage like a drum. She opened the plastic bag that contained Cole's T-shirt and lowered it so that Robo could get a whiff. As she sealed the bag and tucked it into a pocket where she could reach it easily, she continued to rev up Robo's prey drive with chatter.

He danced beside her until she gave him the direction: "Let's go. Let's find Cole."

Though her dog had to be tired, it didn't take much to make him excited. Work was what he lived for. And oddly enough, he'd searched for Cole before during their many practices while training Bruno and Belle for search and rescue.

Robo lowered his head and gave the ground a brief sweep. Mattie turned on her head lamp and could detect the faint outline of a horseshoe on the damp ground. The scent trail that Robo picked up was off to the side by several feet, where the wind had scattered the skin rafts that Cole had shed as he passed this way, thus leaving his scent on a track parallel to the visual one the horses had made.

Mattie murmured words of encouragement as she and Robo took the lead. The moist conditions were perfect for tracking scent, and Robo set a fast pace through the blackened area of the forest. Mattie was vaguely familiar with this landscape, since she'd struck out in a similar direction the night she escaped from the cave, trying to beat the fire as the prevailing wind pushed the blaze downhill and toward the east.

"We're definitely headed for the Balderhouse trail," Brody called from behind. "I'm going to contact the sheriff and tell him to set up a perimeter at the base of that trail in case that's where Cole leads Hauck."

Unless Hauck kills him before they reach the base of it. A chill passed through Mattie at the thought. "Sounds like a good plan."

She didn't want to interrupt Robo's search, so she kept up with him while Brody fell behind to make his call. Her head lamp lit the area at her feet, and she placed her steps carefully to avoid tripping over stones or getting tangled in the new growth that had taken over the burnt mountainside. The lower the altitude, the less snow they had to contend with, but the ground beneath their feet was still treacherous.

Though Brody had fallen behind, the wind drove the noise his horse made toward her, helping her keep track of his whereabouts. She wondered how Garrett was faring as the darkness deepened. Did he have a flashlight? Was he still able to follow Cole's track?

A shout came from a distance, somewhere in front of her but distorted by the wind. It might be closer than it sounded. Her head lamp shone on Robo as he paused with his head up and ears pricked. "Who is it?" she murmured to her dog, afraid to call out, fearing it was Hauck.

Robo put his head down and continued on the track, and Mattie removed her head lamp and held it away from her body to avoid making herself a target. Boulders and stones were strewn over the ground among the skeletons of trees, and the earth shifted beneath her feet into a steep incline.

Another shout, and this time Mattie thought she heard her name. Was that Garrett? Cole? Robo paused to listen, and she decided to call back. "I'm here!"

"Over here, Mattie!"

She followed the sound while Robo continued to follow Cole's scent. Both were taking them the same direction. Within minutes, Mattie glimpsed a light shining through the blackened tree trunks. "Who's there?"

"Garrett. Watch out for a sudden drop-off."

"I see you." And there he was, behind the flashlight as he directed its beam toward the ground to light her way. She and Robo clattered down a sudden downward pitch while stones rolled beneath their feet. "Thank goodness we caught up with you."

"I'm sidelined, Mattie." His face looked drawn with pain as he gestured toward the horse behind him. "My horse took a fall. Looks like he bowed a tendon, and he's all bunged up. I hurt my ankle. We're a sorry pair."

He turned his flashlight toward his horse's legs, which were scraped and bloodied, and it stood with one hoof cocked.

"Oh no. Are you all right?" Mattie grasped the handle on Robo's search harness and stroked his back, letting him know she wanted him to wait.

"I'll be okay." He sounded disgusted. "I've got something wrong with my ankle. Might be broken. But I can't ride this guy. He's got to be led."

"Brody's right behind me." She turned and called Brody's name into the wind, and she felt relieved to hear him shout a reply. As he approached, his horse's metal shoes clanged against the outcropping of stones. She called out a warning to be careful.

"What happened?" The concern on Brody's face was evident in the glow of their flashlights as he dismounted and led his horse toward them.

Garrett briefed him on his status. "But you two have to keep going. I'll make it to the tree line and set up camp. I didn't want to leave this trail until I turned it over to you."

Gusts of wind buffeted them and howled through the dead trees. Mattie pulled up her collar and shrugged deeper into her coat.

"We can't leave you exposed on the mountainside like this," Brody said. "Let me help you onto my horse."

"I have a bad feeling about Cole," Garrett said. "My horse is lame, and I can't leave him here by himself. You go on without me. I'll be all right."

Brody handed his horse's reins to Mattie. "Can't do that, Garrett. Let's get you up on this horse."

Garrett groaned as Brody helped jostle him into the saddle. He settled into the seat, letting his injured leg hang free of the stirrup while he took the reins from Mattie. He leaned toward his lame horse, trying to grab the reins that dangled just beyond his reach in the howling wind. Brody stepped over to grab them and tucked them into his hand.

"All right, I'm good," Garrett said. "You two go now. I'll find the Balderhouse trail and go downhill from there at my own pace."

Mattie worried that they shouldn't leave Garrett alone under this set of circumstances. A quick check with her head lamp revealed that Brody shared her concern. "Robo and I can go on our own," she said to him. "We'll make less noise and have a better chance of catching Hauck unaware."

"We need to stay together."

This was always Brody's go-to when they were in the wilderness, and though it made sense most of the time, Mattie couldn't accept it tonight. "Cole would have taken Hauck back down the Redstone trail unless he was under duress."

"She's right," Garrett said, his voice a deep rumble. "Going across country like this late in the day wasn't Cole's idea."

Brody hesitated, obviously thinking things over. "You've got your radio, right?" he asked Mattie.

"Yes."

"I'll stay with Garrett until we find him some shelter. We'll stay in touch by radio, and I'll come back you up."

Even with the help of the GPS system on their radios, reconnecting with Brody in this wilderness sounded iffy. But

Mattie didn't care. She figured she and Robo could cover more ground by themselves. "Sounds like a good plan. I'll contact you if I find them and give you my location."

"Ken, you need to go with her," Garrett insisted, sounding upset. "I can handle myself."

Mattie patted Robo on the shoulder. "Come," she told him, moving away from the two before Brody could change his mind. "I'll check in soon, Brody."

As she went, she pulled out the bag that held Cole's shirt. It took only a moment to refresh Robo's scent memory as she chattered about finding Cole. Her dog trotted off and she followed, adjusting her head lamp to aim at the ground in front of her. Robo took a few valuable minutes searching for Cole's scent trail again, and Mattie cursed the wind for scattering it around. Robo finally picked it up in a brushy patch where the skin rafts must have clustered.

Darkness closed around her as the unrelenting wind pushed her on. Having seen firsthand how dangerous the footing could be, she focused her attention on each step as she picked up the pace to keep up with Robo.

It took about a half hour to reach the living forest, which offered respite from the cruel wind. Mattie paused to check in with Brody, giving him her coordinates. At the pace he and Garrett were forced to use to accommodate the lame horse, it would probably take them an hour to cover the same distance and reach shelter.

She encouraged Robo to go on, and within minutes they reached the cleared pathway of the Balderhouse trail. Wind whistled through pine boughs on both sides, racing down the trail. Robo appeared to still be on the scent as he alternated between nose up and nose to the ground. If only they'd been headed into the wind, her dog might have been able to find Cole by tracing him through the air. She could tell that's what Robo was trying to do.

He was several feet ahead of her on the trail when he stopped suddenly, his nose to the ground, his head moving back and forth as if sweeping for scent. Had he lost Cole's track? Her heart fluttered as she stopped beside Robo, her lamp trained on him to read his body language.

He sat and stared up at her, a strange white powder covering his nose and his muzzle. Alarm shot through her as confusion filled his eyes and he looked away. He stood, trembling and swaying. Within seconds, his bowel evacuated and he went down, banging his muzzle against the ground.

Fentanyl! A voice in her head screamed at her to hurry. She grabbed Robo by the haunches and pulled his limp body away from the white particles she could now see on the trail. Without thinking, she brushed the powder from his nose with one hand even as she reached with the other for her pocket.

After snatching out one container of Narcan, she pulled off her gloves and plucked at the edge of the packet. She peeled it open and took out the premeasured dose. Placing the injector firmly against Robo's nostril, she pressed the red plunger to deliver the spray.

She shrugged off her backpack and dumped it on the ground. After unzipping it, she reached inside for her water supply, ripped the bladder free from its Velcro mooring, and poured water over Robo's muzzle, brushing at his fur and nose with her bare hand to wash them clean.

She felt a brief euphoria as the world around her whirled and her vision blurred. Her chest tightened and her gut lurched.

I've been exposed to it too.

TWENTY-SEVEN

It felt like swimming upward through dark, oily fluid to reach the air—a snatch at a breath before sinking back down. Then—a soft, wet cloth washed her face. Mattie awakened with her arms wrapped around Robo. He lay in her embrace, licking her cheeks.

She groaned, disoriented and too nauseous to move. *Where are we? What happened?*

Robo tried to wriggle free, but a voice in her head urged her to hang on to him. *Keep him safe.* "Stay," she murmured.

He sneezed and then settled in, resting his head near hers. Gradually, it came back to her. Before she went down, she'd used her second dose of Narcan and grabbed hold of Robo to keep him from going back to the powder when he awakened.

Thank goodness the naloxone was doing its job. But she knew the effect could be temporary, and one dose might not be enough. Protocol ran through her mind: after an exposure to opioids severe enough to result in unconsciousness, both dog and handler needed to seek medical care immediately.

She sat up carefully, fighting dizziness. Robo moved beneath her hand as if to get up, but again she told him to stay. She sat cross-legged and leaned forward, directing her headlight toward her backpack to find water. Shivers racked her body, and she realized her bare hands were numb.

Clenching and releasing her fingers to force the blood flow and warmth back into them, she searched for her water until she spotted the plastic bladder lying open near her pack. Though two-thirds empty, it still held some of the precious fluid. Feeling as if everything moved in slow motion, she used a few splashes to wash her hands and then dried them on her pant legs, hoping they were free from fentanyl powder.

She found a pair of latex gloves in the bottom of her pack and slipped them on, then bathed Robo's nose again for good measure. He licked at the droplets.

"No licking," she told him quietly, hoping to keep him from swallowing any remaining particles. She poured a portion of water into his bowl and let him drink while she pressed the bite valve between her teeth and sucked a few swallows. She rinsed off the latex gloves and decided to leave them on for what little warmth they could provide, because her runner's gloves had been contaminated with the powder.

Thrusting her hands into her coat pockets, she sat for a while, thoughts about nothing and everything floating through her mind like bubbles she needed to chase. She and Robo gazed at each other, his presence an anchor. She felt mindless, like a zombie.

Gradually, her brain sorted itself out enough to formulate a plan, and she put everything away in her backpack. She was beginning to feel halfway human, though her stomach still gurgled and her head remained woozy.

"Stay there," she told Robo as she managed to stand without falling. Her pack felt like it weighed a ton as she tugged it back on. "Now come. Heel."

Her dog seemed to be doing better than she, and he rose to his feet without struggle and moved to her left side.

"Are you okay?" He seemed to be, and she turned her head lamp to light the trail, searching for the beginning and end of the powder. A line of it lay across the trail as if someone had deliberately set a trap for her dog. Hauck. Anger surged through her, giving her renewed strength.

Being careful to keep the powder from going airborne, she kicked dirt and gravel to cover it. Then she grasped the handle on Robo's harness and led him carefully around the spot to the other side. "Let's put on your leash."

Though she hated to impede Robo's ability to search for Cole, she couldn't let him go out in front and fall into another trap. Besides, she didn't know if Robo's sense of smell would be hampered at the moment. Though research showed that nasal delivery of Narcan didn't decrease a dog's sense of smell, would Robo be able to follow a scent track this soon after the dosage? Would he feel up to it? She'd never had this experience before and wasn't sure.

Picking her way carefully, she led him down the trail, using her head lamp to search for the dangerous white powder. After about one hundred yards, a boulder rose up like a monument, and she stepped into its leeward side to block the wind. She felt like her head was beginning to clear. "Let's call Brody."

She keyed on her mic. "Brody, this is Mattie. Do you copy? Over."

Seconds passed before her speaker crackled with a broken transmission. ". . . coordinates . . . over."

The terrain must be playing havoc with their signal.

She checked her GPS and read him her coordinates. "Brody, where are you? Over."

Nothing but a few crackles.

Mattie stepped out from behind the boulder and tried a few more times to connect, but to no avail. In case he could receive her signal, she told him about their fentanyl exposure and asked if he'd brought Narcan. When there was no reply, she gave up and signed off for the last time.

Robo might be okay, but she had a strong suspicion that she was going to need another dose of Narcan, and Brody was her best hope for providing it up here on the mountain. She hoped he'd at least received the coordinates for her location. Maybe she should go uphill and try to find him.

Robo came to stand beside her, lifting his nose to the wind. As she was returning her radio to the inside pocket of her coat, he raised his head and barked, his front paws lifting off the ground. He walked out the full length of his leash and tugged against it, trying to draw her forward into the wind. Then he stopped and stared at her, giving her a full alert.

Her dog had caught someone's scent in the wind. Cole?

She studied Robo's back—no raised hackles. No guarded stance—he appeared excited, not wary.

If Robo smelled Cole's scent, was he still with Hauck?

Prior to getting messed up with the fentanyl, they'd been following Cole's track. But if she'd been reading her dog's body language right, he hadn't smelled Cole on the wind. Now, though, Robo seemed excited about catching scent from upwind.

How could they have managed to pass Cole? Maybe it was Brody, coming from uphill behind them, that Robo smelled.

It was a dilemma. She needed to know who was out there. If ever she'd wanted her partner to be able to talk, now was the time. She removed her hands from her coat pockets to retrieve Cole's scent article from her belt. When she opened the bag for Robo, he remained intent on staring uphill, ignoring it as if not wanting to bother.

Okay, he's telling me we need to follow the scent, so that's what we're going to do.

She put the bag away and thrust her hand through the loop at the end of Robo's leash. The frigid wind chilled her to the bone, and she couldn't stop shivering. "Let's go, Robo. Find Cole."

He hit the end of the leash and almost tugged her off her feet. Thank goodness she'd secured him rather than trying to hold him in her cold hands. "Easy," she murmured, forcing him to move forward at a pace she could match. Her feet were so heavy . . . she was just too tired to run.

Robo followed the wide trail uphill for a bit before heading into the trees on the side opposite where she expected Brody would come. She stumbled over rocks and tufts of foliage as she tried to keep up with him.

Soon the ground tilted downward and she sensed they were heading into a ravine. She grabbed tree limbs to help keep her balance and slid most of the way down. When she reached the bottom, burbling water told her a small stream ran past on her right. Robo continued to pull her uphill, and she felt as if she was in a dream, slogging through mud.

Fatigue threatened to overwhelm her, and she knew she needed another dose of Narcan. She had to keep moving. A cliff face loomed on her left, and Robo pulled her along its base. He barked again, tugging harder.

"Robo!" The call came to her on the wind and pierced the fog in her mind. "Mattie! Is that you?"

"Cole!" She picked up her pace, stumbling forward. "We're here."

"Thank God."

Robo reached him first, jumping up to greet him. Cole was on his feet but he moved toward her awkwardly, using both hands to deal with Robo's exuberance. Tears came to her eyes, blurring the image of his battered face. She reached for him and pulled him into a tight hug.

He didn't hug her back . . . and it dawned on her why. "Your hands are bound."

"Zip tie." He raised his arms, slipped them over her head, and pulled her close. "Thank goodness you're both all right. Hauck set a trap for Robo. I hit my head when I escaped. After I came to, I've been trying to find a way back to the trail."

"We were both exposed," she murmured into his coat. "Here, let me cut that off you."

He loosened his hug and raised his arms to let her go. Mattie ducked under as she reached for the Leatherman tool he'd once given her for Christmas, both of them never guessing it would be used for this purpose. Though her hands were clumsy, she made short work of cutting him free from the zip tie.

He chafed his hands together before reaching for her again. "You were exposed to the fentanyl? How are you doing?"

Mattie pressed close to his warmth to stop her shivers, her cheek on his chest. His voice rumbled against her ear. It was hard to string words together to answer. "Mmm . . . getting sleepy."

Her legs felt like rubber, and she leaned on him heavily. "I need . . ."

And then she slipped away into nothingness.

★ ★ ★

Cole knelt, carefully lowering Mattie to the ground while keeping her upper body braced on his knees. Robo rushed forward to hover over her, and Cole had to push him back. He told him to sit, a command the dog ignored, but at least he gave Cole some space. He reached inside his coat to the inner breast pocket, his fingers clumsy and stiff. Hauck had taken everything else from him, but he'd missed the Narcan doses he'd brought with him today in case one of the dogs ran into trouble.

He struggled to open the packet and finally extracted the dispenser. He used light from Mattie's head lamp to find her nose and injected the dosage. He held his breath as he watched her eyelids flutter. He had three more doses in his pocket, but he knew he needed to be patient and see how she reacted to this one.

It didn't take long. Soon she struggled to sit up, and he helped support her.

"What . . ." she murmured, reaching for Robo, who licked her face. "Is he okay?"

"He looks like he is." Cole held her to keep her from trying to stand. "Wait a minute until you get your sea legs back. Hold on to Robo while I check him out."

He used her head lamp to check both her and Robo's pupil responsiveness. He then pulled Mattie close, placing his fingers against her neck to monitor her pulse. Strong and steady, maybe a little fast, but without a watch it was hard to tell.

Mattie raised her head from his shoulder. "Where did Hauck go?"

"He probably thought I was dead when I fell down that cliff. As far as I know, he headed down the Balderhouse trail. I told him it wasn't public access, hoping he'd stick to it."

"We thought that's what you planned. Brody alerted the sheriff to set up a perimeter at the base. We need to get moving so we can push Hauck from behind in case he decides to turn around and come back up."

She tried to stand again, and this time Cole helped her. Her legs seemed to support her, but she swayed, and he braced her until she could get her balance.

"Let's get back to the trail so I can try to radio Brody." Mattie took a few tentative steps, heading downhill. "There's a place we can climb up just beyond here."

With her head lamp to guide them, Cole kept his arm around her to steady her while Robo trotted ahead. He could feel the shivers course through her body, and he knew what she truly needed was to get down to a warm place. Though at first she wobbled and shook, the Narcan seemed to kick in as she walked. "How are you doing?"

"Better. I think I'll be all right this time."

He hoped that would be the case, and though he knew she was tough, he planned to stay close to keep an eye on her. Robo led the way, and they found the spot where they could climb up to the trail. Cole stayed behind Mattie to make sure she didn't fall backward. The wind careened down the trail when they made their way back to it.

Mattie spoke into her radio, calling for Brody.

His voice crackled to life from the speaker. "I'm here, Mattie." He gave her his coordinates. "Where are you? Over."

"Oh my gosh," she said to Cole before keying her radio back on. "I'm near. Stay put. We'll be right there. Over."

After she ended the transmission, she turned to Cole and grasped his arm. "He's right down this trail beside a boulder I was at before. Let's go."

★　★　★

Brody used the sat phone to contact McCoy and learned that the sheriff had called in help from Colorado State Patrol. Special Agent Rick Lawson from the CBI had arrived as well. Reinforcements were in place, and they'd established a perimeter near the Balderhouse trailhead. Mattie could imagine a dragnet of officers hidden behind trees, waiting to close in on Hauck when he rode down the trail.

"Garrett's waiting up above, off the trail in a sheltered spot." Brody briefed Cole on how Garrett and his horse had been injured. "I hated to leave him alone, Cole. Will you ride up and stay with him until this thing is over?"

Cole looked at Mattie as he took the reins that Brody thrust into his hand, and she could tell he was torn.

She wanted Cole somewhere away from harm. "Go to him, Cole. We can't leave him alone and unprotected. Do you have a gun?"

"Hauck took it."

"Here, take my backup." Brody bent forward to extract the revolver he carried concealed above his boot and offered it to Cole.

"Where will I find him?" Cole asked, taking the gun.

Brody gave directions and landmarks, explaining that Garrett waited not far from the trail. In return, Cole gave Brody strict instructions to keep an eye on Mattie for symptoms of renarcotization as he split his remaining packets of Narcan between the two of them. "Do not leave her side, Brody. You got that? Not for at least two more hours."

"Got it, Doc."

Mattie felt a wave of melancholy as Cole rode up the trail. She told herself it was a residual from coming down from the fentanyl, though she knew it was much more than that. Now that she'd found Cole, she hated to part from him again. She turned to Brody. "Let's go. We'll keep to the trail so we can move faster."

"You set the pace."

Her body felt tired, but her head was now clear. She didn't feel up to running on a rocky trail in the dark, so she pushed forward at a fast walk, pounding down the steep parts, using the rocks as steps when she could. Robo's head was up now as he trotted beside her, but she still kept an eye on the trail for powdery white poison.

After fifteen minutes, Brody checked in with McCoy again. "He said they're all set, but Hauck hasn't come down. I figure he's got to be close to them by now."

"The wind is at our backs and should carry sound down-hill. Let's give him some incentive to hurry up."

"What do you have in mind?"

"He tried to knock Robo out of the game, so he must be afraid of us tracking him. Let's use Robo as a threat."

"How?"

"Let him speak up."

"We risk Hauck setting another trap, but maybe it'll push him forward instead. Go ahead."

Mattie stripped off the oversized gloves that Brody had given her and stroked Robo's head. She dug a treat from her pocket and told him to sit, facing him downhill; then she asked him to "speak up."

Robo barked, sharp yips that carried on the wind. He kept it up while she gave him a treat every few barks. She couldn't help but think of Pavlov's dog experiments and the power of intermittent reinforcement, which worked well with dog training.

They hurried down the trail, pausing occasionally to have Robo "speak up." Juniper and piñon trees grew intermingled with spruce and ponderosa pines beside the trail, telling Mattie they'd reached the lower altitude. Robo had just sounded off again when the sat phone rang inside Brody's pack. She paused while he answered the call and listened.

"Mission accomplished." He was speaking into the phone but grinning at her. "Bring us another pair of gloves, would you? Mattie's got wrecked."

He signed off and summed up the situation as he put the phone in his pack. "Your plan worked. I guess the guys at the top of the perimeter could hear Robo barking as we got closer. Hauck barreled through like he had the hounds of hell chasing him. They closed around him and took him unaware before he made it to the bottom of the trail. They arrested him with no shots fired. He's in custody and demanding why."

"Ha! He doesn't realize yet that Cole's still alive." Mattie returned Brody's grin. "Robo took down two fugitives today without a single bite. Now that's fierce!"

"Stella and Agent Lawson are taking Hauck to the station, and McCoy's on his way up, riding Cole's roan horse to help us retrieve Garrett and Cole."

"Mountaineer?"

"He came down the trail earlier and someone caught him." Brody shone his flashlight on her face, evidently checking her for signs of the fentanyl exposure. "Do you want to go down to warm up and catch a ride with the state patrol?"

Though Mattie wanted a crack at Hauck herself, she figured the CBI agent would get the first shot at him. Right now, above anything else, she wanted to make sure Cole and Garrett were safe. "Get that light out of my eyes, Brody. I'm fine. I'll go back uphill with you."

"I thought you'd say that. Let's find a sheltered spot where we can wait. Okay with you, Robo? Speak up."

Robo sounded off, making Mattie laugh. She gave her dog a treat and handed Brody's gloves back to him before shoving her hands into her pockets. She and Robo followed Brody to a rocky outcropping that would block the wind, where they waited in companionable silence for the sheriff.

TWENTY-EIGHT

Early Monday morning, approximately two AM

Though they'd come down the mountain together, they'd all
gone their separate ways. Sheriff McCoy had driven off with
Garrett, taking him to Dr. McGinnis. Cole had loaded Garrett's
lame horse into his trailer beside Mountaineer and headed for
his clinic. Brody had gone to stand guard at the lower site on
the Redstone Ridge trail.

And Mattie and Robo had headed to the station in her
Explorer. Many hours had passed since their exposure to
fentanyl, and she was no longer concerned about renarcotization. Technically she should have Dr. McGinnis check her out,
but she thought there was no need at this point. Cole had given
Robo a clean bill of health, and that was all that mattered.

She found Stella and Agent Rick Lawson in the briefing room, both working on laptop computers. When Mattie
entered, Stella raised her eyes from her screen and studied her.
"I hear you and Robo were exposed to fentanyl tonight. Are
you both okay?"

"Doing fine."

"Hmm . . ."

Her friend's reaction told Mattie that she might not look as
well as she hoped to portray.

Stella nodded her head toward Lawson. "You know Rick."

Mattie offered a handshake as he stood to greet her. Of
average height and muscular build, the agent wore his dark hair
in a buzz cut that showed a sprinkling of gray at his temples,
and he met her gaze with intelligent dark eyes. "It's good to see
you again. I'm glad you and your dog recovered."

Mattie acknowledged his words with a nod but wanted to get straight to the point. "Have you interrogated Hauck?"

"I tried to. He asserted his right for legal counsel."

Though disappointed, Mattie had thought that would be the case. "I want to talk to him. Off the record."

Lawson narrowed his eyes to study her.

Stella cleared her throat. "Let us brief you on what we've found so far. You don't want to go in without all the information."

Mattie took a seat at the table, and Robo circled before lying down beside her. He heaved a sigh and lay his head down on his front paws. She figured he'd be asleep within seconds.

Stella flipped a few pages back in her notebook. "I have a lot of information to share with you, and I'll try to keep it linear. First, Deidra Latimer—she confessed to *accidentally* killing Tonya with fentanyl patches she obtained from Jim Hauck. She says he coerced her into providing this baby for him to sell on the dark web and that she feared for her life. My take? I think they're a couple and she's worked with him for years. Rick and I have found a smattering of missing mom and infant cases in Southern California that we've been able to link to the midwife clinic she worked at out there."

"Geez." Mattie released a shaky breath. "Tonya appeared safe when we saw her on the store film. How did Deidra get to her?"

"It was in the store parking lot. She spotted Tonya sitting out there, approached her car, and apologized to her. Then she manipulated her into going to her house for lunch. I think Tonya was lonely and vulnerable, so she went. Deidra drugged her tea and restrained her." Stella's expression was grim. "Deidra has more on-the-job training than she initially let on. She's skilled in establishing IVs, and she proceeded to deliver the baby under a rapid Pitocin drip. Labor was fast and painful. Deidra says she started with one fentanyl patch for the pain and then added more . . . but honestly, her story falls apart there. We believe Tonya was conscious when she delivered and then Deidra administered the overdose. She claims she was busy cleaning up the baby when Tonya accidentally died, but again, we believe otherwise. The DA hasn't filed charges yet, and I'm hoping it will include murder one."

This was hard for Mattie to take in. "Why dump her body at that campsite? Why not somewhere closer to Hightower?"

"She'd camped there before and knew the layout. She said she was surprised to see so many campers there and was unaware that it was hunting season. But when she realized most of the campers weren't present in the campground at the time, she went ahead with her plan to leave the body. She and Hauck wanted to take the baby from Timber Creek to Denver last night, but they didn't count on the storm. Deidra ended up taking care of the baby one more day."

"Did she confess to hitting Johnson?" Mattie asked.

Stella's eyes narrowed. "She did. After she dumped Tonya's body, she waited for nightfall in a grove of trees near the Balderhouse trailhead. She thought it would be better to sneak through Timber Creek after dark, and Hauck planned to help her ditch the car. The storm slowed her down and the baby was hungry, so she pulled off to the side of the road to try to pacify her. She said when Johnson pulled up behind her, there she was with Tonya's baby in the car, and she panicked."

Mattie had to stop herself from grinding her teeth. "Any news on the grave site near the Redstone Ridge trailhead?"

Stella nodded. "We've got matching dental records for Rose Marie Harlan, the missing mom from Denver, and there were no infant remains in the grave."

Mattie's body tensed. "Did Deidra confess to killing her?"

"Not yet. A lot of this has come in since my first interrogation." Stella gestured toward the two computers. "We're building a case against her. By the time we talk to her again, I think she'll cave. And she'll have incentive to share all that she knows about Hauck."

"Is Carla Holt part of the baby trafficking operation?"

"There's no evidence of it, and she sent proof of credit card postings that appeared on her account for items purchased in Willow Springs. I also talked to the barista at the coffee shop and confirmed that Carla had been there on Friday afternoon.

We'll check out the midwife in California as well, but so far it looks like Deidra acted alone."

Thinking about the children who were still missing hit Mattie hard. She turned to Lawson. "Is there hope of reuniting these missing babies with their families?"

"If we can gain information from Deidra or Hauck about who these children were sold to, there's hope. Kidnapping and the potential of crossing state lines means the FBI will become involved. There's a lot of work to be done."

Fatigue threatened to overwhelm Mattie. She needed to stay focused on what she could accomplish right now . . . tonight.

"There's more info from the lower site," Stella said. "The bomb squad dug up what looks like a kill kit. A waterproof case containing a sawed-off shotgun, ammo, zip ties, knife, duct tape, and a Taser. Also a black powder pipe bomb with wiring that hadn't been attached yet. We think this kit was all John Cobb's work. Whether or not he left it for others besides himself to use remains unknown at the present."

"That sounds like John Cobb."

Stella nodded. "The bomb squad will move up to excavate the site at the midpoint tomorrow morning, and they think they'll find a similar kit. The forensic team will work on the suspected grave site by the cave. If we find a body up there, we'll see if the remains are from our missing mom from Colorado Springs—Kaylee Cunningham."

"What's your theory on who buried these women? I don't see how Deidra could have done it."

"Right," Lawson said. "The most likely suspect is John Cobb. His markings on the map correspond to the burial sites and the kill kit. And Hauck wanting to come here to investigate that map indicates he didn't know what was buried there. So I believe Cobb buried those bodies as well as the kill kit, but I don't understand why he would go to the trouble of taking these women up into the mountains to bury them. Why would he risk being seen on a trail that others use for hiking?"

Mattie thought she knew the answer. "John Cobb liked to burn bodies up in the high country, and his MO was to use a large fire pit. He transported me at night, so that's probably what he did with these women."

"Hauck recovered several bags of drugs and money hidden in that cave," Lawson said, his gaze intense. "That's what he was after all along."

Mattie's face warmed with embarrassment. "Right. He used the fentanyl on us. There was money too?"

Lawton nodded. "Two bags of cash in large bills, equaling about a million. Deidra told us that Hauck knew Cobb had stolen from the operation before he got arrested in May, but he didn't know where Cobb hid it. He needed you and your dog to find it for him. I wondered why Robo didn't find the other bags of fentanyl when you searched that cave."

Mattie wanted to kick herself. "After we found the first bag, I left Hauck there so I could return a call from the sheriff on the sat phone and give Robo his reward for working. I didn't ask Robo to sweep to the end of the right wall or the far corner. When I returned, Hauck had been digging, and he said he didn't find anything more. I shouldn't have believed him, and I should have never left him alone in that cave."

Lawson shrugged. "He's a chameleon. There are lots of people who never should have trusted him."

"Have you talked to Hauck's superior back in San Diego?" Mattie asked.

"Yep. He is not pleased, and he's not getting any sleep tonight either."

"Could others be a part of this?"

Lawson raised his chin as if to acknowledge her concern. "I'm sure internal affairs will investigate."

Mattie looked at Stella. "I still want to talk to Hauck, but not about any of this."

Stella's eyes narrowed, and she nodded slightly as if acknowledging that she could guess Mattie's goal. She turned to Lawson. "What are the odds that Hauck has information about a homicide that occurred thirty years ago that involved the Cobb brothers?"

Lawson raised a brow. "What are you talking about?"

Stella briefed him about the shooting death of Douglas Wray as well as why it interested them.

Lawson looked at Mattie. "We haven't had time to go back that far. We don't even know yet when Hauck turned—before or after he joined the force in San Diego."

"I want to find out if he knows anything about my father's death. That's all I need."

"And you think he'll tell you?"

Mattie straightened. "I doubt it, but I have to try. This won't be a formal interview. I just want to talk to him."

Her shoulder muscles tightened as she waited for Lawson to mull things over.

"I think Deputy Wray should go ask our prisoner if he needs anything," Stella said quietly.

Lawson put his hands up in surrender. "See what he has to say."

"Deidra's in the private cell," Stella said. "Hauck's in the block."

When Mattie stood, Robo awakened and followed her down the hallway that led to the jail. She keyed in the code that released the lock on the door into the jail lobby, where she noticed that Terry Simpson was on duty. Terry was a beefy guy and one of their younger corrections officers. He looked up from his computer screen. "Hey, it's Mattie and Robo."

She raised her hand in greeting. "I'm here to talk to Jim Hauck. Do you have any other customers in back?"

"Nah, just the woman you brought in earlier, but she's in the private suite." Terry quirked the corner of his mouth at his joke. "Do you need some help?"

"No, thanks." Mattie scanned the lobby, locating an aluminum chair that looked like it wasn't too heavy. "I'll take that chair in with me. Would you release the lock?"

The lock buzzed and clicked and Mattie opened the door, directing Robo to come with her and then telling him to heel. Four cells lined the left side of the room with a walkway to the right, allowing a wide berth for passing. Solid walls separated the cells, which each contained a sink, a toilet, and a built-in platform holding a mattress, but bars at the front limited total privacy.

Since it was the middle of the night, the cells were dark, but dim lighting lit the passageway. Mattie carried the chair to the second cell, where she saw Hauck rise from the bed.

"So it's Mattie Wray and her dog," he said as he walked toward the bars. "Did you bring that chair to break me out of here?"

The strip of lighting behind her glowed enough for her to see his engaging smile, which she now recognized for what it was. Pure cunning and manipulation.

She set the chair outside the cell, staying well beyond his reach, and sat and studied him for a minute while she stroked Robo, who settled down beside her. She was surprised that Hauck looked tired and worn as he sank to sit on the end of his bed. Though she felt nothing but contempt for this man who'd stolen babies to sell and then tried to kill Cole and her dog, she refused to let that show. "Did you get some sleep?"

Again with the smile. She remembered how Rainbow had called him the Silver Fox. The nickname suited him well.

"Some," he said. "The accommodations are comfortable enough."

"Do you need anything?"

"An attorney. But I hear I've got an appointment with one tomorrow."

She sat and waited for a few minutes while they studied each other. Finally, she spoke. "I want to talk to you off the record."

"That's not how this works, Deputy. You know that."

"It's how this works for tonight."

"You're wearing a wire."

"No, I'm not, and I don't want to talk to you about things that happened here in Timber Creek anyway. I want to talk about only one thing."

He continued to smile. "And that would be your interest in your father's death."

Mattie nodded slowly. "What do you know about it?"

He leaned forward, placing his elbows on his knees and spreading his hands wide in an open posture. Mattie recognized the pose—friendly, honest. But she remained fully aware that he knew all the right postures as well as she did. "I can tell you that I'd never before heard the name Douglas Wray until your sister called me a couple years ago," he said.

266 | Margaret Mizushima

"What did you learn about the case after you looked into it?"

"I know nothing more than you know."

Mattie continued to study him. Was he telling the truth? She could usually tell when suspects lied, but not Hauck. He was polished.

Hauck leaned back slightly, moving his hands to his knees. "I've looked at a lot of cases over the years, Deputy, and I've solved some tough ones."

It felt bizarre listening to him talk as if he was a hotshot detective. Maybe he had been at one time.

Hauck went on. "I can tell you that the Douglas Wray case has been looked at many times by some of the best, and until you came up with the John Cobb lead, everyone had hit a dead end. It's too bad we weren't able to interrogate him."

It felt like he was taunting her. Deidra had told them that Hauck had ordered John Cobb's death, and Mattie believed that to be true. But Hauck seemed willing to talk, and even if he was spinning his words to make himself look innocent, she wanted to know what he had to say. She nodded, leaning forward slightly to imitate his posture, encouraging him to keep going.

He snorted his amusement and shook his head as if he was onto her game. But he didn't shut down. "I looked into John Cobb's record the same as you. I know it's long, and he served a lot of time. I believe he or his brother pulled the trigger on your father the night he died, but Douglas Wray was clearly involved with that gang. Your dear old dad was a dirty cop, Mattie. I think you've got to face it."

Mattie shrugged. According to her mother, he'd been coerced and threatened, but she would never share that with Hauck.

"I have no direct knowledge of your father's shooting, but as far as I can tell, your mother is the only living witness. Unless you can find her, you are out of luck." He folded his arms across his chest, telling her he'd said all he was going to.

Mattie kept on her cop face. She had one message she wanted to send loud and clear, in case Hauck ever made contact with his cronies on the outside. "I think my mother's dead. My grandmother and sister have hoped to hear from her for decades, and they've never heard a word. I think she would have contacted them if she were alive. We've all given up hope."

He shrugged as if it didn't matter, even though he'd asked Mattie if she knew her mother's whereabouts only days ago. "Maybe you're right."

"What else do you know?"

This time he snorted with laughter. "You're kidding me, right?"

Mattie slid forward to the edge of her chair, hard enough that it scooted on the tile, making it shriek. Robo jumped up to stand guard. "You robbed me of the chance to talk to John Cobb. Give me something."

Hauck narrowed his eyes, using that speculative stare she'd grown familiar with. "Oh, I have no doubt you'll turn up something . . . or you'll die trying."

She sensed the threat behind his words.

"That's about all I have to say, Deputy." Hauck stood. "Now if you'll excuse me, I need to get some sleep. And from the looks of you, you could use some too."

Disappointed, Mattie stood and picked up her chair, turning to leave.

"On second thought." Hauck waited until she faced him. "Just a word of advice from an old cop to a younger one. If I were you, I'd be careful about investigating this any further. It's been my experience that some things are better left alone."

Without acknowledging him, Mattie turned and walked away, Robo at her side.

TWENTY-NINE

Two days later, Wednesday afternoon

Though it was her day off, Mattie had been at the station all day, wrapping up her part of the case and filing final reports. She also planned to meet with Sheriff McCoy and the rest of the team before Agent Lawson left town.

Hauck had been transferred to a detention center in Denver where he would be housed in isolation awaiting trial. The investigation for kidnapping, child endangerment, and murder conspiracy charges that had been filed against him had been transferred to the CBI, who would be calling in the FBI to help locate the missing babies. The CBI would also get involved with investigating the murder of John Cobb to see if they could verify Deidra's statement that Hauck had ordered a hit on him.

Since she and Stella had been largely responsible for exposing Hauck, it was a shame that they were losing control of the investigation; but even though it was a disappointment, she knew this case was too huge for the department's resources. If there was to be any hope at all of recovering the missing children, it was best left in the hands of the feds.

But the charges against Hauck for Cole's attempted murder would definitely stick, and Mattie thanked all of Cole's angels for looking out for him. Since he would make a valuable witness against the accused when the time came, she feared for his safety even more now, and she planned to help his angels keep an eye on him.

Mattie hit send on the last report she'd typed and glanced at the clock. *Time to meet.* Robo was sleeping on his cushion, curled into a furry ball with his nose tucked under his paw. She bent to place her hand on his side, and he blinked awake, looking up at her with sleepy eyes. He rose, yawned, and stretched before trotting to the door. He knew the routine.

"Let's go to the briefing room," she said, sending him in that direction. He stopped when he reached the closed door and waited for her.

Stella and Lawson were sitting at one side of a table with Brody and McCoy on the ends, leaving the other side for Mattie and Robo.

Though the others were engaged in conversation, McCoy smiled at her as she settled in. He handed her a small black plastic envelope containing something hard and rectangular. "Thank you for working on your day off, Deputy."

"No problem," she murmured, rubbing the hidden object between her fingers. "How's Johnson feeling today?"

McCoy sobered. "Rough. He'll be in the hospital for quite a while, and then his mother plans to come take care of him at home when he's discharged, so that's good. But we're going to need more help. I don't think I'll have trouble convincing the county commissioners to let me hire an additional deputy. When Johnson returns to the force, we'll be more adequately staffed."

"We do need more help. I hope we can get it." The object inside the wrapper felt like a name tag, so she decided to open it, keeping it below the edge of the table for her eyes only. It contained one of the gold name tags the department used, with black lettering that said **DEPUTY MATTIE WRAY, K-9 UNIT**. Her sight blurred with tears as she looked up at the sheriff. "Thank you."

"For when the name change comes through." McCoy's gaze swept the table to include the others. "Okay, let's wrap up so Agent Lawson can get on the road."

Stella looked up from her side conversation with Brody and Lawson. "All right. The latest information this morning is that dental records confirm the charred remains recovered from the grave site up by the cave belong to Kaylee Cunningham. DNA confirmation is yet to come. Rick, do you want to summarize our interrogation of Deidra Latimer?"

Lawson leaned forward. "Latimer has confessed to infant kidnapping in the cases of both Kaylee Cunningham and Rose Marie Harlan, but she continues to deny conspiracy to commit murder. Her statement says that both Kaylee and Rose were alive when she turned them over to John Cobb. She says she never knew of their demise or of their final disposal, and she transferred their infants to Hauck. She swears she doesn't know how he sold the babies or to whom. She still claims she feared for her life and acted under duress. We've found similar cases of missing women and their infants associated with the midwife's clinic in California, and those have been turned over to the California Attorney General's Office for their division to investigate."

Mattie had suspected this would be the way it would go. "Did Deidra elaborate on how she seized Rose and Kaylee in the first place?"

Stella nodded. "She knew both babies had been born, and she stalked the mothers' homes, Kaylee's in March and Rose's in April. Since they both knew her, it was easy for her to lure them into her car when they took walks outside with their babies. She turned the moms over to John Cobb, who took them at gunpoint, and she transported the babies to Jim Hauck, who reportedly sold them to—and I quote—very good homes. The infant trafficking operation appears to have started about five years ago."

Long after her father's death. "Have you turned up anything that ties Hauck to John Cobb's activity thirty years ago?"

Lawson shook his head. "I've turned up nothing that goes beyond this recent infant trafficking operation, and as far as I can tell, that's when Hauck turned. Someone must've gotten to him, and his department is working on finding out who. I think he ordered the hit on John Cobb to protect himself from exposure. Cobb had little to lose, and he might have been happy to let you in on the secret. Why else would he have marked those spots on the map? I even wonder if he headed to his cell to retrieve it before he succumbed to the fentanyl."

Speculation about that might be all they'd ever have. "What does the prison investigator, Russo, have to say? Has he determined how Cobb was dosed with fentanyl?"

"No. It's still under investigation. Russo admits that smuggling fentanyl into the prison is completely possible, and it could have been forced on Cobb by any number of inmates."

Probably another permanent dead end. Mattie felt all hope of clearing her father's name trickling away. But there were other detectives in San Diego she could contact. She would follow up in time, but for now she needed to spend time with the living, with her friends and family here in Timber Creek. And as soon as she could, she would go back to California to visit her sister and grandmother and maybe even go see her mother in Mexico.

Though she and Cole had spoken to each other over the phone, they'd not spent more than five minutes alone together. They planned to remedy that this evening. As soon as the kids got home from school, they would all go visit the puppies. After that, they would return home to eat dinner with Mrs. Gibbs. Though typically Mattie lived for work, she could hardly wait for this meeting to end.

After Lawson and Stella wrapped up the final disposition of the Hauck case, McCoy adjourned the meeting. Mattie hurried to her office to gather her things while her dog stayed with Rainbow in the lobby.

When she returned, she lingered at Rainbow's desk to make plans for dinner together on Friday. Stella and Lawson left the detective's office and headed toward the front door. The two had been working together nonstop for days, and something about them caught Mattie's eye.

Their arms brushed as they walked closely together, Stella's smiling face turned upward, his head bent toward hers. They held their farewell handshake far too long.

Stella paused at the door, obviously watching Lawson walk to his car until she waved a final good-bye and turned. Her eyes met Mattie's, and Mattie raised her brows. Stella winked, giving her a grin as she passed by to go back to her office.

For the first time in days, Mattie felt truly happy.

★ ★ ★

Mattie thought the evening had been perfect. Little Velvet had definitely turned a corner and wasn't looking back. She'd gained strength, could nurse on her own, and though smaller than the other pups, she was plumping up nicely. Mattie had enjoyed visiting with Mrs. Gibbs and the kids while they set the table and put the finishing touches on a delicious dinner, and then they'd all shared a cozy time in front of the fire in the great room watching a movie while the dogs slept on their cushions and Hilde the kitten nestled on Angie's lap.

And now she and Cole were headed into town for dancing at the Watering Hole, just the two of them—Robo had stayed at the Walker home with Belle and Bruno, even though he'd given her sad eyes at being left behind.

"I don't think I told you that Tonya's dog Kip is going to live with Garrett and Leslie," Cole said as he turned onto the highway.

Surprised, Mattie turned to look at him. "How did that happen?"

"Corey Greenfield called and asked if I could recommend a good home for her. Evidently Tonya's parents didn't want her either. She's a great little dog, and I thought living on a cattle ranch would be just the thing. I called Garrett, and he agreed. He'd been thinking about getting a dog lately."

Mattie felt relieved. "That's perfect for Kip."

"I thought so." Cole grinned as he reached for her hand. "And now . . . I've made you happy and I've finally got you all to myself."

Mattie tilted her head back against the headrest and turned slightly so she could look at this man she loved. It infuriated her that her work had brought danger into his life.

She studied his profile. "You always make me happy. This has been a perfect evening. I hope you know how much I love being with the kids."

He sobered, keeping his eyes on the road. "I can tell."

"But I'm glad we're alone too . . . so we can talk."

The truck slowed as he apparently eased up on the gas pedal. "Yeah, you're right. We do need to talk."

Mattie paused to gather her words. "I feel terrible for putting you in a dangerous situation. If Hauck had killed you, it would've been my fault."

Cole laced his fingers between hers. "No, Mattie. Nothing that happened was your fault, and you didn't put me in danger. I choose to be on the sheriff's posse, because it's something I can do to help my community. It's a decision Garrett and I made together after Grace was killed and Sophie was kidnapped."

Digesting his words, Mattie studied his face.

He tossed her a quick smile. "Besides, it gives me a chance to be with you when you have to work overtime."

Mattie failed to see the humor, and his words made her sad. "Quality time. Tracking down bad guys."

The planes of his face turned serious as he continued to watch the road. "Yeah . . . not an ideal situation, is it?"

"If Hauck had harmed you or . . . What if he still tries to get to you?" She swallowed against a sudden lump in her throat. "I can't imagine going on without you in my life."

"I'll stay alert, Mattie. He's not going to get to me."

She closed her eyes for a moment, taking a deep breath. "We both need to make sure that doesn't happen."

He squeezed her hand. "Do you mind going for a drive? It's too noisy to talk at the Watering Hole, and we can go dancing this weekend instead."

They'd reached the edge of town, and she didn't feel like dancing. "A drive would be great."

Cole steered the truck around a block and turned onto the highway, heading back toward his place. They passed his lane in silence, Cole rubbing her hand occasionally with his thumb as he drove. A half mile farther he signaled left, telling her he was headed toward Lookout Mountain, a hill on the north edge of Timber Creek and one of her favorite spots.

He released her hand to navigate the narrow road, and though the night was cold, she rolled down her window a quarter of the way so she could take in the fresh scent of pine as they made their way to the top. It soothed her.

"There," he said as he parked at the overlook.

The lights of Timber Creek glowed below, cozy and quiet on a weekday night. He adjusted the heater as she rolled her window back up and nestled into the warm seat. She turned to look at him, and he leaned toward her, his eyes dark and serious instead of twinkling with their usual humor.

He placed his hand on her cheek and kissed her, a kiss she could lose herself in, one that was long and deep and, by its end, one that showed her how much he cared. He settled back into his seat, turned off the truck engine, and grasped her hand.

Mattie felt warm and loved, and she pushed away thoughts of Hauck and Deidra Latimer and the painful crimes they'd committed. She wanted to focus only on Cole and this precious time they could spend together.

"I'm pretty sure now that Angie has her first boyfriend," Cole mused, rubbing her knuckles gently with his other hand.

"Ben Greenfield."

He turned to her, one eyebrow quirked. "Yep."

"I saw them together the other day. I could tell that Angie liked him."

Cole huffed an amused sound and looked back out the windshield. "It's sort of obvious, isn't it?"

"Mm-hmm."

"She's old enough that I think I need to have a talk with her. You know . . ." He raised both brows. "*The* talk."

"Oh . . . yes, I suppose that would be up to you."

He smiled. "And I thought I should consult you before I do it."

"Me?" That was a surprise. "You're kidding."

He chuckled. "No, ma'am, I'm dead serious and a little bit terrified."

"I wouldn't know what to say."

"Maybe not, but I bet you could help me figure it out."

"Mm . . . I'll have to think about it."

"But you'd be game?"

"Sure. The last thing I want is for Angie to get hurt in any way."

He nodded, his face turning serious again. "Both of us have jobs that require long hours and an irregular schedule. We can have our quiet times together like this evening, or our days and nights can be filled with chaos. I feel at a loss when I can't see you or talk to you for days at a time."

A sense of alarm made her study his face. Maybe he'd grown tired of having a relationship with a cop. *With her.* She gripped his hand.

"But there's something that could change the situation that would make me tremendously happy." He leaned forward, breaking her grip and flattening her hand on his chest above his heart before covering it with his own. "Mattie, would you marry me . . . and the kids and the clinic and Mrs. Gibbs and all the chaos our life together might bring?"

His proposal truly floored her . . . and yet, at the same time, it felt like the most natural thing in the world. In a flash, she remembered how melancholy and sad she felt when they were apart. How terrified she'd been when she thought she might lose him. "Are you sure you want to marry a cop?"

His eyes twinkled. "I've learned to love the idea. My life would be empty without you *and* your profession."

"Then yes, I'll marry you and your kids and everything our lives together might bring us. But we'll have to check with Mrs. Gibbs to make sure she's still in."

She leaned over the console so she could wrap her arms around his neck to hold him as tightly as the awkward position would allow.

Their kiss was full of love and passion and a promise for their future.

Acknowledgments

Thank you to readers, other writers, reviewers, book bloggers, podcast and radio hosts, and all who've supported this series and helped me along the way. You've inspired me to keep plotting and writing, and I appreciate you so very much.

Thank you to Lieutenant Glenn J. Wilson (Ret.); Charles Mizushima, DVM; Tracy Brisendine, Medicolegal Death Investigator; Kathleen Donnelly, K-9 Handler and co-owner of Sherlock Hounds; Nancy Howard, District Wildlife Manager (retired); and Gretchen Lefever, BS, RN, CCRN, for their time and assistance with procedural content. As always, any inaccuracies or fictional enhancements are mine alone.

Thank you to my wonderful publishing team for their guidance and support: Terrie Wolf of AKA Literary Management; publisher Matthew Martz and the fabulous team at Crooked Lane Books, Melissa Rechter and Madeline Rathle; my editor, Martin Biro; my copyeditor, Rachel Keith; and publicist Maryglenn McCombs.

Many thanks to Scott Graham, author of the National Parks Mysteries, for early input; and to Bill Hazard for assistance with drafts.

Hugs, love, and gratitude go to friends and family who've supported me throughout the years. Your support means the world to me.

And to my husband, Charlie; daughters, Sarah and Beth; and son-in-law, Adam: hugs and a big thank you for always being there.